Bumblebee Season

Also by Eileen Garvin

Crow Talk

The Music of Bees

How to Be a Sister

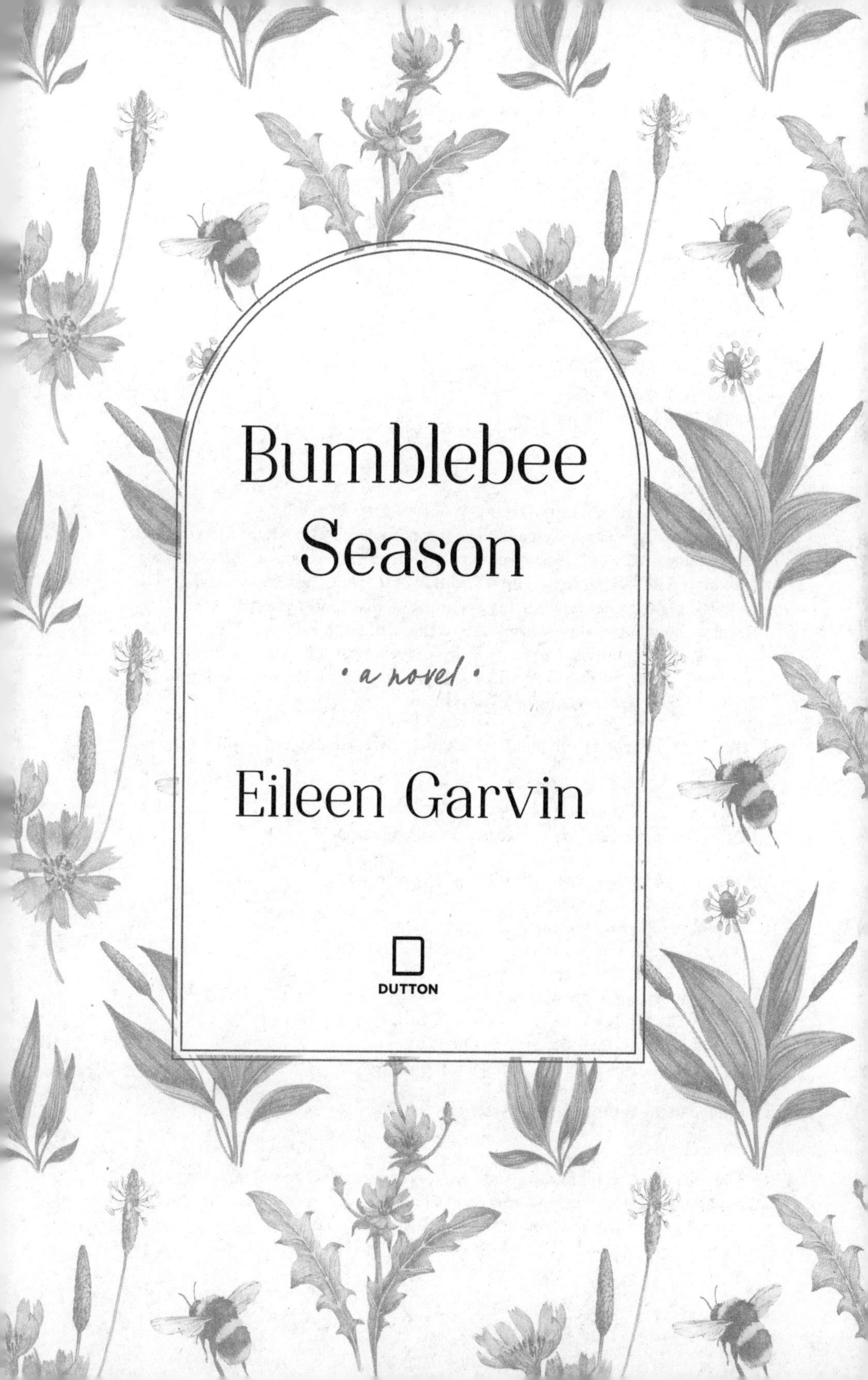

Bumblebee Season

· *a novel* ·

Eileen Garvin

DUTTON

DUTTON

An imprint of Penguin Random House LLC
1745 Broadway, New York, NY 10019
penguinrandomhouse.com

Copyright © 2026 by Eileen Garvin
Penguin Random House values and supports copyright. Copyright fuels creativity, encourages diverse voices, promotes free speech, and creates a vibrant culture. Thank you for buying an authorized edition of this book and for complying with copyright laws by not reproducing, scanning, or distributing any part of it in any form without permission. You are supporting writers and allowing Penguin Random House to continue to publish books for every reader. Please note that no part of this book may be used or reproduced in any manner for the purpose of training artificial intelligence technologies or systems.

DUTTON and the D colophon are registered trademarks of Penguin Random House LLC.

BOOK DESIGN BY ANGIE BOUTIN
Title page background art © Anastasiia/stock.adobe.com

LIBRARY OF CONGRESS CATALOGING-IN-PUBLICATION DATA
Names: Garvin, Eileen author
Title: Bumblebee season : a novel / Eileen Garvin.
Description: New York, NY : Dutton, 2026.
Identifiers: LCCN 2025030869 | ISBN 9798217044900 hardcover | ISBN 9798217044917 ebook
Subjects: LCSH: Bee culture—Fiction | LCGFT: Fiction | Novels
Classification: LCC PS3607.A782894 B86 2026
LC record available at https://lccn.loc.gov/2025030869

Printed in the United States of America
1st Printing

The authorized representative in the EU for product safety and compliance is Penguin Random House Ireland, Morrison Chambers, 32 Nassau Street, Dublin D02 YH68, Ireland, https://eu-contact.penguin.ie.

For anyone who's ever longed for home

This is the bright home
in which I live,
this is where
I ask
my friends
to come,
this is where I want
to love all the things
it has taken me so long
to learn to love.

—DAVID WHYTE, "THE HOUSE OF BELONGING"

Bumblebee Season

1

EMERGENCE

Bumblebee queens, marvelous in their independence,
awake from winter solitude to locate their nesting
sites and establish new colonies.

—D. A. LAVIN, *THE WONDROUS WORLD OF BEES*

ABIGAIL PLUE SURPRISED people, though she didn't understand exactly why. It seemed as if, upon meeting her, they'd been expecting someone else. At least after Abigail had spoken. That was the only way she could explain it. People seemed to harbor some expectation of what she'd say or how she might say it, and when her words came out they were never quite right. No one ever said that exactly, but she could tell it was what they thought.

Before she opened her mouth there was a neutral space, a two-dimensional field that she could exist on, suspended, in orientation to other people. She felt like a stick figure on a flashcard, fulfilling the correct requirements. Human. Woman. Person. But something changed in the air after she spoke. Her voice induced an invisible but tangible shift, a breaking apart of particles. Sometimes she imagined a pungent scent, like the smell of petrichor right after it rained. And then she was Other, Different, Strange. Was it what she said or how she said it? She didn't know. It all seemed terribly unfair to Abigail. How could people have expectations of a person they'd never even met?

When she was alone, though, Abigail didn't feel troubled by how others might perceive her. She simply felt like herself. She enjoyed her own company and found the workings of her brain interesting. Instead of that cramped two-dimensional plane she balanced on so precariously with others, her solitary world was vast—a boundless expanse to observe and explore, to turn over rocks and look under logs, both literally and figuratively. As a girl, Abigail had spent considerable time on her hands and knees observing what was happening on the ground. In fact, it was in this exploratory setting that Abigail first understood she was odd. People also called her strange, weird, and wacky. But "odd" was the first moniker, and one she didn't mind. Odd. Pronounced by Miss Mary Ricketts, Abigail's neighbor, the day they met, when Abigail was seven years old, and already enraptured with the kingdom underfoot.

Abigail's father didn't get home from work until five thirty, so Abigail spent hours alone. Another girl might have felt lonesome. Another girl might have passed the time watching TV or sneaking cookies her father had hidden above the refrigerator where he thought she wouldn't find them. But Abigail liked solitude, was bored by television, did not overindulge in sugary treats, and preferred to be outside. In the soil around the front walk she observed armor-plated pill bugs, which she'd learned from *National Geographic* were called *Armadillidium vulgare*—a delightful discovery because didn't they look exactly like tiny armadillos? She found banded woolly bear caterpillars inching along the underside of the hydrangeas. These fuzzy black-and-red-striped *Pyrrharctia isabellas* looked like bumblebees and transformed into golden-colored Isabella tiger moths.

The day she'd met Miss Ricketts she'd been absorbed by velvety tree ants. A trail of the tiny insects snaked across her yard over the fence and into the neighbor's driveway. Abigail had followed them to the base of a mountain ash tree and was watching them closely when a car pulled up. Since she was not obstructing the driveway, she saw no reason to move.

Miss Ricketts was talking to herself as she climbed out of the car juggling several bags and a purse. She startled at the sight of the small figure and let out a yell. She peered down at Abigail, her eyes covered by large wraparound sunglasses.

"What the heck are you doing down there?!" she barked.

Abigail often struggled to understand the emotion behind people's words. Once she started third grade, she'd begin working with Miss Star—blond, blue-eyed Miss Star, who dressed in soft pastels and whose classroom smelled of peppermint and cotton candy. Miss Star used a set of thick flashcards to help Abigail identify her own emotions, which was difficult enough. Translating other people's emotions was a completely different mystery. What might Miss Ricketts have been feeling when she'd asked that question? Confused was a card that often came up for Abigail. Also, Surprised. However, at the age of seven, Abigail hadn't yet met Miss Star and could only take people's words at face value.

She stood up and pushed her hair out of her eyes.

"Research, ma'am. I'm doing a field study on these velvety tree ants," she replied. "Did you know that colonies of velvety tree ants can be as large as sixty thousand workers and they'll forage up to six hundred feet from the nest?"

Miss Ricketts recoiled slightly, peered at the column of ants climbing the tree, and sniffed.

"I was unaware," she said. "But I do know it isn't polite to do a 'field study,' as you call it, without asking permission to be on someone's property."

Abigail cocked her head and didn't say anything. She watched Miss Ricketts's nostrils flare. She would later learn this was something that happened when Miss Ricketts was feeling Irritated or Annoyed. She would also sigh in a groany way, as she did that first day.

"Young lady. If you want to conduct a field study in my yard, you need to ask *first*. *Before* you begin your *research*."

Abigail blinked. Her mouth gaped. Her mind worked furiously to try to solve the problem. How was she supposed to ask *first* when she'd already begun her study? She didn't know what to say.

Miss Ricketts sighed again and leaned against her car. She removed her wraparound sunglasses and blinked.

"I suppose you are my new neighbor. My name is Miss Mary Ricketts. You and your folks moved in last week?"

Was that last part a question? The sound went up at the end, but Abigail wasn't sure. And as for her folks, well, it was just her and Dad. As Abigail considered these details, Miss Ricketts's nostrils flared again.

"Young lady, what is your name?"

Abigail straightened.

"My name is Abigail Elizabeth Plue," she said, holding out one hand and tucking the other behind her waist like a little duke. "Pleased to meet you, ma'am."

Abigail's father had taught her it was important to introduce oneself and to be especially polite to older people. She couldn't appreciate how the gravity of her tone contrasted with the dirt under her fingernails and the muddy knees of her jeans and her short hair, cowlicked and uncombed.

"Odd child," Miss Ricketts whisper-breathed, shaking the dirty little hand and replacing her glasses.

As the older woman looked down at her, Abigail thought Miss Ricketts's wraparound sunglasses made her eyes resemble the complex foci of the housefly she'd found on the windowsill of her new bedroom. But she didn't say that.

"You may continue your research in my yard," Miss Ricketts said. "Just don't dig any holes."

Abigail said thank you and returned to her spot at the foot of the mountain ash, where she watched and watched until the light faded and it was too dark to see the ants any longer. Then she climbed back over the fence between their yards and went in the house to wait for her dad to come home. She told him she'd met the neighbor.

"Her name is Miss Mary Ricketts. She's old. She said I was odd," Abigail reported over dinner. "What does it mean, exactly? Odd."

Abigail's father looked thoughtful and gazed up at the ceiling.

"Well, odd means different from what is expected. Unusual."

Abigail thought that sounded nice. Praying mantises seemed unusual, the way they could turn their heads 180 degrees like little green robots. Dragonflies were unusual, with their uncanny ability to fly forward and then suddenly reverse.

"Do you think I'm odd, Dad?" she asked.

He smiled, his eyes crinkling in the corners.

"I think you are perfectly yourself, Abigail."

That wasn't an answer, but that was Dad.

Unlike Miss Ricketts, other children didn't call Abigail odd. At school they called her a weirdo, a wacko, a retard. By the time she and her father moved next door to Miss Ricketts, Abigail had attended four different elementary schools. And it was the same at every school. Once she opened her mouth, she felt all wrong. She knew they didn't like her but didn't know why. She didn't like them either, or at least the way they made her feel, which was Scared and Lonely. And Unwelcome. Unwelcome was not among Miss Star's flashcards, but it described how she often felt—through grade school, high school, and even college. Unwelcome.

Feeling unwelcome was no longer surprising to Abigail. She felt out of place in school, at work, and in social situations. But at the age of twenty-three she'd finally found a spot that fit. Her teaching assistantship in the entomology department at Oregon State University had felt like a safe haven, at last. Until this unfortunate meeting with her adviser, Dr. Thomas, when the familiar feeling descended. Unwelcome.

Abigail folded her arms and watched Dr. Thomas's mouth. His

lips were thin and pink. A tiny scar on the right side of his upper lip thickened the flesh there. Under his bottom lip, a small patch of facial hair danced and twitched as he talked. The day Abigail had met Dr. Thomas, at a mixer for freshmen six years ago, Abigail thought he'd missed a spot shaving. She'd felt compelled to point it out, and he laughed, explaining it was intentional.

"It's a soul patch," he said, tapping it with his index finger. "I've had it since undergrad."

Abigail stared at it, troubled. It was too small to rank as a beard and, being under the bottom lip, could not be correctly characterized as a mustache.

"But why?" she blurted. Another student snickered, and Dr. Thomas reddened and said soul patches were cool when he was their age.

"Times change," he said, and shrugged.

"Oh," Abigail said.

For the rest of the mixer, her eye had strayed to the tiny pelt on Dr. Thomas's upper chin as she tried to process the idea of what might be cool now and how the definition of cool could change. She knew enough to know she would not know what was cool. She could ask Dad later, she thought, but she stopped herself from pulling out her notepad. She knew from experience that making notes about what people said in casual conversation was definitely not cool.

The soul patch had continued to distract her whenever she talked with Dr. Thomas over the years, which happened often since he was her adviser. There was something about how it jumped and twitched that fascinated her.

Now she realized Dr. Thomas had asked her a question.

"Pardon?" she said.

"I asked you if you knew why you were being transferred," he said. His voice rose in what Abigail understood from experience was Frustration. And yet, that puzzled her. She was the one who should feel Frustration at being fired. Dr. Thomas kept insisting on using the word "transferred," but she knew it was the same thing.

Abigail pondered the question.

"Because I'm not a good teacher?"

It was the only thing she could think of. Abigail didn't have any idea why she was being removed from the teaching assistants pool and sent to work in research. She wasn't interested in why. All she could think of was the tragedy of leaving her lovely quiet office with its perfect view of the sidewalk outside Stellar Hall.

Dr. Thomas's face grew pink, and he swore softly under his breath. Abigail suppressed a laugh. She was not amused at her supervisor's distress. It was just that she found swearing and swear words hilarious. She also tended to laugh when she knew it was inappropriate to laugh, which made it even harder to stop.

Dr. Thomas closed his eyes and breathed in and out through his nose. When he reopened his eyes, Abigail noticed, as she had before, the lack of symmetry in them. The left eye drooped slightly, which made that side of Dr. Thomas's face look sadder somehow, though he was generally a cheerful person. Abigail had the urge to share these thoughts but bit her tongue.

"Abigail. You are a satisfactory teacher as far as your command of the material. You're being transferred because you yelled at your students. Often. Also, you don't answer their questions on the Canvas portal."

Abigail thought the Canvas portal was excessive. She delivered the information in class, perfectly clearly. Why should she repeat what she'd said in written form to students who were too lazy to take notes or too distracted to remember what she'd said? Or had skipped class?

"The Canvas portal is not a requirement of my job," she said.

She'd checked.

Dr. Thomas sighed.

"But it's a courtesy, Abigail. It helps create rapport with the students. Which is something else you could be better at. For example, you failed one student outright because you didn't like the topic of his semester project."

Abigail crossed her arms.

"But it was a stupid topic. The assignment was to investigate an important environmental concern affecting *invertebrates*, and he wrote a paper about advances in drone technology. Drone technology has no place in the study of *biology*. I just told him what was obvious. We study *creatures*. *Living* things."

The student had seemed to agree with her, hadn't he? He'd said something like, "Of course you think it's stupid." From which she took him to understand that she, being his instructor, would know better. But if he'd agreed with her, why had he gone complaining to Dr. Thomas? It didn't make any sense.

". . . can't behave like that, Abigail," Dr. Thomas was saying. "You can't fail people because the paper doesn't interest you. We have specific grading guidelines. And you can't yell at people! Our institution does not tolerate heated displays of emotion, even if your heart is in the right place. That's not how we communicate with each other! It's the twenty-first century!"

Abigail uncrossed her arms, propped her elbows on her knees, and leaned forward.

"You are yelling at me right now," she said.

She was genuinely curious about the contradiction between Dr. Thomas's words and actions.

Dr. Thomas closed his eyes and whisper-swore again. Abigail suppressed a chuckle. She felt bad for upsetting him because she really liked Dr. Thomas. He dragged his palms down his face, which made the skin under his eyes sag. He looked tired. She probably should not tell him that, she decided.

"Abigail," Dr. Thomas said, his voice level. "You have your new assignment and keys to Dr. Mora's lab. Good luck and let me know how things go with the research group."

Abigail exhaled and nodded. She would do that. Even though he was banishing her to the research wing, he'd still be her adviser so of course she would tell him about her work, which she expected to loathe.

"I will take notes," she said.

Behind Dr. Thomas, she observed a row of spider plants on the sunlit windowsill. Their leaves were yellow and droopy. Why did people keep plants when they didn't bother to take care of them? Didn't they feel a sense of responsibility to the living things they'd purchased? She wondered if Dr. Thomas's wife had put them there. Was he married? Was he straight? Maybe he had a husband. Maybe he had a baby. Was that why he looked tired?

Her gaze returned to Dr. Thomas's face. His lips were pressed together, and the soul patch trembled. He looked like he might laugh or cry, but Abigail couldn't tell which. She wondered if he was feeling sick. The clock on the wall ticked loudly and the overhead light hummed.

"Ms. Plue. Our time is up," Dr. Thomas said. "I have another meeting and I need. You. To. Go."

"Oh!" Abigail said, jumping up. "Well, thank you so much for your time today, Dr. Thomas. I do appreciate it."

She stretched her hand across his desk. Her father had also taught her that it was important to thank people for their time. She wondered if Dr. Thomas knew that because he stared at her hand for a long moment before shaking it.

"Abigail, you are one of a kind," he said.

As she walked down the hall, she thought she heard him laughing, which was odd. Perhaps Dr. Thomas was odd too.

Abigail Plue couldn't have known that her appearance was part of what made her seem odd to others. Specifically, that she looked so approachable. She had an appealing face with wide-set green eyes and short dark hair that she'd worn in a pixie cut since eighth grade. Her willowy frame was pleasing and androgynous. She had beautiful hands and there was a softness about her features that made people believe she would be helpful and friendly. Abigail looked like the kind of person you might ask for directions or engage in small talk in line at a restaurant. But Abigail was not that person. She knew her voice was part of the problem. Since she was little, she'd been told repeatedly that her voice was too loud. But too loud for what? Nobody ever explained.

Abigail returned to the office she shared with two other TAs. "The Dungeon," as they called it, sweated moisture year-round and retained a constant chill by virtue of its north-facing orientation. Abigail's colleagues grumbled about it, but she loved the gloomy embrace of the exposed-cinder-block room.

She felt despondent and the weather did not help. Outside her office window, it was sunny, too sunny. Positively glary. The walkways and benches along the quad were crowded with undergraduates in shorts and T-shirts. The trees were fully leafed out and stirring in a light breeze. Abigail preferred the view in fall or winter when she could count on a low gray sky or at least a few substantial clouds to break up the too-bright blue.

Her throat constricted and she turned away from the window to the task of packing up her desk. Sad, she thought, recalling the downcast eyes and downturned mouth of the little blue Sad person on Miss Star's flashcard. Banished from the Dungeon, relieved of her teaching duties, she'd been reassigned to a research group in the entomology department. How strange that Dr. Thomas seemed to think he was doing her a favor.

"Teaching is just one way of participating in the academic setting, Abigail," he'd said. "The research group is a fine way for you to contribute. This will be a good change. You'll see."

Abigail doubted that she would see. It wasn't that she particularly loved teaching three sections of Environmental Biology 101. But she'd been doing it for the entire academic year, and it was part of her routine. Abigail didn't like change, especially abrupt changes like this one, which was taking place right before summer break. And then there was the fact that Dr. Thomas was shifting her to a research group. A group. Abigail did not like group activities. She was not a team player or a collaborator. She'd been told so many times.

It didn't take long to clean off her desk—a few print publications, a photo with her dad at the Grand Canyon, and a fish fossil that Miss Ricketts had brought back from a cruise to Greece when Abigail was in high school. Her office mates, Linda and Diane, were in the kitchen with everyone else for the end-of-year TA potluck. Since she was no longer a TA, Abigail decided it would be inappropriate for her to attend. She passed the open door to the kitchen without pausing to say goodbye and carried her things down to the south wing of the building, where the research group was housed.

The overhead lights buzzed, and her footfalls echoed in the empty corridor. The acrid smell of fresh paint hit the back of her throat. Every step forward was a step away from what she knew and toward the unknown. Away from teaching her classes, which she did not particularly like but knew how to do. Away from her fellow teaching assistants, none of whom were her friends, really. But they were familiar, especially her office mates—Linda, who sniffled in a maddening, rhythmic manner while grading student work but was generally congenial, and Diane, who never remembered to shut the door when she left, which Abigail and Linda both preferred. Diane made up for this shortcoming by bringing in freshly baked cookies on a regular basis. Linda would probably take her desk by the window with the view of the maple trees and sidewalk. Linda would get to watch the clouds descend in fall and the rain come down in sheets all winter. Lucky, lucky Linda.

Sunshine streamed through a bank of south-facing windows at the entrance to the research wing. "Welcome to the Honeybee Lab!"

was painted on one wall. Undulating golden honeycombs created a border around a series of figures illustrating the life cycle of *Apis mellifera*: egg, larva, pupa, callow bee, and adult worker. The bodies of a petite worker and big-eyed drone flanked a queen, distinguished by her long, tapered abdomen and short wings.

Abigail glanced at the sticky note from Dr. Thomas. He'd scribbled, "Stellar Hall South, Dr. Mora, Room 208 and Lab 4."

The entomology research department included agricultural research as well as the Oregon Master Beekeeper Program but was universally known as the Honeybee Lab.

"Oh, *I Heart Honeybees*!" people would exclaim, if Abigail chanced to mention her area of study, naming the podcast produced by the Honeybee Lab graduate students. Everyone on campus had listened to at least one episode, it seemed.

Abigail was not a fan of the Master Beekeeper Program. As a requirement of her graduate work, she'd been obliged to spend a week helping teach community beekeepers. She found their enthusiasm tiresome and the other graduate students unbearably arrogant. The way they carried on you'd think honeybees were the only pollinators. What about native bees, bats, birds, and small mammals that were also key to pollination? Even beetles? What about the humble stink bug? But Abigail never had a chance to bring up the stink bug or anything else, what with the backyard beekeepers' endless repetitive questions and worries. And the graduate students with their smug answers and quaint stories: Bees could count! Bees could recognize their keepers! Bees could play! Their enthusiasm was exhausting. She was glad when the week finished and never thought she'd find herself back in the Honeybee Lab.

No one was at the reception desk. Out in the sunny apiary, several people in white canvas jackets stood over an open beehive. Honeybees buzzed around their heads as one person lifted a frame free of the hive and held it up. The others leaned in to observe. The person holding the frame said something that made the others laugh.

Abigail turned away. She wanted to find her new desk, unpack her box, and go home to her familiar, quiet apartment and draw the shades. She would lie on the floor and think about things and reorder them in her mind. She would envision her new office and the view outside the window, if there was one. She would think about how to introduce herself to her office mates and explain about how important it was to shut the door when coming and going. And to leave the overhead fluorescent lights off. She would compose a script in her head, and she'd say it over and over so it would come out sounding natural. Then she'd probably feel well enough to get up off the floor and review the materials she had on *Apis mellifera*. She'd read up on the latest research the Honeybee Lab was doing and by Monday she would feel Calm. Or less Depressed, anyway.

She continued down the hall and located office number 208.

"Dr. Nicolette Mora, Professor, Graduate Adviser," the placard read. Adjacent, a cartoon figure of a honeybee danced on two legs, holding daisies in each of its other four feet. "I'm a Bee-liever!" the bee proclaimed.

Abigail sighed.

"Hello, Dr. Mora. My name is Abigail Plue. Dr. Thomas sends his regards. Can you please direct me to my new office?" she muttered to herself.

She'd written this on the back of the sticky note Dr. Thomas had given her so she wouldn't say the wrong thing, or A Wrong Thing.

No one answered her knock. Abigail continued down the hall to the laboratory area and found Lab 4. The door was closed and the light was off. She heard a loud thump and a muffled exclamation.

"Hello?" Abigail said, knocking. She heard another thump. She put her hand on the knob, and it turned in her grasp. She pushed the door open. Someone crouched near the floor in the dimness. The light from the hallway behind Abigail illuminated a slice of the far wall. As Abigail stared at it, the wall appeared to move. She heard a rising buzz and realized the wall was covered with a velvety mass of pulsing, undulating insect bodies.

She stared, dumbstruck.

A voice, sharp and urgent, came from the figure huddled on the floor.

"Get in and shut the door! Quick!" the figure said.

Abigail stepped into the room and pulled the door shut. Everything went dark.

2

NEW SEASON

Of the world's twenty thousand species of bees,
only about seven are honeybees.

—LAVIN, *THE WONDROUS WORLD OF BEES*

JAKE STEVENSON WAS the first honey producer in the history of the West Coast Food and Wine Classic to win a Feastie award, as insiders called the prize bestowed by the esteemed culinary trade show. Never mind that the year he won was also the inaugural year for the honey category at the Classic. No one could deny that Queen of G Honey, a humble farm from Hood River, Oregon, had triumphed. Jake was immensely proud of that.

Even now on this bright June morning eight months later, the sight of the Feastie award hanging on the kitchen wall gave him a thrill. Jake paused over his breakfast and considered the plaque. It was emblematic of so much more than just victory in a competition of hundreds of honey producers from around the country. The award encapsulated many other successes—owning a business, buying a house, being a known person in his community and even an expert, on honeybees anyway. On a good day, this all felt miraculous. Five years ago, when he'd first become acquainted with honeybees as a clueless teenager, he couldn't have imagined this life.

Jake pushed himself away from the table and pivoted his wheelchair into the kitchen. He poured a cup of coffee and wheeled out to the porch. The sun had climbed over the east hills and now cast its tender spring light across the rows of gleaming white beehives in the apiary. The honeybees had been up for hours, buzzing through the blooming fruit trees in the orchard next door, which belonged to Jake's business partner, Alice Holtzman. The bees were doing double magic—pollinating the trees and provisioning the beehives.

"Spring baby boom," Alice had said recently as they sat at the picnic table near the apiary. All around them, the white blossoms of apple trees were alive with the murmuring golden bodies of honeybees.

"Our biggest yet," she said. "Can you believe this bonanza? And this expansion!"

She rubbed her eyebrows and frowned.

"I can't decide if we'll look back and say this was a brilliant move or the stupidest idea we ever had."

Jake scoffed.

"How could you even ask, Alice?" he said. "Of course it's stupid. We're both out of our minds."

He made her laugh, as he'd hoped, because he didn't want her to know he was worried too. As business partners they had an unspoken agreement that they couldn't both freak out at the same time.

During the years Jake and Alice had worked together, the apiary had grown to two hundred hives here on the land between their houses. Last year had been their busiest ever as they sold out of the nearly fifteen hundred gallons of honey they'd harvested. That success alone was fantastic. But then they'd applied to the West Coast Food and Wine Classic at the encouragement of Stefan Bertoli, a local winemaker and one of Queen of G's first wholesale customers. Stefan served tasting plates at his winery—locally made cheeses, seasonal fruit, fresh bread, and honey, all produced in the Hood River

Valley. Jake had never heard of the West Coast Food and Wine Classic until Stefan mentioned it one day when he stopped by to pick up a case of honey.

"They're including honey this year, I read. You should apply. Getting a bit of regional visibility could be great for Queen of G."

Stefan loaded the honey in his truck and waited while Jake wrote him a receipt. He'd tried to convince Alice to at least use Venmo, but she was so old-school. Anyway, customers didn't seem to mind.

"We have plenty of business, Stefan," Jake said. "Between you and Celilo and our farm stand, we're selling out."

"Sure, but that's small potatoes. No offense. The show could open new markets for you. All the best chefs go—from Seattle, Portland, the Bay Area, and LA, of course," Stefan said. "They're all into hyperlocal food right now."

Stefan said his own small winery had gained a new category of business from the show. The volume he could get from restaurants far exceeded what he could make from seasonal tourists at the tasting room and locals who joined his wine club. That new revenue had allowed him to produce smaller batches and experiment with different grapes.

"For me it's about artistic freedom," Stefan said, tucking the receipt into his pocket. "You should think about it."

The idea of artistic freedom did appeal to Jake. He wanted to experiment with single-source honeys—blackberry, huckleberry, and fireweed. Alice was won over by the idea that new business might allow them to add more hives. Alice always wanted to add more hives. For Alice, the honeybee farm and her adjacent orchard were a recently realized lifelong dream. At the age of forty-nine, she was keen to make up for time she'd lost working for the county—a job she'd quit five years ago. Jake was only twenty-three but had deep-seated ambitions too, though different from Alice's. So they'd applied to attend the show and forgot about it in the rush of the season.

One September morning the acceptance email dinged into Jake's phone. He scanned it with growing excitement, then raced out the door to find Alice. Speeding down the ramp and across the yard, he followed the sound of the tractor to the orchard. Alice was steering the chubby orange Kubota between rows of trees. She had her headphones on and was yell-singing.

"Glory days, well, they'll pass you by! Glory days, in the wink of a young girl's eye!"

Jake planted himself at the end of one row and waved his arms. She threw the tractor into neutral and pulled off her headphones, releasing Bruce Springsteen's tinny hoots into the air.

"We got in! To the Food and Wine Classic!" he yelled, waving his phone. "We're going to the show!"

Alice whooped and clapped her hands and shut off the tractor.

"Hot damn!" she yelled. "I can't believe it!"

"I know!" he said. "Oh. My. GOD! Road trip!"

"Look out, LA!" Alice yelled, and then her face fell. She glanced down at her Carhartt overalls, which were her daily uniform.

"Oh hell. Wait. Do I have to wear a dress? I can't wear a dress. If it's, like, a dress thing, I think I'm out, kid. Seriously."

Jake chortled giddily. Alice worried about the weirdest things.

"Yes, you do, actually, Alice. It says in the email that you will not be allowed into the exhibit hall unless you wear a dress. And it has to be slightly inappropriate for your age. With heels."

She jigged in place and chucked her gloves at him.

"We're going to the show!" she yelled.

"The show!" he yelled.

That excitement buoyed them through the weeks before the show—a three-day affair held in October. On the flight to LA, they were upgraded to first class, and during her second in-flight cocktail, Alice made bold pronouncements about taking the Classic by storm—dominating breakout sessions, attending networking mixers, even throwing down at late-night karaoke. But once they entered the exhibit hall, her bravado evaporated, and Jake felt cowed too. To call it overwhelming was an understatement. As they wandered through the giant rooms looking for their booth, they passed hundreds of exhibitors. The show was, after all, a gathering of the best purveyors of food and drink in the country. Such beautiful food—wild mushrooms of all varieties, dried chilis and spices in a rainbow of colors, enormous wheels of gorgeous aged cheeses. Huge blocks of bean-to-bar chocolate. There were cured meats from all over the country, otherworldly fruits and vegetables, and wine, beer, mead, and spirits of all kinds.

After the initial journey through the show floor, Jake was content to spend the weekend at the Queen of G booth. The crowd was difficult to navigate in his chair, and anyway, he preferred chatting with chefs, winemakers, and natural grocery buyers who came by to taste honey. Alice didn't like talking to people. She wandered the big halls and came back loaded with samples and wild stories.

"There's a guy here who forages for sea beans. *Sea beans*, Jake. What the hell is a sea bean? And the seaweed people? There must be a dozen of them. And this one company 'hand harvests ashwagandha for small-batch, mood-enhancing non-spirited spirits.'"

This last she read from a pamphlet.

"What the hell does that even mean?"

At the awards ceremony Alice fidgeted like a kid. Jake faced the stage and tried to ignore her whispering and jokes. He knew she was nervous. Neither one of them cared who won the honey competition. They were outclassed by bigger, more successful producers, and they knew it—companies from Santa Barbara and Seattle and Portland. But they hoped to be named among the Exceptional First Timers. EFTs were automatically invited back the next year and skipped the application process. But the EFT names in the honey category were read out, and Queen of G was not among them. Alice swore under her breath and Jake tried not to let his disappointment show.

Next year, he thought. Then the emcee announced honorable mention, and third and second places, handing out the awards to the happy winners, who posed for photos with the judges.

"Last but not least, first place! This one was a surprise," the emcee said, his mustache twitching. "From our neighbors to the north, we are pleased to award Best in Show to Queen of G Honey! Mr. Jacob Stevenson and Ms. Alice Holtzman of Hood River County. Are you in the house?"

Alice yelped and Jake couldn't breathe. They looked at each other and he saw bright tears in her eyes. As usual, Alice tried to mask her emotion with a joke.

"Get a move on, Mr. Jacob Stevenson of Hood River County."

"Age before beauty," he said, gesturing for her to lead the way to the podium.

He wasn't just being polite in letting Alice go first. He needed a minute to navigate the ramp adjacent to the stage stairs. The past six years had shown him that ADA requirements didn't always mean true accessibility. But the ramp was manageable, and Jake found himself onstage shaking hands with the judges and looking out at an audience of more than a thousand people. The emcee, who seemed vaguely familiar, like an actor from a long-ago sitcom, looked momentarily surprised at Jake's wheelchair but kept talking as Alice and Jake were photographed with their Feastie award.

"Oh, this is extra special," the emcee said. "I've got a note from the judges here. 'While this is the inaugural year for honey at the classic, we were astonished by the quality of the entrants. And Queen of G Honey rose above this talented showing. With a complexity of flavor, and notes of huckleberry and salmonberry, this medium-tone honey seems to conjure the verdant, sunny meadows of the Hood River Valley itself. We're awarding this producer with a ninety-nine out of one hundred points!' Well, what do you have to say about that, Mr. Stevenson?"

Jake leaned toward the mic.

"Um, thank you," he said. "We're just so happy to be here and grateful and . . . this is an unexpected . . ."

He looked out at the auditorium and felt woozy. He'd never been in front of so many people, and his own words seemed to echo back at him like the dumbest thing anyone had ever said. Alice reached past him and plucked the mic from the emcee's hand. She wasn't wearing her Carhartts, as she had threatened, or a dress. In her sensible navy slacks and beige sweater, she looked very much herself. Somehow Alice, introverted by nature, was strangely comfortable in front of a crowd. She held the microphone easily and her voice rang through the auditorium.

"Five years ago, Queen of G Honey didn't exist. It wasn't even a pipe dream. I grew up on an orchard that my parents were forced to sell. I was working an unfulfilling job and thought I'd put in my time until I retired to my beekeeping hobby. Then I met this kid."

She gestured at Jake.

"Jake Stevenson helped me grow from a few hobby hives to a thriving small business. Without his imagination and hard work, I wouldn't be here today. He changed my life, and I'm forever grateful. To me, this award is all about Jake's talent and grit. Thank you for having us."

Jake's vision blurred.

"Allergies," Alice said, wiping her own eyes as they left the stage. "Yellow star thistle is a bitch."

Later they were interviewed by all the big culinary magazines—*Food & Wine*, *Bon Appétit*, and *Saveur*. The *Los Angeles Times* Food section was the one Jake remembered most. The reporter was young, about the same age as he was. She was very attractive and quite nervous, directing all her questions to Alice.

"How do you account for—for—the quality of the honey produced in your hives?" she asked, her eyes darting from Alice to Jake and back to Alice.

"You'll have to ask Jake. I'm just the brawn in this operation. The kid is the brains," Alice said.

The young woman looked confused.

"I'm in charge of the honey classification and sorting," Jake said. "Alice and I share hive-tending duties. We both work the hives during the season, but I do more of the processing-related work—grading and tasting and things like that."

The young woman seemed to be listening but didn't write down anything he said. He tried to quell his creeping frustration. Do not let it ruin this moment, he thought.

". . . seasonal work," Alice was saying. "Tasks vary all summer, but it's all-hands-on-deck during honeyflow. Madness. You should see this kid and me—dueling forklifts."

The reporter glanced at Jake's wheelchair and blushed deeply. Jake felt a spike of anger.

"But how do you— What do you—" the reporter stammered.

Alice exhaled loudly through her nose.

"How do we what, hon?" she asked testily.

If Jake didn't want his own anger to show, it never helped when Alice got her back up about people's discomfort with his wheelchair. He'd told her that many times. Anyway, he knew this reporter, who was now flushing the color of an heirloom tomato, did not mean to be rude. She was just young. But shit! She was his age! Wasn't Gen Z supposed to be more enlightened?

"Well, I mean. Sorry—I didn't— It's just not typical to see—" she stammered.

Jake smiled, almost feeling sorry for her then.

"It's okay. I understand. We get that question all the time. Most people don't know there are all kinds of technologic and mechanical assistance these days," Jake said. "It helps make up for any lack of ability for someone of advanced age. Like Ms. Holtzman here."

Alice snorted and the reporter blinked rapidly and thanked them for their time. Jake watched her hurry away, feeling wistful. She'd been so pretty.

Alice hooted and slapped her knees.

"I think we made a friend there!" she said. "You should put me in charge of your dating life!"

And then she was the one flushing.

The image of Ruby flashed through his mind—Ruby laughing and tossing her red hair. His heart folded in half.

"Shit," Alice mumbled. "Sorry, kid."

"Sure, Alice," he said, pretending he hadn't heard her apology. "Let's do our victory lap and find you some sea beans."

Now Jake set his coffee cup on the porch railing and banished the memory of Ruby. He spun around and wheeled back into the house, checking his email for the third time that morning to see if anyone had answered his help wanted ad.

The question of Jake's dating life, or lack thereof, had been eclipsed by Queen of G's success at the West Coast Food and Wine Classic. Since then, business had ramped up. As Stefan predicted, they had new interest from all over the West. Previously, the wholesale business had been small and local. Queen of G sold a few thousand jars to Little Bit Grocery and local restaurants and wineries as well as through its seasonal farm stand. But now they were getting orders from restaurants in California, Oregon, and Washington—fancy restaurants. Award-winning restaurants. The kinds of places that liked to include the name of each farm on the menu—Carlton Farms pork shoulder with Los Osos Valley Organic Farm Broccolini and Rainshadow Organics' purple potatoes. Artisanal cheeses from Ferndale Farmstead, Tamiyasu Orchards' Honeycrisp apples, and Queen of G Honey. Some of the restaurants sent them sample menus to show how their honey would be presented. It was thrilling to see Queen of G's name printed on the elegant little menus. The sales quantities were smaller, but the price point was higher and the financial influx from those orders had been considerable.

This change of fortune was then surpassed by an unexpected

development—inquiries from patrons of those fine restaurants that had featured Queen of G Honey on the menu. It had started around Christmas—orders trickling in through the website. And the messages! They were like love letters—little joy bombs every time Jake opened his email in the morning.

Dear QOG,

We tasted your beautiful honey at French Laundry in San Francisco when we celebrated our tenth anniversary. My wife said your honey reminded her of summers when we were college kids living in Eugene. This year I would like to surprise her with a jar of your honey for her birthday. It's the best gift I can think of.

And

Your honey brought back memories of my childhood in Oregon!

And

I'm a professional musician and Queen of G Honey cured my sore throat. It's magical and I love it so, so much!

The unexpected messages were delightful at first, but then the trickle grew to a flood, with messages coming from besotted diners in Portland and Seattle and San Francisco and LA. Then, last week, an email from the inestimable Blue Hill at Stone Barns in Tarrytown, New York, with an order for twelve cases. Last year's harvest had sold out and Queen of G was into preorders. Scanning his email now, Jake noticed more order notifications and felt his stomach drop. He'd stopped opening them last week.

Honeyflow was just around the corner, and it would be massive—a fact that made Jake feel even worse. Queen of G had never been more in demand, had a bonkers honey harvest just weeks away, and absolutely didn't have the staff for it.

Jake looked in his email for any responses to his help wanted ad. Nothing. He pulled open Gorge Classifieds and refreshed his entry.

"Help Wanted: Seasonal laborers for Hood River Valley farm. Must be able to lift sixty pounds. Will train. No equipment skills necessary. Starting immediately. $15 an hour with a guarantee of 20 hours per week and up to 40."

A week had passed with no responses. Local kids, it seemed, would rather work at one of the coffee shops around town or Dairy Queen. In 2019, farming was not cool.

Jake tried to feel optimistic. Hood River Valley High School let out soon. Maybe he'd get more interest then. His email dinged. The subject heading read: "Your honey changed my life!" Feeling queasy, he shut his laptop.

Alice would understand, of course. She'd brace her hands on the worn knees of her Carhartts and whistle long and low.

"The misery of success, kid," she'd say. "Look at us poor suckers."

But Alice didn't say anything because Alice wasn't there. Alice had left for a backpacking trip to Alaska with Stan, her man-friend, as she called him, three weeks ago. They'd be gone for eight weeks and unreachable much of that time. Even if he could call her, he wouldn't. He knew she'd come straight back, and he didn't want to ruin her trip—the first vacation she'd taken in years. And with wonderful Stan. He wanted them to have this trip.

It had been a struggle to get her to go in the first place. It had taken all of them—Stan and Sergio, who was the foreman on Alice's orchard, and Jake himself—to convince her. Stan insisted it was the trip of a lifetime. Sergio told her she'd only get in the way and slow everyone down, which made her laugh.

"Seriously, Alice. We'll be fine and the fruit won't be in for months," Sergio said.

Sergio had overseen the orchard since before Alice bought it, and she trusted him completely. She loved Stan. So it had come down to Jake.

"Be honest, Jake. Can you handle the honeyflow without me? It's going to be a big one this year."

"Alice, I'll be fine, I swear. Noah and Cece and her family are going to help me, and Stokes might even be back mid-season."

The part about Harry Stokes, his roommate and dear friend, was a fib. Stokes was teaching kiteboarding on South Padre Island and would not be back until autumn. But Noah Katz had said he'd absolutely help, and his girlfriend, Cece Martinez, said probably. Though the two of them were busy running their small bakery, they could arrange their schedules to help. Noah was dependable, mostly, and Cece was strong for her size. Plus, she had a passel of burly little brothers who did whatever she told them to. Jake had known them both long enough to know that Cece's "probably" was more reliable than Noah's "absolutely."

In any case, he, Stan, and Sergio had convinced Alice to go. She looked so happy the day they left. It made him glad, despite how things looked now.

Jake swiveled from the desk and glanced at the fridge, where he'd stuck the latest postcard from Noah and Cece, this one from Mexico City.

"Help! Being dangerously overfed by future in-laws!" the card read in Noah's terrible scrawl.

Things had changed with Noah and Cece's recent engagement, which set in motion a series of imperative family visits—down the coast of California—to the homes of several Martinez aunts and uncles and dozens of cousins. Then on to the state of Michoacán to see Cece's abuelita and all her sisters, who were Cece's tía abuelas, and the associated family members there. Cece's entire family was going along, including those strong little brothers Jake had been counting on. The itinerary got longer as more stops were added. When they left two weeks ago, they did not know when they'd be back.

"Dude, I had no idea. I'm so sorry, man," Noah had said when they stopped by to say goodbye. "Her gramma is really old and can't travel so we have to go to her, and there's all these other relatives to meet . . ."

He trailed off, looking pale.

Cece was radiant and unapologetic.

"That's why I said *probably*, Jake. I thought we might take this trip. You'll be fine. I'll send my neighbors over. They're good boys, and they work hard."

True to her word, Cece sent her neighbors over. But Jake didn't know if the seventeen-year-old Salazar twins were good boys or hard workers. They hadn't come back after the first day. They took one look at the rows of hives and bees flitting through the morning sunlight and refused to move a step closer.

"We'll do anything but that," one of the twins said, and the other one nodded.

"Not that."

Jake had found about three hours of work for them to do that was not bee-related and asked them to come back the next day to watch him work a hive.

"Then you can decide."

They had not returned.

The refrigerator hummed, and Jake realized how quiet it was in the house. He'd been alone so much the past two weeks. With Alice and Harry and Noah and Cece gone, he felt increasingly besieged by his thoughts. The worst thoughts threatened to intrude—specifically, thoughts of Ruby. He hadn't seen Ruby since last spring when she breezed through town, gorgeous as ever. One wonderful night and months of devastation had followed. Alice was furious. Wanted to track her down and give her "a swift kick in the ass," as she said. But there was no tracking Ruby down. Soon after that scorched-earth visit, she announced on her IG feed that she was taking a break from social media. He had no idea where she was or what she was doing. He knew it was for the best. Nothing about Ruby Jones was good for him.

He pushed out the back door and zipped down the ramp, crossing the yard toward the apiary. In a flash of brown and thunder of paws, Cheney flew down out of the trees and streaked toward him. Jake threw on his brake to absorb the impact of his fireplug of a dog and his traditional morning greeting.

Cheney slathered him with kisses and pushed off, scooting in ecstatic circles, a middle-aged puppy with so much joy.

"Morning! Isn't this awesome?!" his wiggling body seemed to say.

And there was nothing to do but watch him and wait. Jake knew if he tried to keep moving, Cheney would pummel him with kisses and whirl about the chair, making it impossible. "The Long Hello," Alice called this morning routine. Jake scratched the white star of fur on Cheney's sternum until he quietened. Then he rolled toward the apiary with the dog trotting alongside.

He passed Alice's farmhouse. The blinds were drawn, doors and windows closed. In the distance he could see Sergio talking to his crew in the orchard. Jake raised a hand, and when Sergio waved back, Cheney galloped off to greet the men.

Queen of G's apiary was set off to the side of Alice's orchards, facing south toward Mount Hood, which seemed to fill the sky. Rows of hives gleamed white in the morning sunlight. Foragers zipped throughout the orchard and the air was filled with the comforting drone of the colonies, which now numbered two hundred.

Inside each hive, one queen labored to build up her colony. At this time of year, she'd be laying about three thousand eggs per day. And her hardworking daughters, as many as sixty thousand, would be creating space for the young bees—forming sweet-smelling white honeycomb in which to nurture baby bees and sealing every crack with propolis to keep the hive cozy. Foragers would fly from dawn to dusk retrieving pollen and nectar for the young brood. Each member of the hive would be working toward the honeyflow, the period of plenty that peaked in summer in the Hood River Valley.

Jake checked the weather forecast. It was warmer than it should be for June. This meant everything bloomed earlier and could accelerate harvest timelines. There was also the danger of bee habitat drying up too soon and leaving them without midsummer sustenance.

The scent of beeswax and honey wafted through the warming air. The bees droned and Jake felt the hum in his own body, his own heart. Even after all these years, he still felt that golden thread connecting him to the honeybees and their hives, the feeling he'd experienced the first time Alice had shown him the apiary.

He thought of the Machado poem Cece had written in his birthday card last month.

Last night as I was sleeping,
I dreamt—marvelous error!—
that I had a beehive
here inside my heart.

He had it memorized and loved, especially, the lines about the bees making honey and comb from old failures. Cece had included the original Spanish next to the English translation for him.

Miel dulce de mis viejos fracasos. Sweet honey from my old failures.

The golden buzz dimmed, and his heart felt heavy.

Fracasos. Failures. The Spanish word felt more visceral, like the splinters he felt in his heart when he thought of Ruby. Beautiful, terrible Ruby. Ruby whom he'd loved so much, even after she'd broken his heart the second time.

Cheney cantered back across the field and nosed Jake's hand, forcing his thoughts to the present. He looked at the apiary and then up into the thick foothills around Mount Hood. He needed to get up there today to check the meadow apiary and the two hundred new hives there.

This thought, like the love letters from the foodies, filled him with joy and dread at the same time. He wondered if there was a word for that in Spanish—dread mixed with joy. He'd have to ask Cece when she got back. Whatever you called it, the dreadful joy in his heart also included the Mount Hood meadow that he and Alice had established last summer. This was the business expansion Alice had mentioned and that they both felt rueful about now.

"Two hundred more. Hell, kid. Why not?" Alice had said initially.

She loved the idea of growing the business, and Jake was curious about what kind of flavors might emerge in the honey produced at this pristine, high-alpine location. Tansy Stevenson, who was Jake's mother as well as the Queen of G bookkeeper and the oft-ignored voice of reason at the farm, had made cautionary noises about overextending themselves, but neither of them had listened.

In their defense, Jake thought, that was before the food show. They'd signed the lease, prepared the site, built the hives, and installed the splits the month before they'd gotten accepted to the West Coast Food and Wine Classic. Though they'd hoped the show would open new restaurant markets, they'd never foreseen the prospect of direct sales and how time-consuming it would all become. Everything was coming to a head just when it was time to start summer hive checks. Jake turned away from the apiary, made his way to the barn, and loaded his tools into the truck. He opened the truck door and Cheney leapt onto the front seat. Jake climbed in and pulled his chair up and in, folding it down in the back.

He sat in the truck looking out over the apiary—spring was peaking and he had four hundred productive hives just on the edge of bloom time. Jake Stevenson was facing an epic honeyflow and the most epic season of his entire career. And with Alice away, Noah and Cece in Mexico, and Harry in Texas, without a single worker to help him, Jake Stevenson also knew he was epically screwed.

Fracasos. It would not be his first failure, and that was some kind of cold comfort. He drove on toward the mountain, his heart brimming with dreadful joy.

3

SCOUTING

In the case of solitary bees, the queen creates her nest, lays her eggs, and raises her offspring without assistance from any other bees. The majority of the earth's bee species are solitary.

—LAVIN, *THE WONDROUS WORLD OF BEES*

FLACO WAS BRAVE. At least his mother said so. Flaco was one of the quickest strikers on the fútbol field. He took after his father in this, or so he was told. Flaco was smart and spoke better English than anyone in his class and even in the whole town. Maestra Monica had repeated this often and everyone respected Maestra Monica. But in the present moment, none of that mattered at all. All that mattered was that Flaco was hungry.

Flaco was hungry and hungrier than he could ever remember having been hungry before. Hungry in a way that seemed primal and urgent. Hungry, yes, but a hunger that was complicated by the fact that he also felt sick. Almost crudo, not that being hungover was something he was overly familiar with. He'd only gotten drunk with Carlos the one time they'd pilfered some beer from his older brother. But he'd felt similarly then—unsteady, sweaty, and aware that though he had just evacuated the contents of his stomach, part of the remedy lay in putting something else in the now empty space that yawned within him—his belly, his heart, his very soul, it seemed.

He sat up and leaned against the tree he'd been lying under. The horizon tipped slightly but held and he was able to remain upright, which was an improvement. His clothes were damp with spring dew and his tongue stuck to the roof of his dry mouth. He was so hungry.

Un milagro, a miracle, his mother would have teased. Because Flaco was never hungry. His lack of appetite was universally known within the small borders of his hometown.

"El muchacho loses weight while eating," his abuela often complained about her grandson when Flaco was younger.

His friends teased that they couldn't see him when he stood behind the flagpole in the schoolyard. Nobody had called him by his given name since he could remember—Sebastián, or Sebastián Santiago Luna López in its entirety. Everyone called him Flaco, "Skinny," or Flaquito, little skinny boy. Flaco, who was never hungry. Flaco, who often forgot to eat and had to be prodded to the table.

As Flaco grew from a boy into the fourteen-year-old youth he now was, his slightness became ever more apparent. He added inches to his frame and limbs but not his girth. His knees grew knobby; his wrists poked out of his shirtsleeves. His friends teased that his elbows were sharp enough to wound when they played fútbol.

"Ah, you cut me wide open, Flaco!" Carlos would yell and fall to the ground writhing in mock agony. "Machete elbows!"

In recent months, Flaco's Adam's apple had begun to poke out of his drainpipe of a throat. His ears flapped out from the sides of his head. He wished he could put on weight, but he just wasn't interested in food. If it weren't for his mother's insistence that he come to the table, it's true that Flaco might have forgotten to eat altogether. He just wasn't hungry. He had better things to do.

Like reading about geography and natural history, for example. Flaco had first discovered old copies of *National Geographic en Español* in the church basement during primary school. By the time he'd reached secondary school, he'd developed a passion for the world's remotest landscapes—Antarctica, the Himalayas, Ittoqqortoormiit in Greenland, and Easter Island. He was also drawn to the natural wonders of his own country, like Barranca del Cobre, Copper Canyon, which plunged to a depth of 4,600 feet in places, and the Great Pyramid of Cholula, the largest pyramid in the world by volume.

He became obsessed with Mexico's volcanoes, including Pico de Orizaba, the third-tallest peak in North America at 18,491 feet, and Pico de Tancítaro, the highest point in his home state, at 12,615 feet. It stirred Flaco's imagination to think of these now-dormant volcanoes gushing with molten lava many years ago, or more recently, like Volcán de Colima. Volcán de Colima had exploded dramatically in May 2005, on the very day Flaco was born, which made him feel an affinity to the old stratovolcano, and again just that spring. It seemed like a sign that Flaco should make a pilgrimage to witness his volcanic sibling's reawakening in the state of Jalisco. However, his path had not led him to Volcán de Colima. It was Mount Hood he saw from where he sat now in the damp grass.

Flaco had been following Oregon's peaks—Mount Bachelor, South Sister, Middle Sister, North Sister, Mount Jefferson—since Bend. The snow-covered stratovolcano hadn't been visible from Bend, but he knew it was close to Hood River, this northernmost volcanic peak in Oregon's Cascade Range. When he'd finally caught sight of Mount Hood, his heart leapt, as it signaled that he was close to his destination after days of walking. Mount Hood had seemed to tip its witch's hat peak at him in congratulations. He should have felt a sense of accomplishment, but by then he hadn't eaten in days and celebrating anything other than locating food seemed nonsensical. He walked along tortured by memories of his mother's home cooking and the ready availability of calories that he'd once declined. What wouldn't he give for a big bowl of caldo de res with a stack of hot corn tortillas on the side? Or even a plate of leftover beans.

No food would materialize here in this high mountain clearing.

Mamá's caldo de res was three weeks and more than two thousand miles behind him. He was painfully aware that he was on his own, he felt terrible, and he had to find something to eat. Grasping a small pine tree with both hands, Flaco eased himself to his feet. The world slanted ninety degrees, and he slid back down to the ground and closed his eyes.

Time had taken on a strange dimension since he'd left home. The days seemed impossibly long without the structure of school and chores and church. The last five days had seemed especially weird since he'd become separated from Luis. Flaco had never been truly alone before in his life. His own household was relatively quiet, just him and Mamá since Abuela had passed. But in Las Lunas everyone was connected—by blood, marriage, or the nearly family feeling that comes from having known each other for generations. He'd grown up under the constant observation of the adult population of the village, who did not hesitate to correct, castigate, tease, embrace, or scold him or any of the other local kids. He wasn't even aware of that benevolent umbrella of supervision until it was gone. At first that security had been replaced by the excitement of traveling with a group of other young men—Flaco being the youngest among them—on the bus, a truck, the train, and then a van as they made their way north. But these last five days, since he'd been completely alone, Flaco felt exposed and vulnerable like he never had in his entire life. Or, more accurately, only once before: on the day his mother, Beatriz, told him she was sending him north.

Flaco pictured his mother in the kitchen, chopping onions, her eyes streaming as she laughed and wiped her tears with the back of her wrist. Her long, dark hair pulled back and piled into a messy bun on top of her head. He liked to think of her that way—cooking and singing and chatting to their neighbor, Frida. That image was better than thinking of the last time he'd seen her, when she'd said goodbye. Then, she'd looked impossibly sad and tried to smile.

"You're brave, and you're so smart. You'll be fine, Flaco," she said.

"Stay close to Javier until you get to Cousin César. Call me when you can."

She kissed his forehead and breathed a prayer over him and walked away. Flaco watched her go and waited for her to look back, but she disappeared into the crowd. Flaco wanted to run after her, to throw his arms around her neck, breath in the scent of her—vanilla and cinnamon and soap. Beg her to let him stay. But he would not shame her. He turned and climbed onto the bus with the others.

Flaco opened his eyes to the sunny clearing. The birdsong increased, and the sun moved across the sky. Mount Hood's majesty broke through his fatigue. The massive white body of it was grounding somehow. Flaco prodded his stomach lightly and decided to stand. This time he was successful. He pulled his shoulders back, feeling a hollowness in his belly.

It must have been the hongos that made him sick. The pale, rubbery heads and stalks were all he'd eaten in the past few days. He'd found them in the shade of a large grove of firs and eaten three before he began to feel terrible. Flaco had never eaten a mushroom before. But he was hungry and knew he'd have to get used to new things in the north, including food.

Javier, one of the older guys, had tried to prepare him and the other first-timers.

"Things are different—the food, the way people live, everything."

Different how? the others wanted to know. That was the first night, when they were still in Mexico. They were sleeping behind a llantera on the edge of a larger town north of Las Lunas. The owner had collected their money and disappeared into his shop tucked away behind piles of used tires. Later his wife came out and invited them to come eat in the cramped yard off the kitchen. Then they lay in the sand with their jackets under their heads and waited for sleep.

Javier lit a cigarette and blew smoke, considering the question.

"Well, everybody drives, for one thing," he said. "So you have to have wheels or take the bus."

They all knew that from the movies, one of the other boys said.

"Pues, sí," Javier said. "But what I mean is that nobody walks. So in some cities it's hard to get around. Some places you can't walk where the cars are driving. They'll, like, arrest you."

Flaco tried to imagine what he meant. In Las Lunas, most families had a truck. But trucks were for work or taking everyone to church or going very occasionally to Morelia. Everyone walked in Las Lunas. Flaco tried to imagine a street so full of automobiles that you couldn't walk there.

"And when you do walk," Javier continued, "people don't look at each other or say anything. Especially in the cities. If you look at some guys and say hey or something, they get pissed off or worse. It's better to keep your eyes down and act like you know where you're going even if you're lost."

Nobody asked him to elucidate. Flaco shuddered. He thought of the cartel members outside his school, scanning the crowd of kids. He thought of Alán.

". . . but there's other stuff that's great," Javier was saying. "Beautiful women and parties. All kinds of different food and fun stuff to do."

Flaco asked Javier if it was in true that in Oregon, where he was headed, there were volcanoes covered in snow that you could ski on. And if you could really walk right up to the mouth of Mount Saint Helens and look inside the crater. Javier said he didn't know about the skiing or volcanoes.

"You can go hiking and all that. But in those woods, you have to watch out for wolves and bears and stuff. Coyotes. I'm serious, dude," he said, pointing his cigarette at Flaco. "Wild animals up there like we don't have back at home. Better the wild animals than the gringos locos, though."

And by coyote, Flaco knew Javier was talking about the animal, not coyotes like Señor Rivas, whom they'd paid to escort them north. That's what he said his name was anyway. Flaco knew he couldn't trust Señor Rivas, not really. His mother had told him that.

"Listen to Señor Rivas and do what he tells you, but remember he's not your friend, not family," Mamá had said.

Javier, on the other hand, was from the next town over. Almost like a cousin. He seemed trustworthy if not always completely truthful. He was probably making that stuff up about the lobos and osos and coyotes just to tease. Flaco wondered if he was joking about the wild animals being less dangerous than white people. Javier had been to the north several times, so he did know a lot. Javier had been nice to him the whole trip. Flaco had heard his mother ask Javier to keep an eye on Flaco and saw her try to give Javier some money, which he refused. He called her "tía" and told her not to worry.

"He's a smart one, that Flaco. He'll do fine, auntie."

It was true that Flaco was smart. His book smarts were part of the reason Mamá was sending him north, she'd told him. Also, the fact that he was a boy, which would make things easier, she'd said. Her eyes had strayed to Frida's daughters, who were playing just outside in the yard, when she said that. Flaco looked at the two little girls, Rosa and Sofi, who were five and six but looked like twins and were playing an elaborate game involving a battered doll's pram and an old bucket. He didn't ask his mother what she meant.

"Cousin César will be there to meet you. But if it happens that you get picked up by la migra, don't panic. Use your head. Tell them your name and that you need help and ask to speak to the person in charge. Tell them you have family waiting for you in Hood River. They will help you get to César."

She repeated these instructions to him in the days leading up to his departure. The last time, right before he boarded the bus, her voice broke as she said "family." Then she forced a smile and squeezed his shoulders.

"Everything is going to be fine," she said, but she didn't sound so sure. "And Javier will be there too. He'll help you."

Javier had different advice about la migra, having been picked up by U.S. immigration officers twice in the past.

"You don't want to end up there, Flaco. My advice is if you see them, fade back and then run like hell, güey."

Flaco had not seen Javier since California. After riding the buses together, and crouching in the back of the big truck, they'd huddled on the top of La Bestia for two days, which was nothing compared to some of the others who'd suffered weeks on the terrible train. Then they'd crossed the river in the dark and climbed through a hole in a fence and run toward a van waiting for them in the desert borderland. Flaco lay in the back with the others for hours, feeling the American highway vibrate along his spine. Their actual arrival in Central California had been anticlimactic. The driver opened the back, and they all climbed out into the moonless night at a truck stop just outside Fresno. Señor Rivas was nowhere in sight and Flaco couldn't remember when he'd seen him last.

Javier was the first to leave. He threw his bag into an idling car and walked back to the clutch of teenage boys who sat on the curb shivering like rabbits in their light jackets.

"Good luck, chamacos," he said. "You got my number, right, Flaquito?"

Flaco nodded. He put his hand in his pocket and gripped the phone his mother had given him.

"Call me if you get in a jam, little man. I'm sure your primo will be here soon."

Then he was gone. Flaco and the other boys passed the night sleeping fitfully up against the side of the building. Flaco went inside once to use the bathroom, and the clerk, who spoke Spanish, was friendly. Vehicles came and went all night. It was relatively quiet except for a commotion right before dawn when two drunk white men started fighting next to the dumpster. Flaco averted his eyes and hoped the fight wouldn't spill closer. In the morning, the others left one by one until it was just Flaco, Pedro, and Luis still sitting at the truck stop. Pedro and Luis were a couple of years older than Flaco and had begun to fill out. They had muscular arms and downy mustaches. Flaco felt somewhat safer in their company. There was still no sign of Cousin César. After a shift change at the truck stop, the three were told they had to leave the property.

They moved across the dirt lot to a wreck of a building that was still within sight of the truck stop and waited. The day passed and it grew hot. They told stories and dozed in the shade. When the night clerk came back and began her shift, she brought them bottled water and some food—hot dogs smothered with carne and cheese. Flaco ate half of one and felt queasy.

"Gracias, señora," he said.

The woman lit a cigarette and flicked her eyes over the trio of boys.

"You shouldn't stay here," she said in Spanish. "This is not a safe place. All kinds of crazies around."

They argued after she left.

"She didn't say we *can't* stay here, she said shouldn't," Pedro said.

Luis wanted to walk up the road and wait where they could watch for his uncle, who had promised he'd be there by morning. Flaco didn't know what to do. He hadn't received any instructions about how to proceed if his cousin didn't show up. And he'd discovered his phone didn't work in California. When he tried to dial Cousin César, he heard a querulous beeping and the voice of a woman saying something in English he couldn't understand. As the others argued, he thought about what the clerk had said and what Javier had said.

"*Better the wild animals than the gringos locos.*"

Now, standing in the meadow, Flaco knew he couldn't think about all that. He had to start moving and find himself some food. He stepped unsteadily through the trees toward the sound of running water. A clear stream burbled along the rocks under the shade of big pines. He knelt and drank and splashed his face. He felt a little better and returned to the path.

As he walked, he fantasized about what he'd eat when he reached a town. There were lots of Mexican people in Oregon, Luis had told them while they waited near the gas station. Luis was bound for Bend, Oregon, several hours closer than Flaco's destination with Cousin César in Hood River.

"Tacos and enchiladas, tortas, and sopes. As good as home. You'll see," Luis had said.

Flaco's stomach yawned widely. He imagined a table covered with food. Somehow just thinking about it made him feel better, but only briefly. The feeling of want inside him deepened then. It wasn't just the food, of course. He missed Las Lunas, his friends, his familiar routine. He missed school and he even missed church, which bored him. But most of all he missed his mother. His heart ached thinking of her standing over the old stove making breakfast for them before she hurried to work. All the days he took that for granted, that simple daily offering of food. But more than that was the hunger he felt deep in his heart—a lack that all the food in the world could not fill. Mamá.

He found himself at the edge of the trees looking out into a sunny meadow. He hesitated, afraid to leave the cover of the forest after what had happened five days ago. The shaggy branches of the huge firs felt safe, though their shade chilled him to the bone.

Out in the meadow, the green grass rippled like water as a gentle wind blew through it. It seemed to beckon him. Flaco stepped out of the forest and the warmth of the spring sunshine hit him like a hug. He tipped his face up to the sky and wandered into the sea of green grass.

He noticed a rough road off to the west of the meadow. Though it made him nervous, he knew it was a sign that he was closer to people and towns and food, closer to his destination and closer to Cousin César. He made his way through the grass toward the road, rounded a corner, and stopped. There, arrayed across a section of meadow, were hundreds of white boxes. Each one was the size of a large suitcase. A raised wooden boardwalk ran alongside the white boxes. Flaco walked closer, watching and listening for any sign of danger.

His nervous system had been on high alert for weeks. There was the strangeness of being away from home but also the unexpected change in plans that had landed him here—not in a car driving the interstate to Hood River with his cousin but walking alone through the woods along the backbone of the Cascade Range.

It had happened like this: Pedro left and then it was just Flaco and Luis in the dusty lot across from the gas station. And when Luis's ride showed up, the sun was setting and there was still no sign of César. Luis's uncle seemed nice enough and offered to call César since Flaco's phone wasn't working. It went straight to voicemail. Just César's voice saying, "You know what to do, güey." And then the beep.

"You can come with us, mijo," Luis's uncle said. "We can take you to Bend, and you can meet up with your cousin. It's on the way to Hood River."

Flaco hesitated. He wished he could call his mamá but was too afraid to ask the man for another favor.

"Come on, Flaco," Luis said. "You don't want to stay here on your own another night, do you?"

Flaco looked around the dusty parking lot and at the broken fence banging in the dirty wind. The drunk men had disappeared, but who knew if they'd be back? No, he did not want to stay here another night.

So he'd gone with Luis and his uncle, who never did introduce himself by name. By the time they got to Bend, Flaco had worked up the courage to ask the uncle if he could call home. He wanted to weep when he heard his mother's voice.

"¡Gracias a Dios, mijo! I've been so worried. César texted that he was delayed and that he hadn't heard from you. Where are you?"

The worry in her voice made Flaco choke back his tears. He told her he was fine; he was with a friend's family in Bend. He could wait for César there. He didn't know why the phone she gave him wasn't working, but he gave her Luis's uncle's address and phone number to relay to his cousin.

His mother told him how much she missed him and how proud she was of him. Flaco couldn't speak. I want to come home! he wanted to say. I'm scared, Mamá!

In the silence he heard his mother's friend Frida talking to her little girls in the background. He remembered his mother saying he was lucky he was older and lucky he was a boy. He remembered how much she'd paid Señor Rivas. Her life's savings.

"I'm fine, Mamá. Everything is fine," he lied. "I'll wait here for César, and I'll call you when we get to Hood River."

"You take care of yourself, mijo. And remember, just do your best. Remember what my father always said?"

And he said it with her, the mantra of his long-dead grandfather, Sebastián, for whom he was named.

"El éxito no es definitivo, el fracaso no es fatal. Es el valor para continuar lo que cuenta." Success is not final, failure is not fatal. It is the courage to continue that counts.

She told him she was praying for him and that she was so proud of him. And he had to hang up to keep from crying.

Would his journey have been successful if César had picked him up? He'd never know now. His mother had said César would be there in a couple of days. So when Luis's uncle asked if Flaco could do some work, he didn't have a reason to say no. After all, the man had driven him from Fresno and given him a place to sleep and food to eat.

"Por supuesto que sí, señor," he'd said. Of course.

Luis told him it was farming work. Maybe that's all he knew. Maybe Luis didn't know that the farm was a marijuana farm. He probably didn't know that the farm, up in the foothills above Bend, was an illegal growing operation in this state that had legalized marijuana. Flaco's first inkling that something might be illicit was after the hour-long truck ride up into the hills outside of town. At the field, Luis's uncle introduced them to the boss—a scary-looking old white guy with long stringy hair under a dirty ball cap. He flicked his eyes at them and away and didn't speak. Luis's uncle told the boys to be on the lookout for any strangers. He pointed out a path under the trees and said it led to the Pacific Crest Trail.

"That sendero goes all the way to Hood River, where you're headed, Flaco, and on to Canada. All the way from the California border with Mexico. It's just hikers up here and not too many this time of year. Nobody to get in our business."

That business was a sprawling field of marijuana plants standing chest high and covered with pungent buds. Luis's uncle told them that though Oregon had legalized recreational marijuana, the black market still existed and paid exponentially better. He showed Flaco and Luis how to fertilize the younger seedlings by hand and put them to work. It was not difficult labor, but tedious. Luis had grown slightly imperious by the end of the first day, as if Flaco owed him something for letting him hang with his family. And Flaco supposed he did. So he did not object when Luis insisted he, Flaco, take the farthest side of the field the second day. It was more of a hike from the staging area, where the water and snacks were. But Flaco didn't mind.

He struck out across the field with two buckets of compost. The slight incline on the far side of the field afforded Flaco a view of a snowy mountain peak, which Luis had identified as Mount Bachelor. The slender trail disappeared into the trees as it wound its way north. He could see the other workers pruning young seedlings and the uncle talking to the scary boss, both with their backs to the road. Luis dozed under a far tree in the late morning sunlight. From his vantage point, Flaco was certainly the first person to notice the line of black SUVs tearing up the road toward the field, lights flashing. And in the confusion that followed—workers running, officers yelling—Flaco had instinctively done what Javier advised. He faded into the woods, turned north, and ran as if his life depended on it.

That had happened five days ago. Flaco had stayed on the trail and kept heading north, that direction being the only thing he was sure of because of sunrise and sunset. He'd found a tattered map on the trail that identified the mountain peaks. He'd seen no other people along the muddy and sometimes snow-covered path. He'd found nothing to eat, aside from the ill choice of the mushrooms. Tired, footsore, and nauseated—he found all those feelings eclipsed now by his growing hunger.

He sensed motion and turned his head. An insect flew past toward the boxes. Then another and another. Abejas, he realized, honeybees. Flaco drew closer to the boxes, and the number of honeybees increased. He caught the sweet scent of honey in the warm air. He walked faster and broke into a trot.

When he reached the boxes, he saw they were enclosed by a fence, which looked easy to climb. He grasped the links and fell back with a gasp as an electric shock grazed his palms. The pain made his nausea return, and his head swam. He sat down and leaned his head on his knees, waiting for the nausea to subside.

He raised his head and inhaled slowly. That's when he saw it—a streak of brown out of the corner of his eye, then another and another. They came from behind, galloping as their numbers increased. Flaco could hear the thunder of their feet, could almost feel it reverberate in his body, though he refused to turn and look at the wild animals assembling behind him.

Lobos! he thought. Just like Javier had warned.

"Wild animals up there like we don't have back home."

He knew he should run, but it just seemed like too much. It was all too much—leaving home, missing his mother, being alone for so long and feeling so terrible. He heard the swish of grass parting under the weight of the animals as they moved toward him. He caught their strange musky scent and closed his eyes.

The wind blew through the grass and rushed over him. He thought of his mother then. Suddenly he could feel her all around him as if the wind carried her embrace. He heard her voice in his head.

"*Es el valor para continuar lo que cuenta.*" It is the courage to continue that counts.

And he sprang up off the ground and ran forward to meet his fate.

4

A SOLITARY BEE

She lives for a single year, the bumblebee queen, and the brevity of her life makes her accomplishments all the more astonishing.

—LAVIN, *THE WONDROUS WORLD OF BEES*

ABIGAIL STOOD IN the inky darkness with panic rising in her throat. As her eyes adjusted, she saw a dim red light near the floor and the dark outline of a person.

"Come now, sweetheart, where are you then?" a voice whispered. "I want to have a good look at you. No need to be shy."

Abigail wondered how this person meant to have a good look at her with the lights off.

The voice spoke again.

"Bingo! Hello, lovely! In you go."

The light brightened and the red glow revealed a petite woman bent over an observation table, her face obscured by the darkness.

"Most people don't know that queen bumblebees can sting. No need for such unpleasantness on a Friday afternoon," the woman said.

She gestured at the wall pulsing with the soft bodies of insects.

"I lost track of her when I was moving her colony, but I've got her here now."

Abigail saw that the velvety mass was congregated on the other side of a pane of plexiglass. A buzzing murmur reverberated through the room.

"These are *Bombus occidentalis,* western bumblebees. Not wild bees, though. These were bred for commercial use—hothouse tomatoes and blueberries. We're studying them to try to understand more about native *Bombus occidentalis.*"

She held up a small cage, which she then slipped into a larger screened compartment, and turned back to Abigail.

"Now then. What can I do for you?"

"I'm Abigail Plue from Dr. Thomas's group. I'm looking for Dr. Mora."

"Ah!" the woman said. "Well, you found her. I forgot you were coming. Let's go back to my office."

In the bright light of the hallway, Dr. Mora shook Abigail's hand. She was short and plump and had an easy smile. They walked past the window to the apiary. The beekeepers had taken off their veils and were still chatting. Dr. Mora waved at the group and led Abigail into her office.

"Have a seat," she said. "Abigail, is it?"

Abigail nodded and sat.

"Nice to meet you. Now, tell me. Do you know why Dr. Thomas sent you over to work with us?"

Abigail thought about the conversation with her adviser.

"Because our institution does not tolerate heated displays of emotion?"

Dr. Mora laughed with surprise.

"Well, I don't know anything about that," she said. "But I believe Dr. Thomas thought you could help me with a new project. He said you were very bright and attentive to detail. And a hard worker. Is that right?"

Abigail didn't know how to answer. Had Dr. Thomas said she was bright, attentive to detail, and a hard worker? What was the question exactly? Dr. Mora waited for an answer.

"I like to work," Abigail said. "I like details and observing, especially insects."

Her answer seemed to satisfy Dr. Mora, who nodded.

"We've been studying honeybees and their commercial applications for almost twenty years here in the Honeybee Lab. And our community beekeeping curriculum is in its tenth year. Both programs are quite robust," Dr. Mora said.

Abigail recoiled internally. She was not interested in honeybees or their commercial applications. Or community beekeepers. She could still hear them out in the apiary laughing and talking. So annoying. Was someone playing the *guitar*?!

". . . a small team to help me develop a new study cohort," Dr. Mora was saying. "I need a few enthusiastic people to get it started."

Abigail sighed. She wanted to be back in her damp, gray office. She did not want to be around a few enthusiastic people. Enthusiasm made her feel Tired and Lonely.

Dr. Mora narrowed her eyes.

"Forgive me, Ms. Plue. Am I boring you?"

Abigail blinked and sat up, acutely aware that she needed to make an effort. Dr. Thomas had told her in no uncertain terms that she could not return to teaching.

"No, Dr. Mora. I'm sorry," she said. She closed her eyes and thought of the sentence her father had helped her craft so many years ago.

"It's just that sometimes, I forget myself."

There was a pause as Dr. Mora considered her.

"I see," Dr. Mora said. "Well then. Tell me, what do you know about bumblebees?"

Abigail did not, in fact, know much about bumblebees. She thought they were beautiful in their own way—clumsy and fuzzy and slow. But all those years working at the nursery and studying as an undergrad, she'd been drawn to insects that others might call pests—spiders and aphid lions and ants and box-elder bugs and beetles. Creatures that were reviled, it seemed, for their very success in surviving in the human-dominated world. This was possibly why she disliked honeybees—they had too many fans. Bumblebees seemed to exist in that camp as well. If honeybees and bumblebees were the dolphins of the insect world, Abigail was interested in the sea lice. At least Dr. Mora's question was easily answered.

"Dr. Mora, I know nearly nothing about bumblebees," she said.

As soon as she said it, she was worried that it was A Wrong Thing to say. She was worried that Dr. Mora would fire her too and that she'd no longer have a home anywhere in the entomology department. She'd have to find a new job, probably at a plant nursery, and be around customers who wanted to make small talk, and she was bad at that and her supervisor would tell her she needed to be more outgoing and she'd have to quit that job too. She'd have to ask her father to loan her some money until she found a new job and he would be so disappointed. He'd try not to show it, which always made it worse.

Dr. Mora interrupted her mental journey down this path of despair.

"No problem. You can learn everything you need to know. Let me show you your office and I'll get you started."

Dr. Mora led Abigail through the department and down a flight of stairs into a small, quiet room far from the center of things.

"It's not a great space, but it's the best we can do right now. We're a little crowded in this wing. You'll be sharing with Casey Antica. She's out in the field right now, if I'm not mistaken, but should be back by Wednesday or Thursday of next week."

Daylight windows offered a view of the sidewalk, but only enough for Abigail to see shins and ankles and shod feet. The small room had two desks, one obviously occupied. The other bore only a laptop and a stack of publications, which Dr. Mora gestured to.

"This is you. I pulled a few studies to get you started. Dr. Thomas said you're self-disciplined and good at working on your own."

Abigail nodded.

"I am not a good collaborator nor a team player," she said.

Dr. Mora regarded Abigail with a faint smile.

"Collaboration comes in different forms. Let's get together early next week after you've had a chance to review this material and you can tell me what you've learned. Have a good weekend," she said and left, leaving the door open.

Abigail shut the door behind her and looked at the pile of publications Dr. Mora had left for her. On top was *Journal of Insect Science*. Next was *Current Opinion in Insect Science* and under that, *Nature*. She sat down and flipped to the first article Dr. Mora had marked. As she read, the facts of bumblebee life began to fill her mind. The information crept into her brain—each piece of data like a solitary bee—and amassed there. She felt the pleasant, growing pressure of facts building inside her head.

Abigail had found her way to the entomology department by chance during her freshman year. Oregon State University was large enough that an undergraduate could bumble through an entire semester without finding a clear path. Abigail's dad, loving as he was, was of no practical help. He only asked if she was enjoying school and if she needed money—closed questions. Yes and no. She was fascinated by her classes, which she'd chosen on her own and which varied widely—English 101 (required), Advanced Calculus, History of World Religions, Ceramics, and Volleyball. Abigail had chosen these classes mainly because they all took place in the afternoon, and she liked to sleep in. By Christmas break, the results were clear: With the exception of calculus, Abigail was bombing college.

English and History of World Religions puzzled her. In both she was expected to "read and respond to the material" and was told that her personal opinion was the most valuable part of the class.

"What you feel truly passionate about," her young English teacher insisted.

But when she turned in her paper, she received a barely passing grade. Her ten-page treatise on the heroism of the common earthworm—something she did feel truly passionate about—did not model the five-paragraph essay the instructor had taught.

World religions baffled her. Raised in an agnostic household, Abigail found it impossible to get past the obvious contradictions between the principles and actions of every major creed.

In ceramics class, she enjoyed learning about the physics of the kiln fire, which heated to over two thousand degrees. She loved the feel of the wet clay under her hands too. But she found the mechanical sound of the wheel upsetting and worked on her projects free form instead. She created a beautiful model of a *Chinavia hilaris*—a bright green stink bug—but it fell apart in the kiln. The teacher was apologetic when she explained that Abigail had to master the use of the equipment to pass the class.

Volleyball confirmed that Abigail had no natural athletic ability, though her teammates marveled at how far she could send the ball in the wrong direction.

She'd aced calc.

At the end of Christmas break her father asked to see her grades. And then he pulled his hair from both sides of his head in that way he did when he was worried. That's when he called the school to see about getting her an adviser.

At her first meeting with Dr. Thomas, he'd asked what classes she'd liked best in high school and if she had any work experience. Abigail had not liked anything about high school but told him she'd worked at DeSilva's Nursery for years.

"Are you interested in plants, perhaps? Horticulture or ag might be a good fit."

Abigail considered the question. Was she interested in plants? What qualified as interested? Was this another trick, like the English teacher telling her to write about what she felt truly passionate about?

While she was still thinking, Dr. Thomas spoke again.

"What did you like most about working at the nursery?"

"Oh! The spiders," Abigail said.

"The spiders," Dr. Thomas repeated.

"Yes, the spiders."

"What spiders?" Dr. Thomas asked.

Where to begin? There were so many spiders. Abigail decided to tell him about the crab spiders at the nursery, which seemed to prefer blanket flower and lupine and had mutualistic relationships with these flowers and did not use webs but captured prey with their forelegs. She curled her forearms to illustrate.

Dr. Thomas listened, nodding, and Abigail kept talking. Nobody but her father had been interested in the spiders.

"Was there anything else you particularly enjoyed about working at the nursery? Your coworkers or talking with customers, maybe? Or anything else?"

She thought about that. None of her coworkers were memorable and the customers made her feel Annoyed because they interrupted her work and asked for advice on which plants to buy. How would she know what they would like?

"I did like the aphid lions," she said.

"The aphid lions," Dr. Thomas said. "What's interesting about aphid lions?"

Abigail was surprised that a biology professor of Dr. Thomas's experience wouldn't know about the fascinating lives of *Chrysopa perla*, also called green lacewings, also called aphid lions in their larval stage. She explained how they appeared each spring in the rose section of DeSilva's during the aphid population explosion and devoured armies of the tiny green invaders.

Dr. Thomas suggested then that Abigail take some biology classes, specifically in entomology. And for the rest of her college career, that's what she'd done, starting with ENT 101, an introduction to crop, soil, and insect science.

That had been more than five years ago, and Abigail felt like she'd found a place for herself. The entomology department understood the underfoot kingdom—the magical teeming universe of invertebrates that existed alongside the human world. All you had to do was turn over any leaf or stone and there was a portal into a fantastic other world. Abigail had immersed herself in the lives and habits of aquatic insects and forest insects and ecosystems and pollinators. She never really thought about graduation or a career, though she did accumulate enough courses for a bachelor of science degree. And against Dr. Thomas's recommendation she'd stayed on at OSU and enrolled in graduate school.

"Take at least a year and get some more work experience, Abigail," Dr. Thomas had said.

"But you said I could work here," she said. "Teaching undergraduate classes."

Abigail felt Content where she was. That was all she had to say to her dad and she knew she could stay. Dad wanted her to be Content.

Content was how she felt now as she began to understand the lives of bumblebees. She read and took notes and fell headlong into the life cycle of genus *Bombus*.

Monday morning, Abigail stood outside Dr. Mora's office. It was early and the Honeybee Lab was mostly empty. People began to trickle in alone and in pairs. Nobody paid any attention to Abigail. She was tired and sat down with her back against the door. She closed her eyes to rest for a minute and fell asleep, then jolted awake to the sound of Dr. Mora's voice.

"Sorry to disturb you, Ms. Plue," she said. "If you don't mind, I'd like to get into my office."

Abigail sprang up and followed close on Dr. Mora's heels. The professor turned, frowning.

"Ms. Plue," she said. "If you have questions about departmental processes, please check in with Deirdre at the front desk. I have a very busy morning, and I need to get to work."

Abigail stared, her mind clicking through the words and trying to understand. Dr. Mora's voice rose.

"Ms. Plue. Could you please leave my office?"

"Oh!" Abigail said, stepping back.

"But I—I—I—" she stammered. "You said I should fill you in on what I'd learned about bumblebees."

Dr. Mora's laugh was bright and surprising.

"I didn't mean first thing Monday morning!"

She looked closely at Abigail.

"Abigail. Have you been here all weekend?"

Abigail wasn't sure how to answer. Almost all weekend, anyway. She'd left the lab four times to visit the vending machines near her old office. The walk to and from gave her a chance to clear her head. In the hallway she did push-ups and sit-ups like she always did when taking a break. There was no one around and she was glad. Sometimes people stared and she thought they might be critiquing her form.

Dr. Mora gestured at Abigail to sit.

"Okay then. Let's hear what you learned."

Abigail sat. She held a sheaf of papers in her hands—the notes she'd compiled over the last three days. She didn't need them, but it felt good to have them as backup as she reported on the state of Oregon's bumblebee population.

Of Oregon's estimated five hundred distinct species of native bees, thirty were bumblebees. Bumblebees were directly responsible for pollinating much of the food people eat, including Oregon's signature blueberry and cranberry crops as well as the common backyard tomato. Bumblebees also pollinated wildflowers—lupine, goldenrod, aster—which, in turn, provided food for birds and other animals in the ecosystem.

Oregon's native bumblebee population had plummeted recently.

Their decline was linked to habitat loss, pesticide use, climate change, and cattle overgrazing, as well as competition with commercially raised bumblebees like the ones in Lab 4. The commercial bumblebees escaped from the greenhouses they'd been raised for, spreading diseases among native pollinators and outcompeting them for habitat and food.

Three species of particular concern for Oregon were the western bumblebee, Morrison's bumblebee, and Suckley's cuckoo bumblebee. The western bumblebee, for example, was once the most common in Oregon, but their numbers had fallen sharply since the 1990s and none had been seen on the western side of the Cascade Range in about fifteen years. The western was considered an indicator species for the health of other native pollinators and therefore particularly concerning.

"The main question is if the decline can be reversed. And how reversal might best be approached."

Her notes were damp with sweat from her palms.

"And that . . . that's what I learned about bumblebees this weekend," she said. The end.

She said the last part in her head. She knew you weren't supposed to say it out loud. That it would be weird. But she needed the closure of it.

Dr. Mora nodded slowly.

"Excellent, Abigail. I'd like you to present this information at the department meeting on Friday. It's everything the students need to understand, the most imperative information they'll get at this meeting, really. If you could, put together some slides to go with it. And you can ask Casey if you need help."

Abigail nodded, trying to remember who Casey was.

"And, Abigail, go home and take a shower and get some sleep, okay?"

At her apartment she fell asleep listening to the drone of a lawn mower, which in her dreams became a huge bumblebee that circled round and round. Abigail followed it and it grew as large as the Goodyear blimp. She ran to catch up and it spun around like an enormous piñata. The bumblebee had a human face and it was her mother.

"Abigail!" her mother said. "I've been waiting for you! Let's go!"

And she zoomed away.

"Wait!" Abigail called, but the creature had disappeared.

Abigail awoke feeling overcome. How could she even describe what she felt about her mother, Elizabeth Plue, whom Abigail hadn't seen since she was almost three?

For the next two days she spent hours working on her talk. She wrote up the text and downloaded images and graphs from various research papers. She compiled her PowerPoint slides and reviewed them repeatedly. She practiced her presentation aloud over and over again. Though Dr. Mora had suggested she ask Casey for help, she'd forgotten all about Casey until Wednesday afternoon when Casey rudely interrupted her by barging into the office and flipping on the lights.

She shrieked when she saw Abigail sitting in the dark, which made Abigail yell, and Casey shrieked again, and then laughed.

"Holy moly! I didn't know anyone was in here," she said with a hand on her chest.

"Well, you could knock first," Abigail huffed.

Casey bit her lip.

"Um, this is my office," she said. "I don't usually knock?"

She put her backpack on the other desk.

"Oh," Abigail said.

"I'm Casey," she said. "Dr. Mora said you'd be starting soon. You're Abigail, right?"

Abigail nodded, stood, and stuck out her hand.

"Pleased to meet you, Casey," she said.

Casey's hand was soft, and her face dimpled as she smiled.

"Pleased to meet you too, Abigail," she said, sitting and pulling out her laptop.

"Were you practicing your talk for Friday just now? I'm giving one too. Pretty exciting! I mean, mine is just a brief introduction to bumblebees for the undergrads. Sounds like Dr. Mora has you working on the new research. Maybe we could practice together?"

"No, thank you," Abigail said, and swiveled back to her computer screen.

She resumed practicing her talk, though in her head and not aloud. She'd learned from Linda and Diane that people did not like it when someone talked out loud to herself. It was perfectly okay to talk and laugh with *another person* in the office, but to speak aloud to yourself was *disruptive* and *weird*, Linda had explained. She hoped Casey could appreciate how polite she was being by not practicing her talk aloud, but Casey didn't say anything.

On Friday, Abigail entered the conference room to find Casey setting up the projector.

"Hey, Abigail! How's it going? Are you nervous? I always get a little nervous when I do talks. I don't know why. It's silly, I know. I've been doing them for ages and it's just the department. I know everybody here, and sorry. Sorry! I talk a lot when I'm nervous. I don't know why I'm nervous. It's just Bumblebee 101. No big deal!"

She snapped open the projector window and a close-up of a bumblebee filled the screen. She advanced through the slides, and Abigail watched them flash past.

"I think that's about right. Do you want to check your PowerPoint? I'm the unofficial tech person if you need anything."

"No, thank you," Abigail said.

She did not want to check her PowerPoint. She knew it was fine.

"Okay," Casey said, glancing at her watch.

"We have half an hour. Want to go grab a coffee?"

"No, thank you," Abigail said again and sat down.

"Are you sure? We have plenty of time."

"I'm sure," Abigail said. "I do not want coffee."

Abigail did not like coffee and never drank coffee. But something in Casey's face as she left made Abigail think she had said A Wrong Thing. Was the right answer to like coffee?

Gradually Abigail became aware of the room around her. The conference table was too large for the space and the puffy pleather chairs too tall for the table. The fluorescent lights buzzed and flickered. The odor of old banana wafted from the garbage can in one corner. Abigail rose and set it outside the door. People began to arrive, and Casey returned, coffee in hand, and smiled as she sat across from Abigail. So maybe it wasn't A Wrong Thing to not like coffee.

Dr. Mora called the meeting to order and introduced Casey. Casey stood at the podium and snapped on the projector. She smiled, and Abigail watched her for signs of the nervousness she'd described, but Casey didn't seem nervous at all.

"Hey, everyone! I'm Casey Antica. I'll start by explaining the life cycle of native bumblebees, which is quite a contrast to the honeybee, *Apis mellifera*, which most of you are familiar with."

Casey advanced the slide to show a close-up of a large, fuzzy bumblebee with mostly black pile and a bright yellow stripe around the midsection. Her voice was warm and steady and easy to listen to. Abigail could feel her brain organizing the information Casey provided.

"Each bumblebee colony starts from one solitary queen emerging alone after her winter hibernation. She creates a ground nest—often in an old fence post, a rodent hole, or a tree snag. Next she forms a small honeypot out of wax extruded from her abdomen and regurgitates honey she's stored all winter. She forages for pollen, which stimulates her ovaries. She lays her first eggs—four to sixteen at a time—which take up to five weeks to mature. Those offspring are nonreproductive female workers, which become house bees and forager bees. Unlike a honeybee colony, which can number sixty thousand, a typical bumblebee nest will have closer to one hundred members.

"At the end of the season, the queen produces drones," Casey said.

She advanced to a slide of a plump bee curled up in a thistle blossom.

"Drones leave the colony as soon as they mature and live outside. You might find drones at dawn or dusk asleep in flowers."

By the time drones appeared, Casey explained, the cycle of the colony was complete. The female workers developed sexually, and the old queen died; new queens mated with drones. With the arrival of winter, each queen found a place to hibernate alone. If she survived the winter, she'd emerge in the spring and the whole cycle would begin again.

Casey continued to advance her slides as she spoke at length about the native flowers, shrubs, and trees that bumblebees foraged on. She finished her talk with a slide of brightly colored produce arranged at a farmers market.

"Native bumblebees are key pollinators. Here in Oregon, they're essential to our blueberry, watermelon, and cranberry crops as well as red clover—an important hay crop. That's to say nothing of tomatoes, strawberries, eggplants, and other fruits and vegetables in backyard gardens. Lesser known than their nonnative cousin *Apis mellifera*, the *Bombus* genus is key to our ecosystem. Okay! That's all I've got. Thank you!"

There was a smattering of applause as Casey returned to her seat.

"Thank you, Casey. That was a great introduction for our next talk," Dr. Mora said.

She nodded at Abigail.

"Abigail Plue has come to us from the teaching cohort. She's only been here a week, but she's gotten up to speed quickly. Abigail will summarize the key bumblebee research to date to give a snapshot of where we are. Go ahead, Abigail."

Abigail made her way to the podium, squeezing behind the too-big chairs as she went. She inserted her thumb drive into the laptop and watched the projector screen fill with a triptych of a western bumblebee, Morrison's bumblebee, and Suckley's cuckoo bumblebee. She glanced around at the faces of professors and students. She thought of how Casey had begun her talk. Abigail hadn't practiced any introduction and now tried to imitate Casey's breezy tone.

"Hey, everyone. I'm Abigail Plue. Most of you know plenty about honeybees, but you probably don't know anything about bumblebees other than what Casey just told you."

What was it Casey had said about her talk?

"Casey gave us just a brief introduction to bumblebees. Bumblebee 101. No big deal!" Abigail said.

Someone snickered.

"I will begin by telling you . . ."

What had Dr. Mora said?

"Everything students need to understand, the most imperative information you'll get at this meeting, really."

Dr. Mora cleared her throat.

Abigail looked back at the photo of the three bumblebees.

"Oregon's native bumblebees are in trouble," she began, just as she'd practiced a hundred times that week. "Their numbers have declined exponentially over the past decade, and we want to understand why."

Someone's phone dinged. A student gazed at his phone, chuckling.

"We want to understand why," said Abigail again.

The lights hummed, and Dr. Mora coughed. A man blew his nose. Out in the hall someone swore and banged on the copy machine. The scent of old banana wafted through the room.

"The main inquiry," she said, and the student's phone dinged again and then again.

Chairs squeaked as people shifted, the projector motor whirred, the student to Abigail's right unwrapped a piece of gum and began chewing. Dr. Mora coughed again. People were looking at her. So many faces. So distracting. Were they tired? Bored? Hungry? How many eyes were there?

"Excuse me. Dr. Mora?"

Casey's voice rose above the cacophony of other noises.

"Would you mind if I adjusted the projector? The lighting seems off. I meant to change it before we got started."

"Sure, Casey. If you think so. Thank you," Dr. Mora said.

Chairs squeaked and rolled as people made room for Casey. She bent over the projector, fiddling with the controls, and then straightened.

"I think we can see better with the lights off, actually."

She flipped off the lights on the way back to her seat.

"Sorry for the interruption, Abigail!" Casey said.

Abigail stared at the screen. The slide looked the same to her. But in the dimmer light, she felt calmer. All the information, which really was so interesting, came flooding back.

"The main inquiry," she said, "is to determine the greatest threats to these three species of concern."

Her presentation flowed easily then—her photos and maps and data tables flashing by as she summarized the most recent scientific research on the plight of Oregon's native bumblebees.

She became engrossed in the story all over again. When she was finished, the applause startled her. She'd almost forgotten anyone else was there. Someone flipped the lights back on and Abigail sat down.

"Thank you, Abigail. That was a great roundup of where things stand," Dr. Mora said.

Dr. Mora worked her way through the agenda, and when the meeting ended, Abigail was the first to get up and leave. She squeezed past people and stood at the door wondering why they were still sitting. Wasn't the meeting over? She confirmed people were just socializing, which was not on the agenda, so she left. In her office she kept the lights off and took out her lunch.

Sitting in the dark, she rewound the meeting in her mind, knowing she should be Happy. It had gone well. But she could only see Casey's face when Abigail had referred to her talk as "no big deal." Her face looked like . . . Embarrassed or Scared? But wasn't that what she'd said about her talk herself? Abigail heard dinging phones and squeaking chairs and coughing. She felt again the frozen moment with too many faces, too much information.

Abigail realized she was crying. Sad, she thought, and put down her sandwich because it was hard to cry and chew at the same time. Plus, it was her favorite sandwich—chicken salad—and she didn't want to be Sad eating her favorite sandwich.

She wished Casey would come back to their office and eat her lunch too. Abigail wanted to say something to Casey. What should she say? What was the right thing to say?

"Thank you, Casey," Abigail said aloud, practicing.

It seemed like the right thing to say. But Abigail didn't know for sure. She so often said the wrong thing. Or A Wrong Thing, as she preferred to think of it. Because there was more than one wrong thing to say, wasn't there?

"You just said the wrong thing," her father had told her, countless times, when she came home wailing about some mishap at school.

"Don't worry about it, Abigail," he'd say. "Nobody will remember."

But people did remember, and Abigail kept saying A Wrong Thing all through grade school and high school and college. It was why she didn't have any friends. It was why, she now realized, she'd lost her position as a TA. Yelling at your students was A Wrong Thing. Telling a student his topic was stupid was A Wrong Thing. Refusing to use Canvas to communicate with students was A Wrong Thing.

She wondered if she might have been different with her mother around. Her mother, Elizabeth Plue, was good with people. That's what Abigail's dad always said.

Through the daylight windows, Abigail watched people's feet moving down the sunny sidewalk. Sneakers, boots, open-toed sandals, flip-flops. Any one of them could have been her mother and Abigail wouldn't have known because she didn't even know what her mother looked like. Elizabeth Plue had disappeared right before Abigail's third birthday.

Anguish.

Longing.

Sorrow.

Abigail rewrapped the remainder of her sandwich and put it away. She lifted the hem of her T-shirt and wiped her face. Then Abigail Plue got back to work.

5

STUNG

Apis mellifera, the western honeybee, is especially noteworthy for its adaptability, including its skill at creating nests in various spaces.

—LAVIN, *THE WONDROUS WORLD OF BEES*

JAKE DROVE SOUTH on Dee Highway, one hand on the wheel and the other on the hand lever that depressed the accelerator. He had rolled down the windows so Cheney could hang his head out and smell the great blooming world. His big dog stood on the armrest with his chin to the wind, ears flapping.

The white stone walls of the Oak Grove Schoolhouse rose above the orchards. The trees here had blossomed and were fully leafed out. The shapes of small fruit hung in the branches. As he rounded the curve and sped through the straightaway, his heart swelled. His mind slipped back to the evening he'd met Alice. Here, on this very stretch of road, a moment that had changed his life.

Jacob, nearly nineteen then, had the tallest mohawk in the history of Hood River Valley High School. He'd also lost the use of his legs and his music school scholarship in one fell swoop following an accident at a high school party. The night he met Alice Holtzman was near the anniversary of that accident. Discharged from the rehabilitation center, he was stuck at his parents' house, smoking weed, playing video games, and lifting weights. He was so fucking lonely but couldn't bear to see his friends. He'd fled the house that spring evening and out along the country road had pushed himself into a sweaty, heart-pounding mess, confronting the impossible reality he found himself in. Flooded with emotion, Jake didn't notice Alice's truck coming at him in the twilight. She swerved to miss him and smashed into a fence post, scattering a dozen hives from her truck bed.

Jake's enduring memory was the look on Alice's face as she bent over him—a mohawked teenager spilled out of his wheelchair onto the road. The worry on her face reminded him of Cheney the time his dog had found a box turtle by the river and carried it to Jake with a furrowed brow. The memory made him laugh, and Alice had reared back, her concern coming out as anger.

"What the hell are you trying to do? Get yourself killed?!"

He teased her about that later.

"Talking to teens in crisis, Alice. You really ought to teach a class."

Though he could joke about it now, at the time he'd sensed that their meeting would be either his undoing or his remaking. That evening was lodged in his body forever—the clean, bright smell of cold water from the irrigation ditch, the lingering scent of linden tree blossoms, the sound of the chorus frogs singing through the twilight. They sat on the shoulder of the road and Alice told him about her honeybees, those scattered by her crash. Under the sound of her voice, he heard the bees resettling into their family groups and calling to each other. We are here. We are together. All is well.

Jake, who'd been uninterested in talking to anyone in months, hung on to every word. Alice told him how a honeybee hive had a single queen who was mother to tens of thousands of worker bees. The workers were her daughters and acted as veritable Cinderellas—cleaning the brood nest, feeding eggs and larvae, storing pollen and nectar, guarding the hive, and foraging in the field. They also cared for their mother, who was busy laying up to three thousand eggs a day. A small number of drones, males, were produced when a hive was strong enough for excess. The hive was a perfect system, with each member carrying out the work it was meant to do for the sake of the colony as a whole.

Alice drove him home that night and made the acquaintance of his crappy dad. Soon thereafter, Alice surprised everyone, including herself, by inviting Jake to come live with her. What made her do that? he'd asked her, later, when he knew her well enough to understand how private she was, how solitary. Invite a teenager into her home?

"I had no idea what I was even saying! I certainly didn't expect you to take me up on my offer. But then there we were. You and me and the dog. Then Harry. Holtzman's Home for the Feral and Friendless. I ought to file a 1099 for all that."

Jake's reverie was interrupted as he passed a large billboard. Red lettering on a white background stated, "Vote E.W. Dewitt: Your Law and Order Candidate!" The photo showed a stern-looking man with his wife and three sons arrayed around him.

The billboard bemused Jake. It was only June and the election for Hood River County sheriff, months away, was heating up. Ron Ryan, longtime deputy sheriff, had seemed like a shoo-in to win after the retirement of the current sheriff, Dennis Hartford, until E.W. Dewitt launched his campaign. Dewitt announced his run with an appearance on *Faith Matters*, a local Christian talk show hosted by Aaron Scott, which Jake and Alice had heard part of while searching for the weather forecast. Aaron, who'd gone to high school with Alice, had served time for a larceny charge in the nineties and reinvented himself as a spokesperson for the Christian right after finding Jesus in jail. He called Dewitt "the godly choice for sheriff." Dewitt, in turn, had warned that the very fate of Hood River County was in the hands of voters.

"Make no mistake. The woke revolution is coming for our kids," Dewitt had said.

He made a series of wild, baseless claims about urban liberals importing anti-Christian values into schools and funneling county money into social services for "illegal aliens." Alice snapped off the radio.

"Horseshit," she said.

Now Jake entered the little town of Odell, slowing as he passed the taquería, the market, and the school. At Duckwall Fruit he noted the high towers of empty pallets. In just a few weeks they'd be packed full with fruit as cherry season ramped up. Then came blueberries, then peaches and nectarines, and finally apples and pears. Hood River Valley's fruit calendar ran parallel to the beekeeping season, and Jake loved the rhythm of it all.

After Odell he popped out on Highway 35 and headed south. He accelerated around a set of curves and passed the pullout for Tamanawas Falls. The road banked left and the east fork of the Hood River spilled out of the thick forest into the sunshine. The river caught the light, throwing diamonds through the air as it surged alongside the highway. Cool air rushed in the window, and the temperature dropped as the road climbed and the trees thickened. He sped straight at Mount Hood, still buried in snow with the blue light of the glacier glinting near the summit.

Just before the Mount Hood Wilderness boundary, Jake slowed at a narrow dirt road. He put the truck into neutral and shifted into four-wheel drive. The road was rough and Jake had a moment of gratitude for his big Dodge diesel, as he always did on this stretch or any difficult terrain. The truck was not new—a 2010 he'd bought three years earlier. But it had low mileage and a monster engine and could get over anything. He'd been so proud the day he'd bought it—flush with cash after a great harvest.

Cheney began to pace the length of the bench seat, walking across Jake's lap and shoving his nose out the driver's-side window.

The dog whined with excitement and wedged his body between Jake and the steering wheel.

"Off, monster! I can't see!"

The first time they'd come to the meadow, Alice had driven while Jake navigated with the directions she'd scrawled on the back of an envelope. The road seemed even worse that first time and Jake grew skeptical as they crawled along.

"Alice, are you sure? This doesn't even look like a proper road. Or if it is, it's bound to have some unfriendlies at the end."

They passed a "No Trespassing!" sign nailed to a tree.

"Seriously, I don't want to surprise some militia members in the woods."

Alice snorted.

"Don't be a ninny," she said. "I am one hundred percent confident in my directions. You'll love this spot. It's going to be epic. Epic, Jake! Or, what is it the kids are saying these days? Fire!"

He cringed and she cackled.

"Okay, Alice," he said. "If you say so. Fire."

The militia had not appeared, and the road split, as Alice's directions said it would. The right side continued to climb up toward the mountain. Alice took the left and proceeded through the trees, which opened suddenly to the meadow, and stopped at the edge of it. Jake was stunned by the beauty of the view. A long-ago receded glacier had left a pristine alpine field in the shape of a teardrop. A small pond reflected the face of the big mountain on one end. On the far side, a stand of enormous Douglas firs marked the beginning of the wilderness area and old-growth forest—hundred-year-old giants stair-stepping up toward Mount Hood.

The meadow was a unicorn for beekeeping—exposed to the sunny south but protected from winter snow by the southeast-leaning aspect and thick woods. This swath of private land surrounded by national forest was also clean and open. No orchard spraying to negotiate, no potential pesticides from lawns and gardens, and no other honeybees to compete with. Best of all, there was plenty of habitat for the two hundred hives they wanted to put there.

"Hot damn!" Alice had said, thumping the steering wheel with her palm. "Look at this place. It's perfect!"

It was far from perfect. They knew that even then. For starters, the thick meadow grass, which rippled gorgeously in the slightest breeze, was impossible for Jake to navigate in his chair. The road was not maintained by the county, which would make the hives inaccessible in winter. They'd have to pay for spring plowing, and there was risk of wildfire in summer.

Jake's mother, Tansy, ever the voice of reason, had listed all these things and more when advising them against it. But it was gorgeous, and it was a one-of-a-kind spot. It was a dream, and our dreams often include impracticalities that we must overlook in our dreaming.

Jake saw that the location presented the potential for honey like no other, a signature Mount Hood terroir born of the wild huckleberry and bear grass that blossomed there. Alice was won over by the idea of a new product line.

"I'd never have thought of that in a million years, kid," she said. "Mount Hood terroir—like wine. Brilliant!"

Alice had only been half joking when she told the *Los Angeles Times* reporter that she was the brawn and Jake was the brains. When they first founded Queen of G, Alice had only thought of harvesting and selling honey. Jake had better instincts in working with the bees, including an uncanny ability to determine if a hive was queenright by hearing the queen's bell-like ringing of G-sharp in the hive. That talent had led to robust hives and honey production and improved survival rates, which, in turn, had allowed Queen of G to expand. Their expansion included the sale of queens, nucs, and standard Langstroth hives and frames. Single-source honey would be a fitting addition.

Now Jake crept forward in low gear, his heart lifting as he drove into the clearing. He took in the view, the spring sunlight dappling the hives, a chinook breeze rippling the green-gold grasses, and considered his tasks for the day: unloading tools, pollen patties, and honey feeder frames. Opening the first hive to document its status: Was there a queen present? Could he observe eggs and brood? What was the laying pattern? Were there pollen stores, honey stores, and any evidence yet of drones? How many frames were built out? Along with feeding the hungry hives and adding pollen patties, he'd need to take meticulous notes on almost two hundred hives. For after all their fretting through winter and spring, nearly every hive had survived.

There was so much work to do. Jake sighed thinking about his help wanted ad. Maybe he should offer more money. Without another set of hands, he could do only so much. But for a moment none of that mattered. The sight of the hives grounded him, reminded him who he was and how far he'd come since those early days at Alice's place, when he was a clueless teenager learning about bees, navigating his new life, and trying to forgive himself.

The bees had saved him. The first time Alice showed him her apiary, he'd felt a seismic shift. His bruised heart broke open as he watched the tiny golden honeybees going about their business—carrying out their dead, foraging for the young, tending the queen. Jake felt a glimmer of hope that day and eventually saw a new future for himself. He'd grieved all he'd lost—the use of his legs and his college scholarship. But through the bees, he'd gained so much. He wouldn't put the two lives side by side and ask which was better—the one he thought he'd have or the one he had now. It was irrelevant. Most days that attitude served him.

His stillness was too much for Cheney, who resumed his pacing and shoved his nose out the cracked window, snuffling and chattering his teeth and emitting an escalating moan.

Jake eased forward and parked at the start of a wooden boardwalk, built by Harry, that paralleled the hives and allowed him access in his chair. Cheney's moan grew into an anguished yodel as he pawed the door.

"Hang on, buddy!"

Jake opened the door, and Cheney flung himself out, belly flopping into the grass, and bounded across the field like a giant bunny, baying his joy to the bright blue sky.

Jake pulled his wheelchair out of the back seat and lowered it to the ramp. As he swung down, Cheney disappeared into the trees then reappeared, his coat wet from the stream as Jake knew it would be. He cantered around the field and halted outside the electric fence, which deterred honey-seeking bears, and began barking furiously.

Cheney had many barks. There was the morning bark, which accompanied the long hello—a short and pithy yawp. There was the "I think I want to go out" bark, similar to, but discernible from, the "MUST go out" bark. The former resulted in Cheney standing half in and half out of the sliding door. The latter was nonnegotiable. There was the "I want to go see!" bark, an enthusiastic warbling that Cheney often emitted when he saw something new to play with. This was the song he'd performed upon arrival at the meadow. Jake had only heard the dog's worry bark a handful of times in their life together. But he heard it now. There was an urgency to it. This was a bark of concern, a bark that said, "Jake, get over here. There's SOMETHING WRONG!"

Jake swore and released the brake on his chair. Cheney's barking increased as he sped along the walkway. His mind ticked through the possibilities. He prayed it wasn't a skunk. Dog versus skunk wasn't something he felt he could deal with today. Coyote would be worse, though. He couldn't help Cheney in a fight.

Cheney was now bouncing on his front paws with each bark. As Jake drew closer, he saw a dark thing thrashing just inside the fence. Larger than a skunk, it was more the size of a bear cub. He paused. Baby bears meant mama bears. He cursed himself for not calling someone—anyone—to come with him. Even his petite mom could have helped in this situation.

Jake whistled for Cheney, who did not pause his frantic barking.

"Cheney, come! Now, boy," Jake called, but Cheney only barked louder.

Jake scanned the meadow for some sign of the mother bear and did not see her. Steeling his nerves, he rolled closer to the dog and the creature. One of the hives was open and a cloud of guard bees circled the dark, thrashing form. Jake heard a series of short, sharp yelps and the unmistakable sound of Spanish.

It was a boy, rising now. The kid windmilled his arms and reached for the fence, which zapped his fingers. He swung around and looked at Jake. His eyes were huge, and he breathed in short rasps. The kid seemed to gather himself, and his reedy voice rose above Cheney's mad barking.

"Hello! I am Sebastián Santiago Luna López! I need help! May I please speak to the person in charge?!" he yelled.

Then the boy swayed and crumpled to the ground.

6

FORAGING

Bees have a highly developed sense of smell, which helps them communicate within the hive, recognize colony members, and locate nectar and pollen—often at great distances.

—LAVIN, *THE WONDROUS WORLD OF BEES*

FLACO HEARD THE susurration of the long grass parting under the bodies of the creatures as they streamed toward him. He counted twenty or more gray-brown bodies. These were not wolves or coyotes or bears. Nor were they pursuing him. Now that he'd thrown himself up and over the fence, he saw them quite clearly for what they were. Turkeys.

The birds tiptoed past the fence looking sidelong at Flaco. One large tom stalked close enough that Flaco could see its great red wattle and beady eye. The bird emitted a low, threatening purr as if daring Flaco to challenge him. One by one the birds minced past and disappeared into the tall grass of the meadow.

Flaco cradled his hands against his body. He wasn't hurt, though his fingers smarted a bit from the shock. He turned and looked at the beehives lined up in long, neat rows. The air was full of the low murmuring of the bees. A golden knot of honeybees congregated on the face of the closest hive. Some disappeared into a small slot and others launched themselves skyward and departed in the same direction as the turkeys. The air smelled sweet and hot and Flaco's hunger stabbed his belly.

Flaco recalled the old man who sometimes traveled through town selling honeycomb. He'd sit outside the tiendita with his small plastic jars crammed with slices of white wax dripping with honey. Occasionally he brought pollen too—silky golden powders in red, gold, and ochre that smelled nutty and sweet. People said he collected the honey from wild hives in the bosque.

Once the man gave Flaco and Carlos each a taste, slicing off a thin piece of honeycomb and holding it out to them on the blade of a knife. Flaco put it in his mouth and it melted on his tongue like Communion. He closed his eyes and tasted the sunny bosque and the wind in the flowers. Flaco understood it was special that the viejo knew where the bees lived and knew how to collect their honey. He had many questions: Did the bees mind him taking their treasure? How did he do it? Did he get stung? But he was too shy to ask. The next year the man did not come to the little store and Flaco never saw him again.

His mouth watered as he recalled the taste of that wild honey. He considered the closest box and moved to the opposite side from where the bees were congregated. It had some sort of lid on it. Flaco pushed on it but it wouldn't budge. He tried the box next to that one, but it wouldn't move either. Crouching down, he looked at the seam where the top met the bottom of the box. With a shaking hand he pulled out his pocketknife, opened the blade, and jimmied under the lid until he felt it shift. He lifted it and found a fabric cover inside, under which he could hear the muted buzzing of bees. The scent of honey was strong now, and he was so hungry he felt nauseated. Flaco peeled back the cloth and saw honey glistening on the wooden slats like liquid sunshine. He was so hungry he seemed to be outside of his body, watching himself reach in and grasp a wooden frame. It stuck and he levered it out with his knife. When he yanked it free, honey dripped down his arm. He tore a chunk of wax from the frame and lifted it toward his mouth, aware of a strange sensation, like fire, and realized his hands were covered in bees. Then his neck and his face burned. As he brought the comb to his mouth, he realized he was being stung. He managed to swallow once before the fire was too much and he dropped the frame.

He ran, shaking his hands and arms trying to fling off the bees. He felt stings inside his mouth and all over his scalp. He tried to climb the fence again, but without the adrenaline from the fear of wolves that were turkeys he couldn't manage it.

His rational mind deserted him and he threw himself to the ground and rolled. The bees stung him through his shirtsleeves and pants. They buzzed in his hair and climbed in his ears. Flaco curled into a ball and suffered the assault of burning stings. He became aware of a huffing breath. Suddenly there was a creature there, all teeth and snapping jaws—a dog on the other side of the fence.

He heard a voice then, and for a moment he thought it was Javi, who had miraculously found him in this high Oregon meadow. He turned his head toward the sound of the voice and saw a man, a gringo. The man seemed to float through the air and Flaco realized he was in a wheelchair speeding along the wooden walkway.

The man was yelling but Flaco couldn't understand what he was saying.

He remembered what Javi had said.

"Better the wild animals than the crazy white people."

He closed his eyes, wishing he could disappear, and when he opened them, the man in the wheelchair was looking down at him through the fence. He did not feel he was in a position to follow Javi's advice now. Instead Flaco thought of his mother and what she'd said about being polite and asking for help. He pulled himself to his feet and looked the man in the eye, mustering his best manners. He smiled despite the waves of pain coursing through his body.

"Hello!" Flaco said in English. "My name is Sebastián Santiago Luna López! I need help! May I please speak to the person in charge?!"

And then Flaco, feeling hot and cold and fuzzy, passed out for the second time that day.

He awoke to the sensation of liquid running down his scalp and the hot breath of the big dog against his face. He recalled the black beast outside of his school, pacing and snapping its teeth. Fear propelled him into a sitting position. Then the world swung and dipped crazily. Flaco lay back down.

The gringo was sitting next to him on the ground. He said something in English that Flaco didn't understand. Then he said something else that Flaco recognized as Spanish, though the accent was strange.

"Cálmate," the man said. "Todo bien. Okay?"

The gringo tipped a bottle of water and dribbled some of it into Flaco's mouth. Flaco swallowed and felt a little better. He could still hear the buzzing of the bees but did not feel any on his body. He felt the throb of countless stings. After a while he sat up.

"Okay?" the man asked.

Flaco nodded.

The man asked something and pantomimed deep breaths. Flaco nodded again and imitated the gesture and the man watched him. Then he said, "To help you," in Spanish, and gestured at Flaco's arm. Flaco held out his right arm and the man pushed up his sleeve. He peered down at the skin and scraped with his fingernail. The burning seemed to dissipate, and the skin felt tender. Flaco closed his eyes and lost count as the man worked on his left arm and his face. He opened his eyes and gazed at the man's skull, covered with a light stubble. Past his shoulder, the big dog lay panting in the grass next to the wheelchair. It was all very strange.

After a few minutes the man stopped scraping.

"Better?" he asked in Spanish.

Flaco nodded. Yes, it was a little better.

The man nodded and straightened. He pulled himself over to the wheelchair and then up and in. His arm muscles flexed as he settled into the chair and then turned it around.

"Vamos," the man said and pointed to what Flaco could see was a gate. The man pushed himself to the far side of the enclosure with the dog trotting in front, and Flaco followed. Once they were outside, the man closed the gate and typed a code into a keypad. He looked Flaco up and down, and then he shook his head.

"Hambre?" he asked.

Yes, he was still ravenous, Flaco realized as the pain and shock of his encounter with the bees receded.

The man gestured at him to follow and began to roll along the wooden boardwalk. Flaco saw the turkeys emerge from the edge of the trees, and the dog took off toward them, barking furiously. Beyond the turkeys a big white truck sat on the far side of the meadow, and Flaco looked around for the driver. He wondered how many others were with this man and where they were now. The idea of more white people made Flaco nervous as he thought of what had happened in Bend.

He glanced back at the edge of the meadow where the trees started, where he'd found the stream earlier that day. He looked up at the face of the big mountain to the south, the way he'd come. The sight of the white peak of the old volcano steadied him. He could run, he thought. He could jump off the walkway and dash into the trees and the man couldn't follow him. The dog might try, but it was on the other side of the field now. Whoever had driven the truck was nowhere in sight. Flaco could climb a tree and wait until they'd gone.

But he didn't run. He was so hungry and he was so tired. And something about the man's voice made him seem trustworthy. Even if he wasn't, Flaco felt out of options. He followed the man toward the truck with a sense of surrender.

The man opened the driver's-side door. Flaco watched, astonished, as he pulled himself up and in. He opened the passenger door for Flaco and motioned him in. Flaco perched on the seat nervously. The man dug around in a bag and handed Flaco an apple and something wrapped in plastic. Flaco ate the fruit in six bites. He tore open the plastic and ate the rectangle thing without really tasting it. The man passed him a bottle of water and Flaco took great noisy gulps.

The man said something Flaco didn't understand and then: "Slower." Flaco tried to comply and slowed his gulping.

"¿Hablas inglés?"

Flaco felt the jumble of words in his brain. English, Spanish, a couple of dirty jokes in French.

"Me llamo Jake. Jacob," the man said. "¿Cómo te llamas?"

The inglés came to him then.

"I am Sebastián, thank you. It is some pleasure to met you."

The man smiled.

"A pleasure to meet you, Sebastián," he said.

Then his face grew serious. He asked something, and Flaco didn't understand.

"Alone?" the man asked in Spanish, looking toward the meadow. His Spanish sounded strange, but Flaco understood.

Should he tell this stranger he was by himself? He looked out the windshield and down at his feet. Now that the bee stings had subsided, they were beginning to throb again.

"Sí," he said, and nodded. "Estoy solo."

The man sighed and looked out the window at the fenced hives and muttered something. Then he looked back at Flaco, not speaking. Flaco, feeling slightly better after eating, mustered his English.

"I to go Hood River," he said, and pointed back toward the field and the trail beyond it in the woods. "I walk there since five days since Bend. Very close now."

He slid to the edge of the seat.

"I thank you very much sir for your good time."

He slipped to the ground and winced as his feet hit the earth. The man gaped.

"You walked?" he said. "From Bend?"

Flaco nodded and feigned an enthusiasm he did not feel. He recalled the English lesson in Maestra Monica's class about vacations.

"Oh yes. It is a beautiful time of year to visit the country!"

The man stared and Flaco wondered if he'd said the wrong words.

"Hood River?" the man repeated and Flaco nodded.

"I am going for to visit Cousin César. She lives in Hood River, Oregon."

The man gazed toward the beehives, then leaned out the door and whistled. The dog thundered back across the meadow and the man smiled at Flaco.

"Vivo en Hood River," he said and pointed north. He pantomimed driving and motioned for Flaco to get back in the truck. The man said something about a taquería in Hood River and calling his primo.

Flaco considered the offer as the big dog flew up onto the man's lap and licked his face. He laughed and pushed the dog into the back seat. He pulled his wheelchair up, folded it, and put it in the back with the dog. He clicked in his seat belt, shut his door, and started the truck. He looked at Flaco still standing outside the truck.

"It's okay," he said in Spanish. "You can walk or come with me. It's your . . ." He seemed to search for the word. "Your choice?"

Flaco hesitated and felt the pain of his feet and the pulse of the bee stings. His stomach twisted and he thought of the taquería the man had mentioned. He climbed back in the truck. As the truck crept down the bumpy road, Flaco resolved to remain vigilant. He kept the window open and his seat belt off, just in case. He marveled briefly at how the man was driving the truck with a series of hand levers. The big dog began to snore and Flaco's eyes drooped, his head jerked, and he fell asleep.

When he awoke, he was alone. The truck was parked in front of a small building. "Tacos Evangelina," the sign read. Flaco heard the cheerful tempo of a ranchera song and smelled meat and frying onions. An older man stood over a grill under a tree. Nearby he saw the man from the field sitting at a table with a woman. She wore her black hair pulled back from her face into a neat bun like Mamá wore when she went to Mass. His throat tightened.

The man glanced at the truck and, seeing Flaco awake, gestured at him to join them. Flaco walked toward them trying to remember how one greeted adult women in English.

"Hello, I am Sebastián, madame," he said.

The woman rose, her face all sunshine, and addressed him rapidly in Spanish.

"Look at you, you skinny little thing! And all alone up there in the woods. Walking for five days, this one tells me! Come have something to eat, mijo."

She pulled Flaco into a hug as if they were family.

"Sit! You sit here with Jacob and I'll bring you a plate. My name is Señora Evangelina, and everything is going to be fine. We'll help you find your cousin."

Jacob. That was the man's name. The woman disappeared into the taquería, and Jacob smiled, motioning for him to sit.

Señora Evangelina returned with a plate of tacos and a bottle of Coca-Cola. Flaco drank it, cold and sweet, in great gulps.

"Slowly, slowly, Sebastián," the señora said. "You'll make yourself sick! You have a big appetite for such a skinny boy."

He smiled weakly.

"At home they call me Flaco," he said.

She laughed and pinched the skin of his wrist in her fingers.

"Así! Eres flaco, muchacho."

She began to ask him questions. Where was he from? When had he left? Who was he traveling with? Who was he supposed to meet? How had he ended up alone up on the mountain?

Maybe he should have been more guarded. After all, he didn't even know her, but he wanted to be polite and answered her questions. He listened to her translating into English for Jacob. They spoke rapidly in English, and he missed most of what they were saying. The señora turned to him again.

"Do you have your cousin's phone number?" she asked.

Flaco produced the paper with César's number on it, and Señora Evangelina pulled out her phone and dialed the number. She put the call on speakerphone and Flaco heard César's voicemail message.

"We'll try again in a bit," she said, handing the paper back to him. She sounded like Mamá did when she was pretending to be more cheerful than she really was. She said something to Jacob in English in the same tone.

"Have you visited your cousin before?" the señora asked, and Flaco shook his head.

"First time north?" she asked.

Flaco felt increasingly vulnerable. He'd already told so much. Maybe too much. How could he explain to strangers that the journey had been his mother's idea? And that once Beatriz López made up her mind about something, there was no changing it.

Flaco understood his mother's decision had to do with the unfortunate events that had recently shadowed his little town. For most of Flaco's lifetime, Las Lunas had felt like an easy and safe place to live. People made their living growing produce on small farms. Everyone knew of the violence prevalent in the country, especially in the cities. For decades factions had been at war over the drug trade, but in Las Lunas these problems had seemed far away or at least distant enough to ignore. But the darkness had crept into Michoacán too, first its cities and then smaller towns. Even more disturbing, the cartels were not fighting over drug territory there. Now they had invaded the farming industry—limes and avocados, both increasingly in demand with norteamericanos. Cartel chaos seeped into the everyday worlds of small farms closer and closer until it reached Las Lunas.

Ricardo and Manuel were the first young men of Las Lunas to go. The owner of the tiendita described how they'd been accosted on a Saturday night as they stood outside drinking beer. Ricardo managed to send word back to his family that they'd been forced to work on an illegal plantation—cutting and burning the native pine, oak, and oyamel trees to plant avocados. Over time, others were pressured into joining. Cartel members would show up in town or grab them as they walked home from their own fields. Some were able to send messages home saying they were okay; others couldn't.

Then one young man, Alán, had refused to go. He was the only son in his family and his parents were older and needed his help. He explained this to the men who'd stopped him and they seemed to accept his explanation. A few days later, he went to the neighboring town to buy supplies and did not return home on time. His father found him badly beaten on the side of the road. He survived but would never be the same. He stuck close to his family's house and didn't leave the yard. Flaco saw him once up close when he chased a stray ball in front of the house. Alán was sitting outside on a bench. He looked right at Flaco, but there was something wrong with his gaze, like he didn't really see Flaco at all.

After what happened to Alán, nobody resisted. People continued to disappear. Some ran away to avoid being pulled into the cartel's employ. Others seemed to join by choice, like Tonio, Carlos's big brother. Tonio had left more than a year ago. Carlos reported that he'd said it was better to go to them than have them come for you. Soon all the young men were gone.

About a month before Flaco's departure, cartel members had shown up outside the school. They stood across the street, smoking, scanning the crowd of kids. They had a dog with them, a black German shepherd that paced, snapping its teeth, which was terrifying even from a distance. Those men had picked up Jorge, who was only fifteen and in the class above Flaco. Flaco watched him leave with them—a man on either side of him, not touching him, but they might as well have had him tied. And that terrible dog walking behind barking. Jorge's family did not know where they took him. That's when Flaco's mother had decided to send him north to work with this cousin in the estado of Oregon.

"It's not safe for you, mijo. I hate that this is happening in our town, but you can't stay here. I want more for you."

The señora seemed to be waiting for an answer. Flaco looked down, not knowing what to say. They were silent for a few minutes. In the quiet, Flaco listened to trucks driving by, the bark of a dog. The man grilling meat outside the restaurant hollered at someone driving past. The radio started playing a peppy corrido he recognized. Flaco unconsciously tapped his fingers in time to the music and the señora chuckled.

"Oregon has a little bit of Mexico, no?"

"I guess so," Flaco said, looking at his bottle of Coke.

She smiled sadly.

"¡Ay! Mijo, I know it must seem very strange to you here."

Yes, it did seem strange. So far, his experience of Oregon had included only the trouble with Luis's uncle and several days of being alone, scared, and hungry on the trail. But the señora seemed so kind and Flaco didn't want her to worry. He shrugged and tried to smile.

He thought of what he'd learned about Oregon at school. His mother had first mentioned the place more than a year ago, long before she'd announced her plan to send him north. She reminded him that his cousin lived there and had suggested Flaco choose the state for his English presentation. He remembered the opening lines and sat up straighter.

"Oregon is a place of verdant mountains, scenic coastline, and arid deserts," he said in English. "The state includes big cities and small towns."

The details of his presentation came back to him.

"Oregon has a robust craft beer scene," he said. Flaco particularly liked this phrase though he had no idea what it meant.

"And epic outdoor access!"

He looked at Jacob and the señora, hoping he'd impressed them. Jacob looked like he was smothering a sneeze, and the señora laughed and said how smart he was to know so many things.

Flaco nodded. He did know many things. He knew all the states and capitals of Mexico and the United States. He knew the difference between a cinder cone, a stratovolcano, and a shield volcano. He knew that an old volcano like Mount Hood, which had not erupted for hundreds of years, still had seismic activity and one or two earthquakes per month. He didn't know if Mount Hood would erupt in his lifetime. He also didn't know what to do about the fact that Cousin César failed to answer his phone when they tried again and again after that. The afternoon passed, and the sun fell low in the sky.

Señora Evangelina invited them both to her house for dinner. A short distance from the taquería, it was a bright, comfortable home. Her husband was working, she said, and their kids were out. Señora Evangelina gave him some of her sons' clothes to change into. They were too big, but it felt so good to shower and change his clothes after many days in the same pair of jeans and T-shirt.

She made dinner, chatting in Spanish and English from the kitchen. Flaco sat across from Jacob, trying to keep his eyes open. She called him Sebastián repeatedly until he felt compelled to tell her that everyone called him Flaco.

"Okay then, Flaco," she said.

After they ate, Jacob and the señora cleared the table. He could hear them in the kitchen speaking English, but he couldn't understand what they were saying. When they came back, Señora Evangelina explained that Flaco would be spending the night with Jacob. Flaco felt a sudden weight. He would have preferred to stay with the señora, who spoke Spanish and reminded him of his mamá, and who was so kind. But he was too old to cry, and he would be polite as his mother taught him.

"Thank you, señora," he said, swallowing around the lump in his throat.

"Don't worry, Flaco. Jacob is a good person. You can trust him," she said. "I'll see you tomorrow and we'll help you find your cousin. Before you go, is there anyone else you'd like to call?"

Oh, how he longed to hear his mother's voice. But he didn't want to tell her again that he was still not with his cousin. It would only worry her.

He shook his head. He thanked her for dinner and for the clothes and told her it had been very nice to meet her. Before he left, she gave him some English workbooks, some books in Spanish, and a Spanish-English dictionary.

"To keep up with your studies," she said, hugging him goodbye.

It was too dark to see much of the town as Jacob drove. They reached their destination after the truck descended a long, twisty lane to the bottom of a small ravine. The trees opened up to reveal a single-story house, a red barn, and a large stand of trees beyond. The trees were lined up in orderly rows and he realized it was an orchard. Beyond the trees he could see the dark profile of Mount Hood against the dusky sky. Mount Hood, where he'd been that very afternoon. It looked impossibly far. And Mexico was even farther.

The house was small and neat. Jacob showed him a bedroom and bathroom. He pointed down the hall to where he slept and said good night. Flaco climbed into bed still wearing the borrowed clothes and stared at the ceiling. It had been weeks since he'd slept in a bed. It was large and comfortable too, but so strange. His feet throbbed from walking and each spot where the bees had stung him felt alternately hot and cold. He considered how far he'd traveled, seeing the map in his mind. He thought of his little town. He thought of his mother's face the day she left him at the bus. He thought of her plan for him to go north.

It was true what Flaco's mother said. He was brave and smart. And, as his teacher believed, he spoke better English than anyone in his class and perhaps the whole town. It was also accurate that he was one of the best offensive players on the field. Any of his friends would have confirmed the fact. But none of that was any help to him now. Flaco had run into the woods by himself without food or water or any plan. He'd walked for days alone in a strange place. He'd been frightened out of his wits by a flock of turkeys and then tried to quell his hunger by drinking fire from a beehive. His heart burned in him like the magma-filled conduit of a fiery volcano.

Flaco, who his mother said would do great things, lay in the unfamiliar bed in the house of a stranger. A place that was safe but felt impossibly foreign. A home that was not his home. He felt every foot of every mile between himself and his mother. And then Flaco, who was far too old to do so, cried himself to sleep.

7

SPECIES OF CONCERN

Generally peaceful in nature, the female members of the *Bombus* species will sting in defense of their nests.

—LAVIN, *THE WONDROUS WORLD OF BEES*

ABIGAIL CLOSED HER eyes and located the stutter of a large bumblebee probing the head of a mallow blossom. The lab's pollinator garden was a symphony of insect sound—murmuring, buzzing, whirring, and clicking. The bees were hard at work here amid the rabbitbrush, snowberry, and American vetch. Many were native species she'd already become familiar with—the *Bombus flavifrons*, yellowhead bumblebee; *Bombus melanopygus*, black-tailed bumblebee; and *Bombus appositus*, white-shouldered bumblebee—as well as sweat bees, mason bees, and carpenter bees. Occasionally honeybees found their way to the garden as well, though the Honeybee Lab had separate and well-established foraging habitat for *Apis mellifera*, the non-native, much-celebrated honeybees.

In Abigail's brief time with Dr. Mora, she'd learned to recognize the similarities between honeybees and bumblebees. Both species had three main body parts comprised of head, thorax, and abdomen.

They had three sets of legs and two pairs of wings—hindwing and forewing. A long proboscis, antennae, and five eyes—two large compound eyes and three smaller ocelli in the middle of the head—these could all be found on *Apis* and *Bombus* alike. Bumblebees had corbiculae on their legs, which acted like little baskets for carrying pollen, just like honeybees did, and ovipositors, or egg-laying tubes, which had evolved into stingers; though, unlike a honeybee, a bumblebee could sting more than once. That was a surprising fact, really, and perhaps contradictory to their soft appearance.

Abigail found her observations of all native bees absorbing but was taken by the bumblebees in particular—the bright coloration of their soft setae, or hair, which grew in striking sections of yellow, black, brown, white, and rust. Under her fingertips their fuzzy pile felt as downy as an Easter chick. She thrilled to the feel of sticky feet on her palm, looked into the complex faces of the tiny creatures, and marveled at their dexterity and temerity to just keep going, despite the brevity of their lives.

But what she found truly captivating was the bumblebee's unique buzz pollination, or sonification. During this process, bumblebees grabbed onto a flower and used their flight muscles to shake pollen loose. Buzz pollination was particularly useful in plants with tubular anthers, which held their pollen tightly inside. Eggplants, tomatoes, blueberries, cranberries, and many kinds of flowers depended on this strange and wonderful somatic event.

The act created a high-pitched buzz that was not only distinctive, it was also a physical pleasure to listen to. At least Abigail thought so. At work in the pollinator garden, Abigail thrilled to the tone each time she heard it. She could feel it in her body, like a tuning fork against which to measure her own contentment. She'd grown attuned to their droning tones, their rumbling resonance.

She had a knack for locating bee nests—so small, private, and carefully chosen. Each one was like a wonderful secret hidden in plain sight. At the base of a fir tree, a fence post, an abandoned mouse nest. Abigail crouched low to watch the fuzzy insects emerge from the openings and slowly take to the air.

Calm.

Content.

Focused.

Those feelings had dominated Abigail's time working in the pollinator garden. But today, campus was busier than usual, and she was finding it difficult to concentrate. She shut her eyes and strained to hear the bee she'd been following. Someone walked past the garden dragging a stick along the fence. A herd of toddlers trundled by with their minders—holding hands like a string of paper dolls and jabbering to one another. One idiot stood near the gate *smoking* and chuckling moronically as he stared at his phone. Disgusted, Abigail finally stalked over to inform him that OSU was a tobacco-free environment. He'd looked embarrassed and stubbed his cigarette out on the bottom of his shoe before hurrying off. A circle of hacky sack players had set up nearby on the lawn. They shouted their dismay each time someone missed the pass. Like it was some big surprise? Someone always missed! Was anyone ever *good* at hacky sack? Abigail wondered.

Abigail opened her eyes and located a bee emerging from the grass near the ground. The large thorax was ringed with bright yellow stergites—fuzzy stripes on the underside of the abdomen—and a wooly orange rump. The bee was alone and appeared to be larger than the others Abigail had seen that morning. It could be a queen. The queens intrigued her with their solitary winters, their singular purpose in building a nest, constructing a honey basket to feed themselves, and laying their eggs to build a colony. And yet, for all that effort, they had such short lives, lasting only until the end of the summer, when they died and their surviving daughters went into their own hibernation cycles.

Abigail marked the nest location in her notebook and watched as the bee visited a patch of blueberry bushes. The small white blossoms quivered with its buzzing. Abigail gently nudged the fuzzy body into a collection container with her fingertip. With the bee secured, she inspected the coloration and banding more closely and identified it as *Bombus mixtus*, fuzzy-horned bumblebee. She snapped a few photos, opened the collection tube, and watched the bee return to the air.

Dr. Mora had instructed Abigail to use a net when collecting specimens, which Abigail decided was unnecessary. The first time they worked in the garden together, Abigail watched Dr. Mora swing a small net above a large lupine as she explained the best technique. She captured a bee, deposited it in a specimen container, and snapped the lid shut.

"Voilà," Dr. Mora had said. "We want to make sure not to damage the sample before we process it. Now, the next step is to determine—"

"No. I'm not doing that," Abigail interrupted, furious.

"Excuse me, Abigail, but there's no need to—"

"I will NOT drown the SAMPLES as you like to call them."

"Abigail, I never asked—"

"I WILL NOT!"

Dr. Mora's stare made Abigail realize that this might qualify as a "heated display of emotion," which Dr. Thomas had told her was inappropriate. She tried to do the things her father had practiced with her: breathe in and out. Remember where she was and what she was doing. She had closed her eyes and now opened them to see Dr. Mora observing her.

"Abigail. Did I ask you to drown this bee?" she asked.

"No, but that's the MITE COUNT beaker!" Abigail said, struggling to control the volume of her voice. "That they use in the HONEYBEE lab. To drown the BEES."

Dr. Mora glanced at the collection beaker.

"Ah. They are similar. But we are not doing a mite count. We just need to get a couple of photos and measurements."

Abigail felt her heart slow. That had been her main problem with the Honeybee Lab, really—watching the beekeepers cheerfully drown perfectly healthy honeybees in order to count the mites that everyone knew were there anyway.

Dr. Mora photographed the bee and asked Abigail to take measurements. They identified the bee as a healthy *Bombus flavifrons*, yellowhead bumblebee.

"The varroa mite is a major problem for *Apis mellifera*, Abigail," Dr. Mora said. "There is a reason we've developed such protocols as the mite count. But, as I said, that's not what we're doing here, so no need to worry about it."

Abigail scoffed under her breath, unconvinced. But she was relieved to know that her work for Dr. Mora would focus on locating nests, catching bumblebees for identification, documenting their characteristics, and releasing them.

Now Abigail spied a ponderous *Bombus flavifrons* on a rabbitbrush plant. A pungent scent rose as the lacy leaves swished against her pant legs. She nudged the bee into the collection container with her fingertip. She took photos and measurements and released it. The bee drifted back out into the rabbitbrush, bending a stem under its weight and buzzing mightily.

Her new job suited her. She enjoyed the methodical details of research, the processes, the routine. Coming from the teaching pool, she didn't know the first thing about research. Luckily, Dr. Mora had given her very specific directions. Abigail appreciated specific directions. The data sheets Dr. Mora had given her were orderly and methodical: site name, site longitude/latitude, date, number of observers, name(s) of observers. And below that, details like time of day, temperature, wind direction. The meat of the data was about what she actually saw around her—habitat information, flower species in bloom, and bumblebee observations. She felt great satisfaction filling out the data sheets.

Dr. Mora also let her set her own schedule. However, Abigail was required to attend at least one weekly departmental meeting. It could be a visiting lecture, a dissertation presentation, or a panel of undergraduates. Even Fridays in the apiary counted. Abigail silently scoffed at this suggestion.

"Once a week, Abigail," Dr. Mora had said.

Abigail meant to honor this request, but each week she found herself working through the intended hour somehow. She'd failed to show for three weeks, and Dr. Mora wasn't happy.

"Come to the department lecture this week, Abigail. Get there early. It's important."

She told Abigail, in a kind way, that if she wanted to keep working in the pollinator garden, she needed to show up.

"Just do this one extra thing. You're doing good work here, Abigail."

Abigail liked hearing Dr. Mora say that. The research lab suited her in a way that teaching never had. Her dad had noticed when they'd met for breakfast the previous weekend.

"It's great to see you so happy," her father said.

Abigail considered that. Was she Happy? Was Happy something she could feel and also something her father could see?

"I find scientific research reasonable," she said. "It's sensible."

Her father laughed.

"Okay, I stand corrected. It's great to see you feeling reasonable and sensible."

She understood he was teasing her in a nice way. Emotions remained difficult for Abigail to parse, though she'd been trying since the third grade when she worked with Miss Star three times a week. Miss Star polished her nails to match her sparkly pink lipstick. Her desk held a jar of freshly sharpened pencils and full boxes of crayons, all colors intact. Student progress charts, including Abigail's, lined one wall. It gave Abigail a small prickle of pride to see her name there each time she walked in the door. "Abigail Plue!" was printed neatly in block letters—purple, which was her favorite color. Underneath her name was a list of goals: "Naming my feelings! Controlling my emotions! Understanding other people's feelings!" Miss Star always gave her stickers, which made her accomplishments feel more real.

Miss Star's tiny classroom was quiet and cool. It made Abigail feel special to leave the chaos of recess—shrieking girls flinging themselves into the air on swings, boys chasing each other and shoving. Basketballs and kickballs flying across the pavement. Abigail rarely joined in. She was only ever invited to play when there was a shortage in numbers for kickball or four square. She was frustrated by the rules, which lacked clarity and changed all the time. Take Hot Lava, for example. Where you could and could not step on the playground changed from one day to the next depending on who was leading the game. When she asked for clarification, the others made fun of her.

So it was always a relief to see her pretty teacher beckoning from the side door of the school—Monday, Wednesday, and Friday. Abigail loved hearing the sounds of the playground fall away as she walked down the dark and quiet hall. Years later the memory of receding noise and the tap-tap-tap of Miss Star's shoes in the hallway provided Abigail with a deep sense of comfort.

She and Miss Star played games too, but they always had clear rules, and Miss Star answered Abigail's questions when she didn't understand. Often, they played with a deck of flashcards called "Big Feelings!" which displayed cartoon drawings of human faces and defined a range of emotions. A Happy face was laughing. A Sad face had big tears. Angry was eyebrows in a vee and a frown. Scared was wide eyes and gritted teeth. There were many others, but Abigail recalled these four best, these simple, line-drawn emotions on thick off-white cardstock. They were the first she'd mastered. She loved the cards, sturdy in her hands and smelling faintly of her teacher's perfume.

Her time with Miss Star made Abigail feel special, until one day, while waiting for the bus, a classmate told her otherwise.

"You're not special. It's a class for weirdos, wackos, and retards!" he sang out. "Like you, Abigail Poo!"

He swung his backpack and smacked her in the shoulder. Abigail noticed he had rabbity front teeth. When she told him so, he shoved her into the ivy that grew along the wall. It didn't hurt and she laughed, which seemed to make the boy angrier. She didn't know why she laughed and didn't think there was a card to describe how she was feeling. Sad and Mad and Ashamed all mixed together.

In the years since, there were days when Abigail relived those awful feelings from the bus stop and others. Those childhood wounds would resurface when she struggled with work or school. But not now. Now, working with the bumblebees, Abigail experienced a sense of Contentment. Also Calm. And, yes, maybe even Happiness. Abigail watched the *Bombus mixtus* touch down on the lobed face of a delphinium and begin to plumb the depths of the anther. The creature grasped the anther and vibrated its flight muscles to shake the pollen loose. The small miracle of buzz pollination. Abigail, mesmerized, watched the bee at work and startled when the campus clock tower tolled quarter to noon. The lecture began in fifteen minutes.

"*Get there early this time. It's important*," Dr. Mora had said.

Abigail shoved her notebooks and collection materials into her backpack and latched the pollinator garden gate shut. She trotted toward the auditorium, taking the most direct route for efficiency, which led her straight through the circle of hacky sackers. They yelled at her as she shoved past, but she didn't have time to stop and explain that recreationalists must yield to academics, like cars to pedestrians and pedestrians to horses. *Everyone* knew that! And that if they didn't, they should restrict their games to the *campus playing fields*!

The auditorium was packed with students and professors from the life science departments. Many people, it seemed, were keen to hear from Dr. Lavin, a visiting professor from the University of Washington. Abigail lingered in the doorway listening to the hive-like buzz of voices.

She saw Casey sitting near the front. Casey waved and gestured to the empty seat next to her, and Abigail's heart leapt. They hadn't spoken since their presentations. Over time it had sunk in that Casey had helped her by turning off the lights in the conference room. That she'd known it would help, even when Abigail herself didn't. She'd wanted to say thank you and here was her chance. She waved back and moved forward.

"Hello, Casey," she mumbled, practicing. "I wanted to thank you for—"

Someone pushed past her, a boy Abigail recognized from the department. Casey smiled up at him as he sat down next to her. She hadn't seen Abigail at all. Abigail flushed with embarrassment and sat down in the first seat she could find a few rows behind them. Dr. Mora was onstage giving opening remarks.

". . . so lucky to have Dr. Lavin with us today to talk about her latest research in the arena of native bumblebee conservation. Please help me in welcoming Dr. Daphne Lavin."

A young professor stepped to the podium amid the applause. Dr. Daphne Lavin seemed closer to Abigail's age than Dr. Mora's. Tall and broad shouldered, she wore her hair pulled back in a messy ponytail. The fluorescent lights glinted off her glasses, which she pushed up off her nose.

"What a hottie," the boy sitting with Casey whispered, and snickered.

"Good afternoon," Dr. Lavin said. "Thank you, Dr. Mora, for your delightful introduction. I'm so pleased to be here this morning to share the University of Washington's latest research on *Bombus occidentalis*."

Dr. Lavin did not look delighted, and she did not sound pleased. Her face was flat, her unmodulated voice carrying to the far corners of the room. She opened a presentation on her laptop and a large photo of a bumblebee appeared on the projection screen behind her. She looked over the heads of the audience and began her lecture without additional preamble.

The boy nudged Casey and whispered something, and she giggled.

"The plight of the Pacific Northwest native bumblebee population is a microcosm of environmental crises of our times. Drought, habitat loss, pesticide use, newly introduced parasites, and climate change have caused an estimated fifty percent loss in the bumblebee population since 1974."

The boy whispered again, and Abigail felt her blood pulse in her ears. She found it difficult to listen to two things at the same time. She gritted her teeth and leaned forward to say something, but someone else shushed him. The boy slouched in his seat, laughing to himself, but quieter.

Dr. Lavin advanced to a slide with the heading "Species of Greatest Conservation Need," and then went rapidly through photos of several bumblebees.

"Franklin's bumblebee, endangered. Rusty-patched bumblebee, endangered. Crotch's, Suckley's cuckoo, obscure, Morrison's, and western bumblebees—these are all species of conservation concern. The federal government has declined to change the status of these species, which many of us consider imperative to their protection."

Dr. Lavin advanced to a close-up photo of a fuzzy, pollen-laden bumblebee, its bottom striped white and a thick yellow band of pile on the back of its head.

"*Bombus occidentalis* is of particular interest to us. This species was once common in the western United States and Canada—from New Mexico to Alaska and from California to Montana. *Bombus occidentalis* was a frequent visitor to gardens, orchards, and neighborhood parks. But for the past fifteen years, this species has effectively disappeared west of the Cascade Range.

"Theories about the decline of *Bombus occidentalis* include disease, pesticide use, and habitat loss, like so many bee species. *Bombus occidentalis* studies have taken on a tone of postmortem, with most scientists assuming it is simply gone. The disappearance of a species is, sadly, nothing new," Dr. Lavin said.

"Many of you likely believe we are living in the sixth extinction or the Holocene extinction. We know that invertebrate populations have plummeted by almost seventy percent since 1970. In that same period, we've lost three billion birds—more than one in four. And seventy percent of monitored wildlife populations."

Abigail shifted in her seat. Anyone studying science in the twenty-first century knew these things. She'd listened to Diane and Linda debate the issue in the Dungeon. Linda thought they hadn't reached the sixth extinction yet, while Diane did. Abigail didn't join in the debate. The whole idea of the sixth extinction made her feel Anxious and Depressed. It was humankind, after all, that was responsible for the degradation of the animal kingdom. Why even argue among themselves about it?

Dr. Lavin paused and smiled for the first time.

"However, there are bright spots in all this. Last summer, my colleague at UW, James Hall, discovered a *Bombus occidentalis* on Mount Hood."

Dr. Lavin clicked a button and a video filled the screen. Mount Hood rose in the background, and in the foreground, a swath of bright green meadow grass undulated in a breeze. The view zoomed in to a patch of purple lupine where a large bumblebee was at work in the lobed blossoms. A murmur rippled through the audience.

"Dr. Fall's discovery has given us hope that the western bumblebee could be repopulating in areas where it has long been absent. We look forward to continuing our work in the region to assess the current state of *Bombus occidentalis*. This summer we have a unique opportunity to return to the Mount Hood National Forest to canvass for *Bombus occidentalis*. We are pleased that the OSU entomology department will be partnering with us on this study."

Dr. Lavin closed her talk with a summary of recent papers published by a tristate conservation consortium, but Abigail had stopped listening. She was pondering the astonishing possibility of *Bombus occidentalis*'s return. The idea that a species could come back when so many were dying off was simply delightful. Somehow, amid melting ice sheets, deforestation, the global decline of wildlife of all kinds, this bee, this one tiny insect, might be staging a comeback. It was marvelous to consider.

Dr. Lavin left the stage, and people rose and streamed out of the auditorium. Casey, passing, caught her eye and waved.

"Hey, Abigail!" Casey said, smiling.

"Thank you, Casey!" Abigail blurted, half rising from her seat. Casey didn't seem to hear her, but the guy who'd been sitting with her stared as he passed. Abigail sat back down feeling disappointed that she'd missed the chance to speak to Casey, but more than anything, she felt amazed at the wonderful possibility of the western bumblebee's revival.

From the stage, Dr. Mora beckoned Abigail. Abigail's stomach flipped over, and she wondered if Dr. Mora had seen her come in late. She struggled down the stairs against the tide of people leaving the room, who did not seem to understand that someone might need to go *in the other direction*!

Abigail approached her supervisor and braced herself for a scolding.

"Abigail, I'd like to introduce you to Dr. Daphne Lavin. Daphne, this is Abigail Plue. She's recently joined my team and is exceptionally talented in species identification. A beginner, but she's got a real knack for it."

Dr. Lavin held out her hand and Abigail shook it.

"It's nice to meet you, Abigail," she said.

Remembering her father's reminder to look people in the eye, Abigail raised her eyes briefly and noticed Dr. Lavin was looking past her ear.

"Abigail, I thought you might have some questions for Dr. Lavin," Dr. Mora said.

She said it with such certainty, Abigail felt panicked. Was this some assignment she'd forgotten? What had Dr. Mora said at their last meeting? She'd asked for a catalog of species from the pollinator garden, and a working bibliography of research to date. She'd insisted Abigail come to the presentation and arrive early. But Abigail couldn't remember a thing about having questions for Dr. Lavin. Dr. Mora hadn't even mentioned Dr. Lavin!

There was a long pause.

"Why don't we walk and talk?" Dr. Mora said.

Out in the sunlight, they crossed the quad, and Dr. Mora asked Dr. Lavin about the Mount Hood study goals, the timeframe, and the details of the field team. Abigail felt miffed. If Dr. Mora had all those questions, why in the world would she ask Abigail to come up with something to ask about?

Dr. Mora stopped just outside the pollinator garden.

"Abigail, perhaps you'd like to show Dr. Lavin the nests you've located this week?"

Abigail stopped short and blinked. Was it a question? The sound went up at the end but she wasn't quite sure.

"Abigail—"

Dr. Mora sounded impatient, and Abigail felt a mix of Shame and Frustration. What was the right answer?

"Show me the nests you've found, please, Abigail," Dr. Lavin said then, and Abigail felt a flood of relief.

"Oh! Yes. In what order? Day of discovery, species, or location?"

Dr. Lavin said, "Location, please. Working clockwise."

Abigail led the professors through the pollinator garden and pointed out the nests she'd found in the ground, in old snags, and in a fence post. In some cases, they observed bees flying in and out of the openings. She recited the species from memory as she identified each nest—mason bee, sweat bee, carpenter bee, and then the bumblebees, including *Bombus flavifrons*, *Bombus huntii* or Hunt's bumblebee, and the most recent that day—*Bombus mixtus*.

Dr. Lavin nodded and Dr. Mora beamed.

"As I said, Abigail has exceptional skill in locating nests as well as talent for the methodology of identification. Perfect skills for the wilderness field team."

Dr. Lavin looked over Abigail's head, nodding, and explained that the wilderness field team would survey a sample area of the Mount Hood National Forest, including the portion of land where the western bumblebee had been spotted. Dr. Lavin and a small group would be canvassing the region to determine if *Bombus occidentalis* was, in fact, recovering, or if the sighting had been a one-off.

Abigail liked how Dr. Lavin did not look directly at her when she spoke. It was easier to listen to her somehow.

"There's some urgency in the timeline. The forest service permit is only for two weeks. We're bumping up against nesting season for the white-headed woodpecker, which is a strategy species for Oregon conservation. But this is the best time, really. It's peak bloom time on the mountain and will give us our best shot at locating *Bombus occidentalis*. If we can confirm Dr. Hall's sighting, we can apply to protect the area. It's quite exciting but also important that we move as quickly as we can. There's been a bit of—" Dr. Lavin paused and looked out over the playing fields.

"A bit of conflict in the area. There's a group that wants to build on the land—a hunting camp. Hunting is part of the multiuse regulations of the forest, of course, but permanent structures aren't allowed. I personally think such an operation would be inappropriate. It would be a year-round lodge of sorts. Conversations have been . . . volatile. There's a coalition working to try to restore dialogue. But interactions with some of their supporters have been . . . dispiriting," Dr. Lavin said.

"I read about that. It sounds quite divisive," Dr. Mora said.

"The hunting camp owners are reasonable people. It's the online community where things get heated. I read through some of the comments. It's appalling, the tone some of them take."

At the mention of the hunting camp, Abigail recalled an afternoon with a neighbor when she was nine. Her dad was working and had arranged for Abigail to spend the day with the neighbors and their kids. The parents took them to Cascade Lakes for picnicking and swimming. After lunch the dad set up a target for shooting practice. He gathered the kids and demonstrated how to hold the gun, load it, release the safety, and aim. Abigail found it all interesting at first, the mechanics anyway. But at the first report of the .22, she'd disappeared into the woods. It was like her body had made the decision without telling her mind and just took off running. Hiding deep in the trees, her heart thudding, she tried and failed to unhear the sound. She didn't know how long she was there before the other kids found her, but the parents were both mad at her for running off. Abigail didn't hang out with those kids again.

She thought of the *Bombus occidentalis* from Dr. Lavin's video, the broad yellow band of fuzzy pile just behind the head, the corbicula chunky with pollen, the drone of the bumblebee as it worked in the lupine blossoms.

She thought the video had also shown glimpses of the surrounding forest—towering Douglas firs, the stream splashing through a meadow tangled with wildflowers. The idea of gunshots disrupting the quiet seemed appalling.

Dr. Mora and Dr. Lavin had stopped talking and were looking at her. Had they asked her a question?

"Pardon?" she said.

"Do you think you'd enjoy working on Mount Hood?" Dr. Mora asked.

What kind of a question was that? Abigail thought, furious.

"At a *hunting camp*?" she said. "No, I would NOT enjoy that!"

Dr. Mora sighed.

"Abigail. Dr. Lavin thinks you'd be an asset to the western bumblebee study."

"Oh," Abigail said, still not understanding.

Dr. Lavin turned toward her with a hint of a smile. Again, she seemed to be looking just past Abigail's ear, which made it easier somehow to talk with her.

"I'd like you to join the research group. Would you join our *Bombus occidentalis* study on Mount Hood?"

"Oh!" Abigail said. "Yes! Yes, please! Thank you!"

Abigail did not take in many details after that. They walked to Dr. Mora's office and Abigail floated behind them, carried not on her own feet but on the invisible wings of thousands of bumblebees. She felt Delighted, Excited, Elated. She waited in the hall while the two professors finished their conversation.

Three days later, she collected the equipment she'd need to take to the field site in the Mount Hood National Forest. Dr. Lavin had directed her to set up the camp and establish the boundaries of the research area and said she'd follow with the other students later that week. Abigail would drive up with all the camp gear, and the other students would hike in from a drop-off point about three miles below the campsite.

Deirdre, the department administrative assistant, provided Abigail with a list of the camp gear she'd need—tent, sleeping bag, cooking items, lantern, and other sundries.

"I've been doing this job forever, so forgive me if you know this stuff already. I always tell people to bring twice as much water as you think you'll need. And don't count on the filter. If it fails, you'll want iodine pills as backup."

Abigail, who hadn't even thought about bringing any water at all, nodded.

"Now, it can still snow on Hood in June, but it's been pretty warm already, so who knows what kind of weather you might get. Pack layers," Deirdre went on. "You understand good layering, right?"

"Layering. Layering of what, exactly?" Abigail asked.

Deirdre paused and regarded Abigail.

"Dr. Mora said you might need specifics."

She rummaged through a filing cabinet and pulled out a small booklet, which she handed to Abigail. *US Forest Service Field Camp Handbook*, the cover said.

"This is ancient, but you might find it useful."

Deirdre handed her a gear list to take to the equipment room. She also explained where to pick up a university vehicle. Abigail signed the forms Deirdre slid across the desk at her.

"You must be pretty special, heading up the field team," Deirdre said, taking the forms.

Abigail blinked.

"It's a privilege. You get that, right? That Dr. Mora picked you to set up camp?"

Dr. Mora had not, in fact, picked her to set up camp. Dr. Mora had said that Abigail did not seem like the right student for the task. That's what Abigail heard her say. Or overheard, rather, while she'd waited outside Dr. Mora's office. She had not intended to eavesdrop, but Dr. Mora had failed to shut the door completely and had told Abigail to wait outside.

Abigail heard Dr. Lavin say she was impressed with the species catalog Abigail had established in the pollinator garden and the detail with which she'd documented the nest locations, foraging habits, and plant preferences of the various native species.

"She's done an impressive amount of work on her own. I'd like her to be field camp leader for this trip," Dr. Lavin said.

Abigail liked hearing someone say nice things about her.

Proud.

Grateful.

Pleased.

"Yes, she's done strong work in the pollinator garden. But she's never been out in the field. I have many students with far more experience than Abigail," Dr. Mora said.

"You said yourself that what she lacks in experience, she makes up for in commitment and hard work," Dr. Lavin said.

"I did say that, Daphne," Dr. Mora replied. "But you have to understand that Abigail, well, she doesn't approach things in a typical way."

"And you have to understand that doing things the typical way isn't the only way, Nicolette," Dr. Lavin responded. "We neurodiverse folk can teach you neurotypicals a thing or two."

Dr. Mora chuckled.

"I don't know, Daphne."

"Truly, Nicolette. I think she'll figure it out. She reminds me a bit of myself at her age."

"Well, it's your field camp, so it's your choice. Maybe she'll be a natural. Abigail tends to surprise me."

"I tend to surprise Dr. Mora," Abigail told Deirdre, who shook her head and wished her luck.

After a struggle with the clerk in the equipment room, Abigail found herself behind the wheel of an enormous SUV. The motor-pool guy asked if she knew how to engage four-wheel drive. She sniffed and said of course she did. Every car she'd ever driven had had four wheels.

He said that wasn't exactly what four-wheel drive meant and that he'd be happy to show her.

"That will not be necessary," Abigail said, wanting to avoid more conversation.

"It's nothing to be ashamed of," the motor-pool guy said, smiling. "I just want to make sure you're a qualified driver. That you're not some kind of hazard behind the wheel."

Abigail, bristling, informed him she had an immaculate driving record and that he was wasting her valuable time. And as soon as she said it, she knew it was A Wrong Thing. He stopped smiling and gave her paperwork to sign and left her alone to figure out how to turn on the vehicle. Unlike her father's car, there was no fob, but an old-fashioned *key*! This took some time to sort out.

She drove north on I-5, hugging the right shoulder of the highway as cars and trucks blasted past her, and realized two things: one, that her immaculate driving record might be due to the fact that she rarely drove. And two, that the motor-pool guy had been, possibly, *flirting* with her!

Shame.

Embarrassment.

Regret.

She exited the interstate with relief and took slower OR-214 through the little towns of Molalla, Estacada, and Eagle Creek. She headed east on OR-26 and scanned the signposts for Forest Service Road 2308. The trees grew thick and dark and obscured Mount Hood. The road twisted and turned and narrowed the higher it climbed. Then the pavement ended and the road grew rough. She wondered if this was what the motor-pool guy meant about needing four-wheel drive.

She wondered if she was lost and considered turning around. Then she realized the road was too narrow for that and she would have to back down to turn. So she kept going, creeping forward along the road as it tapered down to a narrow track. The trees opened up in front of her and her heart lifted. She paused there and noticed a truck parked in the sunny meadow. Beyond the truck, past the tall grass, she saw two figures out in the clearing near a series of small structures.

What had Dr. Lavin said? Someone had started building a hunting camp but had been told to cease and desist. No one was supposed to be up there right now. And yet there they were, building their illegal camp anyway.

Appalling, like Dr. Lavin had said. The memory of gunshots echoed through her mind and her body felt hot with fear. Fury rose in her like a living thing.

She forgot herself then, as she would say later, trying to explain. She pointed the SUV at the two figures and stomped on the gas.

8

SANCTUARY

Wild honeybees prefer to make their homes in tree cavities, as elevation makes them safer from predation. However, they will settle into human-made spaces like mailboxes, porch columns, and even within the walls of houses when the opportunity presents itself.

—LAVIN, *THE WONDROUS WORLD OF BEES*

JACOB WATCHED THE time on his phone tick from 6:28 a.m. to 6:29 a.m. and shut off the alarm before it sounded. He hadn't slept well, listening for sounds from the room down the hall, worried that the kid might need something in the middle of the night.

Cheney, hearing him stir, thumped his big tail against the floor. And then the dog rose, blocky head first, paws following as he stretched his thick neck. His mouth snapped open in a yawn that ended in a high-pitched yip. Cheney loved morning and its routine: Jake getting up and dressed. Jake letting him out the slider for a big lap in the yard and the chance to mark all his spots and smell what had happened in the nighttime. A bowl of kibble and a good scratch behind the ears as Jake drank his coffee and read the news on his phone.

Jake usually loved their morning routine too. Alice liked to tease him that he was old before his time—twenty-three going on sixty, pottering about in the morning. But nothing about today felt routine. Today he was faced with the responsibility of hosting this unexpected teenager.

"Only a day or two, Jake," Evangelina had said. "I'm sorry to ask, but we can't have him here right now."

Jake understood why Flaco couldn't stay with the Ryans. Evangelina and Ron were consummately generous to friends, family, and even strangers like this boy. Evangelina was such a community resource that Ron teased she was a one-stop shop. If you were looking for a place to rent, a new job, childcare. If you needed help with your visa application, filing your taxes, getting your kid signed up for school, or a good lawyer, just ask Evangelina.

"Saint Evie," her kids teased her, but she just smiled and said, "We all do our part."

However, at this particular moment, with Ron running for sheriff in a county divided over immigration, they couldn't shelter an undocumented minor. The Hood River County Sheriff's Department had been under fire from some members of the community for being "soft on crime" and "turning a blind eye to the 'illegals' invading the county." The voices were few, but vocal. People mostly complained online. But increasingly this kind of sentiment was voiced at city council meetings and letters to the editor in the paper. Their talk was amplified and encouraged by Ron's opponent in the race for sheriff, E.W. Dewitt, who was, one might say, soft on truth.

Last week the *Hood River News* had published Dewitt's letter to the editor, in which he wrote, "Deputy Sheriff Ron Ryan is directing his officers to ignore illegals in Hood River County. It's the responsibility of the sheriff's office to monitor and apprehend anyone suspected of being an illegal alien in our fine county."

Jake bristled at the language—"illegal" and "alien." He also knew it was not, in fact, the responsibility of the sheriff's office to police immigration law. Oregon's sanctuary laws, first passed in 1987, stated the opposite, in fact. In passing House Bill 2314, Oregon became the first state in the nation to establish sanctuary laws, which forbade local police officers from enforcing federal immigration law. That fell under the purview of Immigration and Customs Enforcement officers out of Portland. Hood River County, along with the rest of the state, had overwhelmingly voted to uphold the state's sanctuary laws in 2018. Still, Ron had been pressured to defend county policies. He couldn't risk someone discovering he was sheltering an unaccompanied, undocumented minor.

"We'll get it figured out," Evangelina had said when she walked them out to the truck after dinner. "I'll call you tomorrow."

She turned to the boy and spoke to him rapidly in Spanish. The boy nodded and glanced at Jake.

"By the way, he says everyone calls him Flaco, not Sebastián. And I told him your Spanish is good, but he needs to talk slow," she said.

"That's generous, but not exactly accurate, Evangelina," Jake said.

She laughed.

"Okay, I didn't want to hurt your feelings. I told him to keep it simple."

She kissed Jake on the cheek.

"I'll call as soon as I can, Jacob. And one more thing."

A truck sped by, diesel engine roaring, and she paused until it passed.

"Don't pressure him to talk about his home. Sometimes these kids leave traumatic circumstances, and they need space."

He nodded.

"Thank you, Jacob."

"No problem," he said. "Happy to help."

It was true that he was happy to do this for her. Evangelina, Ron, and their sons were Alice's family. Alice had been married to Ron's brother, who died before Jake and Alice met. When Alice had taken him in five years ago, so had the Ryans. They were his people now too. Hosting Flaco briefly was a minor inconvenience considering all they'd done for him.

The boy was quiet on the way to the house. He watched Jake drive, curious probably, about the mechanical adaptations of the truck. At a four-way stop sign, Jake idled and a young family crossed the street—two little kids whooping and running ahead while their parents hollered at them to wait.

"Esperen, niños!"

Flaco followed the family with his eyes and wiped his palms on his jeans.

"Is okay? Walk here?" he asked, his eyes following the family down the sidewalk.

Jake didn't understand what he meant.

"Yes," he said. "They're fine walking."

Did the kid think they needed a ride or something?

"Todo bien," Jake said.

Flaco nodded and braced his hands on his knees. He stared out the window as the town receded and the land opened up into the orchards.

At the farm, Jake had shown the boy around the house with Cheney following on their heels, which seemed to make Flaco nervous. Cheney was a lover, but he was also a very big dog. Jake told Cheney to sit. He complied, drooling with the effort of holding still.

Jake scratched the dog's ears.

"Es amigable. Friendly," he said to Flaco.

The kid looked unconvinced, and Cheney wagged his tail so hard he moved the kitchen table. Jake shut Cheney in his room and showed Flaco to the guest room at the front of the house. He passed a restless night with one ear cocked toward the front bedroom. It had been Alice's room before she bought Doug Ransom's house and the orchard. Now it was the guest room. Harry lived in the bunkhouse and Jake hadn't had a guest in the nearly five years he'd been living there unless you counted Ruby. Ruby had not slept in the guest room.

Thinking about Ruby would not help now, he thought. He sat up and pushed Cheney away. He transferred into his chair and rolled into the bathroom to get ready for the day.

He did feel better once he'd showered, brushed his teeth, used a catheter to empty his bladder, and pulled on his favorite jeans and Smiths T-shirt. He opened his bedroom door and watched Cheney's brindled hips swivel as he jogged down the hall. Cheney accelerated and skidded out of sight. Jake heard a high-pitched yelp, a thud, and percussive banging.

Flaco was flat on the floor, pinned under Cheney's paws, the dog's tail thudding a happy tempo of greeting. Cheney assumed everyone would love him as much as he loved them. He'd even been sweet with Jake's father, Ed Stevenson, who'd dumped him high up in the woods above BZ Corner years ago, while Jake was in rehab recovering from his accident. Jake could picture Cheney willingly leaping into the back of Ed's truck, certain that fun was afoot.

The day Jake had returned to his parents' house and realized the dog was gone had been one of the darkest in that terrible year.

"Like I said. Take care of the dog or it goes," Ed had said, cracking open a beer and turning back to the TV.

Cheney's unlikely return to Jake's life was one of his brightest memories. Instead of canceling it out, his grief seemed to enhance his joy, the feelings necessary partners in some way.

So he'd never had the heart to train this annoying behavior out of his dog.

He grabbed Cheney by the collar and hauled him backward.

"Outside, big boy," he said, and opened the sliding door. Cheney bounded outside baying his joyful morning song to the world and made a beeline for Alice's place, as he did every morning, even when she was out of town.

"Lo siento, Flaco. Sorry," Jake said. "El perro—wants lots of friends. Amigos."

The kid sat up and wiped Cheney's slobber off his face with his sleeve and pulled himself up to standing. He had wet his hair and was wearing Evangelina's son's old Hood River Valley High School track sweatshirt. He shifted nervously from foot to foot.

"Flaco, how old are you?" Jake asked. "¿Cuantos años?"

"I have four-ten years," the boy said.

"¿Catorce, sí? Fourteen?"

"Sí, fourteen," Flaco said, nodding. "I no am tall, but I to grow."

He held out a thin arm and encircled it with his skinny fingers.

"Estoy flaco. Y soy Flaco," he said.

He almost had a twinkle in his eye.

"Flaco es flaco," Jake said.

Flaco smiled.

"Are you hungry? ¿Hambre?"

The boy nodded, looking bashful, and Jake rolled into the kitchen to make breakfast. Flaco demolished a stack of pancakes while Jake eyed the clock. Evangelina had said she'd call by noon. That was hours away, and he needed to get to work.

"Señora Evangelina, she'll call at doce," Jake said. "I have to work this morning. Trabajo."

The boy nodded, stood, and pulled on the ball cap Evangelina had lent him.

"I to help," he said.

The boy's left cheek and temple were still swollen from yesterday's stings.

"You don't have to help. No necesitas. But come watch."

Jake led the way across the yard as the morning wind gusted down from the west, stirring the branches of the apple trees. The white blossoms formed a canopy overhead and Jake could hear the bees at work as he and Flaco made their way to the apiary.

Jake stopped at the fence line and took in the view. This was another part of his morning routine that never failed to please him. Amid the fenced acres, two hundred white hives sat in orderly rows facing east and cast the morning sunlight back at itself. Jake recalled his first time in Alice's apiary, which had been so much smaller then, just twenty-four hives. That day had changed him forever. The honeybees had seemed magical to him with their graceful flight patterns, their murmuring tone, and their orderly work. That first encounter had cracked his broken heart open, left him feeling the golden buzz of those bees as if they'd lodged in his chest cavity and resided there, glowing. The feeling had never really left him.

"You can watch, okay?" Jake said to Flaco and gestured to the picnic table near the apiary.

He retrieved his tool caddy from outside the fence and opened his logbook. Today he'd confirm which hives needed honey supers added atop their swelling brood boxes. At last check, three days ago, twenty-five of the two hundred hives were nearly ready for supers. He'd start there.

Queen of G used the same hives as most commercial beekeepers. Named for Lorenzo Langstroth, the nineteenth-century clergyman, teacher, and farmer who designed them, the Langstroth hives resembled file boxes stacked on top of one another. Two brood boxes tall was typical for a strong hive, and those boxes would hold up to sixty thousand bees at peak population. The shorter boxes, called honey supers, were added on top of the brood boxes. The bees would build those out with surplus honey, which was considered fair game for beekeepers to harvest.

While the Langstroth hive had made beekeeping easier for most people, the design was not ideal for Jake. Once the hive was two brood boxes tall, Jake couldn't lift that second brood box. To solve this problem, Harry Stokes, his roommate and a carpenter genius, had installed a ramp system along one side of the hives, giving Jake an extra two feet of height. The ramp allowed him to work the second brood boxes by opening them and pulling frames to check on brood development and honey stores.

Good old Harry. They hadn't spoken since he'd left in March for

South Padre. Harry did not like to talk on the phone but sent cryptic text messages: a screenshot of the route he had driven on the way to Texas. A Strava log of his kiteboarding hours in the bay. Random photos of people on the beach, and funny road signs. "Make America Mexico Again," the last one read.

Jake moved down the row of hives to begin his checks. Once the honey supers were full, not even the ramp would help him. That was why he needed helpers, he thought now, and he felt his pulse accelerate. Summer was a ticking clock and honeyflow was just around the corner. He felt the edges of his anxiety begin to peel up, and he caught himself. Jake knew the bees would read his mood, and that calmer was better. He forced his worry away and moved carefully down the row of hives. Working swiftly, he confirmed that this first row of twenty-five hives was ready for supers. Jake retrieved two supers from a stack just inside the apiary gate and returned to the hives. He removed the first hive top and inner cover, set them gently aside, and installed the empty super. The honey frames swung and clacked with the movement as he pressed them together. Then he replaced both covers and repeated the tasks with the second hive.

It wasn't hard work, but it was slow going ferrying the supers two at a time on his lap. As he installed the fourth honey super, he looked at the picnic table and saw Flaco was gone. Scared of the bees, Jake thought. But here was the boy coming across the field with the wheelbarrow from the barn. It was stacked high with supers Harry had left piled inside the shop.

"I get," he said. "Is correct?"

"Yes. Gracias," Jake said.

With the wheelbarrow and an extra set of hands, the twenty-five hives were quickly supered. Flaco seemed at ease in proximity to the hives, so Jake kept working, evaluating the others. By the end of the morning, they'd installed supers on eighty of the two hundred hives.

They sat at the picnic bench and Jake pulled cans of Coke from the cooler. After entering his notes in the logbook, he checked the weather forecast and temperature, estimating that the remaining 120 hives would need to be supered sometime in the next week. It was warmer than he'd expected and forecast to get hotter fast, which would speed up honeyflow. That was worrisome. He would update his help wanted ad again today and raise the hourly rate. Maybe he'd reach out to River and Tierra—Amri's little brothers. Amri was his first love and still his friend. Her siblings had always liked Jake and might be willing to help. River was the same age as Flaco. He looked at the boy, who was picking at his right temple. A stinger glinted in the sunlight, and Jake motioned him to turn his head.

"Okay?" he asked and reached toward the boy's face. Flaco nodded, and with a quick flicking motion, Jake scratched the stinger free.

"It's strong. Fuerte," he said. "Venom."

Flaco nodded.

"Veneno."

"Veneno," Jake repeated.

Jake gestured toward the hives.

"Are you afraid?" he asked, searching for the word. "¿Miedo?"

Flaco shook his head.

"Las abejas. The bees only . . . protejer? The home."

"Yeah," Jake said. "Protect. Right."

Flaco looked out at the hives.

"Any bee any house?" he asked.

Jake shook his head.

"Each bee has one house."

"How?" the boy asked, watching the bees zip up and away from the hives.

Jake couldn't explain the queen pheromone or the bee waggle. Not in Spanish. So he told Flaco about the beeline, how each bee learned the location of the hive and was able to find its way home from out in the field.

"Beeline," Flaco said, and smiled.

Cheney barked somewhere beyond Alice's house and the neighbors' dogs talked back. Flaco's head jerked toward the sound.

"You don't like dogs?" Jake asked. "¿Perros?"

Flaco looked down at his hands and then back at Jake.

"Some dogs," he said. "No good dogs."

He looked like he might say more, but then he didn't. He swigged the last of his Coke and stood.

"I put for garage," he said, and grabbed the wheelbarrow.

Jake watched him walk toward the barn. He looked so skinny and young. How had he managed the journey alone? How long had he walked? Why had he left his home in the first place? But Evangelina had warned him not to pry.

Cheney returned at a full gallop with a large, slobber-covered stick. He discarded it and threw himself into Jake's lap. Jake cradled the dog's upper body and pulled on his big ears.

"Listen, Godzilla. You need to take things down a notch, okay? Remember how you used to clobber Mom when you were little? Flaco is scared of dogs, so you need to chill."

The dog caught sight of the boy crossing the field with the wheelbarrow and began to whimper and wiggle.

Jake held his collar and pushed him off his lap.

"Cheney, sit."

Cheney sat. Then he was up again and racing toward the long driveway, where a black Jeep was descending. Ron Ryan raised a hand in greeting as he stepped out. Jake waved back and went to meet him. Cheney leaned against Ron, who had squatted down next to the Jeep door. He stood, looking harassed.

"Why hasn't Alice fixed the driveway? Look—I dinged the door on that big sinkhole. Is this her way of keeping people away? Making the road impassable?"

He sounded irritated and amused. Alice brought out mixed emotions in people.

Jake shrugged.

"You know Alice. She's petitioned the county that it's not her responsibility because Pacific Power uses it as an access road. She told me any repairs made before the case was settled would look like a concession. 'Can't let the bastards see me blink' were her exact words, I believe."

Ron chuckled and ran a hand through his hair.

"One hundred percent Alice Holtzman," he said.

Ron looked past Jake and gestured toward the apiary and the orchard.

"Everything good over here? I wondered about the bees during that April cold snap."

"All good," Jake said, pivoting to look toward the barn. Flaco had disappeared.

"The bees had three solid weeks to forage before it got cold, and they were flying again the next day. The trees are fine too. Looks like a good yield year."

Ron nodded and chewed his bottom lip, squinting toward the orchard. Jake knew from the look that Ron had something on his mind.

"You have time for coffee?" Jake asked.

Ron shook his head.

"No, I have to get to the station. But I promised Evie I'd stop by and fill you in about the boy's cousin. Where is he, anyway?"

Jake gestured toward the barn.

"He's putting the wheelbarrow away. He's been working with me all morning."

Ron nodded.

"Evie said he's a nice kid. Good manners. What is he, fourteen?"

"Yeah, but he looks younger. Tall and skinny. Like Victor. Early years."

Victor was one of Ron's many nephews. He'd been a pipsqueak all through high school and came back on Christmas break from his first semester at college so bulked up from a growth spurt that his own mother didn't recognize him when he walked in the door. He'd played football at Washington State University and now worked in tech but maintained his build with club rugby.

Ron chuckled.

"Hard to remember that Big Vic was a skinny little guy once."

His face grew somber.

"Well, the good news is we found the boy's cousin. Bad news is he's in NORCOR."

Jake grimaced. Being in the regional jail explained why Flaco's cousin had not answered his phone.

"On what charge?"

Ron sighed.

"He got pulled over for a broken taillight, but it turns out he was driving with a suspended license for a failure to appear at court. His work permit had expired, it seems, but he didn't show up to address that. He's going to have to sort things out. Not really in a position to help his cousin right now."

Jake swore softly.

"Yep. Not great news," Ron said. "Evie asked the ROP folks to let him know that Flaco is here if they get a chance to meet with him."

"Are they still out there every day?"

The Rural Organizing Project members had held a daily vigil outside the county jail for months now to support people who'd been incarcerated for violating immigration laws. The protest had started in 2017 with a hunger strike over inadequate food, unaffordable phone rates, and lack of access to family and legal counsel. Organizers were demanding an end to NORCOR's contract with ICE, saying that it was a violation of Oregon's sanctuary laws.

ICE paid NORCOR a daily fee to house immigration detainees, and it came out that NORCOR would routinely tip off ICE when they were about to release someone who'd completed their sentence for a civil crime, which the ROP members saw as a clear infringement of the Fourth Amendment. Amri had been actively involved with the protest before she'd left for college.

Ron nodded.

"Yep. Evangelina would be there too if she wasn't busy running the taquería and trying to save the rest of the world," Ron said. "She sends food out every week."

Jake felt ashamed of himself for not keeping up with what was happening there. He would ask Amri about it next time they texted.

"So what happens with Flaco if his cousin can't help?"

Ron sighed and rocked back on his heels.

"Evie is going to make some calls. For now, she asked if you could hang on to him for a bit. She's trying to find him a lawyer and a place to stay. I wish we could have him at our place, but I'm taking a bit of heat at the department right now, as I'm sure you've heard."

Jake shook his head, thinking of Dewitt's letter in the paper.

"I don't get it. Oregon voted to uphold our sanctuary laws last fall, right? And Hood River was declared an inclusive city?"

Ron frowned and shook his head.

"Yes, but immigration is still a divisive issue."

He squinted past Jake toward the barn. Flaco appeared in the open doorway and then disappeared again.

"Can he stay a few more days?" Ron asked.

Jake thought of all the work to be done. He was irked to have lost an entire day at the meadow apiary yesterday in the course of taking Flaco to Evangelina. Flaco had been helpful with the honey supers that morning, but Jake didn't have the time to babysit a teenager right now.

"I know it's not convenient, but you know we can't have him at our place, at least not right now. Or with any of the extended family," Ron said, his face flushing. "Dewitt is turning up the volume on this thing."

Jake thought of Dewitt's interview on *Faith Matters*. His wild claims about "the illegals" taking funding away from other kids.

Using fear to divide neighbors. What a mess to have this small town so divided. It made his own problems seem less urgent for the moment.

"Sure, Ron. Tell Evangelina to keep me updated. If anyone can figure this out, it's her."

Ron's face relaxed into a smile.

"Don't I know it."

"What should I tell Flaco? About his cousin, I mean?"

"Don't say anything just now. Evie will stop by when we have more information, probably tomorrow. No use upsetting him now."

Ron left and Cheney trotted across the yard and into the shop. Jake followed, hearing a muted tapping. In the barn, Cheney lay in a beam of sunlight. Flaco stood at the workbench piled high with disassembled honey frames. Harry had cut them before he'd left but hadn't had time to assemble them. Flaco tapped a small nail into the side of one frame and held it up for Jake to see.

"Is okay? ¿Está bien?"

Jake took it from him and nodded. He was a self-starter, this kid.

"Yes. The next part goes here."

He picked up a piece of waxed foundation and snapped it into place.

"Now it's ready for the honey super. Listo."

He dropped the frame into a nearby honey super and showed Flaco that each super took ten frames.

"Diez," Flaco said. "Tin. I do."

"Okay," Jake said. "Thank you. I'm going back up to the house. Come up for lunch soon. Almuerzo."

Back at the house, he checked his email and found one response to his ad—a guy in Seattle who was interested in the job but needed a flex schedule because he really wanted to prioritize his kiting time this summer.

Jake sighed. Honeybees were anything but flexible. Honeyflow time was a magnificent upwelling of sunshine and blossoms and nectar and the hard labor of millions of golden bees. Magnificent, and at this very moment, overwhelming.

Jake thought of Flaco, who had much bigger problems. When Jake was fourteen, his biggest concern had been trying to land an ollie at the skate park and having an unrequited crush on Cristina Rae, who sat in front of him in Algebra I.

He thought of his conversation with Ron about Hood River being an inclusive city and pulled up the *Hood River News* archives.

> RESOLVED, that Hood River is an inclusive city. We will not turn our back on the men and women from other countries who help make this city great, and who represent over one third of our population. We endorse ORS (181A.820), the state law which forbids local jurisdictions from using their resources to enforce immigration law. Our police are busy keeping our residents safe from crime; they will not act as agents of or for federal immigration. We will continue to be a place of sanctuary and safety by nurturing a culture of trust between police, immigrants and communities of color so all residents feel safe in their neighborhoods.

What did that mean, a culture of trust, for one boy all by himself? Would he be counted among the men and women from other countries "who help make this city great"?

A search showed that 30.7 percent of Hood River County's 23,000 residents identified as Hispanic or Latino in 2018. Oregon's immigrant population was 432,410, or about 10 percent of the population. Of that number, 36 percent were from Mexico and 24,167 were kids. About 48 million immigrants lived in the United States, representing more than 14 percent of the national population. An estimated 11 million people in the country and 120,000 in Oregon were undocumented.

Jake closed the search and returned to his labor question. He emailed friends and farmers he knew. He texted Amri's little brothers. While he was at it, he sent Amri a quick text. He noted another influx of honey orders in his inbox but did not open them.

Jake returned to the barn and found Flaco snapping foundations into frames. He'd racked the completed frames into honey supers, spacing them neatly and stacking them near the shop door. Jake observed his economy of movement, his diligence, and his self-discipline.

Jake's own father, Ed Stevenson, had taught him a few shop lessons when he was young. Measure twice, cut once. Keep things neat. Use what you have on hand before going to the hardware store. Weekends he tinkered in the carport outside their manufactured home and always fixed things for Jake's mom. Those were good years, before something had changed in Ed.

Jake tried to think of his question in Spanish.

"¿Trabajas con tu papá? Your dad?"

The boy shook his head. He looked so young then, like he had up in the meadow when they'd first met. He looked down at the pieces of frame in his hands.

"Mi mamá," he said quietly.

Evangelina had cautioned him not to pry. But something about the boy's tone made him ask.

"Your mom? What's your mom's name?"

"She is Beatriz," Flaco said, his voice dropping to a whisper.

Jake thought of his own mother and how she'd sat next to his hospital bed after the accident and visited him in the rehab center and encouraged him to call his friends during those dark days. No matter how horrible or angry he'd been, Tansy Stevenson showed up every day. After that awful time, he understood how much he needed her, his Jesus-loving, uncomplaining, faithful, unassuming mom. Tansy Stevenson was bulletproof.

When had Flaco spoken to his mother last? he wondered.

"Do you want to call your mom?" Jake asked.

There was a long pause and Jake thought he'd gone too far.

But then the boy's face bloomed with the sweetest smile, tears shining in his eyes. He did not speak but only nodded and the meaning was clear in any language.

Yes, yes, please, and thank you.

9

UNFAMILIAR TERRITORIES

How does a bee hear? A fascinating question. Specialized organs in their legs and antennae allow them to pick up vibroacoustic signals.

—LAVIN, *THE WONDROUS WORLD OF BEES*

THE MAN INTRODUCED himself as Señor Sergio. He was originally from Uruapan, he said, which Flaco knew was southwest of Morelia, and smaller than the capital, but still a big town. His eyes were sad or tired, Flaco couldn't tell which. He did not seem pleased to make Flaco's acquaintance, although that is what he said.

"A pleasure to meet you, son."

His sonorous and gravelly voice reminded Flaco of the older men back home. He shook Flaco's hand with formality and folded his hands on the picnic table between them. There was something watchful in his gaze.

Señor Sergio said he was the foreman for the orchard next to the apiary. Jacob had asked him to come over to explain a few things to Flaco.

"I work for Alice Holtzman. She owns this place," Señor Sergio said, gesturing around them. "She lives in the big house and sold the little one to Jacob. Alice and Jacob own the bee farm together and I run her orchard."

Flaco had noticed pictures of an older woman on Jacob's refrigerator and wondered about her. Alice was not Jacob's mother or aunt or relative of any kind, Señor Sergio clarified. They were business partners, he said. Flaco had never met a woman who was business partners with a man she wasn't married to.

"And her husband?"

Alice was a widow, Señor Sergio said.

Flaco nodded.

"My mother too," he said, and the man's gaze softened.

"My condolences. You must miss your father."

"I didn't know him," Flaco said, and did not say more, and Señor Sergio did not ask.

"Jacob and Señora Evangelina will help you," Señor Sergio said. "They're fine people. The thing is, the señora, she's married to the sheriff. That's why you can't stay with her."

Flaco nodded. The señora had not returned but had sent word through her husband that she'd be in touch. Flaco had not met him. He'd stayed in the barn, frightened by the sight of the police Jeep, and was relieved when Jacob had explained who it was.

"He would have to put me in jail for not having papers?"

Señor Sergio said no. Sheriff Ryan was a good man, but some people were criticizing him about immigration. There was lots of fighting about it right now—in the town, the whole country.

"Their president, you've heard about him, no?"

Flaco nodded.

"A little. Our teacher said the Americans elected him because he said Mexicans are bad people."

Señor Sergio clicked his teeth.

"Not all the güeros think like that, but things are hard right now. I've lived in this country for thirty years and I've never felt so unwelcome," the older man said.

Flaco had many questions. When had Señor Sergio arrived and how had he found work? Was he a U.S. citizen now? Was it true you could make so much money here? But nothing about Señor Sergio's demeanor welcomed questions.

"For now, you'll stay here. Jacob says Señora Evangelina is trying to find you a lawyer."

Flaco nodded, wondering why he needed a lawyer.

"And if I don't find a lawyer, they would send me back home?"

Señor Sergio sighed and leaned on his forearms.

"Didn't your people explain deportation to you, son?"

Flaco tried to recall what his mother had said.

"Mamá said if I got caught by la migra, I should ask the person in charge for help. She said to explain that I was good at school and wanted to learn English. And to tell them she wanted me to come here because our town is not safe anymore. She said that if they sent me back, all the money she saved would be wasted so I should try really hard to explain."

Señor Sergio wagged his head.

"Mijo, if you get deported, they won't just send you back to your little village on a bus. Once ICE has you, you enter the system. You could end up in a detention center for months. And far away, like Texas or Arizona. They might not even notify your family, and if they send you back, they'll only take you as far as Tijuana or Mexicali. Just dump you off there alone—no money, no nothing. You do not want to get deported, son. I promise you."

Flaco felt cold all over. He thought of the train ride, the little girl in the rebozo and her sister. He thought of his days wandering the trail from Bend by himself. He did not want to be alone like that again.

"So . . . I wait here?" he said.

Señor Sergio nodded.

"Yes. You wait here. Jacob likes you. He said you helped him with the bees."

Flaco nodded.

The dog barked and came bounding across the field toward them with Jacob following. Flaco was no longer afraid of the dog, who was friendly like Jacob had said.

"Has Jacob always used the wheelchair?"

Señor Sergio shook his head.

"No. He had an accident."

"What happened?"

"I don't know. I never asked."

His tone told Flaco it would be impolite to ask.

The older man looked him over.

"He said you got stung up in the meadow."

Flaco touched his forehead and shrugged.

"You're not afraid of them?"

As he'd tried to explain to Jacob, he said he understood the bees were just protecting their home.

"It hurt at first, but not too bad," Flaco said.

"That's good of you to help out," Señor Sergio said.

Jacob pulled up to the table and set down three bottles of sweet tea, which sweated in the morning sunshine. Señor Sergio said something in English and pointed his chin at the orchard. Jacob nodded and gestured at the tea, but the older man shook his head and said something in a demurring tone.

They glanced at Flaco and had a quick exchange that he did not catch most of. He heard "Señora Evangelina," "cousin," and "work."

Señor Sergio stood and shook hands with Jacob, then held out his hand to Flaco.

"Good luck, son. I hope everything goes well for you."

"Thank you, señor," Flaco said.

Señor Sergio began to leave and turned back.

"Listen, son, I'm sorry I can't be of more help to you. I'm trying to bring my mother here. She's very old and sick. I don't want anything to complicate my application. Things are really crazy in this country right now. You understand."

Flaco did not understand. What did it mean that he could complicate Señor Sergio's application? But he didn't want to be impolite.

"Of course, señor," he said.

Señor Sergio looked at Jacob and then back at Flaco.

"If I can help answer questions, you let me know, okay? I'm over here every day but Sunday."

He pointed toward the orchard.

Flaco nodded, thinking of all the questions he wanted to ask that he felt he could not ask, and Señor Sergio walked away.

Jacob smiled and pushed a bottle of tea toward him. Flaco thought about what Señor Sergio said about Jacob having an accident. Flaco didn't know anyone who used a wheelchair other than Señora Ofelia, an old lady in Las Lunas. He often saw her pushing herself along the sandy road through the village. She'd park herself outside the church during school days and talk to herself. Jacob did not talk to himself and was not old either. Flaco had been somewhat fascinated watching Jacob do things like cook, drive, and work in his wheelchair.

And yet, he was keen to avoid offense. Jacob had been so kind to him, like yesterday when he asked Flaco about his mother.

"When did you last call her?" he'd asked.

Flaco had shrugged and guessed it had been about a week. Truly, he'd lost track of the days.

Jacob muttered something and pulled out his cell phone. He called someone and jotted down some numbers on a piece of paper. He punched a few numbers into the phone, then asked Flaco for his mother's number, dialed it, and handed him the phone.

When Flaco heard her voice, his heart leapt.

"Mamá," he said, and then he couldn't speak for fear that he'd cry.

"Flaco, I've been so worried! Where are you? Are you with César? He isn't answering his phone. Are you okay?"

He wanted to tell her that he was not okay. He wanted to tell her that César was unreachable and that he was with güeros, gringos, strangers. He wanted to tell her he was scared and lonely and wanted to come home. But the fear in her voice made him swallow his own.

"I'm fine, Mamá. Everything is fine."

He told her he'd left Bend and had arrived in Hood River. He was not yet with César, but he was with nice people.

"I'm staying on a beautiful farm. They raise honeybees and I'm helping out until I can get to César."

This white lie felt like the right thing to say.

"I'm so glad, son. I'm praying for you. God bless the people who are helping you. And when you're with César, he will help you with everything."

She had sounded so relieved and told him she was proud of him. They talked for a little while. She told him about work and asked him to describe the farm to her. She said that they would talk again soon and to be good and remember she was praying for him.

"One more thing, amorcito," she said. "Never forget how much I love you. You are all I have."

And then Flaco did cry, turning away from Jacob after he handed back the phone. He heard Jacob introduce himself to his mother and tell her in clumsy Spanish that her son was a good boy and safe here. By the time he hung up, Flaco had composed himself. They returned to the work they'd been doing, and Flaco was grateful not to speak.

Now Jacob put the lid on his sweet tea and said something Flaco didn't understand.

"Sí, gracias. Sorry. My English," he said, and seesawed his hand. "Not always good."

Jacob looked pensive.

"What about Oregon's robust craft beer scene? Hood River's epic outdoor access?"

Flaco recalled the snippets of his school presentation he'd repeated to Jacob and the señora.

"Oh yes! I memory, for class. ¿Memoria? ¿Memorizar?"

"Memorize?" said Jake.

Flaco nodded.

"Sí. Still I am to learn much English."

"Y yo español," Jacob said.

Jacob said he needed to get back to work.

"I to help," Flaco said and insisted when Jacob told him he didn't need to.

They returned to the barn to continue assembling frames and transferring them into freshly painted boxes. It was not difficult work and satisfying—the click of the foundation piece as it snapped into place, the scent of freshly cut wood, the frames clacking against each other as he positioned them in the small boxes.

While Flaco was placing frames into supers, Jacob left the barn. Flaco heard the sound of an engine starting and the growling whine of its approach. The dog barked raucously. Jacob reappeared atop a small tractor with a front bucket, with the dog bounding in front trying to play.

"Cheney, no! Leave it!" Jacob yelled.

He motioned Flaco to load the supers into the bucket. When it was full, he reversed out of the barn and drove toward the apiary.

The air had warmed considerably and Flaco shed the sweatshirt the señora had lent him. Jacob stopped the tractor on the far side of the apiary and lowered the bucket. He unfolded his wheelchair and lowered it to the ground. Flaco moved to help steady it, but Jacob shook his head.

"It's okay," Jacob said. "No problem."

He sounded annoyed, and Flaco wondered what he'd done wrong. But then Jacob smiled at him, and it seemed okay. He swung down into the wheelchair, grabbed three supers from the tractor bucket, and carried them, stacked on his lap, down the raised platform. He repeated the steps he'd done the day before—jimmying the lids open and off, removing another layer of wood from inside, positioning the new super on top, and putting the other pieces back. Flaco followed along bringing supers to Jacob in a wheelbarrow. They worked until the tractor bucket was empty, then returned to the barn for more. They continued this way until all the supers were in place.

Jacob set the last one and Flaco noticed a line of boxes in the field that were different from the others. Instead of rising vertically from the ground up, three boxes high, these were single horizontal boxes set atop small stands. Bees zipped in and out through small openings on one side. They looked like the boxes in the meadow, he realized.

"Is different?" Flaco asked, pointing to the horizontal boxes.

"Both kinds of boxes are hives, or colmenas, and the low hives are new," Jacob said. And, yes, different. He began to explain, but Flaco was quickly lost in the host of unfamiliar words. He felt bad, as he could tell Jacob was excited about whatever he was saying. Jacob halted, registering his confusion.

"Later," he said. "Está bien."

Back at the house that evening, Jacob pulled out a notebook and sketched a beehive, then next to it, the parts of the hive. He labeled them in English, then slid the notebook across the table to Flaco along with a Spanish-English dictionary.

Flaco understood and went to work translating the various elements of the hive. He became engrossed in the puzzle of words while Jacob made dinner. As they ate, he showed Jacob what he'd translated: Hive cover, inner cover, honey super, super frames, brood box, brood frames, hive stand, entrance reducer, screened bottom board. All the parts of a beehive, or colmena.

Jacob nodded and took the notebook back and drew a picture of a frame standing by itself, labeling various areas, which Flaco translated as honey, pollen, and brood.

"Brood, cría, babies?"

"Yes, bee brood," Jacob said.

Jacob got on his computer and looked at his email while Flaco continued to work on the catalog of bee terms.

"Queen bee, worker bee, drone," Jacob had written.

"La reina, el obrero, el zángano," Flaco translated.

"La obrera," Jacob corrected. "Feminina. Hembras. Female."

"¿Hembras?" Flaco said, surprised. "No man?"

"Just the drones, zánganos. And later in the summer."

Through the screen door, twilight hung on late. Birds twittered in the falling darkness and a small wind blustered across the yard as Flaco searched for words. It felt like school, which Flaco had always loved, and it made him forget, if only briefly, his worry about reaching his cousin. And what Señor Sergio had said about deportation. And how much the sound of his mother's voice made him want to weep.

"*I'm so proud of you, Flaco,*" she'd said.

The next day, Jake explained that he needed to return to the meadow to visit the bee colonies there. Flaco could come with him, or he could stay at the house.

His mother had not raised him to loaf when there was work to be done.

"I to help," he said.

As they drove away from the farm, Flaco realized it had been nearly dark when he'd arrived days earlier. Now the view looked entirely different. The truck left the dell and ascended a narrow, winding track up into the sunshine. Due north, Flaco saw a great snow-covered mountain rising in front of them like a mirage.

"Mount Adams, or Pahto," Jacob said, pointing. "Old volcano."

Along the road they passed restaurants and churches, a gas station and a bank. The truck descended a steep hill and the northern volcano disappeared behind a tall bluff.

They drove past houses clinging to the hillside, an assortment of one- and two-story homes with green yards and leafy trees. A broad river lay at the foot of town, flowing east to west. Flaco knew from Maestra Monica's books that this was the Columbia River. It began in Canada and ran for more than twelve hundred miles to the Pacific Ocean. A green steel bridge spanned the width of the river, and trucks and cars streamed across it. Near the bridge the river was nearly bisected by a large sandbar. Flaco saw large colorful objects flying over the water.

Jacob glanced at him and pointed at the activity on the water.

"Kiteboarding," he said. "Wind sports. Un poco loco."

They drove past neatly planted rows of fruit trees stirring in the wind. Workers walked the rows with ladders and pruning equipment. At a stop sign the sound of a ranchera drifted in the window. A man leaned out of a food truck and yelled something in Spanish to the driver next to Jacob. The man laughed and called back.

"Andale, pues!"

The orchards went on for miles and miles. Men on ladders, men driving tractors, men and women carrying buckets, and the acrid smell of something chemical hung in the air.

This was the kind of work César did and where he'd promised Mamá he could find Flaco a job. Cherries came in first, he'd said, then apricots and peaches before apples and pears. There were blueberry fields too. Flaco had never worked in an orchard before, though many families in Las Lunas grew avocados and limes. He didn't know what it might be like, only that it would be a way for him to earn money to send to his mother. And it was the only concrete element of this trip to the north he understood.

After miles of orchards, the view opened up to a small village and Jacob slowed. A grocery store, a gas station, a few tienditas. To the west, the forest sloped up steeply to a summit where several radio towers lined the ridge. A large playing field stretched out to the east. There was a fútbol game going, teenage boys playing hard. The ball soared through the air and one of the offensive players sprinted for it. He left the rest of the field far behind. Flaco could see the joy on his face, then he heard a whistle blow and a man's voice calling offsides. The boy with the ball swore in Spanish, laughed, and kicked the ball backward with his heel.

Jacob pulled over near a cluster of food carts. He leaned out the window and waved at someone. A young woman appeared at the window of the truck. Her black hair fell over her shoulders in twin braids. She smiled shyly, revealing a gap in her front teeth.

"Hello, Mr. Jake," she said.

Jacob said something to her in English and then introduced the girl to Flaco as Barbara. The girl looked bashful and said hello. Jacob said something else and then turned to Flaco.

"Barbara is one of my student of bees," he said in Spanish.

Flaco didn't know what that meant, and the girl giggled.

"He taught us a class at school," she explained to Flaco in Spanish. "About beekeeping and honeybees."

Jacob ordered some food and Barbara ducked back inside the food cart.

"Poco tiempo," Jacob said, and his phone rang. He answered it and began speaking rapidly to whoever was on the other end, and Flaco couldn't understand most of what he said.

There was a thump against the truck door and Flaco saw the checkered balón spinning away across the parking lot. He jumped out and retrieved it, then turned toward the field. One of the boys raised a hand, and, without thinking, Flaco returned the ball. It felt so good—the swing of his leg, his foot connecting in the sweet spot, the satisfying thunk on contact. He sent the ball up in the air in a beautiful arc. Somebody yelled, "Ese!" and the boy trapped it under his foot and waved. The game continued.

"Mijo," someone said.

Flaco turned and saw an abuela sitting at a fruit stand. She motioned to him.

"Venga, por favor."

She said more but turned her head away and he couldn't hear her. Flaco approached and understood something had fallen under the platform. He bent down and retrieved a glasses case from the ground and handed it to her.

"Oh, thank you, mijito. Such a relief!" she said. "I just couldn't reach the darn thing."

Her smile bloomed through the wrinkled walnut skin of her face, reminding him of his abuela Patricia.

She asked his name and if he was on the team, gesturing at the field. He said no.

"Where do you live, mijito?"

Flaco said he was staying in Hood River and fear rippled across her face.

"You be careful in the city, mijo. La migra, they'll snap you up in broad daylight just like that man at the bank! And they're doing raids in the orchards and packinghouses."

Flaco didn't know what she was talking about, but she seemed genuinely frightened. He told her he would be careful. She gave him a white paper bag full of cherries and asked God to bless him. He felt embarrassed. He wanted to stay and talk with her, but he didn't know what to say, so he thanked her and said goodbye.

Flaco wandered toward the field, watching the players match up for a corner kick. They were wearing lights and darks. Not pickup, then. It was some kind of practice. The man with the whistle caught his eye and nodded.

"Nice foot," he said in Spanish. "What position do you play?"

"Center forward," Flaco said.

The man nodded.

"Will you be at the high school this fall or are you still at the middle school?" he asked.

"Um, I don't really know yet," Flaco said.

He hadn't thought about school.

"This group is practicing for junior varsity tryouts. You're welcome to join us if you want. We meet up twice a week. It's casual, but it's a good game."

"Um, thank you," Flaco said. "But I don't—"

"Coach!" one of the boys yelled. "This clown. Seriously!"

The man blew his whistle and walked, laughing, toward the players.

Flaco watched them play for a while. The boy who'd gone offsides was really, really fast. But Flaco thought he himself might be even faster.

Jacob called his name and held up a bag from the food cart. Flaco trotted back and climbed into the truck. As they drove through the town, he read the signs on businesses they passed: Michoacán Grill, a tiendita called La Popular, Gustavo's Auto Repair, Diamond Fruit Growers.

"What is called this town?" he asked Jacob.

"Odell," Jacob said.

"Is many Mexican people here?" Flaco asked.

Jacob nodded.

"Mexicanos y norteamericanos."

They turned south on the highway and soon Mount Hood appeared, rising in the distance and filling the sky. Flaco quailed, remembering his long walk, and his stomach roiled, recalling the mushrooms. He could almost taste the awful tang of them. His feet felt better in the boots Jacob had given him but were still a mess of healing blisters.

After some time, Jacob turned off the highway and the truck climbed into the trees on a narrow road. As he drove, Jacob quizzed Flaco on beekeeping terms in English: cover, inside cover, frames, honey, brood, and pollen. Then the gear they would use: smoker, hive tool, hanger, brush, gloves, veil. He asked Flaco to translate the words in Spanish and repeated them. It was like a game and Jacob's funny accent was a distraction from the disquiet Flaco felt at returning to the woods.

When they arrived, the sheer face of the mountain rose from the field, massive and white. Flaco's breath caught at the sight of it. How magical that this once-explosive volcano was now transformed into a silent snow- and ice-covered peak.

Jacob parked and unloaded his chair and his tools from the truck. He handed Flaco two pairs of hedge trimmers to carry and set his tool caddy on his lap. As they approached the hives, Flaco noted that they were all horizontal like the little coffin-shaped ones at the house. The night before, using a translation program, Jacob had tried to explain how these hives were different from the ones down at the house, and for the most part, Flaco understood.

Unlike the hives at the farm, Jacob didn't add frame-filled boxes on top of each of these. Instead, he added frames to a single interior compartment. The process was easier for a beekeeper and less disruptive to the bees. The bees in these hives were calmer, Jacob said. Flaco liked the sound of that. Though he'd grown accustomed to the process, each time Jacob had removed the inside cover of one of the vertical hives, Flaco had startled at the small crowd of bees that boiled out. They did not seem to bother Jacob, who did not even wear a veil. Occasionally Jacob had used the smoker to get the bees to settle back inside before replacing the cover. The smoker would go out and had to be relit. The process made Flaco nervous—the waiting and the bees' agitation, though Jacob remained calm.

Now Jacob opened the apiary gate and progressed down the wooden ramp toward the closest hive. He maneuvered his wheelchair to the front of the hive and cut back the meadow grass that grew there.

He set the trimmers aside and opened the top. It rested in place on its hinges, so there was no need to take it off or put it down. The inside cover, instead of wood, was made of thick canvas. Jacob folded it back slightly so Flaco could see the edges of the frames. He counted sixteen already in place. Then Jacob folded the canvas cover back on itself to expose an empty portion of the hive.

"Four frames, please," he said.

Flaco passed him the frames, which he dropped in place, then replaced the canvas cover and shut the lid. A couple of bees buzzed languorously out of the hive to investigate.

"No worried bees," said Jacob. "Much easier."

He looked so happy when he said that, and Flaco had a glimmer of understanding about why this lower hive design made the work easier for Jacob. Flaco watched as Jacob moved on to the next hive, deftly swinging the tool caddy and setting it next to his chair. He had so many questions, questions he wouldn't have known how to ask even if they'd had a common language. Had Jacob been a beekeeper before? And by before, he meant before whatever accident had left him unable to walk. Or had it been an illness? Señor Sergio had said he'd never asked Jacob. Was it wrong to ask?

"How long you keep the bees?" Flaco ventured.

Jacob looked puzzled as if trying to work out what he meant. His eyes shifted past Flaco at something behind him. Flaco turned to follow his gaze and saw, just beyond Jacob's truck, a black SUV zooming into the field. The vehicle swung wide and the sun bounced off a logo on the side door.

Fear shot through his body as he thought about the raid in the Bend field. He heard Señor Sergio's voice in his head.

"*You could end up in a detention center for months . . . They might not even notify your family.*"

The SUV roared toward them and Flaco turned and ran.

10

ADAPTATION

Many bee species can tolerate colder temperatures thanks to their ability to thermoregulate with endothermy, or rapid muscle movement.

—LAVIN, *THE WONDROUS WORLD OF BEES*

THE SUV ACCELERATED toward the apiary, bouncing wildly over the uneven ground. There was a sharp crack and the vehicle halted, engine whining. It was too far away for Jake to make out the seal on the door. Was it someone from the ranger station? Alice was friendly with the ranger, who sometimes came by with staff to see the hives when they were working in the area. They were all nice enough, but this person was driving like a jackass.

The door swung open and the driver scrambled, slipped, and honked the horn. A lanky figure with short dark hair marched toward Jake. It was a young woman—nobody he'd seen before. Perhaps a new hire? Whoever she was, she seemed to be yelling at someone. Her voice carried across the meadow in snatches. Was she on the phone?

". . . wilderness area?! . . . have the RIGHT to . . . and DESTROY everything!"

As she drew closer, he observed her flannel shirt, jeans, and work boots. Not a forest service uniform. She didn't appear to be on the phone but seemed very angry. When she reached Jake, she fell silent and turned in a full circle, gazing across the meadow.

"Hi," Jake said. "Are you looking for someone?"

The young woman spun around and gaped. A honeybee zipped past her head, bound for home. Then another and another. For a long moment she watched the bees in flight. Her silence was unnerving.

"Are you . . . lost?" Jake ventured. "Can I—"

The woman boiled over then.

"HONEYBEES?!" she shouted. "These are honeybee HIVES?!"

Her voice was high-pitched and gravelly and louder than one might expect. Jake blinked and glanced at the hives. In all his years of beekeeping, he'd seen people delighted by, afraid of, or interested in his bees. But never had they provoked anyone to rage. How could honeybees make anyone angry? He suppressed the urge to laugh.

"Yes, they are honeybee hives," he said. "Carniolan colonies, to be exact."

She stared, silent again, and the silence lengthened. It was strange.

"Do you need—" Jake began.

"Why would you put honeybee hives at a HUNTING CAMP?!" she yelled.

The urge to laugh deserted him, as she was obviously confused.

"Um," he said. "I don't know anything about a hunting camp. Just bees here. Maybe there's a camp on that side?"

He waved east toward the ski resort.

The woman began to pace and mutter. He looked past her at the SUV, its driver's-side door still flung open, and recognized the logo.

"Oh, are you with the OSU Honeybee Lab? I did my master beekeeper training with them. It's a great program," he said.

The woman stopped pacing and eyed him warily.

"I am NOT with the Honeybee Lab. I am working with Dr.

Daphne Lavin on native pollinators, specifically bumblebees. I am not *interested* in honeybees."

She sounded disgusted and he choked back a laugh. How could anyone be so put off by honeybees? he wondered.

"Well, that sounds pretty cool," Jake said. "I didn't know about the native pollinator program. You're in the right place, though. I've seen all kinds up here—sweat bees and mason bees and bumblebees. Big ones."

The woman regarded him coolly.

"Oh," she said. "Well. That is quite interesting to hear. We are looking for the western bumblebee, *Bombus occidentalis*."

"Huh," Jake said. "I don't know much about bumblebees. What's special about *Bombus occidentalis*?"

The young woman watched an approaching honeybee land on the hive and crawl inside the entrance.

"Quite a lot," she said.

She seemed calmer now.

"Bumblebees, in general, are in decline," she said.

She leaned a hip against the ramp and crossed her arms. Habitat loss, pesticide use, and climate change were among the reasons for decline, she explained. The western bumblebee, once ubiquitous from California to British Columbia and from the coast to Montana, had disappeared. It was thought to be an important indicator species for the health of the ecosystem as a whole, and understanding its disappearance could help with habitat restoration for many species.

"Something interesting occurred recently, though," she said, her gravelly voice quavering.

"A UW biologist sighted a *Bombus occidentalis* up here on Mount Hood. OSU and the University of Washington are collaborating to investigate the possibility that *Bombus occidentalis* is making a comeback."

There was a research team dedicated to the endeavor, and she was the first to arrive.

"It is a very exciting opportunity," she said. "To be a steward of this one wild bee."

Her words were stilted and halting, but Jake sensed deep emotion behind them.

"Interesting," Jake said. "All those things you mentioned—pesticides, climate change, habitat loss—those concern me too as a beekeeper."

She nodded at him, still looking wary.

"But I have to ask, what does that have to do with a hunting camp?"

She stared at him as if he were deranged.

"Earlier you mentioned putting honeybee hives at a hunting camp?"

"Oh!" she said. "Well. Some people want to build a hunting camp in the Mount Hood National Forest. Somewhere near the Eliot Glacier. I thought that was what you were doing here."

"Ah," Jake said and looked south toward the mountain. "That's Eliot Glacier up there."

He pointed to the slab of ice and snow that lay across the saddle of the northwestern flank of the mountain. It glinted blue in the sunlight.

The woman gazed up at the glacier. The field team would set up its research camp near there, she said.

"It is our summer research project."

"You're close, but this is private land, not national forest. It's the last private acreage before the wilderness boundary. You just turned too soon. I can tell you how to get there."

He tore a page out of his notebook and drew her a rough map.

"The road isn't well signed, but once you see the wilderness marker you'll be in the right spot. You can't miss it," he said.

The woman folded the paper carefully and stuck it in her back pocket.

"Thank you. I appreciate your help. I am sorry. Sorry for—for the . . . yelling," she said and sighed, looked away, and looked back at him.

"I made a mistake. I forgot myself."

"Don't worry about it," Jake said.

She didn't look embarrassed exactly. But her impassive apology seemed sincere. Something about her reminded him of Harry. Harry too was prone to blurting information that sometimes took a while to parse. But he usually made sense and was always well intentioned.

"Your honeybee hives are . . . different," the woman said, turning to face the meadow.

"Yeah," Jake said. "I guess you could say this is *my* summer research project. Are you familiar with the Langstroth hive design? That's what you use at the Honeybee Lab, right?"

The woman closed her eyes, exhaling loudly, and Jake wondered if she was going to yell again. But she responded in a regular voice that, yes, she was familiar with the Langstroth hive.

"We were required to volunteer in the apiary," she said stiffly.

Had he offended her?

"Sorry, I just didn't want to assume. But if you're familiar with the design, you know that the hives expand vertically as the population increases."

"Yes," she said. "The typical hive at the Honeybee Lab is two brood boxes high and two to three supers."

"Right," Jake said. "Well, that design is not ideal for me. I can't work the bees past the second brood box from a seated position."

She nodded, looking thoughtful. She did not, however, look embarrassed as strangers sometimes did when he referenced his wheelchair.

Managing the loaded honey supers, he went on, was out of the question for him.

He did not explain his frustration at how the design limited his access to the hives, which had led Harry to begin tinkering with alternative designs. First he'd built a hive based on the nineteenth-century leaf hive. It extended horizontally instead of vertically. Harry reasoned that the bees would just build out instead of up.

"*They nested for thousands of years in logs and random holes before humans made hives, so why not?*" he'd said when Jake looked skeptical.

He was right about that. Honeybees had thrived for millennia before human interference, so why not consider their natural inclinations?

Jake used the leaf hive with some success, but there were problems—a cumbersome top, multiple inner covers. Harry kept tweaking things, but the hive never yielded much honey and had not survived the second winter. Then, two years ago, Harry learned of a beekeeper in Bend who used a wheelchair and had created a hive that was easier for her to use. She claimed the design was better for the bees too. Harry Stokes—quiet, awkward Harry—came home from that visit to Bend talking nonstop about Naomi Price's Valkyrie hive. With her blessing, Harry built half a dozen hives for Jake with her design.

"The design is better for the bees too—insulation from heat and cold, a canvas inner cover, which is less disruptive to the colony, a higher entrance to protect them from rodents. And the honey frames can be taken out one at a time, which is easier for me to manage," Jake said now.

"A full honey super can weigh up to sixty pounds," the woman said.

"Right," Jake said.

"May I see the inside?" the woman asked.

"Sure," Jake said and motioned her up onto the ramp.

She pulled herself up next to him and stood. Tall and lanky, she folded her arms across her chest and hunched forward.

"I'm Jake, by the way," he said. "Jake Stevenson."

The woman straightened and stuck out her hand.

"My name is Abigail Plue. Pleased to meet you, Jake Stevenson," she said.

Her tone was polite and formal. Such a contrast with her angry arrival. She had brilliant green eyes.

He demonstrated the hive's external advantages starting with the long, low body. The insulated stand kept the hive warmer in winter but was also situated at the ideal height for someone sitting. The hive entrance, he showed her, was high up to protect the bees from predators as they landed. Two observation windows made it possible to do a quick hive check anytime without disturbing the bees. He pulled down the shutter to reveal the plexiglass window.

"See how this last frame is nearly three-quarters filled out? That tells me it's ready for more frames."

He reached to open the lid of the hive and Abigail stepped back.

"You are not wearing protective equipment, and you do not have a smoker," she said.

She sounded like a stern teacher and Jake suppressed a smile.

"Just watch."

He loosened the lid with his hive tool and raised it slowly to rest on its hinges. He removed the wool insulation pillow and touched the inner cover with his hive tool.

"This is canvas, not wood. So I can just fold it back."

The cover was sticky with propolis but came away easily and revealed one side of the hive empty of frames. The inhabited section of the hive remained covered, so no bees were disturbed. Jake advanced the blocker board, quickly added four frames to the hive, unfolded the canvas, and closed the lid.

"Done," he said.

The woman stared at the hive, silent, and her face was unreadable. Again, Jake thought of Harry, his quiet, thoughtful friend. The moments ticked by.

"The frames are all the same size," she said after some time. "All like medium Langstroths."

"Right," Jake said. "So I can add in a frame of honey here and there if they need a little extra. It's part of the experiment."

It also helped with feeding and transitioning to foundationless frames and mite checks, but he wouldn't get into all that.

"What is your research project?" Abigail asked.

Jake swiveled to face the mountain. From this vantage point, you could see all two hundred hives. The Valkyrie hives Harry had installed thrived that first summer. In the fall they decided to replace a few retiring Langstroth hives with the new design. The orchard apiary now had about ten Valkyries. They'd done so well that Jake had convinced Alice to try them out on a large scale in the meadow here. That was the most magical part of the meadow apiary for Jake—every single colony in this apiary was housed in a Valkyrie hive.

"My partner and I are hoping they will outperform our Langstroths. And we suspect they will be better for the bees too."

"How could they be better for bees?" she asked.

Jake thought of the advantages Naomi Price had documented at her farm—lower mite counts and queen mortality. Greater success overwintering. Protection from rodents and heat and cold. They even seemed gentler. But he didn't want to run on, as Alice accused him of, and he needed to get back to work.

"Lots of ways," he said. "You'll have to wait for our results."

He meant it as a joke, but she nodded soberly.

"I will await your results, Jake Stevenson," she said.

She looked past him then.

"Your partner," she said. "Where did he go?"

Jake realized she meant Flaco, and that Flaco had disappeared. He felt a stab of concern. The kid hadn't run off, had he?

"Oh, that's not my partner. He's my . . . friend," he said, thinking it sounded simplest. "He went for a wander, I guess."

Abigail glanced at the sun, which had passed over the meadow and was traveling westward. She pulled out the map Jake had drawn for her, looked it over, and tucked it back in her pocket.

"I need to go make my camp," she said.

She stuck out her hand again.

"It was a pleasure to meet you, Jake Stevenson. I hope your project is a great success."

Her strange formality was charming if a little odd, Jake thought, shaking her hand.

"Thanks, Abigail. I hope your project is a great success too."

She jumped down from the platform and strode off, then turned back.

"I invite you to visit my campsite if you are interested in our research," she said. "It is a fascinating opportunity."

Her arrogant tone couldn't be intentional, he thought, chuckling to himself as she walked away. Abigail climbed back into her SUV and cranked the engine, stalling it twice. She then endeavored to turn the vehicle around, which took considerable time and much lurching. Jake thought he could hear her yelling through the rolled-up windows. She finally bumped off toward the road.

Alone in the field, Jake scanned the tree line for Flaco with growing concern. What the hell was he supposed to do if the kid had taken off? He couldn't go after him. He thought of calling Evangelina but decided against it. If Flaco wasn't back by the time he finished with the hives, he'd call her then.

After some time, he heard Cheney's announcement bark and turned to see the dog's brown body streaking through the sunlit grass. Cheney flashed his dopey grin, leapt up on the platform, and threw himself at Jake, resting his heavy head on Jake's knees. Jake pulled on his ears and looked at the tree line where Flaco stepped out into the sunshine and stood unmoving.

Jake raised a hand and whistled.

"Flaco!"

The boy made his way back and Cheney dashed out to meet him. Jake felt relief and a spark of anger. He didn't want to be responsible for this kid in the first place. He certainly didn't have time to wait for him if he decided to wander. He tried to think of how to say those things in Spanish as Flaco approached.

The kid was pale, and his eyes were huge in his face like the first time Jake had seen him. He looked toward the road.

"¿Policía?" he asked, his voice shaking. "Is Immigration?"

Jake felt terrible then. Flaco had run because he was scared.

Jake shook his head.

"No, no. It was just . . ."

He didn't know how to say biologist or scientist in Spanish. Caretaker was the closest thing he could think of.

"Cuidadora," he said. "Cuidadora de abejas."

Flaco looked relieved and they returned to work, adding frames to the growing hives. Jake glanced at him from time to time and thought how young he looked. What circumstances could have made him leave home so young? And all alone?

They worked through the afternoon and made their way down the mountain after sunset. The sky was green in the north and the tree line black against it.

After dinner, Flaco shyly asked if he could call his mom. Jake gave him the phone and the boy went into the guest room but soon returned.

"No answer," he said.

Jake asked if he wanted to try anyone else.

"Your dad, maybe?" he asked without thinking.

The boy looked embarrassed and shook his head.

"Is went," he said. "Is gone."

"I'm sorry," Jake said.

"Is okay," Flaco said.

The boy was quiet as he did the dishes and went to bed early.

Jake sat up late transferring notes from the bee logbook into his database about the day's work: temperature, wind speed, tasks completed, and the status of each hive. This was a tedium of the job that he loved and Alice hated. She preferred the paper logbook alone, but Jake liked to have the year-over-year data for a fuller picture of how each hive was doing.

After five years of commercial beekeeping, Jake appreciated the routine. Though beekeeping could be unpredictable—weather, food sources, summer heat—much of it was cyclical. He loved the seasonality of it—spring emergence, summer honeyflow, autumn taper, and winter cluster. He loved teaching classes to the kids at May Street Elementary, which he did each spring. He enjoyed the occasional conference, which was a place to connect with other beekeepers.

And yet, even amid the rhythm of beekeeping, he hadn't felt like himself lately. He'd passed up invitations from friends, made excuses to the local beekeeping group. He told everyone he was busy, and the new apiary certainly created a credible reason. People took him at his word, everyone except Alice, who saw right through him. One night, before she'd left for Alaska, she called him out.

They were sitting at the picnic table near the apiary. The brilliant blue-sky day had faded and a chill had fallen with the sunset. Over dinner they'd discussed the seasonal tasks that would happen while she was away. It was a long list and they both loved the minutiae of it.

Alice finished her beer and set the bottle on the table.

"One more thing for the list. Aside from all the bee business, you need to get off campus. Go hang out with some other humans before you get insanely busy here."

Jake shrugged and said of course he would. But Alice persisted.

"When?" she said. "Who? Specifics, please."

There were, of course, no specifics. He knew Alice knew that. She understood that he was, simply, heartbroken. It had been a year since Ruby's reappearance and heart-stomping departure, and the anniversary weighed on him.

"Don't mom me, Alice Holtzman," he said lightly.

She knew him well enough not to push.

"Well, I'm here to help you with your dating profile when you need it. On Bimble or Tumble or whatever. Teach you a thing or two."

"Great, Alice," he said, laughing. "You can be my dating mentor."

Alice and Stan had not met online, but during a community effort to pressure the county to ban certain pesticides in the orchards.

"We met the good old-fashioned way," she liked to joke. "A lawsuit."

Jake had met Amri during that same time that Alice had met Stan. Sweet Amri, his first love, still his friend. Amri did not stomp on his heart when she left town for college. They kept in touch and saw each other when she was home for holidays. She'd texted him just a week ago about her struggle to choose a major. Law, veterinary medicine, or dance. "Or maybe all three?" Followed by a laughing-crying emoji. He replied with an eye-rolling emoji. They'd always be friends, he and Amri.

But not Ruby. Had he and Ruby ever been friends? Ruby had stormed into his life like a gorge wind.

The day he met Ruby, he'd been hanging out at the waterfront watching Harry give a land lesson. There was a timelessness there—the broad swath of lawn, the rushing westerly wind, brightly colored kites flying over the water with people skimming the swell underneath, the sunshine on the waves. Jake felt so at ease there.

Cheney, who'd been napping at his feet, rose, shook himself, and ran out to the sandbar to wrestle with a pair of fat yellow labs. Kites in every color were stacked close together on the grass. People milled about rehashing the details of their sessions on the water—women his mom's age, older dudes, dozens of twentysomethings, and a pack of rowdy teenagers. It was like this every day all summer.

Ruby strode through that crowd—tall, broad shouldered, fire-haired, with a bright blue kite tucked under one arm and her board under the other. She was wearing an orange shorty wetsuit that revealed the tattoo of a flower-adorned serpent winding around one of her gorgeous, muscular calves. People turned to stare as she passed.

Jake had noticed her before. It was impossible to miss Ruby, but he turned away. He didn't like it when people gawked at him, though that was for different reasons.

Ruby dropped her gear near him. Straightening, she smiled that million-dollar smile, her long hair dripping with river water. She introduced herself and asked if he was Jake Stevenson.

"That's me," he said.

"Thought so. Are you coming down for Kiteboarding for Cancer?"

"Wouldn't miss it," he said.

He'd gone every year since Harry had begun participating in the annual fundraiser. The money raised was used to support young adult cancer survivors.

"I'm riding in the Gold Supporter level," Ruby said. "I'm trying to raise at least three thousand dollars, and I need one more corporate sponsor to make my goal. Stokes tells me you own a honey company. It's tax-deductible. You game?"

Jake looked past her to Harry, still giving his lesson, who gave him a double thumbs-up.

"Sure," Jake said. "I'm game. Put Queen of G down for it."

He didn't even ask what the financial commitment was. He would have said yes to anything Ruby had asked of him. He'd fallen for her as soon as she'd said his name.

Later Ruby told him that the fundraiser had been a ploy to introduce herself to the hottest guy at the kite beach. That was the kind of thing Ruby said. Jake wanted to believe her, though he knew by then that Ruby said a lot of things, many of which turned out to be untrue. But what Ruby had never said when she left was "I love you" or "I'm sorry" or even "goodbye."

Jake logged out of the database and shut down the computer. He got ready for bed and lay awake watching the moon rise over the shoulder of the east hills.

He thought of Abigail Plue and what she'd said when she apologized.

"*I forgot myself*," she'd said.

What a curious, old-fashioned thing to say, but how apt, he thought now. For that's how he felt when he lapsed into the shadow of heartbreak. Like he'd forgotten himself and who he was and everything that had come before Ruby.

The moon sailed from east to west across the sky and Jake imagined its light shining down on the meadow apiary. He was exhausted by the day's efforts, but sleep eluded him. He lay awake thinking of Ruby. He could recall every line of her face, every curve of her body, the feeling of her skin on his skin. In her absence and in his deep loneliness, he forgot himself and felt forgotten. If only Ruby could be forgotten instead.

11

BEELINE

Bees have five eyes—two on the sides of their heads and three smaller eyes, or ocelli, in the middle of their heads. Ocelli are key in finding nectar sources and in navigation.

—LAVIN, *THE WONDROUS WORLD OF BEES*

THE EARLY BIRD catches the worm," Flaco wrote. Then: "A bird in the hand is worth two in the bush." And, "An ugly duckling becomes a beautiful swan."

While much of this English lesson seemed easy, Flaco couldn't make head or tail of the dichos he'd translated so laboriously, which seemed weirdly focused on birds.

On the whole, the English workbooks from the señora were a mix. Some too easy, some too difficult. Collectively they'd confirmed one thing for Flaco: While he might have spoken English better than anyone in his class or anyone in the whole town of Las Lunas, he really didn't know English very well at all.

At least it was nice working in the barn. The wide door let in the sunshine and breeze. Flaco could see part of the orchard and the pretty white farmhouse that belonged to Jacob's business partner, who was out of town. Sometimes he could hear music as Señor Sergio and his men worked in the orchard.

Here he was out of the way. After breakfast, Jacob had become absorbed in his computer and seemed angry. Flaco did the dishes quietly, not wanting to contribute to his host's ill humor. He didn't know what to do with himself then. There was nowhere to sit in the bedroom he was sleeping in, and when he tried to occupy the living room area, he felt like every cough and sniffle was an annoyance. Finally he gathered the English workbooks and told Jacob he was going out to the barn to study. Jacob, frowning at the computer screen, didn't even look up when he said okay.

Flaco paced the length of the barn from the shop area to the bunkroom. The open door revealed a pair of twin beds and a small nightstand. A bookshelf stood just outside the door with a guitar leaning against one side and a skateboard on the other. Flaco glanced through the books. Judging from the covers, they seemed to be about hiking, natural history, flowers, and birds. He pulled down a pocket atlas of the United States and flipped it open to the map of Oregon, tracing the route he'd driven with Luis and his uncle and the path he'd walked past Mount Hood. He located the dot of Hood River on the edge of the Columbia River. He looked at the pages of California, Arizona, and Texas. Their southern borders were squared off like the earth ended there, no sign of Mexico at all. He followed the Columbia River from its mouth at the Pacific Ocean backward to its source—through Washington and up into Canada.

A poster on the wall showed a bare-chested man hanging suspended over cerulean waters with a red and yellow kite above him. Next to that poster was an illustration of Mount Hood in the act of erupting. A wave of lava and debris coursed through a forest into the Columbia River. The words "500,000 years old" were written at the center of the mountain and "100,000 years ago" within the molten lahar. In the Columbia River, a huge wave of water was labeled "Missoula Floods, 10,000 to 30,000 years ago." Flaco looked at the basalt cliffs, the upthrust of a syncline, and saw tiny human figures drawn at the bottom near the river. "First Humans, 13,000 years ago," was written there.

Two long paragraphs of text followed, but Flaco could only pick out a few words—volcano, lava, flood. Frustrated, he returned to his English lessons, spreading the workbooks on the shop counter.

He flipped past the bird exercise to "The Family Tree." Flaco leaned an elbow on the counter and dutifully translated the words arrayed around the tree drawing: brother, sister, mother, father, aunt, uncle, grandmother, grandfather, great-grandmother, great-grandfather, cousin. He flipped to the next page, "My Family Tree." He wrote his name in the center, filled in mother, Beatriz, and grandmother, Patricia. Then he was stumped. Who else was there? He couldn't even put César on there as a primo. He wasn't a real cousin, was he? Was César his mother's cousin? Flaco sighed and put his pencil down. His family tree was a scrawny shrub with a couple of leaves.

From the time he was small, Flaco had known there was something different about his family. In the village of Las Lunas, most families were large. His classmates all had brothers and sisters and aunties and uncles to spare. And abuelas and abuelos. It was not unusual to have bisabuelos, great-grandparents, all living under the same roof. His friend Carlos complained about his crowded house, his grandfather's snoring, his older sister hogging the bathroom, doing her hair in the mirror for hours.

But Flaco loved the warm chaos of Carlos's house. By contrast, his own home was quiet and sometimes a little lonely. Flaco had no siblings or aunts or uncles. His mother's mother, Abuela Patricia, had died when he was five. He didn't remember his father or when his father had left. Flaco's father was not a subject his mother cared to discuss. Flaco had learned over the years not to ask questions about David Luna, but sometimes the questions came unbidden.

Springtime, second grade. Math class had just broken for recess, and Flaco was chasing Carlos and Fabian out of the building to the sandy playground.

"I'm first!" Fabian called, streaking ahead toward the monkey bars.

"Nobody cares!" Carlos yelled, but of course they all cared who got there first, and Carlos and Flaco raced to catch up.

Flaco heard a low whistle and saw a man standing on the edge of the school grounds. The man beckoned him, and Flaco trotted over. Was he looking for someone? He was nobody Flaco knew—a stranger with a serious face. The man squatted down and took Flaco by the shoulders.

"Mijo, look at you. Growing to be such a big boy, aren't you?"

Flaco didn't know what to say and stared at his sandaled feet, covered in red dust from the playground.

"You are Sebastián, yes?"

Flaco nodded, still looking at his feet.

"My name is David. I'm your papá."

Flaco startled and looked up into the man's face. His papá? It was true that his papá's name was David. But what did he look like? Flaco had seen a few photos—some of his parents' wedding day and one of his father holding him as a baby with his mother standing next to him. But he could not remember the living, breathing person, could not recall any particulars about his body or his voice. In the photos, his mother's face looked the same mostly. Did this man resemble the man in those pictures?

Flaco scanned the man's brown skin, his eyebrows, his generous mustache hiding his mouth.

"My father does not have a mustache," he said finally.

The mustache lifted then as David laughed, and Flaco could see all his teeth.

"Mustaches come and go, my son," he said, standing. "But I'm your father. I promise. Let's walk a little."

They paced the perimeter of the playground together, David

resting his hand on Flaco's shoulder from time to time. David talked and Flaco listened, though later he couldn't remember what David said. He was thinking of all the questions he wanted to ask. But he only got the chance to ask one.

"Are you coming to live with us now?"

David lit a cigarette, looked away toward town, and blew smoke over Flaco's head.

"Not now," he said. "But soon. Very soon."

The bell rang for the end of recess, but David continued walking and Flaco followed, unsure of what to do. He heard his teacher call his name and swung around to see the others lined up in front of her.

"I have to go back to class now, señor," he said to David.

He wanted to call him Papá but it didn't seem right.

David nodded and gazed down at him.

"Can you do something for me?"

Flaco nodded.

"I have to go back north. You take good care of your mamá, okay? I'm counting on you."

Flaco had so many questions: Where in the north was David going? How long would he be gone? Could they come with him so they could be a family?

But he just nodded and said yes, he would take care of Mamá. David squatted down again and embraced him, and Flaco breathed in the scent of him—cigarette smoke, chewing gum, and woody cologne. He felt a strange ache at how unfamiliar his own father was to him and how he wished it was different. Then David released him and walked away. Flaco never saw him again.

Where had his father gone and why? Where had he been before? These were questions he'd asked his mother that night. But she wouldn't answer him and his questions made her cry, so he stopped asking. He also never asked why she'd told him David was dead. Had she, or was it something he assumed? People in the village referred to his mother as a widow, which was why he'd told Señor Sergio that without thinking. For all he knew, his father might be dead, but Flaco didn't know. It was more accurate to say, as he'd told Jacob, that his father was gone.

Flaco often recalled the memory of this single conversation with David—his words, his clothes, the unfamiliar scent of him—until he wasn't sure what was memory and what was his own fabrication. Years later, the only thing he remained certain of was David's one request.

"*You take good care of your mamá*," he'd said.

But Flaco hadn't done that, had he? She was still taking care of Flaco. He was ashamed that he was here now so far away at her urging. Shouldn't he have been man enough to resist? To convince her that he could stand up to the pressures of Tonio and his boss?

She wanted better for him, but he didn't know if this was better, living with strangers in a place where people behaved so weirdly. Like that woman in the SUV shouting at them in the meadow. Back at the house, using Google Translate, Jacob explained she was a biologist studying bees. But he didn't explain the yelling, and Flaco didn't ask. It was one more thing he didn't understand.

He stayed out in the barn until Jacob called him in for lunch. Jacob still seemed preoccupied or maybe annoyed, and Flaco went back out to the barn for the rest of the day. In the passing hours he felt bored and sleepy with inactivity and also a growing sense of his deep loneliness at being so far from home. His stomach ached and so it wasn't a lie when he told Jacob he wasn't hungry and went to bed early.

That night, Flaco dreamed he was at home in the kitchen with his mother. She stood over the stove, chatting about a problem with the horno at work, stirring the caldo de res that she always made on the weekends. It was so comforting to see the familiar house he'd grown up in. His whole body felt warm with contentment. The rich aroma of the caldo de res filled the kitchen. His mother turned up the flame on the stove and smiled at him.

"Listen to me, mi amor," she said, shaking her spoon at him. "Don't ever forget what I'm about to tell you. This is the most important thing. If you remember this, it will be the answer anytime you have trouble in your life."

He leaned forward, desperate to know what it was, this one answer. But then she seemed to be speaking a different language, and he couldn't understand a word she said.

"¿Me entiendes?" she asked.

But he didn't understand at all and felt panicked.

"Mamá, I don't understand. Say it again?"

"Good boy," she said, as if she hadn't heard him, and turned back to the stew. She grasped the heavy cast-iron lid and set it on the pot with a clang.

At the sound, Flaco awakened with a jolt. He saw checkered curtains, the photos of white strangers smiling down from the wall, and remembered he was not at home. He was in Hood River, Oregon, and his mother was thousands of miles away. His heart seemed to wring itself out. The dream had felt so real, his mother's voice, her closeness. He could almost smell the caldo. He could hear Jacob talking to someone as he got up and pulled on his clothes. From the doorway he smelled the very real and rich aroma of caldo de res wafting down the hallway.

Señora Evangelina was sitting with Jacob at the kitchen table and rose to greet him.

"Good morning, Flaco! Did you sleep okay?"

She embraced him and Flaco was embarrassed at how pleasant it was, how comforting, though he barely knew her.

"I made caldo de res," she said. "An ocean of it! Too much! And I thought you and Jacob might like some."

She moved to the stove and ladled the stew into a bowl and urged him to sit and said something to Jacob in English. Jacob nodded at her and looked at Flaco.

"Stew good," Jacob said in Spanish.

Flaco's stomach twisted on itself with homesickness. Caldo de res was his mother's dish. Eating someone else's seemed like a betrayal. But his mother had raised him to be polite. He dipped his spoon and raised it to his mouth, and suddenly he was ravenous. The bowl was quickly emptied and Señora Evangelina, still talking to Jacob in English, rose and refilled it. She pulled a plate of tortillas out of the oven and placed them on the table. Flaco scooped the stew up with one and bit into it—tasting the corn, a touch of salt, and the flavor of home.

"A little more?" Señora Evangelina asked.

"No, thank you. It was delicious," he said.

The señora pulled a notebook out of her bag and sat down.

"Jacob says you're being a good guest and that you had a chance to talk to your mom too. Are you doing okay, Flaco?"

He was homesick, he was confused, he was scared. But he was doing okay, all things considered, so he nodded.

"I'm fine, señora," he said.

She smiled at him, but her eyes were sad, like she understood. Of course he wasn't fine, and the mix of feelings in his heart was impossible to name. She opened her notebook.

"I've learned a few things about how we can help you," she said. "But first, I have some bad news. I'm very sorry to tell you this, but your cousin is being deported. There's nothing we can do for him. If he already had a lawyer, we might have been able to slow things down. But his work permit expired some time ago and he missed a court date for that. I'm really sorry, Flaco."

César been pulled over for a broken taillight. He had missed a court date for an expired work permit, which was a problem. Now he was being deported.

Flaco looked down at his empty bowl, dejected. César was supposed to help him get a job. He'd said Flaco could live with him in the housing provided by the orchardist. That's all his mother had told him. What in the world would he do now?

It wasn't all bad news, though, the señora was saying. As a fourteen-year-old on his own, Flaco was classified as what was called an unaccompanied minor. The first thing they needed to do was get him a lawyer.

"What would a lawyer do?" Flaco asked.

"Protect you and help you apply for residency."

"I can apply without papers? And without my cousin's help?"

"Yes, even without papers. It's the law here."

He thought about that. It didn't seem to make sense. He thought of what Señor Sergio told him about the danger of deportation, of getting left in a border town in the north of Mexico.

"If it's the law, then why do so many people get sent back?" he asked.

Señora Evangelina frowned and shook her head.

"It's complicated. The laws keep changing. Some Americans want to help. Others believe things . . ." she trailed off.

"Like their president?" Flaco said.

She nodded.

"Yes. He says many rude and untrue things, and some people listen to him. So, for you, it's important to get a good lawyer and start your petition immediately. I know someone who can meet with you tomorrow. She's going to ask you lots of questions. About where you came from. And why you want to be here. Are you willing to talk to her, Flaco?"

He thought of Tonio telling the others it was only a matter of time. Telling them not to be stupid and to go to Morelia. He thought of Carlos's face the last time he saw him, his best friend's words hanging over him forever.

He nodded to Señora Evangelina.

"Okay," she said, unsmiling, as if she knew there was nothing easy about it. She told him she'd take him to the lawyer the next day. She'd brought him some more of her son's clothes and told him to wear something nice. She hugged him and Jacob both when she left, answering her phone on the way out the door and waving goodbye to them.

Flaco cleared the table, washed the dishes, and prepared to return to the barn.

Jacob looked up from his computer and smiled.

"Thank you, Flaco. Do you want coffee?" he asked.

Flaco did not drink coffee, but Jacob had pulled out two cups, so he nodded and said yes, thank you. Flaco brought his workbooks to the table and sat. He did a lesson to pass the time. This one was all about a couple of work colleagues on a trip to Boston. The weather was very cold. One needed to buy a coat and never seemed able to find one. Her male coworker was looking for a dry cleaner, whatever that was.

After a while, Jacob shut his laptop and moved to the sliding door to let the dog out. He seemed irritated, and again Flaco felt uncomfortable, an unwanted guest. He watched Jacob out of the corner of his eye making notes in his notebook and staring out into the yard. When he saw Flaco looking, he dropped his frown.

"What's that one about?" he asked, gesturing at the book.

"A trip to Boston," Flaco replied. "Is cold, Boston."

"Yes, so they say."

"So they say," Flaco repeated. "No more work today?"

Jacob frowned again, but then he shrugged.

"Let's go for a drive," he said.

They drove past the orchards again and through town, but this time, instead of heading up the winding highway toward the mountain meadow, Jacob turned down the hill and drove through Hood River. They passed shops and cafés and sidewalks teeming with people. Jacob drove toward the river and pulled into a parking lot across from a bright green belt of grass. The dog jumped down and Jacob got his wheelchair out. Flaco stood next to the truck and surveyed the scene.

The world was a carnival of color and sound. On the grass, scores of large nylon kites in every color were stacked together against the whistling wind. Some people seemed to be inflating them with pumps. Men and women in tight, funny athletic clothes milled around on the lawn like it was a weekend party, not a weekday morning. Kids flew down the sidewalk on bikes, skateboards, and scooters. Someone's stereo was pumping out a perky American pop song. Everyone seemed white. And out on the river, dozens of the brightly colored kites swooped over the water, dwarfing the pilots below them.

Jacob appeared at his side and gestured grandly.

"Bienvenido to the Hood River Event Site."

He led Flaco through the throng and Flaco tried not to stare. Javier had been right about the beautiful women. He'd never seen so many young women in one place in such short shorts and bikini tops. Beautiful bare legs and arms. Swelling breasts in small tank tops. He didn't know where to look.

Everyone seemed to know Jacob. Fist bumps, high fives, back slaps. Some of the girls hugged him and were so close Flaco could smell the sweet scent of their hair. They glanced at Flaco, smiling with huge white teeth, but Jacob didn't introduce him to anyone. He kept moving through the crowd until all the people were behind them. There, where the lawn began to slope toward the rocky beach, they had a full view of the river.

The face of the Columbia was dark green and riffled with whitecaps. The spray from the waves threw back sunlight like bright embers. The current surged visibly westward and the wind blew to the east, working at cross-purposes as if trying to keep the water at a standstill. The water was crowded with people doing all kinds of sports Flaco had never seen before.

Jacob pointed to the various recreational crafts, naming different activities, words Flaco had never heard—kiteboarding, windsurfing, foiling, paddleboarding. A deep horn sounded and an enormous barge bore down the center of the river. It appeared to be heading straight for the carefree recreators, but they moved easily out of its way as if in a choreographed dance. How did they not run into each other? How did the different watercraft work? How did people learn it all? So many questions and he didn't have the language to ask.

"Much, much things," Flaco said.

Jacob laughed.

"Yes, many things. Too many things."

The dog leapt up, tore across the grass, and threw himself into the water. Crossing a short channel, he ran out onto a large sandbar spilling into the river. Jacob gestured after the dog and said something Flaco didn't understand.

"Go look," Jacob repeated. "It's beautiful. Una buena vista."

Flaco stood and waited for Jacob and realized he could not enter the water in his wheelchair. He felt embarrassed and didn't know why.

"Go see," Jacob insisted. "It's super cool."

Flaco proceeded to the water's edge and took off his shoes and socks and rolled his pants to his knees. A small girl was paddling in the water and yelled to some adults on a picnic blanket nearby. From the ease with which she managed the water, Flaco could tell the channel was not terribly deep. Someone called back to her in Spanish. The little girl swam over to a group of women—her mother and aunts maybe—then swam back to where Flaco stood on the bank. She clutched her life jacket with small hands and kicked her feet. Flaco stepped in the water and recoiled, gasping. He'd never felt anything so cold, like ice and fire at once.

The little girl laughed.

"It's not that cold! Watch me," she said in Spanish. She dunked her head, then came back up, water streaming into her eyes.

"It's easy!" she said.

Flaco inhaled and plunged into the water, which came up past his knees. He pushed through the shock of the cold and surged out the other side onto the sandbar. The wind was stronger there and blew cold on his wet legs.

He looked back at the lawn for Jacob, who was still in the same spot and talking to someone. Flaco heard the dog bark again and turned. Cheney was running along the shore and biting the waves. The sand was soft under Flaco's feet and warm from the sun. To his left, a kite rose slowly in the air, piloted by a man in the shallows. A stand of small trees rose out of the mud flats, and as he passed, an eruption of goldfinches filled the air, twittering as they flew around him. An osprey, keening, hung fluttering above the river, and a lone heron stalked in a shallow pool of the wetland. Flaco kept walking, and the crowd of people thinned and soon he was alone at the far edge of the sandbar.

He looked out at the water and recalled the map of the river from the atlas he'd found in the barn. This waterway began in a humble spring in Canada and wound its way south into the state of Washington and then Oregon, bending back on itself and heading west and then south and then west again until eventually spilling out into the Pacific Ocean at the end of its twelve-hundred-mile journey.

Across the water, basalt cliffs rose steeply to form the north bank. Flaco realized he was looking at an accordion of compressed lava. He looked west and saw the slope buckling upward in a dramatic syncline and east to see the downward curve of the anticline. Turning, he found Mount Hood rising out of the valley floor in the south. He thought of the poster in the barn detailing the last volcanic eruption, the terrible floodwaters, the lava cooling into ribbons of basalt. The late morning light drew his gaze west down the long tunnel of the gorge, the soaring hills overlapping each other like buttresses on a cathedral, one after another heading west and away toward the Pacific Ocean. The water, the sand, and the hills were all gilded gold by the sun.

Yes, it was, as Jacob had said, a beautiful view, una buena vista. But it was also something more than that. A moment of serenity in a world that was constantly shifting underfoot. He was overwhelmed by the beauty of it and the sense that this beauty was the aftermath of so much destruction. He wanted to explain it to his mother. And Carlos. He felt a lump in his throat thinking of his friend.

He thought of what Jacob had told him about the beeline, the direct path that a honeybee knew to follow back to the hive from the field—confident and unwavering. He turned south and closed his eyes and thought of his home. Las Lunas called to him. He could feel the tug of that invisible line connected to his heart. Maybe it was like this for honeybees, the gravitational pull he felt within his body.

His heart surged with wonderment at the physical beauty in front of him and grief for his home and the people he'd left behind. A confluence of the most wonderful and terrible feelings he'd ever had—two opposing currents crashing together in his heart.

He glanced back at the channel to where the little girl and her family had been and saw they were gone. He felt the depth of his loneliness then, his terrible homesickness. Deeper and wider and longer than this gorge or this river pushing westward, wild and unceasing. His sorrow could fill the ocean.

12

HABITAT

Solitary or social? Some solitary species living in peaceful parallel can look like a colony but are, in fact, a series of individual nests.

—LAVIN, *THE WONDROUS WORLD OF BEES*

ABIGAIL STOOD, SHOULDERS slumped, surveying the heap of nylon fabric and aluminum tubing that was supposed to be her tent. She wanted to howl with frustration. She kicked at the pile and tripped, nearly falling, which made her feel even more impotent. She was so furious she wanted to cry. How hard could it possibly be to erect a simple *tent*?!

Getting to the field site alone had taken some doing. After she left the beekeeper's meadow, the SUV had felt funny, vibrating and clunking as she drove. Following the beekeeper's directions, she'd located the rough double track heading up to the field. The three-mile route was steep and exposed. She crept along, teeth rattling in her head until she couldn't stand it anymore. She gripped the wheel, hit the gas, and shot up the hillside. The vehicle leapt over rocks and ruts until Abigail could see the meadow opening in front of her. She depressed the gas pedal as long as she could stand the shaking and wobbling. At the top, the vehicle halted with a terrible clunking sound. Abigail slid out the door, sweating as if she'd run those three miles uphill.

She stepped into the meadow and gazed up at Mount Hood rising in front of her, the sheer walls of snow and the blue glacier glinting like a mirage. The mountain was magnificent and intimidating. She felt uneasy and it dawned on her then that she didn't have the slightest idea how to begin the task assigned to her—setting up a field camp.

She glanced at her watch and chewed her bottom lip. Tent first, she decided. She located the tent bag from the pile of gear in the back of the SUV and upended it, strewing the contents onto the ground. The bag was holding the tent itself—a large piece of nylon fabric—as well as five aluminum poles, several stakes, a few bungee cords, and another smaller sheet of nylon fabric. Laid out flat, the tent revealed sleeves on the exterior, presumably for the aluminum poles. She selected one pole and inserted it in the top sleeve and proceeded with the others until the tent was a five-legged creature. But no matter how she bent the poles, she could not force the nylon into a tentlike shape. She tried moving the poles around. She worked from the top down and the bottom up. She struggled to pull the poles into the corner insertion points, sweating and staggering until the entire thing sprang out of her hands like a live creature. It collapsed, enfolding her with menace. As she fell, she heard the fabric tear underneath her.

The grass warmed her back through her shirt as she lay there wondering why things that were easy for others seemed so difficult for her. What was she feeling? Anger. But she knew it was really Frustration and maybe even Shame.

Abigail had never erected a tent before. She'd never even been camping before. But nobody had asked her that. They'd just given her directions. Dr. Lavin had told her to set up the field camp before the others arrived. Dr. Mora had directed her to Deirdre for details;

Deirdre had said to check out a vehicle from the motor pool and gear from the equipment department. The motor-pool guy had explained how to get to the field site. He'd also offered to show her how to engage four-wheel drive, which she had, regrettably, declined. And the student in the equipment department had told her to go fuck herself.

She'd recognized him as the guy who'd been sitting with Casey in Dr. Lavin's lecture, the one who'd been whispering and snickering. He was tall and thin, but somehow flabby at the same time. His skin was oatmeal-colored and his hair reddish brown. When Abigail approached the equipment room, he was absorbed by his phone. She stood at the counter waiting for him to look up.

"Excuse me," she said finally when he did not.

He put down his phone and rose, sighing.

"Things to check out?" he asked.

This seemed an obvious and unnecessary question. Why else would she be in the equipment room? To pay a social call? She slid the gear list across the counter, and he scanned the paper.

"Okay. Let's see. You need a sleeping bag?"

He looked at her, eyebrows raised.

"Seriously. You know the department sleeping bags are ancient, right? You don't have your own sleeping bag?"

"No, I do not," Abigail said.

He scoffed and continued to scan the list.

"Tent, water filter, stove, camp kitchen setup for fourteen. Fourteen adults?"

He looked up from the paper with narrowed eyes.

"Wait, what's this for?"

"It is for Dr. Lavin's Mount Hood field camp."

The boy dropped the gear list and frowned.

"Wait. You're setting up the field camp for Lavin. Why you?"

Abigail shrugged.

"Dr. Lavin asked me to."

He snorted.

"Yeah, I get that part. But aren't you the reject from the TA pool? You got here, like, what—five minutes ago. Jesus! They're sending you. Fucking figures. Do you know how long I've been working with Mora?"

Abigail did not like being called a reject and did not know or care how long the boy had been working with Dr. Mora, but he did not seem to expect an answer to either question. He'd turned away and began banging through the shelves, pulling gear down and tossing it on the counter, grumbling. He swung around to glare at her.

"Headlamp. Seriously. You don't even have the rudimentary gear. Have you ever set up a camp before?"

Abigail found it impossible not to answer direct questions.

"I have not," she said.

The boy swore again and gripped the counter with both hands. She wondered why he was so angry.

"But they're sending you. You know why? Because women hire women. The estrogen Mafia. It's so fucking unfair."

The boy turned back to the shelves and continued to locate supplies, throwing items into a growing heap as he continued to mutter to himself. He shoved a waiver across the counter and snatched it back when she'd signed it.

"This place is so screwed up. Three years I've been here. I've done all the shit jobs with a smile on my face and Mora never even puts me on a field team. You just got here and you're *leading* a team. What does a guy have to do around here? I mean it. What am I doing wrong?"

Abigail wasn't sure why he was asking her, but there was nobody else there, and he was looking right at her now.

"Well, you are acting like an asshole."

It was the simplest suggestion she could think of, but the guy didn't seem to appreciate it. That's when he told her to go fuck herself.

Now, in the meadow, she sat up and looked at the horizon. The sun was swimming west and would soon be lost over the rim of the Cascade Range. Abigail shivered. It would be a cold and uncomfortable night if she didn't get her tent up. The thought made her think of her father, and the list he'd created to help Abigail remember important routines when she left for college. "Nighttime Routine," he'd written. And under that, "Eat dinner, wash dishes, wash face, and brush teeth." There was a daytime list too: showering, breakfast, packing for class. Abigail had scoffed that she wasn't a dumb kid anymore. But her first night in the dorm, when her new roommate asked why she was going to bed with her clothes on, she'd had to say of course she wasn't. She was just resting. Then she'd pulled out the list, sheepishly adding, "Put on pajamas," and silently thanked her dad.

Abigail, who thrived on good directions, now remembered the handbook Deirdre had given her when she was getting ready to leave for the field.

"*Dr. Mora said you might need specifics*," Deirdre had said.

Abigail found the slim green volume in the chaos of her belongings. *US Forest Service Field Camp Handbook*, the cover read. Opening to the table of contents, she felt a flood of relief.

Abigail was great at following clear directions, and this book was full of them: from choosing a camp site and locating a water source to setting up a kitchen and maintaining a safe fire area. "Your step-by-step guide for establishing an organized and efficient study site," the introduction promised.

Abigail flipped to the section on tent setup. She quickly surmised that the tent poles, though they looked very similar, must be different sizes. And slowing down to count the sleeves, she realized there were six and understood she was short one pole. She organized the poles by length, and it became clear where each belonged. Inserting all five, she found herself with a good enough tent, albeit sagging at the end that lacked a pole. She identified the ground cloth and spread it out, set the tent in the middle, and attached the rain fly. She stood back, feeling satisfied. Consulting the handbook, she worked her way through the checklist for her own primary needs—securing her food from bears, filtering enough water for the night's cooking and drinking, establishing a latrine area, and setting up a kitchen. By the time the sun slipped behind the mountains, Abigail was tucked into her sleeping bag with a belly full of soup and fell asleep almost instantly.

She startled awake to the blare of horns in a traffic jam. But no, it was a great vee of geese sailing above. Climbing out of the tent, she saw Mount Hood awash in the alpenglow of dawn—pinks and oranges and soft grays. She turned north and saw Washington's massive old volcanoes lined up on the horizon—Mount Adams, Mount Rainier, and the lopsided mouth of Mount Saint Helens, which had exploded sixteen years before Abigail was born. A breeze blew cold on her face and the meadow came awake around her. The melodious song of a meadowlark ascended through the grass. A covey of quail took to the air in awkward flight, calling to each other. The sun lit up a ring of ancient gray snags rising out of the bear grass like ghost trees, and a white dot on one became a woodpecker drumming away for breakfast, surely the white-headed woodpecker Dr. Lavin had mentioned. The creek rushed and burbled at her back and a chorus frog called from the mossy bank, then another and another until their voices overlapped and she lost count of them.

Abigail, who had never camped. Abigail, who had always lived in cities. Abigail, who had never slept outside, was simply enchanted. She stood in the meadow listening and turning and listening more, astonished by the simple beauty of the high mountain meadow under the gaze of Mount Hood at dawn.

After breakfast, she reviewed Dr. Lavin's instructions and was relieved to find them clear and straightforward. In addition to setting up camp, she was to measure the study area using the GIS coordinates provided and mark the boundaries. Dr. Mora had said she'd probably only need a day to set up camp, but Dr. Lavin had urged her to go up earlier if she needed more time. Abigail didn't like to be rushed and had given herself an extra day and was glad now. It was so peaceful, walking through the wilderness area toward the north boundary. No stereos playing out of open windows. No cars accelerating past. She didn't hear the annoying chatter from the kitchen near her office or the unending construction noise from the new dorms being built on campus. No hacky sackers calling out a chorus of disappointment. She heard the wind, her own breath, the buzz of bees, the click of beetles, and the hum of crickets. A pair of ravens cronked overhead, the wind in their wings. She lost track of time pacing through the hip-high meadow grass.

She felt she was part of the rhythm of the world around her. It was like a return to her earliest of days as a watcher of creatures—the velvety tree ants and the caterpillars and the pill bugs in the yards of every childhood house. To some this might have sounded so sad, so lonely—that image of a little girl in the yard with no company but a kingdom of invertebrates. But to Abigail, it was the very definition of heaven—quiet, private, and focused. It felt like home.

The time between the velvety tree ants and landing at Dr. Mora's lab had been difficult for Abigail. Her academic record was uneven, though she generally excelled in science and math. Socially, she was like a tent with a missing pole—never quite erecting the structure of lasting friendship. By the time Abigail was in junior high, she'd given up on having friends and hoped instead merely to avoid outright persecution.

Eighth grade was surely the worst year. Why was she a target for such cruelty? Something about her made other kids dislike her. If only she knew what it was. The things people told her didn't make sense. That she stared. She stuttered and said weird things. She smelled her food before she ate it and had been observed smelling her own armpits during assembly. Didn't everyone do those things?

She came home in tears after a classmate opened her *Beauty and the Beast* backpack and unearthed her baby blanket. Why was it weird to bring your blanket to school if you didn't take it out in class?

"Just ignore them, sweet pea," her father counseled. "They are teasing you to get a rise."

But teasing wasn't the word for it. There was a deep unkindness there, a message that she would never belong no matter how hard she tried. Tripping her when she walked in the cafeteria. Sticky notes on her back that said, "Kick me!" And worse. It was that eighth-grade year that a pack of boys followed her home laughing and saying horrible things. She started taking a shortcut through an alley to avoid them. It seemed to work, until the day she stopped to admire the ants crawling on the face of a beautiful peony. Suddenly they were right behind her, three of them. She turned to run, but they caught her. She felt their hands all over her body as they pressed her into the dirt. Two of them held her down while the third put cockleburs into her hair. They ran away laughing and Abigail walked home covered in dirt. Her father was at work so she went to Miss Ricketts's door, bawling her eyes out. The burrs hurt when she tried to pull them free, but mostly it was her feelings.

Fear.

Humiliation.

Mortification.

Miss Ricketts told Abigail to wash her face and then come out to the patio. She handed Abigail a fizzing glass of Coke and gestured for her to sit. Miss Ricketts stood behind her with a comb and examined the damage. Abigail smelled the smoke of her menthol cigarette.

"I'm going to have to cut them out, Abigail. But I don't want you to cry over this. It's just hair and it will grow back."

Abigail sniffled and nodded.

Miss Ricketts inhaled and set her cigarette in the ashtray. Abigail squeezed her eyes shut as Miss Ricketts began to snip the burrs free.

"I'm going to tell you something now. Those kids aren't teasing you, like your dad says. It's plain meanness."

"That's what I told my teacher—" Abigail started, but Miss Ricketts shushed her.

"I want you to listen to me and remember what I'm telling you. I know those boys aren't teasing you. They are little assholes."

Abigail startled and smothered a laugh. She'd never heard Miss Ricketts swear.

"Right now, they'll tell your teacher they were joking and it's all a game. And your teacher will tell you the boys are playing around. But they're not. And when you're older, those little assholes will be bigger assholes, because they'll have grown up learning they can get away with whatever they want. You'll have to work with them and work for them and suffer their idiocy. People will tell you to lighten up and not take everything so seriously. Sometimes you'll have a male supervisor who sees things your way. Some men are great bosses, colleagues, and friends to women. Your dad is one of them. But you can't count on it. You can only count on yourself. And you'll have to deal with unpleasant people sometimes."

Abigail stuttered a sob.

"But if they could only see I'm a good friend—" she said.

Miss Ricketts picked up her cigarette and inhaled.

"Abigail. Do you really want to be friends with little assholes like that?"

No, she did not.

"Don't worry. You'll find good friends, I'm sure. Other than that, I believe the key to happiness is to find something that interests you and work hard at it. Hard work is an offering and a gift."

Miss Ricketts snipped without talking for a while and Abigail listened to the shivery sound of the scissors. When she was finished, she passed Abigail a mirror.

"What do you think?"

Abigail stared at herself. Her hair had never been so short before. The pixie cut revealed her high cheekbones; the bangs emphasized her green eyes and the dusting of freckles across her nose. She looked almost pretty, she thought.

"I like it very much," she said. "Thank you, Miss Ricketts."

"You're welcome, honey. And don't worry. You'll find your people eventually."

They sat in Miss Ricketts's TV room watching *The Ellen DeGeneres Show.* When she went home for dinner, her dad complimented her hair, and she only said Miss Ricketts had cut it. And when Abigail went to school, she walked past those boys like they weren't even there. That whole day, they tried to get her attention—following her, making fun of her hair, and calling awful things at her back. She continued to ignore them, thinking about what Miss Ricketts had said when they were watching *Ellen.*

"*Find a way to work around them.*"

As those boys followed her down the hall, she thought of the major classes of the phylum Arthropoda. Crustacea, Decapoda, Isopoda, Arachnida, Insecta, Chilopoda, Diplopoda. When they crowded close and muttered curses, she'd list the members of each class. Starting with her favorite, Insect: Coleoptera, Blattodea, Diptera, Ephemeroptera, Hymenoptera, Lepidoptera, Mantodea, Odonata, Orthoptera, and Siphonaptera. She lost herself in the singsong rhythm in her head and made herself forget they were there. By the week's end, those boys grew bored and left her alone.

After that, Abigail became okay with being by herself. She did her homework at lunch, which gave her free time after school to read. She got a job at DeSilva's Nursery in high school. In college, after her first terrible semester, she double majored in biology and math. She got good enough grades and was not unhappy. Occasionally, though, she thought wistfully about what Miss Ricketts had said about finding her people. At the age of twenty-three Abigail had yet to make any real friends.

The sun climbed as Abigail marked the four corners of the study area. Then she turned to the work of setting up camp for the others—Dr. Lavin and twelve students who'd be joining the field team. Consulting the *US Forest Service Field Camp Handbook*, she set up a large kitchen area near the stream and established a data-processing spot under the shade of two large Douglas firs. She staked off discreet latrine areas—one for women and one for men—and set up more bear-proofing for food storage and food waste. Consulting the handbook, she noted a sidebar of optional items, including a campfire ring for "after-hours socializing." She paused over that one. She couldn't see herself sitting around with the others after dinner. Or could she? With some effort, she rolled a trio of logs into a triangle on a patch of ground near the kitchen and set a ring of large stones in the middle. Why not?

That afternoon, she began to collect samples. Still eschewing her net, she allowed each creature to settle on a blossom before coaxing it into a collection container. She worked quickly to identify the samples, photograph them, and then release them back into the air, for they had work to do—pollinating the bear grass and wildflowers as well as willow trees and other spring flowering shrubs. By the end of the day, she had a growing list of bumblebee species—*Bombus flavifrons*, yellowhead bumblebee; *Bombus melanopygus*, black-tailed bumblebee; and *Bombus appositus*, white-shouldered bumblebee. She had a good list of other insects too—longhorn bee, sweat bee, mason bee, and wool-carder bee—as well as a fine catalog of trees, flowers, and grasses that the bees were foraging in.

Near the north edge of the survey site she noticed the increasing presence of honeybees in the sampling area. They were easy to identify—small gold bodies with black stripes, wings extending past the ends of their abdomens. Their tone was a consistent murmur, unlike the bumblebees with their stuttering buzz. The honeybees made her think of the beekeeper and his field nearby.

Jake Stevenson had seemed interesting and articulate. He'd explained what he was doing with the long hive and how it was better for the honeybees. They'd had a cordial conversation. He'd been kind to her. With a sinking feeling, Abigail recalled her own behavior at the field. She'd conveniently forgotten that in the moments before Jake Stevenson introduced himself, she'd accused him of violating wilderness rules. She'd yelled all sorts of things at him. Not very nice things. Her face grew hot as she remembered, and she halted. She closed her eyes and thought how she must have looked, how she must have sounded.

She hated herself in that moment. Like always, the remorse came later. She'd come out swinging, as her father liked to say.

"Asshole," she whispered, pinching the inside of her arm hard enough to bruise.

She tried to recall their conversation. What had Jake Stevenson said to her when she left? He'd said it was nice to meet her and he wished her success. She believed him too. Jake Stevenson seemed like someone who meant what he said. She felt slightly better then. Maybe he would come visit the field camp and she could show him photos of the samples she'd collected.

That evening, she tidied the kitchen and double-checked the bear-proofing on her food supplies. She filtered extra water to make sure there would be enough for the field team and cleared debris off the best areas for tent spots. The wood she'd collected in the fire ring lit easily, and she sat up late watching the flames dance in the darkness. The temperature dropped, and the fire felt delicious against the chill. She worried briefly about the state of the SUV, which had jolted and wobbled and clunked to the top of the road, but decided not to think about it for the time being.

Abigail wondered how to welcome the others the next day. Should she make a sign? Should she pick flowers? No, that would be terrible, uprooting wildflowers. But she was the host, sort of, wasn't she? She wondered who else would be coming with Dr. Lavin. A dozen other graduate students from the University of Washington and OSU. Her heart flipped over. Suddenly, the idea of so many people at this beautiful, quiet camp made her feel exhausted. She didn't know why. It just happened. People made her anxious and she felt better alone.

"Your mom was like that too," Dad said once. "Introversion is common in artists and deep thinkers."

What was she like, Elizabeth Plue? Unequivocally beautiful. Anyone could see that by looking at the photos. She was tall and willowy with bobbed, honey-colored hair. She favored overalls and ankle boots, especially when painting. One of Abigail's first memories was of holding a fat tube of oil paint, cool in her toddler hand, and raising it to her mouth. Just before her lips closed over the open top of Scarlet Sunset, Elizabeth had shouted and snatched it away. Abigail had cried—in surprise and in fear but also in disappointment because she was sure the viscous red gel would have tasted like candy. Her mother had laughed and danced her around the room and kissed away her tears. Sometimes Abigail could almost remember her voice.

"Abby-Baby," her mother crooned into Abigail's hair. "Abby-Baby, my one and only."

Her dad had never called her Abby, but told her her mother had. The pet name was like a private room she could inhabit, a place where Elizabeth Plue was still with her, holding her, smiling and calling her name. Abby, she would sometimes say to herself when she was alone and feeling still and quiet. Abby-Baby, my one and only.

Abigail did not remember when her mother left or any specific event that might explain why. She only remembered knowing that her mother was gone. And the ache inside her small body was the color of Scarlet Sunset paint and the size of a ripe strawberry. While her body had grown, the pain remained there, berry-size, just below her heart. Sometimes she woke up in the middle of the night for no reason. She'd put her thumb to her rib cage below her breast and imagine she could feel it. She did so now as she lay in her tent.

The sky grew dark and the stars came out. The fire died into ashes. A coyote sang in the blackness and others replied. Abigail felt the loneliness deep within her, a hunger that was always there, that strawberry-size wound on her heart.

She got up with the sun and consulted the handbook to ensure each area of the camp was set up correctly. She checked and rechecked the data sheets and photos of samples she'd collected to show clear identification. Recalling how she'd enjoyed the fire, she gathered more wood for that evening. Surveying her work, she felt a strange sensation that was hard to identify at first. And then she realized it was pride—a calm, grounded sense of having done good work. She'd made this camp all by herself on behalf of the group. Her anxiety dimmed and she felt a surge of excitement about sharing it with the others.

They arrived near noon. She heard them before she saw them, laughing and chatting. Someone was singing "Oh My Darling, Clementine." They came out of the trees, pacing up the trail in twos and threes, laden with heavy packs.

"Welcome to camp," Abigail muttered under her breath, practicing. "I hope you enjoy your time at Camp Bumblebee."

No, that was stupid. They were scientists, not children. She felt nervous again and didn't know what to do with her hands. What would she show them first? The data-processing area? The kitchen? Food storage? No, she decided, the campfire circle. It would be fun, a fun thing that she had to offer. When they were close enough to see faces, Abigail raised a hand in greeting.

"Hello!" she called. "Welcome!"

She saw Casey first, who looked up, her face blossoming into a smile as she waved..

"Hey, Abigail!" she yelled. "We made it!"

Abigail showed her teeth so Casey would know she was smiling. Then she looked at the man hiking just behind Casey and recognized the guy from the equipment room.

Her heart plummeted to her feet.

13

ORIENTATION FLIGHTS

Wayfinding, home finding. How does the worker bee make her way back to the nest? Or the queen from her mating flight? Bees memorize landscape markers to get home safely. Early efforts in navigation always begin with orientation flights.

—LAVIN, *THE WONDROUS WORLD OF BEES*

THE KID WAS talking, but Jake couldn't concentrate on what he was saying, not the words anyway. He heard the voice, a rumbling male cadence that rose and fell. You could tell the voice had recently dropped in register, changing from a squeaky tenor to a sudden baritone. Jake recognized the gruff bro-speak that he himself had employed when he'd been the kid's age. Only a few years had passed, but it seemed almost like a different lifetime.

Apart from the voice, there was also the body. The size of this kid's muscles was truly distracting. When they'd begun their conversation, Jake noticed the boy used any potential movement as a chance to flex. His biceps rippled as he brushed his blond hair out of his eyes, his deltoids undulated as he pointed a tanned arm up the driveway toward town, his triceps rolled as he cracked his knuckles.

". . . gonna be sick," the kid was saying. "It's the fourth year of the Big Air Classic. You should come check it out."

Jake nodded noncommittally. Not that this boy would have noticed. Chase Deltmore was not the most observant of teenage boys. Adept at relaying the minute details of his latest sesh on the water or a play-by-play of the downhill course he'd ridden at Whistler over spring break—lengthy descriptions of which he'd just recounted to Jake—he was less apt to consider his audience's level of interest in what he was saying. His older brother, Chance, was the same way, Jake recalled. Chance had been in Jake's class. Within the social hierarchies of Hood River Valley High School, the Deltmores were top of the heap. They didn't seem to care what other people thought of them because they'd grown up believing they were awesome. Chance, as blond and tan as his little brother, was a sponsored rider with Slingshot Kiteboarding.

"Chance will be there. He's going to worlds," Chase said. "Mos def. He's doing the whole circuit this year."

Jake didn't respond, not wanting to encourage the digression, but then the kid was off—outlining the North American kiteboarding tour in fine detail: San Diego, South Padre, Hatteras, Los Barriles, and Merida.

Jake sighed and glanced at the time. Chase Deltmore's interview had already lasted longer than Jake had hoped it would, and they hadn't even discussed the actual job. But, desperate for an employee, he tried to be patient. He gazed out over the apiary as Chase talked. Today he was up against mite treatments—hundreds of which would need to happen in the next two weeks to stay on track for honeyflow. As Chase rattled on, Jake considered a plausible schedule for applying miticides now that the days were heating up. It was hotter than the previous June and the June before, according to his records.

". . . it's totally, like, fire, right?"

Chase concluded his story and cracked his thick neck. He bared his teeth in a perfect smile. Great genes or a great orthodontist? Jake wondered. He picked up his notebook and scanned the list of topics he'd outlined to discuss with Chase.

"That's great, Chase," Jake said. "I hope your bro has an awesome time. But let's talk about the job a bit. Cool?"

"Oh sure, yeah. Right," Chase said.

He sat up and appeared to be paying attention.

"As I mentioned in the ad, it will be full time during honey harvest, but the hours will vary before and after. It will be hard to predict the timing exactly, so I need someone who can be flexible and take fewer hours some weeks and more on others."

The squirrely timetable of honey harvest was part of the reason it was easier to rely on friends for labor. A regular summer employee would reasonably expect some kind of base hours. But with Alice, Stan, Harry, Noah, Cece, and Cece's little brothers all gone, Jake couldn't rely on friends this year. He sighed, feeling defeated already, but Chase nodded with enthusiasm.

"Yeah, sure. No problem. I can roll with that. You don't need me one day, I can just have more time out on the water. Working on my frontroll with a downloop, man. It's fucking gnar!"

Jake was skeptical about hiring a kiteboarder. He knew from living with Harry how flaky wind-chasing boys could be.

"Great. That's . . . great, Chase. But when I need you, I'll really need you. It could be seven days straight or even ten. And short notice. Things can change overnight depending on the temperature, you get me? If there's an epic wind forecast, we can't postpone."

The boy nodded amicably.

"Yeah, sure. That's cool," he said. "Whatever you need, bro."

"Okay," Jake said slowly.

It was what he wanted to hear, but something about the boy's interest didn't track.

"Can I ask why you want to work at Queen of G?" Jake asked. "Frankly, it seems like you might have more fun at the waterfront."

Jake knew all the kite schools were still hiring, and even if they paid less, Chase would fit right into the summer scene at the river—hanging out on the beach after the wind died, flirting with girls, and sneaking beer in water bottles. Jake also knew that Chase's parents were loaded. He was pretty sure the Deltmore kids didn't need to work. So why didn't Chase want to spend the summer perfecting his gnar frontroll? Why waste time working on a farm up in the valley?

Chase straightened, put his shoulders back, and smiled that winning smile. He had dimples, for Christ's sake. He smiled like he'd been told he had a beautiful smile his whole life. And he did have a beautiful smile, which was even more irksome.

"The job was my mom's idea. She saw it posted and said it might make me more well-rounded," Chase said. "For college applications. I'm going to try for early admissions this fall."

That sounded like his mom, Jake thought. Rina Deltmore was a typical wealthy Hood River mother—sporty, fit, and involved. She was always in the paper for some nonprofit thing or other. Ribbon cutting at the new dog shelter, handing out summer lunches for low-income kids, the annual education foundation gala. Of course she'd be super involved in her kids' lives too, adding parental attention to the Deltmore boys' privilege pile.

"How would it help with your college applications, exactly?" Jake asked, tapping his pencil on his notebook. "Are you thinking about studying ag or culinary?"

Oregon was now famous not only for its wine and beer, but increasingly for heirloom fruit, farmstead cheeses, and hazelnuts. And honey, Jake thought, thinking of the West Coast Food and Wine Classic and Queen of G's prize. It made sense that more kids were studying agriculture or culinary arts.

But Chase shook his head. He was interested in tech, he said, in AI in particular. He thought the smartglasses were going to change everything.

"Have you read about the Metaverse glasses?"

Jake shook his head.

"They are fucking fire, bro!"

And then he was off, summarizing the benefits of augmented reality technology, which would allow you to feel like you were in the same room as someone who was on the other side of the world and get text and email alerts at the same time, even while you were in a meeting with someone. You could control it all from the screen on the glasses and other people you were talking to wouldn't even know. Here comes an email. Boom. A text. Done. A message from your navigation system about traffic. Got it.

It sounded hellish, Jake thought, wondering how in the world being deluged with more information through augmented reality might possibly be good. Wasn't regular reality challenging enough?

"Anyway, the programs are super competitive, you know," Chase said, winding down. "And Mom just thought it would help on my application for colleges to see that I'd done some work with the, with, you know, with the disability community. Like community service."

His voice was lofty as he made this pronouncement. As his words sank in, Jake felt a heat rush through his body and for a moment he couldn't breathe. There was a pause and Chase's smile deepened as if waiting for Jake to congratulate him.

"Community service," Jake repeated.

Chase nodded, looking so pleased with himself. Then he took in Jake's tone, and his eyes widened and his face reddened. He knew he'd said something wrong but didn't know what it was or why it might be offensive. Jake felt the impulse to be charitable. After all, the kid was only parroting his condescending mother. But then instead of shutting the fuck up and thanking Jake for his time and leaving as fast as he could—which was the only decent thing to do—the boy kept talking and dug himself a deeper hole.

"Yeah, I mean. Yeah," he said, sounding defensive, as if he shouldn't have to explain himself. "Like, like the people who are less fortunate and don't have the opportunities that . . . you know. People that can't do all the regular stuff normal people do."

Rage rose inside Jake like a wall of flame. It almost surprised him that such anger was still there, latent but powerful, like the smoldering roots of a tree after a forest fire.

"Regular stuff. Normal people," Jake repeated flatly.

Chase lurched to his feet and his flush deepened.

"Well, not *normal*. But not like handicapped or whatever. You know what I mean!" His voice rose in frustration as if Jake were the asshole.

"I don't think I do," Jake said, looking up at the angry boy. "What do you mean, exactly?"

"Fuck this! This is bullshit!" Chase said.

He turned on his heel and strode to his truck. It was a brand-new Toyota Tundra, Jake noticed. Much nicer than Jake's old Dodge and undoubtedly a gift from his parents. Or not even a gift. Just something the Deltmores could afford and gave without even thinking. Because their son wanted it. Regular stuff for normal people. Fortunate people with more opportunities.

Chase tore up the driveway, spraying gravel. Jake knew the kid was probably embarrassed and confused. Still, he hungered to punch the ableist, privileged little shit. He couldn't do that, so he went out to the barn to pummel the punching bag instead. He pounded away for a while, trying to flush out his anger. He put on some music—a ska playlist Noah had made him that spring—and cranked it. He moved to the weight set. "What's Wrong with Me," by We Are the Union captured his shit mood perfectly.

I'm just trying to explain
Why nothing feels that good to me
Can't escape the way I feel
Why do I keep
Running away when life gets real?
What's wrong with me?

Chase Deltmore was a privileged little shit, but Jake couldn't blame him for stirring up that old anger. It wasn't Chase's fault that his words made Jake think of Ruby Jones.

Their first date had taken place after Kiteboarding for Cancer two years ago in July. In addition to sponsoring Ruby, Jake had also pledged Queen of G's support to Harry. He sat on the lawn for hours watching the action, which was a bit tedious. Occasionally someone would boost and get some big air, but mostly it was just riders doing laps. Harry offered the best entertainment of the day when he managed to wrap lines with two other participants. The others pulled their safety releases, but Harry held on. The crowd whooped and hollered as Harry was dragged into the sandbar under the power of all three kites, eventually landing safely but disqualified.

Ruby had been among the top three fundraisers of the day. During the awards ceremony, she ascended the podium to receive her medal, her wetsuit replaced by a short red sundress that showed off her incredible legs. The emcee was congratulating the participants for raising more than $250,000, which would be used to pay for outdoor camps for young cancer survivors. Ruby leaned over and grabbed the mic.

"Don't forget our sponsors, man! We couldn't do it without them."

The crowd hollered and clapped.

"I'd personally like to thank Jake Stevenson with Queen of G Honey farm. Where are you, Jake?"

He raised his hand and Ruby smiled right at him.

"There he is. The man himself. Thank you so much for your support today, Jake!"

She said some other things, but Jake didn't hear what. He only heard the sound of her voice saying his name—the sweetest sound he'd ever heard.

Later he'd asked her out or she'd asked him out. He couldn't remember and it didn't matter. She said she liked surprising and unusual first dates, so he took her to a wheelchair rugby match in Portland. When they pulled up at the East Portland Community Center, she scanned the marquee and laughed.

"Pacific Northwest Murderball Championships? Portland Pounders versus Alberta Roughnecks. What the hell is murderball, Stevenson?!"

He smirked.

"Murderball is surprising and unusual."

Inside the arena they watched the final game in the regional series of wheelchair rugby. As he explained the rules, Jake glanced at Ruby's snug jeans and tank top that showed off her beautiful arms. It was a typical match—four on four. The players were all men, aside from one woman on the Alberta team. It was a loud, physical game, the metal hubcaps on the chairs slamming together, competitors yelling and grunting as they collided, the whoosh of the ball in the net, the crash of a chair going over, the referee's whistle. Ruby seemed to enjoy it—yelling and stamping her feet. She rooted for the Roughnecks, who were not favored.

"I love an underdog," she said, flashing a smile.

The Roughnecks lost.

After the game, they went to ¿Por Qué No? with a few members of the Pounders, who were old friends of Jake's from his rehab group in Portland. Ruby chatted with Darren and Topher, laughing at their jokes and teasing back, so at ease with them. He imagined Ruby felt at ease everywhere she went.

"Did you ever play?" she asked as they sped down I-84 back toward Hood River.

"Not seriously, like those guys," Jake said. "I threw the ball around during PT sessions sometimes."

She asked him about his accident then—directly, quietly. It wasn't something Jake loved to talk about, but then people didn't often ask. People stared at his chair and seemed embarrassed when he noticed them looking. But Ruby was so easy to talk to. So he told her about it—an unlucky fall from the roof at a party and the injury to his spinal cord—T11 and T12. Ten months in a rehab center in Portland and then back to his parents' house. Losing his scholarship to Cornish College of the Arts. Ruby listened attentively and was quiet when he finished. Jake suddenly wished he hadn't said so much. This date had been going well. Why did he have to ruin it by oversharing?

Ruby exhaled.

"Well, that fucking sucks, Jake. Must have been really hard."

There was no pity in her voice, just kindness.

"It was, at first," he said. "But life moves on, and you have to decide how you want to show up, you know?"

He figured the conversation would stop there, but she kept asking questions—about how he got into beekeeping and started the business. But also about his physical life—what changes he'd had to make day to day. How he'd learned to drive with the modifications on his truck. He didn't talk with anyone about this stuff outside of his medical team—not even Alice or Harry. But he told Ruby all of it—driving, working at the farm. And before that, learning to transfer from bed to chair to shower, how he had to manage his diet, even bathroom stuff. He felt like he could tell her anything.

They were both quiet for a while then. The sun had long since set and the river was a ribbon of silver in the late summer twilight. As they took the exit to town, Ruby asked one more thing. It sounded like a question, but it was more than that. It was a series of questions, it was a wealth of answers, it was an opening door into a new world. In just three words.

"What about sex?" she said.

It seemed like the most natural thing then, following her into her apartment, finding himself in her bedroom, explaining to her how he needed to position himself. Ruby was the one who'd said she liked the surprising and unusual, and that's how Jake would have described sex with Ruby. She was open and free with her body, and it made him feel the same. She wasn't embarrassed or hesitant, listening to him explain what he needed. When she touched him, she was intuitive and generous. Her skin against his skin, her mouth, her hands, her hair falling around him. Jake felt himself open up and his world expanded. His teenage love affair with Amri, which had reawakened his newly mended body, had been a sweet pleasure. And he'd hooked up a couple of times with a woman in Portland. But loving Ruby was something altogether different. It was intoxicating and all-encompassing. Driving home the next morning he looked at himself in the mirror. He saw himself, for the first time in a very long time, as desirable and attractive. It was a powerful feeling.

"You lucky fucker," he said to his reflection.

For the rest of the summer, they saw each other almost every day. Jake was in love, and he suspected Ruby was too. Sitting together at the kite beach, drinking beer at pFriem, or hanging out at the farm, they were always near each other, touching. Holding hands or leaning shoulder on shoulder, knee to knee. It was everything Jake had ever wanted, everything he'd ever imagined. It was everything. And then one day it was just over.

It happened on the Monday of Labor Day weekend. Jake had been busy prepping for fall harvest and Ruby was competing in the Red Bull Big Air Send at the waterfront. It was the last competition of the summer season in Hood River, and she'd entered it on a lark.

"I really gotta start thinking about snowboarding season," she'd said. "I'll start weight training next week or the kids will ruin me."

Ruby would be teaching youth snowboarding at Mt. Hood Meadows as she had for the past two winters. Jake reasoned that since the farm was closer to the ski area than Ruby's place in town, it made practical sense for her to move in with him. He was going to ask her over dinner. The idea made his heart thrum with happiness, and he sped through his chores that morning so he could make it to her afternoon competition.

Her heat had already started when he got to the waterfront, and Jake hurried to the viewing area to watch. He spotted Ruby in her signature orange shorty wet suit speeding across the river. She turned back toward the judges' platform and loaded up her kite, then boosted hugely. The crowd whooped and clapped.

"Number thirteen, Ruby Jones!" the announcer barked over the loudspeaker. "The Woo Meter just measured thirty-five feet for that boost. Looking good, Miz Jones!"

Ruby, speeding back toward the north side of the river, suddenly reversed direction. She jumped again and when high in the air let go of the bar. She fell back toward the water, arms dangling and twin braids cascading in a perfect deadman. The spectators went crazy for it, and when she pulled out of it and stuck the landing, they roared their appreciation. Ruby's brilliant smile was visible from halfway across the river.

After the competition, it took him a while to find her. The grass was crowded and hard to navigate. He saw her by the judges' table besieged by admirers. Jake made his way toward her and called her name over the thumping bass of the music.

Their eyes met and he raised a hand, thinking how gorgeous she looked. She smiled when she saw him but her smile changed as he neared. When he reached her, he grabbed her hand.

"Babe, you were awesome! Deadman, I mean, deadwoman, right? So old-school!"

She smiled but didn't lean down to kiss him as she normally would have.

"Jake, this is Rob Henly. He works for SkyFly," she said. "Rob, this is Jake Stevenson. He owns Queen of G Honey. They were one of my Kiteboarding for Cancer sponsors."

Jake recognized the guy as a sales rep for SkyFly, one of the biggest local kite companies. Jake had seen him at other events that summer—forty-something, tan, and fit.

"Nice to meet you, Jake," Rob said, nodding. "Will you be sponsoring Ruby for winter too? If so, we should talk so there's no redundancy. Come find me at the booth later."

He pulled Ruby into a side hug.

"Great job today, kiddo. They're going to love you on the south circuit."

He strode off and Jake stared at Ruby, feeling a cold punch in his belly.

"Winter season? South circuit? What's that about, Ruby?"

Ruby sat down on a bench and faced him. She smiled her beautiful smile, and her eyes brightened with tears.

"I got sponsored! SkyFly is going to pay me a salary and cover all my gear and travel for the winter circuit."

Jake stared, his heart slowly sinking toward his feet.

"Travel? Travel to where? And when?"

Mexico, she said, and Brazil and South Africa and Spain if she did well.

"But—but—what about working on the mountain?"

He stammered and hated himself for it.

"You said you loved that job."

Ruby sighed and looked away.

"I thought you'd be happy for me," she said.

She sounded annoyed and Jake felt like everything was sliding away from him.

"Of course I'm happy for you, Ruby. If it's what you want," he said, "I'm all for it."

Liar, he thought. Fucking liar. But she had turned back toward him and was beaming.

"It is! Oh, it is! I'm so stoked. We're leaving next week, and I still have so much to do before I go, but it's going to be amazing!"

"Next week?" Jake said. "Wait. How long have you known you were leaving?"

Her smile dimmed and she looked away again. When she turned back he read the irritation in her eyes.

"Does it matter, Jake?"

He didn't say anything and felt his insides crumbling.

She picked up his hand and kissed it.

"It's been really fun, Jake. But this was never a serious thing. We both knew that, right?"

Jake couldn't speak, and, in his silence, she began talking about everything she needed to do. Finish packing her things and clean the apartment, and sell her car. And how just now she needed to go talk to Rob and the other riders but if he wanted to wait, they could grab dinner in a bit. She kissed his cheek and walked away. He watched her go and then stared out at the river. The wind had dropped and the water was flat, reflecting the fiery September sunset back to the sky. Jake felt like he'd been hit by a train.

He did wait for her. For a long time. He watched her chatting with people at the SkyFly booth—big, burly riders. Chance Deltmore was among them. There was one other woman, a petite blonde named Kitty who'd dated Harry briefly. Ruby finally glanced over at him and held up a finger.

"Who's that?" someone asked.

"Jake Stevenson," he heard Chance say, his voice carrying across the grass. "He was in our class, remember? Fucked himself up right before graduation."

"Oh right, I remember. So what—is he your community service project this summer, Ruby?"

Someone laughed.

"Don't be an asshole, Neals," Ruby said, but she didn't sound angry, or angry enough anyway. Jake turned away so he couldn't see her face. After a few minutes, he left, and she didn't come after him. That night was the first he'd slept alone in weeks, and he'd never felt so lonely in his life.

Ruby dropped by to say goodbye a few days later. Said she was sorry she'd been so busy. She kissed him deeply and said she'd be back for Christmas. She'd keep in touch. But she hadn't been back, and she hadn't kept in touch. Through her Instagram feed Jake watched her travels, her competitions, her wins. He saw her funny pictures at foreign airports and beach bars. He saw her with her team members. Then increasingly the face of Neals. Pictures of the whole team, then just Neals's competition photos, then photos of the two of them—margaritas at sunset and beach walks at sunrise. Jake stopped looking after that. He tried to forget her. He finished harvest and spent winter planning. He leaned hard into the honey business and teaching classes at the elementary school. Then, one spring night, just over a year ago, Ruby had shown up on his doorstep, back in town between seasons. Jake held the door open and thought of every hurtful thing he wanted to say.

"I wanted to see you," Ruby said.

And it was enough for him to let her in.

She was gone when he woke up the next morning. And his wounded heart broke open all over again. He couldn't eat, didn't leave the house for days, wouldn't answer his texts. On the third day, Alice banged on the door and demanded to know what the hell was going on.

"Ruby came by," he said.

He couldn't say anything else. He knew his heartbreak was written all over his face.

Alice paced the kitchen swearing in an extended and imaginative way about throttling the little tart. He was normally amused when Alice got her back up. It would have made him laugh if he hadn't felt like he was dying.

He didn't hear from Ruby again. He worked hard on the company and picked up his trumpet again, playing at a weekly jam in town. He saw his friends and had dinner with his mom once a week. He did all the things to make it look like he was okay, though he was not okay at all.

That summer, he and Alice had entered the 2018 West Coast Food and Wine Classic. That fall they had leased the meadow for the alpine apiary. Jake was feeling slightly better then. Sometimes he didn't think about Ruby all day, though she still showed up in his dreams. But he was fine. He was good. He was solid.

Until now. Until his conversation with Chase Deltmore had brought it all back.

"Community service," he said aloud. "Fucking little punk."

He sat up on the weight bench and transferred back into his chair. He wheeled over to the open shop door and looked out at the apiary. He checked the temperature on his phone and shoved it back in his pocket.

He spun around and returned to the shop, located the mite treatment caddy, and loaded up the equipment he'd need. He considered the day—the light breeze, the impossibly blue sky, the golden honeybees carrying out their tasks. It was gorgeous and perfect, as if heartbreak could not exist in such a world.

He was grateful to be alone. Evangelina had taken Flaco to meet with an immigration lawyer that morning. He liked the kid, who was a hard worker and took initiative. He was funny and a little sweet. Unlike Chase Deltmore, who was destined for a private university bankrolled by his parents, Flaco had an uncertain future. He'd come so far and was all alone.

When she came by to pick up Flaco, Evangelina had recounted the details about the cousin. As Ron said, the officer who pulled him over for a broken taillight found that his driver's license had been suspended for missing a court date for an expired work permit. That landed him at NORCOR, and when he made bail, ICE had scooped him up right outside the jail. Though he knew about the Rural Organizing Project protest, Jake still didn't entirely grasp the relationship between the two organizations.

"So is NORCOR part of immigration now? Like ICE for the county or something?"

Evangelina clicked her teeth and shook her head.

"No, it is not. NORCOR is a private entity and ICE is federal. That's why people are protesting the contract between them. It's a violation of the Fourth Amendment for NORCOR to basically release immigrants into ICE's custody. Not to mention the appalling conditions at the jail. Inadequate food and clothing, lack of access to legal representation. Some people haven't been allowed to contact their families, so nobody knows where they are."

Protesters had assembled daily outside the jail for more than a year now, Jake knew. But none of that would matter to Flaco. All this kid would understand was that his cousin, his one hope of support, was gone. Now he was at the mercy of strangers.

Jake could relate. He'd started over from scratch himself among people he didn't know. Five years ago, he'd moved in with Alice and met Harry and Amri and her family. He'd been taken in by Ron and Evangelina and their kids too. But he'd been older—eighteen to Flaco's fourteen. Moreover, he'd been in his country of origin, not to mention his hometown. Their situations were completely different.

He moved into the apiary and began mite treatments. He opened the first hive, placed the formic acid strips between the brood boxes, and reassembled the hive. He moved down the rows, opening hive after hive. He found contentment in the rhythm of simple labor.

He thought of what Chase Deltmore had said about the less fortunate. People who can't do all the regular stuff normal people get to do—like live with their parents and finish school and grow all the way up in their hometown. Whatever had pushed a sweet kid like Flaco to leave home, and all on his own, to find himself walking alone along the flank of Mount Hood—well, there was nothing normal or regular about that at all.

14

NESTING SITES

When it comes to making a home, the bumblebee queen will line her nest with the softest items nature can supply—feathers, moss, and tender grasses.

—LAVIN, *THE WONDROUS WORLD OF BEES*

THE LAWYER WAS the whitest person Flaco had ever seen. Her skin was milky, almost transparent, so that when she turned her hand, he could see blue veins on the inside of her wrist. Her palms were paler still under the fluorescent overhead light. Her platinum hair seemed to glow, and he had to look closely to see her eyebrows. The white lashes ringing her eyes made their startling violet color more pronounced. And yet her Spanish was perfect. As she spoke, he recognized the crisp accent of Mexico City, like Maestra Monica's. He couldn't guess her age. Her face was unlined, but the shocking white of her hair made her seem old.

Was she una albina? he wondered. He'd never seen a person with albinism. Only pictures in *National Geographic en Español* of people with albinism from all over the world—the South Pacific, Europe, the United States, and Cuba. Now she turned her palms downward again. Her hands moved like small white birds over the desk as she talked. She was weird and strange and fascinating.

"Don't stare at people who are different from you, mijo."

He could almost hear his mother's voice in his head. Ashamed, he raised his eyes and looked into her face. She seemed serious but not unkind.

She'd asked for his full name, and he said Sebastián Santiago Luna López. She'd asked what his mother's name was and he said Beatriz López. She asked what grade he was in, and he said the last year of secundaria. He did not say he was the smartest boy in his class and perhaps the whole village of Las Lunas. But he thought it to himself.

"We're just going to talk a bit today so I can get to know you a little, okay, Sebastián?"

He nodded. He wasn't about to tell her nobody called him Sebastián and that he went by Flaco. She seemed so serious but maybe all lawyers were. He'd never met one before. Las Lunas only had a traveling notary who came to town once a month and took appointments at the post office. Hood River didn't seem like a very big town, but this building alone had twelve lawyers listed in the lobby.

The lawyer was asking the señora a question and Flaco's gaze strayed to the posters on the walls in Spanish.

"All are welcome here!"

"Know your rights!"

"You have the right to remain silent, even if an officer has a warrant. You do not have to let police or immigration agents into your home unless they have certain kinds of warrants. If police have an arrest warrant, they are legally allowed to enter the home of the person on the warrant if they believe that person is inside. But a warrant of removal/deportation (Form I-205) does not allow officers to enter a home without consent.—ACLU of Oregon"

Flaco swallowed hard, feeling sick. None of those bullet-pointed rights made him feel any safer or clearer about what was going to happen to him.

"Señora Evangelina told me you came here to meet your cousin," the lawyer was now saying.

She glanced down at her notebook.

"César Camarillo, is that right? And I understand he's been deported?"

Flaco nodded.

"I'm sorry to hear that," the lawyer said. "I'd like to hear more about how you got here, who you came with. To get a sense of your story."

He thought of Señor Rivas, and an icy fear gripped his belly. That man, the coyote, had stood in the bus aisle, appraising the group. Most were young men Javier's age plus Flaco and one white-haired viejito. Señor Rivas didn't raise his voice over the growl of the diesel engine, but Flaco heard every word. He told the group where they'd be getting off and where they'd be spending the night. He told them to stick together and not lose sight of him. Under no circumstances should they speak to him. Then he told them to keep the details of the trip to themselves.

"If you ever tell anyone you traveled with me, or which route we took, you'll be truly sorry."

His eyes frightened Flaco.

"Your people too," he said.

Señor Rivas walked to the front of the bus and sat alone. Flaco slumped in his seat feeling shaken. What did Señor Rivas mean by that—"*your people*"? Would he hurt Mamá?

Javier plopped down next to him and thumped his knee with a fist.

"Don't worry about that old fucker. Mucho ruido y nada de huevos. Besides—who would we tell, anyway?"

At the time Flaco had planned to tell Mamá about every detail once he had arrived safely at César's. She'd asked him to.

"Pay attention to all the details, mijo. You can tell me about the different mountains you see and the kinds of rock and the trees. Tell me about the little towns and the big cities."

She'd given him a small notebook with a tiny pencil tucked in the side so he could take notes. The idea had comforted him through his jarring departure. Even up to the last minute, he'd hoped his mother would change her mind, that she'd say he could stay in Las Lunas. That she'd been worried about nothing and things would be okay. But she hadn't.

He lost the little book on the third day. By then the group had ridden on two different buses and in the back of a big truck. The buses were okay, and he could pretend he was just heading into Morelia, like he once had to see President Nieto with his school. Even the truck was all right, though being the youngest, he had to ride standing up and the exhaust blowing in the back made him feel sick. But the third day everything changed. The truck left them on the outskirts of a small town in the predawn hours next to the train tracks. Señor Rivas lit a cigarette and gestured to them to gather. He exhaled a plume of smoke and pointed at the train track.

"Today you ride La Bestia," he said. "You need to be ready to climb up. If you don't make it, nobody is coming back for you. It will be here in an hour, so be ready."

He walked away from them toward a small building with boarded-up windows.

Flaco listened for the sound of the train in the distance and heard murmuring voices in the darkness. His worry blossomed into fear. What if he couldn't get up the ladder in time? What if he fell? He'd heard stories about La Bestia from a man in the back of the truck. The train route ran all the way from the Guatemalan border, he said. While they would only have to ride it for two days, some people traveled this way for weeks and thousands of kilometers. In the darkness, Flaco heard the white-haired man in his group ask if they should worry about the conductors.

"They don't mind us," someone answered. "It's the others you have to watch for. Pandillas from the cartels. Keep your guard up and be ready for anything."

Flaco did not feel ready for anything. He stood alone in the dark for a terrible hour growing more fearful. By the time he heard the rumble of the approaching train, his dread had almost reached panic. The rails vibrated as the great iron creature rounded the corner, its headlight like the eye of a monster. Flaco thought he might be sick. The train crawled into view, an ugly, thunderous machine belching black exhaust.

Then Javi was at his side, his face lit with a grin.

"Ready, Flaquito? Don't worry, güey. Just follow me and you'll be fine," he said.

Flaco became Javi's shadow. When Javi approached the track, Flaco approached. When Javi began to trot, Flaco trotted. Javi grabbed the rung of a ladder and Flaco was right behind him, pulling himself up hand over hand until he reached the top and Javi tugged him up onto the dirty roof of the railcar. Javi laughed and clapped him on the shoulder. Flaco felt a surge of adrenaline and something close to joy. He lay flat on his back and breathed and breathed. Javi leaned on his elbows and belted out the chorus of "El Rey."

"No tengo trono ni reina, ni nadie que me comprenda, pero sigo siendo el rey!"

Javi yipped like a coyote and an older man sitting nearby scolded him.

"We're not at a fútbol match, cabrón. Have some respect!"

His Spanish was soft and rounded and Flaco wondered where he was from.

"Don't worry, señor," Javi said. "Nobody cares about us up here. It's easy going from this point. Trust me; I've done this before."

The train passed under a lamppost and illuminated the man's angry face.

"Easy? Some of us have been riding for weeks. Nothing easy about it!"

Flaco saw two little girls sitting with him then. One had her head on his lap and her eyes closed. Sleeping or ill, he could not tell.

The other, sitting next to him, had a brightly colored rebozo wrapped around her shoulders.

Javi looked chastened. He held out his water bottle and the man passed it to the sitting girl. She drank, then leaned down and whispered to the second girl, who didn't move or open her eyes. She handed the bottle back to the man, who drank and returned it to Javi.

"Thank you," the man said.

Flaco lay on his back dozing and feeling the train move under his body and watching the dark sky. Later, the sun rose, and the train slowed. Flaco sat up and saw they were approaching a town.

"Do we get off here?" he asked.

Javi shook his head and began to explain something. There was a loud bang next to him and a splatter of liquid. Flaco startled as objects rained down on them.

He thought of what he'd heard that morning. Robbery and assault from gangs who preyed on the migrants riding La Bestia. "*Be ready for anything*," that man had said, but Javi was laughing and leaning over the edge of the train.

Flaco looked down and saw them running alongside—dozens of women and girls—arms arcing up as they flung plastic bags. The travelers scrambled to collect them—bags of tortillas and beans and rice. Bags of fruit and fruit juice. People yelled their thanks down to the angels on the ground. And those angels chased the train until it picked up speed. Then they stopped and waved and hollered good luck and blessings.

All around him Flaco heard laughing and crying and praises to God. He held a bag of fruit in his hands, still slightly nauseated and not hungry. He ate an orange slice, then turned to the little girl in the rebozo and offered her the remainder of his bag.

"For you and your sister," he said. "If you want?"

She thanked him and took it.

The mood was brighter after that. People talked softly and even laughed a little. Someone began to sing. The train passed under the broad branches of kapok trees. The sun was out but not too hot and the train didn't seem so bad just then. Flaco watched the hills around them grow taller and greener. His mother would like to know about that, he thought. He reached for the little notebook to write down what he'd seen, but it was gone.

"Try to sleep, Flaco," Javi said. "I'll wake you up if anything happens."

Sleep felt impossible with the noise of the train and the voices all around him, but he did sleep. He dreamed he was back in Las Lunas telling Simón and Carlos about how he had tamed the monster train by feeding it bits of fruit.

"It just wants friends like everyone else. It doesn't want to be a scary monster," he explained to them, rubbing slices of orange and piña on the sooty grill of the train.

When he awoke dusk had fallen. Javier looked somber. He heard a muffled sound and sat up. The girl and the old man were weeping over the other girl, so small and so still. Flaco missed his mother terribly then, a physical pain like some part of him was missing. He turned to Javi.

"What do we do?"

Javi shook his head and said nothing. Darkness fell and Flaco heard some of the women praying, murmuring their way through the rosary. In the morning, the old man and the girls were gone and Flaco was too afraid to ask Javier what had happened to them. Of all the miles he'd traveled before and after, that was the moment Flaco remembered most vividly and could never, ever speak of. That little girl who was younger than he was and so small. She looked like his neighbors, Rosa and Sofi.

Now Flaco startled as the electric kettle boiled and clicked off. The lawyer rose and poured water over chocolate in three cups and stirred, handing one to Flaco and another to Señora Evangelina.

"It's okay if you don't want to talk about the journey, Sebastián. Can you tell me about the place you left? It's called Las Lunas, yes? Did you grow up there or did you live somewhere else?"

Flaco sipped the chocolate, which was sweet and tasted of cinnamon.

"I was born in Las Lunas," he said. "I always lived there."

"What was it like? Can you tell me about your home?"

Flaco considered how he might answer. He could tell her that Las Lunas was a small town of approximately four hundred people on the arid side of the state of Michoacán. He could tell her that it sat at an altitude of nearly one and a half kilometers and received an average annual rainfall of less than twenty-five centimeters. During dry season, from April to November, it smelled of dust and drying guava tree leaves. Rainy season brought a carnival of scents—damp earth, wet leaves, and soaked stone. In the morning the arroyos held the prints of all the animals that wandered there at night—plodding cows, trotting foxes, the hopping prints of a pocket mouse, the swerving track of a coral snake. He could tell her about the butterflies that pollinated the mango trees, crowds of them fluttering around the sweet-smelling blossoms that bloomed in spring. He could describe the arroyos flooding in an instant with a rushing brown torrent during the rainy season. And how that water, impossibly, could disappear in a day. The only trace of it could be found in the tiny green bodies of the frogs, which emerged from the muddy banks of the arroyos to sing and lay eggs and then disappear back into the soil. Or of the red shock of nopal fruit that plumped up on the opuntia cactus, the soft mouthfeel of the sweet fruit after his mother removed the spines one by one. And sitting in the yard at sunset as the flycatchers, in soft yellows and grays, warbled sleepily in the spiky thickets of choya where they hid their nests.

Home was playing fútbol in the dusty town square with his friends. The noisy joy of Maestra Monica's classroom during Friday quiz. The church bell calling everyone to Mass. A calf bawling for its mother near an arroyo. The village dogs sending out alerts at dawn and dusk.

Home was the little house he shared with his mother. The

crowded kitchen, the stove, the smell of tortillas on a hot griddle. The neighbors all around and the sound of Frida's little girls calling to each other outside.

Home was his people and a place. It was everything that came before his departure, his journey, and that little girl on the train. Trying to put it into words felt impossible. He looked down at the cup in his hands and noticed his tears falling into the chocolate.

Señora Evangelina lay an arm across his shoulders.

"It's okay, Flaco," she said. "Take your time. Señorita Vasquez just needs to know a bit of information for her paperwork. Señorita, maybe you could tell us about the application?"

Flaco felt both deeply comforted by the señora and terribly embarrassed to be crying. He was far too old to cry and especially in front of strangers. He straightened and wiped his face on his arm.

"Yes, please," he said to the lawyer.

She nodded at him and sat forward.

"Because you are under the age of seventeen and here without parents, you are considered an unaccompanied minor," she said. "In some ways that is a good thing, at least regarding the application."

"For the green card?" Flaco asked.

From what he understood, César would help him get a green card. But what the card was for, he wasn't sure.

The lawyer shook her head.

"No, you can't apply for a green card now. You're only eligible for a green card if you have a parent who is a U.S. citizen. From what I understand that is not the case?"

Flaco shook his head.

"But don't I need a green card to work? My cousin said I could work at the orchard with him. Maybe I still can?"

The lawyer said he was too young to work legally in the United States and working without papers could jeopardize his application.

"For people like you—unaccompanied children—we find the best thing to do is apply for Special Immigrant Juvenile Status," the lawyer explained. "It will protect you from incarceration and deportation."

Flaco shuddered, recalling Señor Sergio's words.

"*You do not want to get deported, son. I promise you.*"

"How do I apply for it?"

She pushed a sheaf of papers across the desk. Flaco, glancing at the first page, saw that the text was in English with a Spanish translation following each line.

"This form, I-360, covers people in various circumstances. For you, we'll be petitioning for this."

She highlighted a section in the middle of the page.

"If you are in the United States and need the protection of a juvenile court because you have been abused, abandoned, or neglected by a parent, you may be eligible for Special Immigrant Juvenile (SIJ) classification. If SIJ classification is granted, you may qualify for lawful permanent residency (also known as getting a Green Card)," it read.

His head swam.

"For this you need to be physically in the United States and must apply before your twenty-first birthday. But it's best to apply as soon as possible to show your commitment to compliance. And you can also access more school resources," the lawyer said.

Flaco scanned the form: "Information About Person or Organization Filing This Petition. NOTE: If you are a Violence Against Women Act (VAWA) or special immigrant juvenile, skip to Part 1, Item Number 7."

Then it asked for things like alien registration number, social security number, passport number, and IRS number. Mailing address and classification requested and, confusingly, a question about spouses and children. Flaco flipped through the pages. The application went on and on. Was he supposed to fill it out in English or Spanish? It said to make a copy, but how would he do that? He didn't have a social security number or a passport number or an IRS number.

He reread the section the lawyer had highlighted: "If you are in the

United States and need the protection of a juvenile court because you have been abused, abandoned, or neglected by a parent, you may be eligible for Special Immigrant Juvenile (SIJ) classification. If SIJ classification is granted, you may qualify for lawful permanent residency."

The words blurred on the page.

". . . can take up to six months to hear back, so it's a good idea for us to get started right away," Señorita Vasquez was saying.

Flaco looked at the pages with dismay.

"I'll help you, Flaco," Señora Evangelina said. "I'm familiar with the process. Don't worry."

"In the meantime, it's important that you stay safe, Sebastián. Señora Evangelina tells me you're staying in a good place, which is great. But you should know that if immigration officers come to the house, you do not have to answer the door. You should stay quiet. Don't run, but don't open the door or let them in, and do not sign anything. Call me immediately. These are your rights, even if they try to tell you differently. Do not go with them."

The lawyer gave him a big envelope for the paperwork. The two women began chatting about something else, but Flaco wasn't listening. He was thinking about his mother. It was growing increasingly clear that his mother didn't understand how things worked here. She'd made it sound simple—the trip, his reunion with César, whom he hadn't seen since the age of six and would only recognize from photos. But then what did she think would happen? Flaco felt disloyal just thinking it but wondered if Mamá understood how strange things would be in this place.

The señora gathered her things and Flaco stood too.

"How do I pay?" he asked.

The lawyer shook her head.

"We're a nonprofit firm and there's no charge for young people your age," she said.

She looked at him kindly, almost smiling, and she did not seem so strange then.

"I'll do my best to help you, Sebastián. I promise," she said and shook his hand.

Flaco followed Señora Evangelina out into the sunshine. He stood on the sidewalk while she made a phone call. Below him, the Columbia River was covered in whitecaps and the trees on its far shore rose in a wall of green. The westerly wind stirred their branches, and snow-covered Pahto, the northern volcano, rose behind them against the blue sky.

A group of white boys on bikes zipped down the street and stopped. Flaco had never seen bicycles like the ones they rode. They had large bumpy tires and dozens of gears in the back. They were shiny and all colors—bright green and orange and blue. The boys wore helmets and gloves and colorful jerseys. They straddled their bikes, chattering and laughing. Flaco listened, trying to understand what they were saying. Their English was fast, and he only understood one phrase.

"More cowbell! More cowbell!" one boy yelled.

They all laughed together, and their laughter was infectious. While Flaco didn't know what a cowbell was or why it was funny, he laughed too. One of the boys glanced his way. Flaco smiled but the boy looked right through him like he wasn't there at all.

The one who'd made everyone laugh took off and the others followed, speeding down the street and around the corner. As they disappeared, Flaco felt his loneliness pierce him to the core.

It hit him then that his long journey, his walk through the mountains, and now this confusing application were all working toward the goal of helping him stay here.

He knew he should be grateful. So many people were helping him—Jacob and the señora and now the lawyer. But staying in the north? He'd been so busy feeling sad about saying goodbye and scared on the trip that this ultimate goal had escaped him. To stay in the north. What did that mean exactly?

A plane passed overhead, and Señora Evangelina turned away

from him. She seemed to be arguing with whomever she was talking to. Flaco heard the warning horn of a barge out on the river. The wind gusted from the west—biting his neck. He thought of the sun rising over his little town, and the dusty path from his house to school. He thought of his friends and his mother, wondering when he would see them again.

His home felt far away, impossibly far. The little house, the schoolroom, the fútbol field, and his friends, all so distant.

Flaco watched the plane as it disappeared over the far hillside. The June sunlight fell full on his face as he stood on the sidewalk, tourists passing by, families on holiday. Nobody noticed him standing there—the loneliest boy in the world.

15

A SOCIAL SPECIES

Solitary bees live alone—building a nest, foraging for food, and raising their offspring without the aid of others. Most of the world's bee species are solitary.

—LAVIN, *THE WONDROUS WORLD OF BEES*

ABIGAIL SEETHED. EVERY step was a stomp, her arms swinging as she strode away from the field camp along the double fall line of the meadow. Her body was electric with anger, her mind racing with everything she could have said. Everything she *should* have said. She halted, whirled around, and headed back toward the field camp toward *him*, toward *Dwight*. That asshole who had ruined *everything*. Then she remembered the look on Casey's face. The look on the others' faces. They thought she was nuts. She yelled her frustration at the sky. She yelled to keep from crying. Then she wheeled around again and kept walking.

When Casey had emerged on the trail, smiling and calling hello, Abigail's heart had leapt. Maybe Casey was excited to see her? Maybe Abigail could still thank her for her help with the slideshow? Could they be friends? Casey's smile broadened and Abigail raised a hand. Then Abigail recognized the guy from the equipment room behind her. The one who'd told her to go fuck herself. Apparently, he'd managed to get himself assigned to the field team, despite all the disadvantages of being a white man among women in the sciences, as he'd raged.

Like the sun ducking behind a cloud, Abigail felt her excitement eclipsed by dread.

"Abigail! How's it going? It's so beautiful up here!" Casey called.

Despite the fact that she was carrying a large pack on her back and a smaller one on the front, she moved with surprising speed. When she reached Abigail, she unslung her baggage and stretched her arms over her head.

"What an amazing spot! Look at this place! It's incredible. I've never been up here before. Dang, that last part was steep. When did you get here?"

Casey's words flowed in a torrent and Abigail didn't know what to say. Casey didn't seem to notice. She continued prattling on about the OSU transit bus dropping them off at the trailhead and Dr. Lavin coming up with the van after her meeting with the ranger.

The guy came up behind Casey and dumped his pack with a thud.

Casey punched him in the shoulder.

"Good job, Dwight! I knew you'd make it. That's a pretty steep trail, though. You should be proud of yourself."

Dwight, sweaty and peevish, forced a smile.

"Oh, it wasn't that bad. I was just trying to make you feel sorry for me," he said.

Casey laughed like he'd made a joke, but Abigail didn't get what was funny.

"Well, here's your other pack, then, you faker! Making me carry it for you!"

She shoved the smaller pack at him, laughing. He took it from her but didn't say thank you.

"Abigail, this is Dwight. Abigail is my office mate. Do you two know each other?"

Abigail wasn't sure how to answer.

"No, we haven't met," Dwight said, smiling and extending his hand.

Abigail looked at him closely. She was sure he remembered her. But his bald-faced lie was such a surprise that she shook his hand.

"Nice to meet you, Abby."

His hand was slick with sweat. She flinched, pulled her hand back, and wiped it on her pants.

"It's Abigail," she said.

There was a strained silence.

"Well! I want to get my tent set up and go jump in the creek," Casey said. "Want to show us around?"

"Sure," Abigail said, feeling slightly better.

They walked into camp and Abigail pointed out the various areas—the spot for tents, the kitchen, the data-processing workstation, and the latrines. She showed them the food storage area and where to hang food bags out of reach of bears. She ended the tour at the campfire space where she'd staged wood for the evening's fire.

She'd followed the *US Forest Service Field Camp Handbook* to the letter, and it all made sense to her now. She felt shy but proud showing it to Casey.

"Awesome, Abigail!" Casey said. "It's so well organized. Don't you think, Dwight?"

The sweat had dried on Dwight's face and formed a rimy crust on his forehead and jowls. He frowned and squinted around.

"Well, it's not the *worst* field camp I've ever seen. But, I mean, you did make some rookie mistakes here."

"Oh," Casey said. "What do you mean?"

He gestured around them.

"I mean, if I were setting things up, I might have put the kitchen over there."

He waved toward the data-processing station.

Abigail felt a wave of nausea. For a moment she doubted herself and all she thought she'd learned. But then she remembered how she'd chosen the kitchen area specifically for drainage and the data-processing spot for afternoon shade because they would need shelter from the sun.

"And the sleeping area is okay, but you didn't seem to take into account the wind factor from the east," Dwight was saying.

Abigail smiled. Of course she hadn't accounted for the wind from the east. The wind almost always blew from the west in summer, and she'd checked the weather forecast to confirm that fact.

"And the latrine area. I don't know. I mean, you only get one chance to make sure you've got that right. Especially for you girls. Know what I mean?"

He snickered and Casey blushed.

"Oh," she said.

Abigail was furious. Of course she'd thought of that. Especially for the *girls*, as this moron had said. Anyone could see that the site she'd chosen was the most private and she'd thought specifically of the *women*.

Dwight was still talking, and with growing confidence, possibly because he'd taken Abigail's silence for agreement.

". . . food storage. Does that seem bear-proof to you, Abby? Again, I mean, all it takes is just one time and they'll be crawling all over this place and there won't be anything we can do about it. We'd have to break camp, you know, and call the ranger and deal with all that mess."

"Oh dear," Casey said. "That sounds like it could be a big problem."

She turned to Abigail.

"I'm sure you did your best, Abigail. But maybe—I don't know. Maybe Dwight could help?"

Abigail's fury rendered her speechless. The other students had begun to reach them in groups of twos and threes, high-fiving and whooping at having finished the hike.

"I mean, sure. I could help reorganize," Dwight said. "We could get everyone to help. It wouldn't take long at all."

He turned to the recent arrivals.

"Hey, you guys. Let's circle up. We need to reorganize some things."

He moved over to the fire circle and started dragging the logs off to one side.

"First things first. Let's get this crap out of the way."

Two other young men joined him and in a matter of seconds had dismantled the cozy fire ring Abigail had so carefully created. Then they moved over to the kitchen area, where Abigail had set up food prep and waste areas.

". . . yeah, let's just put this over there," Dwight said.

He and another guy began to fold up the kitchen tables. More students had gathered now.

"What are we doing?" one young woman asked.

"Um, moving camp around I guess?" said another.

"Why?"

"Dunno. Dwight's in charge," someone said.

"Nnnn-no, he is NOT," Abigail said, speaking for the first time and furious at herself for stammering. "Dwight is NOT in charge! Dr. Lavin sent ME to set up camp!"

Her voice rose in frustration, and she hated herself for it. Casey touched her arm.

"Hey. It's okay, Abigail. He's just trying to help."

Abigail closed her eyes and gritted her teeth. She tried to calm herself with the breathing exercise her father had taught her, to no avail.

"No, he is NOT trying to help, Casey," she said, struggling to control her voice.

When she opened her eyes, she saw Dwight's ugly smirk. She felt like an eighth grader again and Dwight was every bully on the playground.

"Jesus," he said, rolling his eyes. "Why don't you just chill, Abby."

And when he called her Abby for the third time, whatever string had been holding Abigail together came undone. It unleashed in her a torrent of swearing and insults that she hadn't known she was capable of and ended with her returning the invitation Dwight had extended to her in the equipment room: that he go fuck himself. Then she'd grabbed her daypack and fled.

The stomping and the crying made her tired but did seem to help in a strange way. After some time, Abigail stopped, unslung her pack, and took out her water. She rested in the grass and looked out across the expanse of wilderness. Her breathing slowed and she felt better. She ate an apple and closed her eyes, seeing Casey's shocked face and the bewilderment of the other students. She swore softly to herself and pinched the inside of her arm in the same spot as before.

"Asshole," she whispered.

Oh well. It wasn't the first time people would think she was unhinged.

She opened her compass to get her bearings. In her fit of pique, she'd hiked nearly to the northeast border of the survey area. She decided to locate the boundary marker and work her way back from there.

She wiped her face, pulled on her pack, and continued toward the northeast. The spring sunshine warmed her neck, and the western breeze kissed her left cheek. She heard a laughing croak and looked up to see a pair of crows chasing each other through the treetops. A Douglas squirrel scolded from somewhere in the branches of a fir. Feeling herself watched, Abigail halted and scanned the tree line until her eye found a red-tailed hawk perched on a snag. The petite raptor gazed back but didn't stir. As she continued walking, three deer rose out of the grass and slipped away—mother, yearling, and fawn.

Contentment.

Abigail felt it wash through her—a sense of peace that was beautiful and unexpected and so comforting.

She came over a rise and located the study boundary corner where she'd pushed a marker into the earth. Sunshine lit up a line of white on the horizon, and she recognized the honeybee hives belonging to Jake Stevenson. She recalled their meeting and her initial furious salvo, mistaking him for a rogue hunting camp developer. She cringed and wanted to pinch herself again, then saw Jake's truck parked at the edge of the field and Jake himself rolling along the raised boardwalk. Her heart rose and she walked toward him.

"Hello, Jake Stevenson," she said when she reached him.

Jake lowered the top of the hive in front of him and smiled.

"Abigail Plue," he said. "Not lost again, I hope?"

"I am not lost. I am canvassing," she said, and then realized he was teasing her. But it was friendly teasing.

"Thanks to you, I found the field site quite easily."

She gestured back the way she'd come.

"Did your field crew arrive?" he asked.

Abigail flushed remembering the shocked faces of the other students.

"Yes, they did," she said.

She was determined not to think about Dwight, and asked Jake what he was doing.

"Mite treatments," he said. "'Tis the season."

Abigail recoiled, recalling her time at the Honeybee Lab when the lead beekeeper blithely demonstrated how to murder the bees during the mite count like it was no big deal.

"Oh!" she said now. "Did you drown them in alcohol or pummel them to death with powdered sugar?"

Anger spiked through as she waited for Jake to lecture her about the importance of controlling the varroa mite population and how every hive was bound to get them and how researchers had determined this course of action and how anyone who did not follow this specific protocol might as well go ahead and give up the hive for dead. That's what the Honeybee Lab beekeeper had said when she questioned the practice. And the other honeybee cheerleaders had nodded in agreement.

But Jake only smiled.

"Neither," he said. "I use a sticky board to get a sense of the numbers, and I make notes if I see anything like workers pulling diseased larvae out, or deformed wing syndrome. I know every hive will get mites eventually. I just don't see the point in killing hundreds of bees to confirm the fact."

Her anger drained away.

"Now, in this hive, I've got something different going on." Jake said. "I found queen cells, which means this gang is on the cusp of swarming. Want to see?" he asked.

Abigail climbed up on the platform and squatted down. Jake raised the lid, and she leaned away, expecting a phalanx of guard bees, but none rose out of the hive. Jake folded back the stiff canvas that served as the inside cover until the tops of four frames were showing. Using his hive tool, he eased one out and held it up for Abigail to see.

A velvety golden mass moved about on the frame, murmuring tranquilly. Jake pointed to the bottom of the frame, where four wax pods shaped like peanut shells extended off the end.

"New queen cells! And because the bottoms have been sealed with wax, I know they're close to hatching."

"What happens when they hatch?" Abigail asked.

"Well, you're the scientist. What do you think?" he asked.

Abigail thought for a moment.

"Oh," she said. "A battle."

"Right," he said. "There's only room for one queen."

He rested the frame on the edge of the hive. Abigail reached out and touched a queen cell. The wax was warm and pliable under her fingertip. It was a beautiful sensation. How delicate and precarious this young queen was maturing in that small space.

"Just eyeballing the population, I can tell the old queen is still in here and probably preparing to swarm," Jake said. "So the first thing I need to do is split this hive so they stick around."

He opened a small wooden box next to him and slid the frame inside.

"What will you do with that?" Abigail asked.

"This will be the start of four new hives. I'll take these ladies home and separate them out so they can hatch individually. First, I'll need to locate the old queen and make sure she stays here, but otherwise—"

He stopped and looked up from the box.

"Did you hear that?"

He raised an eyebrow, and Abigail cocked an ear toward the box. Above the calm murmuring of the honeybees, a sound rang out, a golden note rising above the buzz.

"What is it?" she asked.

"One of the unhatched queens is tooting. She's letting the others know she's about to hatch. She wants to rally the workers to her cause," he said.

They were quiet, listening. Abigail heard the note ring out over the warm undertone of the murmuring bees. She thought of the bumblebees and the sound of their distinct buzz pollination that she so enjoyed. Jake had his eyes closed and looked reverent. Abigail understood that he was Calm and Content and Happy. She felt a strange mix of emotions herself: Happy, but also Happy that Jake was Happy. What did you call that?

He opened his eyes and smiled at Abigail.

"Never gets old," he said.

Abigail watched as he located the old queen on a frame. Her long, slender thorax and shorter wings distinguished her from her daughters. Jake eased that frame back inside the hive and closed the top.

"Thank you, ladies," he said quietly and turned to Abigail.

"Do bumblebee hives do this?" he asked. "Swarm?"

Abigail shook her head.

"No, not exactly. There's only the one queen for starters."

She explained how the queen overwintered alone and emerged in spring to begin her colony. She'd find a nest, make a honey basket out of wax, and survive on the food she'd stored in her crop. She'd begin laying eggs—female workers first. In this way, *Apis mellifera* and the *Bombus* family resembled each other. As the season went on, Abigail explained, the workers would begin to develop into sexually reproductive females and start to challenge the queen, their mother. She kept them in line physically—by head butting and pulling on their antennae.

"Wow, that is so interesting!" Jake said. "And then what?"

"Well, at the end of the summer, drones are produced and immediately leave the hive. They live outside after that. Those are the ones you'll see sleeping in flowers in summer. The queen dies and the life cycle of the hive is over. Female workers mate with drones. As new queens, they hibernate alone for the winter."

Jake whistled.

"All alone? Where do they hibernate?"

Abigail sat back on her heels and pointed around the field.

"Old rodent nests, tree roots. Any dry, warm spot. And in the spring, each queen starts her own colony. For a social species, they are quite solitary really."

Jake shook his head.

"And they only live for one year. It seems so short."

"Yes, it does," Abigail said. "But they do so much in that one year."

She stood and looked around.

"Is your friend here today?" she asked.

"Or is he"—she paused for effect—"out buying ammo?"

Jake looked confused and then laughed.

"Ah, right! For my illegal hunting camp."

"Kidding," Abigail said, flushing with pleasure.

She'd made a joke, and Jake Stevenson had laughed!

"No, it's just me today. Me and the mites. What about you? Where's your crew?"

A heat rose in her chest as she thought of Dwight telling her to chill out.

"Getting organized," she said tersely.

She didn't care what they thought of her, she decided. But she hated the idea of returning to see her beautiful spot filled with noisy people and her camp rearranged by *Dwight*.

"What is it you're looking for again?" Jake asked. "You said there was some particular bumblebee?"

"*Bombus occidentalis*," Abigail said. "Western bumblebee. They were quite common in Oregon until about fifteen years ago. There was a sighting last summer. Dr. Lavin, our supervisor, is hoping it's a sign that *Bombus occidentalis* is making a comeback. If it is, it could be useful in understanding how to support other bumblebee species and their insect neighbors."

Excited. That's how she felt talking about the humble *Bombus occidentalis*, the fuzzy black-and-white zeppelin of a bee that had been unknown to her just a month ago. Delighted even. She told Jake about the other endangered bumblebee species—Franklin's bumblebee, Suckley's cuckoo bumblebee, and the rusty patch bumblebee—that might benefit from Dr. Lavin's study.

"What do you think caused the decline of the one you're after? The western?" Jake asked.

Abigail pushed her hair out of her face and pondered the question.

"Habitat loss and climate change," she said. "Competition for resources, drought, and forest fire are problems too. Pesticide use, of course, is a major issue."

"Same with honeybees," Jake said. "A few years ago, we had an incident in Hood River. A new pesticide that was really toxic to the bees. A bunch of us got the county to ban it, but sometimes it all feels like whack-a-mole."

He looked at the hives stretched out in front of him, clenching his jaw. Then he smiled.

"I hope it goes well, Abigail. Your study, I mean. It sounds like really engaging work."

She stood up and nodded solemnly.

"Thank you, Jake. I wish you well with your hive splitting and mite killing."

They said goodbye and she hiked back over to the study boundary area. She felt immensely better after talking to Jake Stevenson. She pulled out her notebook, deciding to work the eastern boundary as she returned to camp.

She walked, eyes trained on the flora in front of her, and located her first specimen on the head of a penstemon blossom. She caught it, photographed it, and examined it closely before marking it in her notebook and releasing it into the air. *Bombus flavifrons*, yellowhead bumblebee.

And as she walked, she thought of the bumblebee queens awakening from the cold winter on their own, building their colonies up from nothing, and pushing on through the season. They just kept going, doing the work they were wired to do. They contributed what they could and then they died. There was beauty in that.

She lost herself in her task—paying attention to the tiny inhabitants of the remote mountain meadow waking up for summer. It was a meditation and act of service at the same time, which might be the best definition of work.

Hours passed and eventually she heard voices. She was close enough to camp to see other students scurrying around and setting up their tents. Someone had erected flags—orange and black for OSU and purple and white for UW. She saw Dr. Lavin's tall figure, hands balled into fists on her hips. Dr. Lavin turned in a slow circle and pointed at something, her voice low and carrying across the field. Abigail couldn't understand the words, but Dr. Lavin didn't sound happy.

Abigail halted, heart sinking as she weighed her options. She thought of the SUV, which, the more she thought about it, seemed damaged. Dr. Lavin would add that to her list of sins and would probably not let her try to drive it back to campus. What if she just headed to the road and walked out? She could hitchhike to Government Camp and call her dad. Of course he'd come get her. He always did. But what would he say? He'd say what he always said when Abigail experienced some kind of failure—personal or professional.

"I can't fix it for you, kiddo. You're going to have to figure it out your own way."

And she would cry and feel stupid and want to yell, but she wouldn't because it upset her dad when she did that.

She was a failure. She was a weirdo, a wacko, a loser, like she'd been hearing since she was a kid.

Remorse.

Disappointment.

Regret.

She sighed, thinking of everything she'd yelled at Dwight. She couldn't take any of it back. She didn't particularly want to either. She pulled her shoulders back, brought her chin up. The least she could do was go out with dignity. She thought of the right words to say.

"I'm sorry, Dr. Lavin," she'd say. "Thank you for the opportunity and I regret I did not meet your expectations."

"Forgive me, Dr. Lavin, sometimes I forget myself."

She walked toward the camp to face the consequences.

16

REIGN OF THE QUEEN

Each honeybee colony is united by the pheromone of its queen, who is mother to all the hive's inhabitants. A healthy queen can keep her colony thriving for years.

—LAVIN, *THE WONDROUS WORLD OF BEES*

JAKE SLOWED PASSING Hood River Valley High School as cars spilled out of the parking lot. School was out for summer, but next year's rising seniors were on campus for the annual Oregon Youth Leadership Summit, which took place each June. They yelled to one another over their competing music, laughing and excited. Windows down, stereos blasting, they were impatient to go, get moving, get on to the next thing. So much energy and endless plans for the afternoon, the summer, for their entire lives. He remembered feeling like that. He thought he knew everything back then.

He idled the truck and let a line of cars pull out in front of him. One kid honked his thanks, and Jake recognized the boy he'd seen at Carlene's Floral a few weeks earlier. Jake had stopped to pick up his mother's special order for May Day Mass. This same kid was at the counter paging through a large plastic binder while Carlene watched, arms crossed, plainly amused. She smiled broadly when she saw Jake.

"Hey there, Jacob! I've got your mama's order all fixed up. Be right back."

"Thanks, Carlene," he said.

He pivoted his chair and looked around the shop. The banner behind the counter read "Class of 2019!" The card rack was full of graduation cards. "Congratulations!" and "Felicidades!" and "We Are So Proud!" The front counter displayed prom photos from years past. There was Noah and Cece's—Noah's big hair, Cece's elegant black sheath and impossible heels.

The boy at the counter was mumbling and turning the pages of the binder.

"Damn, I don't . . ."

He turned to Jake, eyes wide.

"Bro. Corsages. I can't even?"

Jake smothered a laugh and cocked an eyebrow.

"Brutal, dude," he said. "Maybe ask Carlene."

Carlene emerged from the back with Jake's mother's May Day arrangements and helped Jake load them in the truck. He wondered how long she would let that boy suffer before suggesting he text his date and ask for a photo of her dress. That's what she'd done two years ago when Jake found himself befuddled by the process.

"It's not rocket science, Jacob," she'd said.

"I don't think Amri is like that. She might just wear, you know, jeans or something?"

Carlene guffawed.

"Trust me, honey," she said. "That girl is not wearing jeans to her prom. Text her."

Amri had responded immediately with a photo of herself in a strapless peaches and cream 1950s gown she'd excavated from her grandmother's closet. She did wear white Chuck Taylors with it, which did nothing to detract from the overall effect of her lithe beauty.

Carlene had looked smug and suggested a wrist corsage of peach and white rosebuds nestled in tiny ferns. Amri had pronounced it perfect.

Now, idling in the truck, Jake read the high school's marquee.

"Congratulations, Class of 2019! Felicidades, Clase de 2019!"

Jake hadn't attended his own graduation because he was still in the hospital. His intended future—music school and life in Seattle—had evaporated in a nanosecond. But now, six years on, the anniversary of his accident no longer weighed him down like it once had. Because the end of his old life had brought the beginning of this other completely unexpected path—meeting Alice and her honeybees, moving to the farm, dating Amri, and starting Queen of G Honey. He couldn't have imagined any of it at eighteen.

Jake began to feel impatient waiting for the line of teenagers to clear the parking lot. He crept forward and a large truck roared out of the driveway. Signs affixed to the sides and tailgate read, "Vote E.W. Dewitt: Your Law and Order Candidate!" Jake shook his head. It seemed early for such an effort with the election more than five months away.

The current sheriff, Dennis Hartford, was a soft-spoken man in his sixties. People liked him and assumed he'd stay on for years. But in March, Hartford had announced he was stepping down before the end of his term. His oldest daughter, who already had two children, was expecting twins. Dennis and his wife, Jan, were moving to Baker City to be closer to their grandkids.

Surprise over Dennis Hartford's resignation was soon eclipsed by the campaign for his replacement. Deputy Ron Ryan was competing for the position against E.W. Dewitt, a local builder. Jake recalled Dewitt's blistering message on *Faith Matters*.

"*I'll be the first to tell you*," he'd said. "*We're facing a reckoning.*"

Host Aaron Scott had egged him on, though others tried to challenge his baseless theories about a flood of "illegals" taking resources from local kids. Noah Katz's sister, Angela, a reporter with the *Hood River News*, had asked Dewitt to provide evidence for his wild claims.

"*No comment*," he'd said repeatedly, according to Angela. "*I can't reveal my sources. Surely you can respect that, miss.*"

Angela was furious and shaken.

"It was maddening," she told Jake and Noah. "He just lied and smiled like it was the most normal thing in the world to make shit up. He just wants to rile people."

A few years ago, Jake would have scoffed at the idea. Hood River was a friendly place where people mostly got along. But the 2016 election had exposed the fault lines among neighbors and even within families.

The tension over immigration was particularly unsettling. Migrant workers had always been part of the community. In the 1900s, when the first fruit trees were planted, Japanese immigrants had worked in the orchards, learned the business, and started their own farms. Latino workers first came as part of the national Bracero Program during World War II. Many stayed, started families, and became permanent residents and citizens. And yet, Jake knew Hood River's immigrant history was braided with racism. He was a junior when he learned about the Chinese Exclusion Act of 1882, which prevented the Chinese men who'd built the western railroad from becoming citizens or bringing their families over. The restrictions had effectively remained in place until Congress passed the Immigration Act of 1965. And, of course, whites had displaced Indigenous peoples in the Hood River Valley before that. The Confederated Tribes of Warm Springs, Confederated Tribes of the Umatilla, Nez Perce, and the Yakama Nation had been forced to cede their ancestral lands with nineteenth-century treaties. During World War II, Japanese American citizens of Hood River were removed from their homes and placed in internment camps around the country. Some lost everything. Their orchards, houses, and businesses were stolen by their white neighbors—some of whom had once been friends. Many never returned and those who did came back to Hood River to see signs in store windows reading "No Japs allowed." They suffered personal harassment and vandalism of their property.

As for the Latino families, the Family Reunification Act of 1987 allowed many to petition for their families to emigrate. Now Latino people accounted for more than 30 percent of the county population. Jake's high school class had been more than 40 percent Latino, yet he'd never thought much about how his Mexican American classmates' experience might be different from his. At the time he'd felt more distance between himself and his wealthy classmates—those who came to school on expensive mountain bikes or were dropped off by parents in sporty vans that cost more than his parents' manufactured home.

But five years ago, when he began teaching beekeeping classes at May Street Elementary, he'd come to understand more. He remembered asking a pair of cousins—Maria and Eugenio—if they'd been down to Mike's Ice Cream yet, which had just opened for the season. The Hood River icon was a gathering place for local families in summer. The children looked at each other and then looked at the ground and said no.

"Why not?" Jake teased. "Haven't done your chores?"

Eugenio, the shyer of the two, said nothing.

Maria's cheeks flamed.

"We aren't supposed to go down there," she said.

Jake understood then that they felt unwelcome, and he felt ashamed. After that he started to see how so many Hood River spaces seemed dominated by white people—the event site, downtown, Post Canyon. Even the beekeeping association meetings.

Now the high school traffic cleared and he drove on, pausing for a stoplight where a Dewitt billboard loomed. Blue lettering on a red background, this one read, "My promise: Anyone who engages in illegal activity in Hood River County will be prosecuted to the full extent of the law. Vote E.W. Dewitt: Your Law and Order Candidate."

The billboard showed a photo of Dewitt with his wife and their three boys, everyone smiling hugely. His wife, Cindy, seemed nice enough. She always looked very put together, as Jake's mother would say—pastel shirts tucked into Western-style jeans, her hair styled and makeup on. Jake's mother had gone to high school with her.

"Those Keller girls were all like that," Tansy said. "Everything matching, always done up and pretty, but not show-offy."

And yet, Jake recalled the time that he'd seen Cindy Dewitt looking noticeably undone. He'd stopped into Little Bit Grocery for milk near closing time. The store was quiet, and when Jake had zipped around the corner into the dairy section, he saw Cindy Dewitt staring into the milk case. She'd turned toward him looking so bereft, he almost didn't recognize her. She didn't say anything or even acknowledge him. Just hurried away empty-handed.

Smaller Dewitt signs were planted at the base of the billboard. Jake felt his pulse throb in his temples. He and Alice had put a couple of Ron's campaign signs at the top of their driveway, but he hadn't seen any others posted in town. It seemed like Ron Ryan was facing a serious PR competition.

That evening he drove to the Ryans' for dinner with Evangelina, Ron, and their sons, Ronnie and Marco. Flaco had not come, saying he didn't feel well. Evangelina looked worried at that and said she'd send a plate home for the boy. The Ryans all tolerated Cheney's banging around the kitchen before dinner, but Jake put him in the truck while they ate.

Over dinner, Jake mentioned the proliferation of Dewitt's campaign signs.

Ron sighed and rolled his eyes.

"Yes, he's been getting them out there. I just got more printed."

He leaned back and pulled a cardboard placard off the sideboard. In white lettering on a navy background it read, "Ron Ryan: Experience, Knowledge, Dependability." The other side read, "Ron Ryan: Experiencia, Conocimiento, Confiabilidad."

Both sides bore a photo of Ron in his sheriff's deputy uniform. They passed it around the table.

Marco whistled.

"Que guapo, Dad," he said. "So professional."

"Thank you, son," Ron said.

"I like how they airbrushed out all the gray hair and wrinkles," Ronnie said.

Evangelina laughed, slapped his wrist, and held up the sign.

"As handsome as our wedding day," she said.

Ron kissed her cheek.

"Dewitt says I'm pandering for the Latino vote," he said.

Evangelina chuckled.

"Obviously he doesn't know your in-laws."

Ron laughed and squeezed her hand.

Jake knew they took the election seriously despite their joking. Dewitt's radical base extended beyond the issue of immigration. Angela had told Jake that Dewitt had recently posted about the 2016 armed takeover of the Malheur National Wildlife Refuge and called the Bundy family "heroes."

"*The comments section was . . . frightening*," she'd said.

"The new signs look great, Ron," Jake said. "I'll put a couple new ones with the others at our place."

"Thanks, kid," Ron said. "I appreciate it. The boys are going to canvass for me too, aren't you?"

Ronnie leaned his chair back on two legs and stretched his arms over his head.

"I'll check my schedule, Pop. Pretty busy with the ladies."

"¡Chamaco malcriado!" his mother said, laughing, and snapped a dish towel at him.

Ron's phone rang and he rose to take the call. Ronnie and Marco cleared the table. In the kitchen they teased each other over the sound of running water and clinking silverware.

Evangelina folded the dish towel and gazed at Jake.

"I have some new information about Flaco's situation, Jacob," she said.

From her tone, he could tell the news wasn't good. He groaned inwardly. What had been an overnight favor had turned into a multiday affair. The boy was perfectly nice—polite and helpful—but Jake was growing eager for his unexpected guest to depart. He didn't want to be responsible for a teenager.

"What's the latest?" he asked.

She told Jake about Flaco's meeting with an immigration lawyer. As Jake knew, the boy's cousin was being deported and could not help. But because he was an unaccompanied minor, Flaco could petition the government on his own. It was called Special Immigrant Juvenile Status.

Ron rejoined them at the table.

"We never used to see this sort of thing, kids arriving without their parents," Evangelina said. "They've always been with families. But cases like Flaco's are becoming more common."

Ron shook his head.

"In Medford they've had kids as young as ten," he said.

He glanced toward the kitchen, where Ronnie and Marco were FaceTiming their cousin as they loaded the dishwasher. The three of them were talking over each other in a mix of English and Spanish.

"Imagine sending your kid off alone like that," Ron said.

His wife looked at him, steely-eyed.

"Exactly. What I keep asking myself, mi amor, is what would drive a mother to such extremes? How bad must things be that she'd feel her child was safer out in the world alone?"

Ron looked chastened and ran a hand through his hair. He took her hand and kissed it. Neither spoke, but Jake saw a whole conversation pass between them. Ron straightened and collected the remaining dishes.

"I have a meeting at the Elks," he said. "Thanks for dinner, honey. Good to see you, Jake."

He left and Ronnie and Marco followed. Ronnie gave Jake a fist bump on the way out and Marco banged out the door singing Lil Nas X's "Old Town Road."

Evangelina smiled.

"Tone deaf. Both of them, Lord help me. ¡Pero les echan ganas!" she said.

They both laughed.

"So, back to Flaco," she said.

"Flaco," Jake said and sipped his water.

Evangelina would help him fill out his paperwork and the lawyer would file it with the immigration court in Portland. That was the good news. The bad news was that it could take months to be reviewed. The court system was overloaded and understaffed. Realistically speaking, it might take 180 days or longer for Flaco's case to be decided.

Jake felt a heaviness in his chest. He'd hoped Evangelina would have better news—about the kid's cousin or some other local family that would be willing to take him on. He felt slightly amused by the fact that she'd said 180 days instead of six months. Maybe she thought days sounded better? She was shrewd, this woman.

"Dang. Well, Evangelina, that's a long time."

She nodded, unsmiling.

"I know it is, Jacob. I'm not asking you to commit to the entire length of time, but if he could just stay with you a while longer. I'll keep looking for other options. Everyone is busy with cherry season starting, but I'll find a family for him to stay with as soon as things settle down."

Jake looked out the window at his truck, still loaded with equipment from the mountain apiary. He had two more interviews for potential helpers tomorrow and so much work to do. If the weather forecast was correct, they'd be in full-on honeyflow soon. He ran his hands over his face.

"I just have a lot going on right now. When harvest starts, I'll have people coming and going. It's hectic. Maybe I can help later in the summer when things calm down."

Evangelina patted his hand and rose, taking his water glass.

"You don't need to decide right now, mijo," she said.

She went into the kitchen and returned with a foil-covered plate for Flaco.

"You sleep on it, and we'll talk tomorrow. I've got to run over to my mom's now, so I'll see you later."

She kissed him on the cheek and then Jake was alone in the Ryan house.

He felt peevish as he got into the truck. Cheney gazed at him from the passenger seat, looking somber.

"I totally just got mommed. She's an old pro."

The dog opened his mouth in a laugh and dropped Jake's phone charger on the seat. It was nibbled nearly clear through. Jake swore and plugged in his phone. The charge icon blinked on and off and on again. Cheney smiled and shoved his nose out the window.

As he drove south, Mount Hood rose black against the green-yellow sky. Nearing summer solstice, the days had lengthened imperceptibly, and it wasn't hard dark until ten p.m. Driving toward home, Jake thought about how he'd explain it to Evangelina. Flaco was a nice kid, and he'd been no trouble. But Jake just couldn't take on the responsibility right now. He had to focus on the farm and the harvest. They could regroup in August, he'd tell her. Evangelina Ryan had connections wide and deep in Hood River County. If anyone could find a place for the boy, it would be her. He just had to say no. Firmly next time.

A truck was pulled over on Reed Road near Alice's driveway. It was a red Ford F-350 with star-spangled mud flaps. The driver bent over next to the front tire. A flat maybe, Jake thought, as he slowed. The man yanked something out of the ground and turned, holding one of Ron's campaign signs. He tossed it in the back of his truck, then pulled the second one out.

“What the hell?” Jake said.

He pulled forward and rolled down the window. The man was hammering a new sign into the ground. “E.W. Dewitt: Your Law and Order Candidate,” it read. He turned at the sound of Jake’s truck, and Jake saw it was Dewitt himself.

“What are you doing?” Jake asked, furious.

Dewitt smiled blandly.

“Puttin’ up signs. Election season, you know.”

“Looks like you’re taking signs down too,” Jake said.

Dewitt flicked his eyes to the truck bed and back.

“Oh. Yeah. Those looked a little banged up, so I thought I should remove ’em.”

“Right,” Jake said tightly. “Thanks for your concern. Now, put them back, please. And you can take yours with you.”

Smirking, Dewitt retrieved the signs and stuck them in the ground and removed the ones he’d place by the mailboxes. He wiped his hands on his jeans, tucked a pinch of chew in his lower lip, and spit. He glanced at the mailbox, which read “A. Holtzman / J. Stevenson. Queen of G Honey.”

“Alice Holtzman. I heard she started up a little ol’ farm after she got fired from the county,” he said.

“She resigned,” Jake said, bristling. “She wasn’t fired.”

“So she says,” Dewitt said, smirking. “Difficult these days, farming. What with this flood of illegals and their phony work papers. Entrapping hardworking farmers. You folks had any trouble with that?”

“No,” Jake said. “And you’re mistaken. There’s no flood of migrants, just the same seasonal workforce as usual.”

Dewitt spit again.

“Hey, don’t feel bad. Lots of people are misinformed these days. Good thing ICE is back to local sweeps.”

Jake felt a chill pass over him.

“Got that one hombre up in the Heights just a couple of days ago. Had to wrestle him down. Law enforcement is hard work.”

Jake didn't say anything.

"They're getting anonymous tips from concerned citizens, so even little farms like this one can be monitored. Don't you worry!"

Dewitt slapped the hood of Jake's truck.

"Well. Have a great day, son," Dewitt said. "Don't forget to vote."

Jake waited until he'd driven away, then got out with the new campaign signs. The old ones were torn from top to bottom. Hot with anger, he tossed the ruined signs into the truck and placed the new ones, sweating with the effort.

Could that be true, he wondered, what Dewitt had said about ICE sweeps? Evangelina and Ron would know. And what about monitoring local farms? Reporting on each other? He wanted to believe the citizens of Hood River County were not capable of such ugliness. But he knew better. As he drove down to the house, he thought again of the newspaper articles after World War II, the threats to Japanese American residents of this same valley. And the broken treaties with the tribes, and local support for the Chinese Exclusion Act. Hood River had a long history of racism and distrust.

As he pulled into the yard, Jake saw the light on in the barn and remembered Flaco was there alone. He shuddered thinking that Dewitt had been just a stone's throw from this unprotected kid. Through the open barn door, he could see Flaco walking back and forth in the light of the shop. He seemed to be dancing or something. Flaco said something aloud, and Jake heard the unmistakable sound of female laughter.

A red Honda Element was parked outside the barn. His body prickled with irritation. Did Flaco have someone over? Had he feigned illness to hang out with a girlfriend? Annoyance surged through him as he got out of the truck and sped into the barn. Flaco turned, jigging in place, with arms akimbo, and Jake saw he was holding a baby. The baby was patting Flaco's cheek with one fat hand.

"Oh, hey, Jake," a voice said, and he turned to see the last person he expected—Ruby Jones, sitting in a chair wrapped in a blanket from the bunkroom. He opened his mouth, and nothing came out.

"Surprise?" she said, and her eyes flooded with tears.

Her thick red hair was pulled back in a messy ponytail, and she was as gorgeous as ever. He looked at the baby, the crown of red fuzz on its head, and back to Ruby. In the silence, the baby gurgled a laugh, and Jake felt an impossible idea rise in him. He thought of that night with Ruby last year and counted forward. He looked from the baby to Ruby with eyes wide.

"Is that—" He couldn't finish the sentence. Was he a *dad*?

Ruby laughed softly and shook her head. Twin tears spilled down her cheeks.

"No," she said. "Jesus. Sorry. I didn't think about that."

She wiped her face on her arm.

"I met his dad in Baja. It's nobody you know. We aren't together. Just a brief thing."

The emptiness in his heart yawned wider. Why did that make him feel worse?

Flaco was bouncing the baby and singing in Spanish. The baby laughed and reached for Flaco's nose.

What the hell are you doing here? Jake wanted to ask. How could you just show up?

"What's its name?" he asked instead.

"Samuel," Ruby said, wiping a hand across her eyes. "After my grandpa. He's a hell-raiser, like Grampy. Doesn't sleep much. Flaco here, he's like a baby whisperer. Finally got him to stop crying."

She looked like she might start crying herself.

"Good baby. Strong toes," Flaco said.

He held up his thumb and Samuel wrapped his tiny fingers around it and laughed. Flaco's smile dimmed.

"I think he make caca?" he said.

Ruby stood and took the baby.

"I'll be right back," she said, and walked out into the night toward her car.

As she passed, Jake smelled the familiar scent of her—citrus and sunlit grass, spring rain and heartbreak.

Flaco looked at him.

"What is baby whisper?"

Jake typed it into his phone.

"¡Susurrador de bebés!" Google Translate announced.

Flaco looked puzzled and Jake tried to explain.

"It's from an old movie. About horses. It means, like, magician. That you're good with babies. You like babies."

"Everyone like babies, no?" Flaco said.

Jake shrugged. Suddenly he felt exhausted.

"Sure, Flaco. I guess so."

Ruby returned with Samuel. He bounced and shrieked, pointing at the overhead light.

"Yes, it's a light, baby," she said and turned to Jake. She was still stunning despite her obvious fatigue.

"Ruby," Jake said. "It's great seeing you, but I have an early day tomorrow. So . . ."

She looked startled and he couldn't quite believe himself either. He was asking her to leave? In the past, Ruby did what Ruby wanted and Jake dealt with the consequences. But now he just couldn't.

"Oh! Sorry! Yeah, of course. I just . . ."

She trailed off and glanced down at Samuel and then back at Jake. Her eyes shone with tears.

"Could I— Could we crash? Sorry to ask, but I'm wiped out. I drove all the way from Bishop today and I don't want to wake up my grandma this late. Just for one night. Do you mind?"

He knew he should say no. He should suggest she go stay with one of her teammates or one of her fabulous friends that she'd tagged in her Instagram feed for the past two years. Or her SkyFly sponsors. They were her people now, weren't they?

"Sure. No problem," he said, hating himself. "Flaco is in Alice's room, but Harry is gone so you can have the bunkroom."

"Thank you, Jake! Thank you so much! I super appreciate it."

Her naked gratitude made him feel worse. He did not want to feel sorry for her. She laughed and it came out as a sob.

"It's better if we're out here because this little guy likes to party late and get up early."

Samuel cooed. He was a very cute baby.

Flaco gathered Ruby's things from the car, and Jake flipped on the lights in Harry's room and found clean towels. Ruby set Samuel down on the bed. She turned suddenly and bent to hug Jake. The familiar scent of her overwhelmed him.

"Let's talk in the morning, okay? I have some things to tell you," she said.

He heard tears in her voice as she whispered her thanks. He couldn't look her in the eye for fear she would see his desperation.

"Sure," he said. "I'll see you in the morning."

He went inside and got ready for bed. Later he heard Flaco's door click shut. He lay awake, exhausted, sleep eluding him. The moon rose over the east hills and sailed across the valley. It hung there luminous and unfeeling as it probed the depths of his heart.

It started to rain. The patter on the roof began lightly at first, and then the sky opened. Thunder rolled across the valley and the room lit up with a flash of lightning. Jake reached up and slid the window open. Cool air rushed across his bare skin. The unexpected rain would bring relief from the rising temperatures and would slow the race toward honey harvest. The unexpected gift of it opened something in his heart.

Of course he still loved her. Of course he would do anything for her. Maybe she needed him. Maybe he could help.

His heart swelled at the thought. She needed him. He could be there for her and help her with the baby. It didn't matter that Samuel wasn't his. They could be a family.

Hope sparked within him. Yes, this was the answer. Ruby and Samuel could stay. He could help her with the baby and she could help him with the farm. The thought filled him with such relief that he almost got up and went out to her. But no, he would let her sleep. He would explain in the morning.

It made even more sense now that Flaco should go. Flaco would go, and Ruby would stay and they would sit under the apple trees and make their plans. Together.

He awoke early with hope blooming in his heart. He got up, dressed, and hurried outside. A fresh breeze gusted across the yard. The leaves of the apple trees glinted with last night's rain and the meadow was alight with the golden bodies of honeybees. The sun winked through the clouds dispersing over the east hills.

Before he reached the bottom of the ramp, he saw that the parking space next to his truck was empty, as empty as the bottom of his broken heart. Ruby's car was nowhere in sight. He crossed the yard and went into the barn. The door to the bunkroom yawned open. The blankets were folded neatly and the towel hung—the only signs that anyone had been there. And just like that, Ruby Jones was gone again.

17

DEPARTURES

As soon as they're able to fly, bumblebee males, called drones, depart the colony. That bumblebee you see slumbering in a blossom at dawn or dusk is likely a drone at rest. They live in the open until the winter ends their brief life cycle.

—LAVIN, *THE WONDROUS WORLD OF BEES*

THE BABY'S LAUGH was a golden bubble floating through the air and out into the night. So round and perfect, Flaco imagined he could catch it in his hand. Such a cute baby. Samuel, the woman had said his name was. Back home it would be pronounced as only two syllables. In English or Spanish, it was a big name for such a small baby.

The baby's laugh woke Flaco from his sleep, and he lay in bed listening for it again, thinking about baby Samuel and his mother.

She said her name was Ruby and that she was an old friend of Jacob's and that she'd come by to surprise him. She'd been living in Mexico for the last couple of years—Baja and Yucatán and Cancún. Her Spanish was good, far better than Jacob's. She was so pretty—red hair and blue eyes. She was easy to talk to and Flaco realized he hadn't spoken to anyone at length in weeks—only Jacob and the señora, and with them it was mostly serious stuff. But talking with Ruby was fun. He couldn't remember the last time he'd had any fun.

She told him about her travels around Mexico and all the towns she'd seen and the different foods she liked. Right before Jacob returned, Ruby had told him about the seven moles of Oaxaca—colorado, negro, poblano, verde, amarillo, manchamantel, and chichilo. She told him about the torta ahogada of Guadalajara. In Baja the thing she loved most was the pitaya fruit. She couldn't get enough of it when she was pregnant with Samuel, she said. She'd wake up in the night thinking about it and couldn't go back to sleep. Flaco felt embarrassed when she talked about being pregnant. His eyes strayed to her belly, which was flat as a rock under her shirt, and then to the baby, with his fat knees and plump arms. The idea that Samuel had been inside Ruby's body made Flaco squirm. And yet he knew where babies came from, knew that he had resided in his own mother's belly before emerging into the world. He'd seen his neighbor, Señora Frida, pregnant with both her girls. It was an amazing thing that mujeres could do. Still, it made him uncomfortable.

Ruby asked what people ate in his village. What was the traditional food of Las Lunas, Michoacán? He shrugged and said he didn't know. Nothing special. Just regular food.

"Regular food," she'd repeated, laughing. "What does that mean?"

"Not fancy, like the seven moles or ahogada. Just normal food."

"Food doesn't have to be fancy to be good," she said. "Like, what is your favorite thing your mom makes?"

He'd answered immediately: Caldo de res. Thick caldo de res with a stack of fresh corn tortillas and piquin salsa. Caldo de res with corn, potatoes, and chayote.

"Everyone makes caldo de res at home, but my mamá's is the best."

"Bingo! Mamá's caldo de res sounds pretty special to me," she'd said, smiling.

She asked if Flaco had met Jacob's friends Noah and Cece. They owned a bakery in town and made the best bread, she said.

"No, I haven't met them," Flaco said.

Now Flaco rolled over in bed and listened as the golden burble floated again across the yard from the barn. Fully awake now, he realized it was not the laughing baby but the extended clucking of a chicken. One of the bigger hens liked to celebrate when she laid an egg.

Flaco rose and dressed quickly, excited to see Ruby and Samuel. He hoped they'd slept well. He'd offered his room in the house, shyly, thinking it a more appropriate place for a señora than the rustic bunkroom. She thanked him but said Samuel woke up during the night and she didn't want to disturb them. Flaco had left her sitting cross-legged on the bed in the bunkroom cradling Samuel, whose eyes had grown heavy with sleep.

"Hasta mañana, Flaco," she'd said. "Sleep well."

He didn't even know her, but she looked so peaceful, so pretty sitting there with the baby, that he wanted to hug her. The thought made his face flame, and he mumbled good night.

Flaco pulled on socks and shoes. Samuel wouldn't have disturbed him if he cried in the night. He'd helped take care of Rosa and Sofi when they were babies. He'd liked holding Samuel. Such a happy baby. Flaco hadn't seen any babies or little kids at all since he arrived in Oregon. Younger kids were such a part of life in Las Lunas, he'd never really thought about it. It made him feel so happy to watch the baby do baby things—try to put his whole hand in his mouth; his surprised laughter when Flaco made silly faces; flapping his fat little hands to the music on Ruby's phone; giggling as Flaco danced him around the barn.

He hurried out to the kitchen, expecting to find Jacob making breakfast. But the room was empty and the counters clear. Jacob's door was closed. He must be out in the barn with his guests or still asleep.

The dog slithered off the couch and stretched, greeting Flaco with a snapping yawn. Flaco opened the door, and the dog ran out toward the orchard.

Flaco walked quickly toward the barn. If Jacob was still sleeping, he would ask Ruby if she was hungry, and he could figure out how to make breakfast. Jacob had shown him huevos revueltos and also fried. And oatmeal. Ruby herself had said good food didn't need to be fancy. Halfway across the yard, he realized the red Honda was no longer parked there. Disappointment stopped him in his tracks and a dark loneliness pressed down on him.

In the barn, he confirmed that the bunkroom was empty. The bed was neatly made and there was no sign of Ruby or Samuel. Had she and Jacob gone somewhere together? Or maybe they were inside the house. He trotted back to the house and stood in the living room. There was no sound coming from behind Jacob's closed door, and his sunglasses, keys, and phone were in the kitchen.

He returned to the shop area and sat in the chair Ruby had occupied the night before. The guitar was still there, resting where she'd left it. While Flaco was holding the baby, she'd pulled the guitar off the wall and sat down.

"Do you play?" she asked, twisting the pegs at the top of the neck and bending an ear to listen.

Flaco shook his head. Abuela Patricia told him his father had played the guitar, but Flaco never had.

Ruby strummed for a while and then picked out a melody. He liked it and he told her so when she finished.

"I used to play more," she said.

Then Samuel started to cry, and she set the guitar aside and took the baby from Flaco. She pulled up her shirt and Flaco looked away, blushing, as the baby nursed.

Ruby smiled at him.

"Don't be embarrassed, Flaco. It's how all baby mammals eat."

He reddened to the tips of his ears and pretended to look at something on the workbench until she pulled her shirt down again. He took the baby back and helped him burp, hoping she would play another song. But she wrapped herself in the blanket and leaned back in the chair looking tired.

"Maybe later," she'd said. "I'll show you a couple of chords if you want."

But now she was gone.

The crunch of gravel under tires made his heart leap; he was thinking she'd returned. But it was only Señor Sergio's truck coming down the driveway. He waved as he passed and Flaco heard him singing along to the radio.

Flaco sat on the stool at the shop bench. There, with the workbooks and dictionary Señora Evangelina had given him, he'd left the paperwork from the lawyer. He pulled the pages out of the big envelope. Though Señora Evangelina had said she'd help him, she hadn't had time since the afternoon she took him to see the lawyer. He thought he'd see how far he could get on his own. Yet even the first page was confusing. It asked for "Information About Person or Organization Filing This Petition." Was he supposed to put his own information there or the lawyer's?

The page asked for things like mailing address. Should he put Jacob's address or his mother's? Or the lawyer's?

Blessedly, some answers he knew: name, date of birth. But then passport number? Social security number? Date of arrival? Arrival where?

Then these questions:

"Has it been determined in judicial or administrative proceedings that it would not be in your best interest to be returned to your or your parents' country of citizenship or nationality or last habitual residence?"

"Has a juvenile court determined that reunification with one or both parents is not viable due to abuse, neglect, or abandonment?

His eyes lingered on the first question.

Not in his best interest. What had Mamá said?

"It's for your safety, Sebastián," she'd said when he'd tried to talk her out of sending him away. She rarely used his given name, which underscored the gravity of the situation.

"I can't protect you if you stay here. Not now, not after Carlos—"

Her voice broke and she didn't finish.

The last time Flaco had seen Carlos, who'd left Las Lunas a couple of weeks before he had, Carlos had bragged about getting a smartphone to Flaco and the other boys. He'd left it at his house, he'd said that morning at school, but would show them TikTok if they came over in the afternoon. Nobody in their school had a smartphone and Flaco didn't quite believe his friend was telling the truth. One of Carlos's pranks, surely. But he'd talked about it all day, bragging about funny videos he'd been watching and cool music.

After school Flaco checked in with his mamá at the panadería and then ran down the path to Carlos's house as he so often did. Simón and Tomás were already there. Sure enough, they had a phone in their hands. They were hunched over the small screen giggling.

"A sexy dance video," Carlos said, rolling his eyes.

"El Guincho," someone said, and there was Tonio leaning in the doorway. "Dude is the shit."

Carlos's older brother, Tonio, had been gone for two years, and Flaco felt happy to see him. He'd always treated Flaco like a little brother. But now as Flaco moved to embrace him, something in Tonio's face made him stop. Tonio held out his palm and Flaco slapped it awkwardly, feeling uncool.

"Flaquito—look at you. Grown so tall, güey."

Tonio lifted a can of beer to his lips and drank. He stepped out of the doorway into the light of the yard. He looked the same to Flaco, mostly. His hair was shorter, and he had a small mustache. His jeans were pressed, and he was wearing a white guayabera like he was dressed up for something. But his face seemed different somehow. His smile had changed.

The phone, it turned out, was Tonio's, and he was letting Carlos borrow it.

"Or maybe I'll let him keep it for a while. Depends on if he's willing to work for it."

Carlos's face lit up.

"Of course I am, Tonio!"

Tonio set down his beer and pulled out a pack of cigarettes. He held it out to Flaco, who giggled, thinking he was joking. Carlos took one and looked at Flaco, defiant, as Tonio lit it for him.

"What?" Carlos said, holding the cigarette awkwardly. "We're old enough now."

Flaco didn't respond and glanced at Simón and Tomás, who were both engrossed in the phone. When he looked up, Tonio was watching him and not smiling. He didn't like how Tonio was making him feel and wished he hadn't come over in the first place.

"I forgot. I have to be home for . . . something," he said finally.

"Stay a while," Tonio said. "I want to catch up with my chamaquitos! I brought you something."

He reached inside the door and pulled out a plastic bag. He upended it on the table and candy poured out. Simón squealed and grabbed a handful of Paleta Payaso. He ripped the wrapper off one and crammed it into his mouth. Tomás took a handful of caramels.

"Thank you, Tonio!" Tomás said. He and Simón stared at the phone, chewing noisily.

Flaco backed toward the path.

"Thanks anyway, Tonio. Bye, Carlos. I'll see you tomorrow."

He turned and ran toward his house, not caring that it might seem rude or strange. He didn't know why but he wanted to get away. Behind him he heard Carlos yelling at him to wait. Flaco slowed to a walk and his friend caught up with him.

"You don't have to go home, Flaco. Why are you being weird? Tonio just wants to hang out and talk with us. He invited me to come visit him in Morelia when school lets out next month. And he said I could bring you guys. He said we could work for him. It would be awesome! We could earn money to buy our own phones and stuff. Real fast, like in a week. He said his boss always needs responsible kids."

Flaco kept walking, looking down at his feet.

"My mamá won't let me go to Morelia to stay with Tonio, Carlos. And I don't think your mamá will either."

Carlos jostled Flaco with his shoulder.

"Don't be such a baby. We're grown now. We can make our own decisions. We're the men of our houses."

Flaco stopped walking and looked at his friend. That sounded like something Tonio would say. Carlos's dad was dead, and Flaco's was gone. How did that make the two of them men?

"I don't think so, Carlos. Thanks for asking, though."

He turned to walk up the path to his house and Carlos grabbed his arm.

"Please, Flaco. Come on. He wants me to go with him. I'm . . . I don't want to go by myself, and Simón and Tomás won't follow through. You know how they are. All talk, no action."

Carlos sounded funny, almost like he was going to cry, and wouldn't meet Flaco's eyes.

"He said we could just be doing errands and stuff for the boss who runs the avocado plantation. He said maybe they would give us bikes. You're smart and good with directions. You'd be really good at it."

Flaco felt proud that Carlos thought he was smart and that he would ask him over the others, but still he shook his head.

"Thanks anyway, Carlos. But I don't think so. I mean, Morelia?"

He thought of all he'd heard about the capital city—the crime there, the way the police weren't even in control of things.

"I don't know. Maybe you should talk it over with your mamá? I mean it sort of sounds like you're afraid."

He meant it kindly. Carlos was his best friend. But Carlos's face flushed with anger.

"Why would I do that? She doesn't know anything! You don't know what you're talking about either. You big fucking baby!"

He threw a fistful of candy at Flaco. The colorful packets hit him in the chest and scattered in the dirt at his feet. It didn't hurt, but Flaco suddenly wanted to cry as Carlos turned and ran down the path back toward his house. That was the last time Flaco saw him. Carlos left with Tonio that same night.

Their mother, Ana, came by early the next morning, her face drawn with worry, asking if Flaco had seen Carlos that day. Flaco told her no.

"Maybe he's with Tonio."

"Tonio?" she said. "Why would he be with Tonio? What are you talking about, Flaco?"

Flaco told her about seeing her older son at the house the previous day.

"He said we could come work for him this summer."

Ana fell to her knees like she'd been struck and began to weep. Flaco stood staring and then Mamá was there, pulling Ana inside. Ana gripped her hand, wailing, and Flaco remembered that Ana had banned Tonio from her house. The last time he'd visited, two years ago, he'd shown up in a new car with presents for her—perfume and nice clothes. He'd bragged about working for the cartel, and she'd told him to stay away. Now he'd come back for Carlos.

"Carlos, my son. My sweet Carlito. He's lost to me. Both of them. My sons, my sons!" Ana sobbed.

Carlos's desk was empty at school. During roll call Maestra Monica asked if Carlos was sick. Nobody said anything. During recess, Flaco found Simón and Tomás sitting in the shade just off the playing field. They were throwing rocks against the side of the bathroom building.

"Carlos didn't want to go," Simón said. "Tonio made him. He said it was only a matter of time for the rest of us."

"He said he'd be back next month," Tomás said. "He said not to be stupid and be ready to go to Morelia. He said to tell you."

Flaco didn't know what to say.

By nightfall, everyone knew Carlos had left for Morelia to work with Tonio. The next day Mamá told Flaco she was sending him north.

Flaco could hear the music from Señor Sergio's truck parked somewhere nearby.

He looked down at the form.

". . . reunification with one or both parents is not viable due to abuse, neglect, or abandonment?"

No, that wasn't it at all. He hadn't been abused, neglected, or abandoned. His mother had sent him away to protect him. But nowhere on the form did he see a place to include that.

He felt a terrible sorrow then, a deep and bottomless sense of loss. Certain things, it seemed, were gone from his life, and he would never, ever get them back.

He'd lost Las Lunas, which had been such a happy place to be a boy. And the "peek peek" of the flycatchers that nested around the village, the plaintive coo of doves. Maestra Monica's classroom, which smelled of the manzanilla that she hung in dried bunches. Her collection of books and maps that had opened the world to him. The playing field, where he ran side by side with Carlos and Tomás and Simón, running as fast as they could, hearts pounding and heads sweating, still feeling like kids. His own house at dusk. He could almost see it—the open door, the sound of the radio playing in the kitchen, and his mother making dinner, his mother waiting for him. Always happy to see him. Smoothing his hair back, kissing his forehead, calling him "mi vida." Calling him "amorcito." "Querido."

It all seemed lost to him, and not just by distance. If he could return this very minute, if by some magic he could be transported to the sandy yard outside his house, things would never be the same again anyway. Those days were gone and so was the person he had been. Who was he now?

His heart was a knot in his chest, a terrible snarl that felt like it would never come undone.

A gust of wind blew across the yard, stirring the branches of the fruit trees, which flung off droplets of water from the night rain. The music from Señor Sergio's truck was more audible now. Flaco remembered hearing this song back home. It was one his mamá liked.

He thought of the little girl he'd seen swimming in the Columbia River. Her mother and aunties nearby on a blanket, laughing and chatting, calling to the girl and the other little kids in the water to stay close, to not go too deep. He saw them holding the smallest children by the hands as they toddled on unsteady legs. His mother would have liked seeing them, those families. She was outgoing and everybody liked her. If Beatriz López had been with Flaco, she would have learned all those ladies' names and all the kids' and remembered them the next time she saw them. She was like that.

He thought of the sandbar, that broad expanse of silty sand spilling into the grand Columbia River, which roiled with whitecaps and wind pushing east. And that river, which had once risen to thousand-foot floodwaters, now placidly flowing west. The sight of Mount Hood rising in the south over the green hills of the valley. The old volcano, now quiet and covered in snow, that had formed this whole valley. She would have liked that too.

¡Qué chido! she would have said. How beautiful! Maybe she would see it someday, Flaco thought. And the idea comforted him. Maybe if he was allowed to stay, his mamá could come visit. She could fly on a plane to the city of Portland, where the airport was. And Jacob or the señora could help bring her to Hood River. And if he was staying at Jacob's house, he would give Mamá his room and he would sleep in the bunkhouse. And Mamá would make caldo de res and it would taste so good that Jacob would tell her she could stay as long as she wanted. He imagined taking his mamá down to the water, calling hello to those tías and mamás and kids picnicking on the grass. And he'd lead her out into the middle of the river on the sand. He'd turn her around so she could see the mountain and tell her how he'd walked right past it. He'd tell her that underneath that beautiful white face of snow there was a heart of fire. When he explained how the rush of ancient floodwaters formed the gorge, her face would open up with surprise and delight. The sound of her laugh would be worth all the sorrow he was feeling in this moment.

"Qué maravillosa!" she'd say.

Jacob would help him, surely. He was generous. He'd been kind to Flaco and he'd been kind to Ruby and Samuel. He would ask Jacob about having his mamá visit sometime. He would just ask.

The big brown dog trotted out of the orchard and loped over to Flaco. It nudged his hand and cantered up to the house. It barked and pawed the door. Then barked again. But the door did not open and there was no motion inside.

The big dog circled once, twice, thrice on the mat and lay down with a thump to wait. And wait was all Flaco could do too.

18

CONGREGATING

Unlike female honeybees,
female bumblebees can sting more than once.

—LAVIN, *THE WONDROUS WORLD OF BEES*

ABIGAIL STOOD AT the edge of the cluster of students feeling pleasantly invisible. She'd assumed that she'd be the focus of the students' disgust and Dr. Lavin's ire. And why not? Abigail had performed heated displays of emotion. And had failed to set up a proper field camp. She'd arguably said more than one Wrong Thing. But no one even noticed her approach. They were all listening to Dr. Lavin scold Dwight.

Dwight stood, red-faced, shoulders slumped, as he received what Miss Ricketts would call "a dressing down" for taking it upon himself to reorganize the field camp, which had already been established. This was a waste of time and energy, and they had such a short window in which to work. Dr. Lavin had sent another student ahead to set up the camp so they could begin canvassing right away. Not only had they lost precious hours, but Dwight had also created confusion among the other team members and undermined the work of that student.

"Furthermore, Dwight," Dr. Lavin said, her voice never rising but every word like the bang of a hammer, "I will remind you that your place here is tenuous. You were a last-minute addition at the request of your supervisor. I would dismiss you immediately if it weren't for the fact that we don't have a vehicle headed to campus until Thursday. That means you have four days to change my mind. If you do, in fact, want to be part of this field team. We are a team, you understand."

The last part did not seem like a question, but Dwight nodded anyway.

Dr. Lavin turned to Abigail.

"Abigail," she said. "Can you orient us to the camp setup so we can get reorganized? We're losing hours here."

Abigail looked at the piles of gear and tables and tents, the dismantled fire circle and the mess of bags and random pieces of equipment. She closed her eyes and sorted it all in her mind. Then she opened her eyes and began to explain.

"The kitchen goes there," she said, pointing to the spot she'd chosen to catch the morning light.

"And the data-processing station is here," she said, and gestured to the area in the shade of the big firs. She outlined the sleeping spot, the food storage, the water collection point, and latrines. Dr. Lavin listened and divided the students into groups to reestablish the field camp.

"Is that everything?" the professor asked.

Abigail hesitated and pointed to the pile of logs that Dwight had rolled off to the side.

"That was a—a—campfire circle. For after dinner. If anyone wants to hang out or, I don't know . . ."

She trailed off, feeling silly, but Dr. Lavin nodded.

"Wonderful idea. Community and connection are an essential

part of a good field team," she said. "Dwight, you can start by putting those logs back where they were. Thank you."

Dr. Lavin's tone was neutral, as if signaling that Dwight would not be scolded every time she spoke to him.

How kind, Abigail thought, as the professor walked away. Dwight glared at Abigail and muttered under his breath.

She approached Dr. Lavin, who was talking to the students tasked with making dinner. She was immensely relieved not to have been dismissed and felt the need to come clean about everything.

"Do you have a question, Abigail?" Dr. Lavin asked.

Abigail shook her head.

"No, there is a problem."

Dr. Lavin frowned.

"What is it?"

Abigail pondered the question, trying to decide how best to explain. What had the motor-pool guy said?

"Dr. Lavin, I am not a qualified driver," Abigail said.

Dr. Lavin frowned.

"I don't understand."

Abigail glanced at the SUV she'd parked haphazardly at the top of the track. How to explain about the four-wheel-drive confusion, her bumpy arrival in the meadow, the alarming clunking sounds?

"Dr. Lavin, I believe I am some kind of hazard behind the wheel."

Dr. Lavin's laugh was loud and unexpected.

"You seem to have arrived just fine, Abigail."

Abigail tried to explain, but Dr. Lavin told her not to worry about it for the time being.

"I'll have a look later. Focus on getting camp set up now," she said.

Abigail helped reestablish the data-processing station and went to her tent. Others had begun pitching their tents facing each other in twos and threes. Abigail moved her tent, sleeping bag, and pad farther east, to the edge of the sleeping area. It felt better on the outer ring somehow. Yet she felt wistful after dinner as the others crawled into their tents and lay near each other giggling and laughing and playing music on their phones.

Abigail crawled into her tent and sat cross-legged looking north toward Mount Adams. The snowy peak had caught the alpenglow and blushed pink in the late evening sunset. Abigail felt her heart expand watching the snowcapped mountain turn from pink to orange and fade to yellow then green. She heard someone stepping through the grass and poked her head out the tent door. Casey stood in the twilight with two small stuff sacks.

"Hey, Abigail!" Casey said. "This is such a beautiful spot. Do you mind if I set up here? I mean, I don't want to disturb your privacy."

Abigail shook her head.

"You won't."

Casey unrolled her sleeping pad and bag and lay down.

"I like to see the sky," she said, shedding her sweatshirt and slipping into her sleeping bag. She stretched and sighed.

"Oh, man, it feels good to lie down! That was a steep trail."

Abigail didn't say anything. It didn't feel like she needed to say anything. The sky darkened and the stars winked on. She lay down with her head at the open door of the tent and listened to the night sounds of the meadow—the chorus frogs, killdeer, a trio of coyotes yipping in the darkness.

"Oh, there's the Dog Star," Casey said. "You can see it so much better up here. Can you see it?"

"No, I don't know that one," Abigail said.

"See Orion's Belt? Just go north from there and you'll see the Dog Star. It's part of Canis Major."

Abigail pulled her sleeping pad and bag out of her tent and lay back down. Orion's Belt twinkled in the dark sky and the Dog Star pulsed off to the left.

"I see it," she said.

"That is one of my favorites," Casey said. "My mother taught me all these when I was little. Canis Major comes from the story about Laelaps, a dog that chased a fox. Zeus turned them into stars and placed them in the sky for eternity."

Casey's voice was a soothing prattle like the burble of the nearby stream. Abigail felt drowsy and closed her eyes. She fell toward sleep. A cool breeze blew across her face, and she inched deeper into her bag.

"Abigail?" Casey's whisper woke her from a light slumber. "Are you awake?"

"Yes," Abigail said.

"Hey, I . . . I want to apologize. I shouldn't have listened to Dwight about the camp. I should have backed you up. I'm sorry."

Sorry.

Abigail felt a warm glow in her chest. She flipped her mind through the memory of the flashcards. What was this feeling? She didn't know the name for it. Something like Happy but more than Happy because it was unexpected and surprising and followed Sad. And Angry. And Disappointed. Whatever it was, she liked it.

"It's okay," Abigail said. "Don't worry about it."

And it was okay and she fell asleep.

In the morning, Abigail and Casey walked back to camp for breakfast. Casey was immediately drawn into conversation with others. The contentment Abigail had felt seeped out of her like a deflating birthday balloon. She sat just a little apart from the others, eating her breakfast and listening to Casey chattering away.

After they'd eaten and washed up, Dr. Lavin gathered them for the morning meeting. Mount Hood rose behind her, a vibrant white cone against a brilliant blue sky. The morning was sunny but cool. She thanked the students who'd made breakfast and those who'd washed the dishes. She reminded them to secure all food from bears and not to leave anything edible in their tents—no snack bars or chewing gum—as they prepared to head out for the day.

"It's a beautiful day for canvassing, but we are pretty exposed up here above the tree line," she said. "Please make sure you have sufficient water, food, sunscreen, and a hat. Don't forget your collection equipment and remember to be very gentle with the specimens you collect. We want to rerelease them carefully to cause as little disruption to the meadow ecosystem as possible."

She paused and scanned the group of students.

"Time is of the essence here. At the outset of this project, the forest service gave us a two-week permit, but they have reduced that window. Our permit now only lasts one week from today."

The students murmured with dismay.

"It is a disappointment," Dr. Lavin continued. "But the regional ornithologist was concerned about our impact on the nesting season of the white-headed woodpecker. So we'll have to work hard and be efficient. If we can confirm the presence of the western bumblebee in this area, it will help the application for protection immensely. With the decreased timeline, it does seem unlikely, but we'll do our best."

Abigail gazed around the alpine meadow. Surely they could find one or two?

"At the very least, we will get a look at the westerns' preferred habitat. We have a rare opportunity to have a direct impact on a disappearing species. Our efforts could help preserve this area and, possibly, save the western from extinction."

The students murmured with excitement. A lanky redhead raised her hand.

"What should we do if we think we have found a western bumblebee?"

"Good question, Tamara. It's imperative to confirm it's a western. Document it like you would any specimen and then bring it to me as quickly as possible. Each team should take one specimen cooler to keep the bees from overheating on the way back. Be quick, but very careful."

Dr. Lavin told them to pair off and mark their canvassing areas on the master map that was tacked up at the data-processing station.

The other students turned to one another and Abigail's heart sank. It was grade school PE all over again. She approached the master map and put her name on the far northeast quadrant. It was the most distant from camp and had, she recalled, a beautiful view of Mount Adams.

Casey appeared next to her and jostled her shoulder.

"Overachiever! That's the farthest corner!" Casey said, smiling and leaning into the map.

Abigail thought of how she'd enjoyed their conversation the night before.

"Casey," she said. "Do you want to—"

"It's your lucky day, Antica!" Dwight interrupted.

He swaggered up to the map and circled a quadrant. Smiling, he revealed a set of teeth that seemed too small for his large head.

"I picked the shadiest spot."

Abigail turned to leave. It didn't matter. After all, she was used to working alone.

"Veteran move, Dwight!" Casey said as she leaned in and wrote her name next to Abigail's.

"Enjoy it. We're taking the northeast boundary. See you later!"

Abigail's heart swelled.

Touched.

Glad.

Elated.

She knew it was silly, to be twenty-three years old and feel like a kid on the playground. But it was the best thing—having someone you liked like you back.

Casey grabbed a specimen cooler. They shouldered their day packs and walked toward the northeast section of the field, quiet at first, and then Casey began to ask her questions. And Abigail, to her surprise, found herself answering.

How had she ended up at OSU? When did she start her master's? How had she liked teaching in the entomology department?

The questions grew more personal. Where had she grown up? Did she have siblings? Where did her parents live?

She thought of her mother then and her answer stuck in her throat. There was a long pause and then she said, "My dad lives in Corvallis. Not my mom."

Casey nodded, as if understanding that was all Abigail wanted to say or could possibly say about her mother.

But then Abigail heard herself saying, "My mom left when I was three, so I never really knew her. Still, I miss her, which doesn't make sense, does it?"

They were walking side by side, and not having to look at Casey somehow made it easier to say this.

"Of course you miss her. She's your mom."

They were quiet again, and then it occurred to Abigail that she could ask Casey questions about herself. That Casey might want to answer such questions. That this was how one got to know people. So she did ask, and Casey told her. She'd done her bachelor's at the University of Minnesota. She'd started her master's the previous fall. She hadn't done any teaching yet but thought she would enjoy it and had applied for the TA-ship for the following year. She'd grown up in St. Paul and had two little sisters, who still lived there with her parents. Thirteen and fourteen—going on forty, she said and laughed. Abigail didn't get the joke but smiled to be polite.

When they reached their area, they split up, Casey taking the eastern border and Abigail the western. Almost immediately Casey slowed, swung the specimen net through the air, and stopped to examine what she'd caught.

"Yellowhead!" she called out, and Abigail gave her a thumbs-up.

Abigail fell into the rhythm of walking, listening to the sounds of the morning around her. A westerly wind moved through a nearby stand of Douglas firs, pushing them this way and that in a tall, shaggy dance. A lone crow flapped overhead, chased by a pair of furious tree swallows. The grass susurrated against her pant legs and the green scent of it rose around her. The buzz of a fly, the click of a dragonfly's wings, the querulous scold of a Douglas squirrel. Then she heard the signature drone of a bumblebee, heavy and sonorous in the morning sunshine. She saw it hovering above a lupine blossom and lowering its heavy body into the soft, downy petals.

Abigail coaxed the bee into a collection vessel, took a series of photographs, and then jotted a list of visual details and species identification.

"*Bombus appositus*, white-shouldered bumblebee," she wrote.

She opened the vessel and tipped the fuzzy creature back onto the lupine blossom.

She traveled slowly through the meadow and within the first hour had cataloged a satisfying list of insect inhabitants. Of bumblebee species she noted, Nevada bumblebee, Vosnesenski's bumblebee, and yellowhead bumblebee. Other native pollinators of interest were red nomad bee, small sweat bee, and carpenter bee. As she approached the edge of the study area, a honeybee buzzed past. Then another, then several more. She raised her head and looked south. She could just make out the low, white shapes of Jake Stevenson's honeybee hives in the distance.

Later, she and Casey met up at the northern boundary and compared notes. Collectively, they'd seen thirty bumblebees as well as an impressive list of native pollinators. Abigail showed Casey the photos she'd taken of the red nomad bee.

"A red nomad bee! I've only seen one once," Casey said. "They're so cool-looking!"

So often people mistook this slender native bee for a wasp, but all you had to do was look at the hair on its body and the pollen-collecting legs to distinguish it.

"I would never have thought of that," Casey said. "You're really good at this, Abigail."

Abigail flushed and shook her head.

"No, I mean it. You have a great eye for detail and an excellent memory. I mean, you're good. You should know that. I'm not just being my regular cheerleadery self. Really."

Abigail blushed deeply but felt a grounding sense that she was, in fact, good at this thing.

"Thank you," she said.

They both turned at the sound of a low drone in the meadow behind them.

"There!" Casey said, pointing to a milkweed blossom and raising her net.

Abigail stopped her.

"We don't need that. Look, she's already landed."

She crept close to the milkweed, moving slowly, and crouched low. There, in the lilac center, was a plump, fuzzy bumblebee—black with double white stripes.

"Oh my gosh! Is it a western?" Casey whispered.

Abigail brought the collection beaker just under the lip of the flower and coaxed the creature inside with her fingertip, then shut the top. Casey took photos and Abigail jotted down the physical characteristics of the fuzzy bee.

She shook her head.

"It's a cuckoo. Definitely. There's yellow on the bum instead of white and the head is slightly smaller than a western. But I thought it was too."

"Shoot," Casey said. "I really thought it might be."

Abigail opened the container and released the bee.

"It would be good to find it," she said. "For the wilderness application."

Casey nodded thoughtfully, then grinned wickedly.

"And also, to be the ones to find it!" Casey said. "I should warn you. I'm ridiculously competitive!"

At the end of that first day, Dr. Lavin read the list of species that had been collected by the team. No one had found a western.

"Congratulations to all of you. You're doing really good work," she said. "Don't be discouraged. Just keep going."

The days passed and Abigail and Casey continued to work together. Abigail, accustomed to being alone, preferring, in fact, to be alone, found herself waking each morning in anticipation. What would she and Casey talk about today?

They all fell into the rhythm of camp life—long hours in the field, cooling off in the stream in the afternoon, dinner with plates in their laps, and time around the fire circle. On the fourth night, Dr. Lavin told them not to make a fire.

"The ranger reported a fire danger level of yellow this morning," she said. "It's better to be safe than sorry."

They sat together looking up at the sky as conversations fell away and the stars blinked on one by one.

As the week passed, the team assembled an impressive number of pollinator species, including many varieties of sweat bees, mason bees, leaf-cutter bees, and bumblebees, but not the western. The students also tallied the flowers, shrubs, trees, and ground cover that created the pollinator habitat. Despite Dr. Lavin's encouragement at evening debriefings, every day without finding the western felt like a failure to Abigail.

Impatient.

Frustrated.

Disappointed.

She knew Casey felt the same way, which was comforting somehow.

The morning of the last day she awoke feeling despondent. Surely today would be no different. The week was over. She sat up to find Casey dressed and sitting with her chin on her fist. Her normally sunshiny face was folded in a frown. She didn't even say good morning.

"This sucks," she said. "I wish we had more time. I really wanted to find a western."

Casey—ever positive and enthusiastic—looked ready to cry.

Abigail was at a loss. She'd never seen Casey down before. It made Abigail sad to see her friend in such despair. She felt an unusual sensation—the desire to comfort her friend. She remembered then what Miss Ricketts had once said to her about work.

"All we can do is try, Casey. Hard work is an offering and a gift," she said.

A small smile bloomed on Casey's face and she shook her hair back and jumped to her feet.

"You're right, Abigail. Let's get to work. One more day!"

"One more day," Abigail repeated, and rallied her own spirits.

That morning they began canvassing at the northernmost section of the field area with renewed determination. Casey's enthusiasm had returned. When they passed near each other, she'd smile and call out the mounting number of specimens she'd found since the last pass.

"Five bumbles and eight more natives!"

They stopped briefly for lunch and then got back to work. As the hours passed, Abigail felt the creep of apathy. They were not going to find the western and their time was up. In the late afternoon, Abigail was hot and footsore. She paused and stretched her back and gazed around the meadow.

Something moved off to her left and she heard the tinny sound of music. She turned and saw Dwight sitting in the shade between the meadow and where the trees began. He was reclining against a log and looking at his phone, laughing. His backpack and collecting materials were strewn around him. She'd managed to avoid Dwight for most of the week. At camp, he had ignored her even if she was in a group with others. That was just fine with her. She turned around and kept walking.

Casey, nearby, called hello to Dwight, and Abigail gritted her teeth. She heard the whiny timbre of his annoying voice as he answered. She strode quickly away from them, irritated by the sound of his stupid music disturbing the quiet and by Casey's ability to be kind to everyone, even the Dwights of the world.

She halted midstride, hearing the warm rumble of a bumblebee in a waist-high patch of lupine. She saw a lumbering black-and-white body land on one of the purple flowers. It calmed her, watching the plump bulk of it clambering around. The bee gripped the blue petals with dexterous feet and extended its long proboscis into the petal of the flower. Abigail felt better just watching its slow, intentional movements. If human behavior confused her, the bees made sense, always. She stooped low and gently scooped the bee into her collection container. What a simple, beautiful thing it was—hindlegs loaded with deep orange pollen, hindwings and forewings stilled. The bee groomed itself—pulling on its antennae with its forelegs and combing stray bits of pollen down in its corbicula. It paused and seemed to be looking right at her.

Abigail held the container with the sun at her back and her breath caught. She gazed at the distinctive coloration and realized she was holding a gorgeous robust western bumblebee.

Her hands shook as she set the container on a stump and prepared to photograph the bee. Her heart hammered. It was a western, she was sure of it. The yellow and black segments of the insect's torso caught the sunlight. This once common and now rare creature was here. Right here. It was incredibly precious, a glimpse of possibility, of survival, of renewal.

An electric current coursed through her. She felt connected to this small creature somehow and to the meadow itself and all the miniature kingdoms contained therein. She imagined herself rooted to the very ground. And in that moment, something lightened in her heart. She almost felt her mother standing with her. It was as if Elizabeth was there too sharing this beautiful moment with Abigail. Laughing, calling her Abby Baby.

"Abby Baby, my one and only."

Her mother was gone, but there was a trace of mothering there.

In this moment, Abigail was certain that she had been loved. Her mother had carried her and held her and loved her. Her mother had danced her around the room, singing to her and crooning her name. That was all part of her even though Elizabeth Plue had left forever.

There was an unweighting in her heart, a release, a surrender. So strange and unexpected.

Behind her, Casey was wading through the hip-deep meadow grass, and Abigail waved and called to her.

"Casey! I think—!"

Her breath caught and she couldn't finish. Casey whooped and broke into a run. She reached Abigail, panting, and clapped her hands when she saw the plump, perfect western bumblebee in the specimen container, a young queen from the look of it.

"I took some photos, but . . . I'm not sure. Can you confirm what I'm seeing?" Abigail asked quietly.

"It is! It is one. I'm almost positive!" Casey whispered with excitement. She took her own photos and jotted down some notes.

Abigail knelt and loosened the top of the container.

"I want to get a couple of photos close up so you can really see the markings," she murmured. "Then we should take it back to Dr. Lavin fast. Ready?"

Casey raised her phone and Abigail opened the container and tipped the bee toward her open palm. Then something flashed between them and the container flew out of Abigail's hands.

19

FRAGILE ECOSYSTEMS

Human dependence on pollinators cannot be understated.
They are responsible for 75 percent of the food we eat.

—LAVIN, *THE WONDROUS WORLD OF BEES*

THE RAIN DRUMMED hard on the roof all day. Heavy clouds hung low and made it seem like late fall, a time of necessary stillness and inactivity, instead of high summer. The storm brought a reprieve from the spiking heat. It would delay, if only briefly, the pressure of honey harvest. This should have felt like a relief.

Instead, Jake felt the weight of his grief as he listened to the rain rattling down the gutters and rushing into the rain barrels outside. He lay on his bed, still in his clothes, where he'd returned after confirming that Ruby was gone. He knew he should get up but simply did not see the point. Along with the summer storm, a darkness had descended on his heart, or rather, reemerged. It was a familiar sensation, though he hadn't felt it for some time. He remembered this same impossible weight from the early days in the hospital after his accident. An overwhelming sense of pointlessness. What did it matter if he ever did anything again? He would just stay there, lying there. Nobody could convince him that he should do otherwise. He hadn't listened to his mother, or the doctors, or his friends, or his teachers, who stopped by the hospital. He'd eventually refused to see anyone but his mother. The days passed as he grew weaker. He pretended not to hear the whispered conversations between his mother and the physical therapist about the waning opportunity of regaining strength and mobility and what it would mean for his future.

"Jacob, you have to get up and get moving," his mother said. And wept when he refused to answer.

Eventually, he did get up and get moving again. He started eating and they took his feeding tube out. He submitted to the PT exercises and then started doing them on his own. He moved from the hospital to the rehabilitation center, and there he'd met Darren and Topher and some of the other guys at the gym. He'd begun to feel not better exactly, but not deeply awful every second of the day. Instead, it was an impassive detachment, which was bearable.

At the time he couldn't have said exactly what it was that shifted in him. It would have been easier to lie there and slowly disappear. But he got on with his life, whatever that life was going to hold. That impulse to move on, even though he didn't know what he was moving toward, was the reason he'd been out on Reed Road in the twilight of an April evening and met Alice Holtzman—beekeeper, grieving widow, and his unlikely savior—who'd nearly run him off the road in her truck. He stared at the ceiling of his room now, recalling their first meeting. Sitting on the shoulder of the road as the darkness fell, waiting for her honeybees to settle down after she'd hit a fencepost with her truck. He'd never forget what she said to him about the bees.

"Well, if they don't make it back to the hive at night, then they die outside."

To his immense surprise at the time, it bothered him to hear that. He cared about the fate of the small creatures that he hadn't given a second thought to before. It was the first time he'd cared about anything since his accident, felt empathy for someone or something outside of himself. Because that was just who he was—someone who had the capacity to care and to keep going. He knew that now, which was why he sat up on a rainy June morning with a shattered heart. He cared about other things besides himself, and he had shit to do.

He transferred into his chair, went into the bathroom and emptied his bladder, washed his face, and brushed his teeth. It was quiet in the house and he thought Flaco must be in the barn. He went out there most days until Jake called him in for breakfast. He could tell the boy was trying to make himself scarce, knowing he was an inconvenient houseguest. The irritation Jake felt at knowing the boy was there was softened by Flaco's nervousness, like the way he tried to help by washing dishes. He often did a terrible job, and Jake had to rewash them. And the way he made his bed, which Jake could see through the open door to his room, the covers pulled sloppily over the pillows, the fabric pooling unevenly over one side of the bed. Like a little kid would do. Well, he was kind of a little kid, wasn't he?

Jake rolled into the kitchen and pulled out eggs, bacon, salsa, cheese, and tortillas. He worked mechanically, making breakfast for the two of them, thinking about what he needed to do that day.

First, he needed to go see Evangelina. He'd tell her he'd considered her request to let Flaco stay longer and realized it was impossible. Even though she said it wouldn't be for the entire six months, she'd need to find someone else. Seeing Ruby again had drained him of any reserves, and he just couldn't help someone else right now. He wouldn't tell Evangelina about Ruby, though. Evangelina's fury at Jake's ex rivaled Alice's. But he would tell her about Dewitt. His talk about anonymous tips and monitoring local farms made him worried too. How could he protect Flaco if someone came snooping around?

Apparently it was true, what Dewitt had said about ICE grabbing a man at the bank. Jake had found a brief mention of it in the *Hood*

River News. In the comments section, someone wrote that they had wrestled him to the ground and hadn't even let him turn off his car. His wife had no idea anything had happened until local police called to say his car was blocking the bank drive-through. The comments section was mostly full of outrage, but a few people praised the work of the ICE officers. That was distressing to read. The whole thing made Dewitt's veiled threats more ominous. Even more reason Flaco couldn't stay.

Second, he needed to attend to his labor problem. Both of his interviews for that day had canceled. He would need to step up his efforts to find someone—anyone—to help with the pending harvest. After the honey was in, he could think of other things—like the retail orders piling up in his email inbox. And his broken heart.

Jake folded four tortillas and popped them in the toaster—a cooking hack courtesy of Cece Martinez, who'd taught him to cook back in his early days at Alice's house. Cece was the oldest child in a big family and accustomed to helping feed everyone. Jake remembered how she'd scoffed at the idea of the West Coast Food and Wine Classic last fall.

"These people clearly have too much time on their hands," she said, paging through the show catalog Jake had brought back from California.

"Food is fuel. Punto."

"Even bread?" Jake teased.

After all, she was a baker herself.

"Yes, even bread. Noah is the creative one. It's just water, salt, flour. I don't know why people get so excited about it."

Ever-practical Cece, Jake thought, almost smiling as he shredded cheese over the scrambled eggs. It was Cece who had reorganized this kitchen five years ago. The upper cabinets were mostly empty now or contained things Alice had left behind when she bought the farmhouse and the orchard across the way. During Jake's first week at Alice's, Cece and Noah had moved things to suit Jake's needs—

pots, pans, mixing bowls, knives, and other essentials within easy reach—in a bid to convince Alice he could be of use, that he wouldn't be in her way. He'd been desperate for Alice to let him stay. Like Flaco, he knew what it felt like to be an unwanted houseguest.

The toaster popped and Jake assembled the breakfast burritos. There was still no sign of Flaco, or Cheney, for that matter. He heard music playing out in the orchard. He covered the plates and pushed out the door and down the ramp. That Alice's house had already been ADA accessible had seemed like a sign when he'd first arrived. She'd modified it years earlier for her parents, but they'd died before they'd had a chance to use it. The accessibility was one of the reasons he'd convinced her to let him stay.

"You won't even know I'm here," he'd said, trying not to sound desperate. Anything to avoid going back to his parents' house, to the sound of the TV as his father watched sports all weekend, his mother on the phone with her friends from church.

Alice had cracked a smile then.

"Right, kid. You'll be like wallpaper."

She made him laugh and that was the first inkling the two of them would become, unaccountably, fast friends.

Now Jake sped across the flat yard toward the barn. Sergio and his crew were working the close side of the orchard and Jake heard someone laugh. The pumping bass of a ranchera song floated on the morning breeze from one of the truck radios.

Flaco was sitting on the floor with his back against the wall of the shop with his eyes closed. He was singing along to the radio in the orchard. Books and maps were piled around him and the breeze riffled their pages. Cheney, lying next to the boy, rose, shook, and bounded over to Jake, shoving his big head into Jake's hands. Flaco started and opened his eyes. It seemed to take a moment for him to come back to where he was. And then he looked embarrassed.

"I am sorry. I use the books."

Jake waved him off.

"It's fine. They're for everyone."

The boy stacked the books into a neat pile.

"Is your books?"

"No, they're Harry's, my friend who usually lives out here."

Flaco nodded and glanced at the yard.

"And your friend Ruby. With the baby? She leaves?"

Jake felt his heart fold in half.

"Yeah. She left."

"She comes back?" Flaco asked.

"No, I don't think so," Jake said.

He knew Ruby was not coming back. He also knew he couldn't trust himself to say anything else about Ruby just then. He told Flaco breakfast was ready. The kid rose and began to reshelve the books.

"You can read them," Jake said. "It's no problem. Bring them in the house if you want."

Inside Flaco ate with enthusiasm. He finished two breakfast burritos and Jake held out his own plate with one untouched burrito.

"I can't finish this. Do you want it?"

Flaco hesitated briefly and then took it, smiling. He ate, humming quietly to himself, and it sounded like the same song he'd been singing out in the barn.

"You have a nice voice," Jake said. "Do you play anything in school?"

The boy looked confused.

"Like fútbol?" he asked.

"No, I mean music, like music class? Band?"

Flaco shook his head slowly.

"No, we have no class of music in school. We have math, writing, sciences, historia, and English, of course. Geografía. But no class of music."

"Where did you learn to sing?" Jake asked.

Flaco shrugged.

"I sing with radio. My grandfather play guitar. And my father, I think."

"You think your father plays guitar?" Jake said, teasing. "What, is he not that good?"

Flaco looked embarrassed.

"I don't know him," he said quietly, looking down at the table.

Jake felt like an utter asshole, remembering that the kid had said his father was gone.

"Well, however you learned, you sounded really good."

The boy looked up, smiling slightly.

"You sing, Jacob?" he asked.

Jake noticed the way he said his name with a soft *j*, realizing he hadn't heard Flaco say his name before.

He shook his head.

"No, but I play trumpet."

He gestured to his horn, sitting on a shelf in the living room, and realized how long it had been since he'd picked it up.

"I was in band in middle school. As a kid," he said. "I met my best friend there, actually."

He rolled backward, pulled a photo off the fridge, and held it out for Flaco to see. Noah towering over Cece, who was leaning on the back of Jake's chair. Alice had taken the picture the first summer Jake had lived with her.

"That's Noah. I've known him forever. He plays trombone. And his girlfriend Cece."

Flaco looked at the photo and smiled.

"Noah and Cece," he repeated, nodding. "Ruby say they have bakery."

The mention of Ruby's name felt almost like a physical blow, but Flaco didn't seem to notice.

"Yes, they do. The best," Jake said, rolling into the kitchen with the dishes so the kid couldn't see his face.

After breakfast, he made some calls to farmers in his network to see if anyone had leads on seasonal labor. He called the president of the local beekeeping association with the same question. Everyone was sympathetic but nobody knew anyone looking for work. They said they'd spread the word. He spent considerable time posting his ad farther afield—in Portland, Bend, and Corvallis. Maybe he could get some college kids looking to spend the summer in Hood River.

Later he told Flaco he had errands to run and got in the truck to head into town. Cheney was nowhere to be seen, still out on his morning tour of the orchards. Jake asked Flaco to keep an eye out for him and make sure the dog had water. As he drove away, he glanced in the rearview mirror at the boy standing in the windswept yard. Flaco waved and turned to go back into the barn. Something about the figure of the boy standing there by himself made Jake feel so lonely, but he shook it off and continued up the driveway.

He paused at the top to check the campaign signs he'd placed. On one, someone had drawn a speech bubble next to Ron's face that said, "Open borders!" And on the other, "Illegals welcome here!" with an arrow pointing down the Queen of G driveway. Jake got out and removed them, feeling more sick than angry.

As he drove into town, he scanned the roadside. All along Tucker Road he saw Ron's signs defaced with graffiti. He recalled the summer of 2014, when a peaceful protest against the county's contract with a shady pesticide company had turned violent. Before then, he'd never have believed his little town could be so divided, and yet he'd seen it with his own eyes—counterprotesters shoving and punching people. It was like a bad dream and the wound had only deepened since the 2016 election.

Jake spent the day doing errands. He went to the DMV to renew his trailer license. He dropped by Mother's Market to pick up empty bulk honey containers and talk about their summer order. He went to the post office and mailed half a dozen direct orders of honey—the last he'd processed before he'd had to stop answering those emails. He got his oil changed and went through the car wash. Everything went more swiftly than he expected, and he knew he was stalling. Eventually he went to the taquería to find Evangelina. He had to tell her he couldn't keep Flaco—for the kid's own safety, he told himself.

As he drove, he heard the spatter of firecrackers and saw kids running away and ducking down side streets. Illegal though they were and with a burn ban on, people still set off fireworks the week before and after the Fourth.

It was early evening and busy when he arrived at the taquería. As he parked, his phone chirped and he plugged it into the charger. The charge sign flickered on and off and then on again. He held up the cord, seeing where Cheney had nibbled it nearly through, and sighed.

Evangelina waved at him from the kitchen doorway and said she'd be out shortly. He sat at a table under the large Douglas fir that presided over the patio. Nina brought him an horchata and wiped down the oilcloth.

"How's that chamaco staying with you?" she asked.

"Pining for you but otherwise okay."

She giggled and snapped the towel at him.

"Tía will be out in a minute."

Jake sipped the sweet drink and listened to the conversations around him. He'd always been able to understand more Spanish than he spoke. Now he heard people talking about the price of gas, the cost of rent. One family was discussing cherry harvest and the work schedule for the coming weekend and who would watch the little kids.

The table next to him grew animated, their voices rising. He heard one of the men say "la migra," and "NORCOR." Were they talking about the protest or the increasing presence of ICE in town? Or perhaps about the guy who'd been grabbed outside the bank? The man speaking saw Jake looking and lowered his voice.

Evangelina came out, cell phone pressed to her ear. Her face was somber, but she smiled when she hung up. She kissed Jake's cheek and sat across from him.

"Oh, it feels so good to sit down," she said. "How are you today, Jacob?"

How was he? That was a question he could not have answered. Not today. Instead, he asked Evangelina about the man who'd been picked up by ICE.

"Did you know him or his family? I mean, how does that happen?"

Evangelina looked tired.

"Yes, I know his wife. He'd missed a court date, so he knew they were looking for him. But it doesn't make it any easier. He's been deported and she's here now with two little ones. He was the one with a work permit."

He asked her if they were doing sweeps at the packinghouses and orchards as Dewitt had said.

She nodded.

"There has been some of that, yes. And in the process, they've detained people who have valid work permits. The community is working to address that."

"How can they do that?" Jake asked. "It's not fair."

Evangelina rubbed her eyes.

"Nobody said it was fair, Jacob."

"But people with valid permits. People with families!"

"Yes, I know. The U.S. immigration system is a mess," she said.

She sounded impatient and Jake felt ashamed making her listen to his outrage.

"The only clear pathway right now is for people who are married to American citizens. Like me."

And even Evangelina, who'd been a citizen for decades, did not escape discrimination. He recalled the smearing she'd endured during the SupraGro conflict—a litany of false accusations from locals. She hadn't done anything wrong. She was simply helping people access the resources that were available—housing, work, childcare, school, legal assistance, and medical access. Evangelina didn't let it go quietly either. The speech she'd made at the city council meeting had been reprinted in the local paper, and then *The Oregonian*, and had even been picked up by the Associated Press. The following year the Hood River Valley High School valedictorian, Maria Jimenez, had quoted Evangelina in her speech.

"*Some may think we have a choice to make—whether or not to care for everyone in our community. But there's no choice at all because that is the very definition of community.*"

Now Jake told her what Dewitt had said about a tip line, and the new defacement of Ron's campaign signs. Evangelina didn't look surprised at either piece of news.

"It's nothing new. Bullies flexing their muscles. There are laws against intimidation, and they can't trespass onto farms."

Jake wished he felt as sure as she sounded.

"But what about the signs?"

"We'll get new ones made and replace them."

"You should make Dewitt pay for the reprinting or something. I mean, he's got to be encouraging it if he isn't doing it himself."

Evangelina shrugged.

"I try not to worry too much about people like E.W. Dewitt, Jacob. I'm playing a long game. Look at this place," she said, gesturing around her at the small café and little store.

"When I first moved to Hood River, this was José's Taco House. It was famous in the eighties. People—white people, mijo—would drive out from Portland to eat here. It was written up in *Sunset Magazine*!"

"Wow! They must have been some tacos."

In the 1980s, Hood River would have seemed as distant as North Dakota to the city dwellers of Portland.

"Not quite as good as mine," Evangelina mused. "Pretty good, though. The thing is, José's was more than a tourist attraction. It was a gathering place for people—new immigrants and families who came for the picking season and those who, like mine, stayed. José's was like a community center—the place you could get information about housing, work, the school system, sending money back home. Finding legal representation. It was all happening here just because people wanted to help each other."

"I never knew that. I thought you started this place," Jake said.

"I made it my own, but I'm carrying on a tradition. When I first came here on a work permit, José's wife helped me apply for my green card and everything. Helped me get residency. Long before I met Ron. I feel the debt of that."

Jake felt ashamed.

"I've never thought about it much. All my Latinx friends were born here."

Evangelina shook her head.

"Not all of them. Cece, for example. Cece's parents brought her when she was little, so she's not a citizen. She's a Dreamer. She applied to be part of DACA."

Cece was a Dreamer? Why didn't he know that?

"I guess I never asked her," he said, feeling like a horrible friend. "But she's okay, right? She can become a citizen now?"

Evangelina shook her head.

"Currently no. The present administration discontinued the program in 2017. Some people were able to apply for renewal, but there's no clear path for citizenship."

"So they're in limbo?" he said.

Evangelina nodded.

"About seven hundred thousand young people," she said. "And the government has all their information."

Cece had never mentioned any of this. But why hadn't he asked?

"Some things are better," Evangelina said. "Hood River has some wonderful immigration lawyers now. I found someone to help Flaco here. It's so much easier than driving into Portland."

"Do they think they can help him?"

Evangelina sighed and held up her palms.

"Vamos a ver, mijo. I hope so. They're doing what they can, like all of us."

Nina leaned out the door and called out in rapid-fire Spanish to Evangelina.

"Ya voy!" Evangelina called back and something else Jake didn't catch.

Nina banged back inside the door, laughing. Evangelina turned back to Jake.

"I haven't been able to find a family who can take Flaco, but there are some other options," she said.

Relief washed over him, and he brightened.

"Oh good! Like what?"

"Well, there's Hood River Shelter Services. They're housing people in the new pallet shelters. And Portland has some temporary housing for youth. They have a pilot project he might be able to get into, but they don't always have translators. It's not ideal."

Jake's mother, Tansy, volunteered for Hood River Shelter Services. It was all adults there, he knew. Mostly single men sharing double-occupancy pods, and many were mentally ill. He thought of Flaco sharing a small space with an adult, a stranger who didn't speak his language and was potentially volatile. Or in a shelter in Portland surrounded by the young adults Jake saw in Pioneer Square—pierced and tattooed and angry. He thought of Flaco dancing with Ruby's baby and making silly faces. Flaco bowled over by Cheney's morning greetings. And the first time they had met—his skinny face ballooning with bee stings.

He's just a kid, he thought.

Evangelina watched him. She must have known what he'd come to say. That he just couldn't take responsibility for Flaco because he had to focus on the farm. That his life was busy and complicated. That he didn't want to get involved if Dewitt or people like him came snooping around the farm. Because that was part of it, he now realized. He didn't want to get involved. How cowardly his worries suddenly seemed in the grand scheme of things.

He recalled Flaco sitting in the barn with his eyes closed, singing along to the music in the orchard, trying to be quiet and not a bother, just as Jake himself had early on at Alice's. She hadn't wanted to let him stay, but she had.

He sighed and cracked his knuckles.

"He can stay with me for a while, Evangelina. It's fine."

Her face bloomed with a smile, and she squeezed his hand.

"You're a good man, Jacob. Thank you for helping him."

He didn't need her praise, but it certainly didn't hurt. Evangelina Ryan was the kind of person who made you want to be the best version of yourself.

She sent him home with new campaign signs for the driveway and chicken enchiladas and caldo de res for Flaco. She hugged him through the window of the truck.

"You're an asset, Jacob. To so many people."

But not to Ruby, he thought.

His phone chirped again, reminding him that it was nearly dead. Jake sighed and tried to remember where his spare charger was at the house.

He headed south on Tucker Road, and Mount Hood was shrouded in clouds. He heard more firecrackers and bottle rockets whistling through the darkening air. Rain spattered the windshield. He paused at a stoplight and checked the weather radar on his phone. A new storm was headed directly over the south valley. The rain would cease in the morning and temperatures would rise for the foreseeable future. Harvest was upon him. As if to underscore the bleakness of his situation, his phone chirped once more and died.

Maybe it wouldn't be a complete disaster, he thought, pretending at hope. But who was he kidding? He knew it was going to be a complete disaster. He paused to make a left turn and a truck blew past—

diesel engine roaring and stereo blaring. The vehicle hit a mud puddle, spattering Jake's windshield as it passed, and he heard a howl of laughter. A large American flag unfurled out the back. As it rounded the corner, the passenger hurled something out the window. A flash followed by the boom of an M-80.

"Idiots," Jake muttered to himself, driving on. Realizing how late it was, he suddenly felt remorse for leaving Flaco home alone all day. Would he have gone inside to make himself something to eat? What had he done with himself to pass the hours? Evangelina's praise felt especially undeserved just then.

When he reached the bottom of the driveway, he could see the house was dark. Flaco had probably stayed out in the barn all this time.

His headlights swept across the ground between the house and the barn, and he slammed on the brakes. The wet earth was a torn-up mess of tire tracks. He felt a stab of fear in the pit of his stomach. He thought of what Dewitt had said to him.

"*Even little farms like this one can be monitored.*"

Jake heard voices—an indistinguishable murmur and then a man's voice yelling. Above it all he heard a sound that grabbed his heart—the sound of Cheney, his beloved dog, crying out in pain.

20

ENVIRONMENTAL THREATS

After thriving for more than 100 million years and adapting to the planet's changes, bees are now grappling with the single biggest threat to their survival—human beings.

—LAVIN, *THE WONDROUS WORLD OF BEES*

FLACO LOOKED NORTH through the barn doorway. The sun had set, and the sky stretched yellow-green under a bank of clouds to the west. It had stopped raining, and the wind had dropped in the wet yard. Flaco had watched the afternoon wane and the light disappear with a growing sense of unease. In all the days he'd been at the farm, he'd never been alone for such a long period of time, and he'd always eaten dinner with Jacob. While it felt awkward at times to sit with this near stranger at the table, the absence of their evening meal made him feel the stark loneliness of his strange, suspended life.

A truck engine rumbled in the distance and grew louder as the vehicle descended the driveway. The knot of anxiety loosened in his chest, and Flaco stepped outside to meet Jacob. He'd been waiting all day to ask if he could call Mamá. He didn't have anything new to report since he'd already told her about his meeting with the lawyer. He simply wanted to hear her voice.

The truck accelerated down the incline and passed into the yard at a faster clip than Jacob usually drove. It roared toward the barn, blinding Flaco with its headlights. A second truck followed and then a third. None of these vehicles, Flaco realized, belonged to Jacob Stevenson. Fear shot through his limbs and he recalled what the lawyer had said to him about la migra. If they came to the house, he should not open the door. He should stay quiet and not run, and he should call her immediately.

But the barn door was wide open, and he didn't have any way to call her. He froze with terror.

The first truck tore in a large circle, skidding as it cornered and throwing up mud. Over the sound of the engine, the driver was yelling and laughing. A large American flag streamed out behind the truck, twisting and snapping as it spun. Flaco leapt into the shelter of the barn doorway and watched the other vehicles follow. They sprayed dirt and gravel as they careened around the land between the house and the barn, tearing up the earth under their tires. These were not law enforcement vehicles, which didn't make them less frightening.

Time seemed to stop as the trucks circled and roared past the open barn door. Revving engines and male voices and loud music made a wall of sound. Flaco stood frozen as the trucks circled. As they came closer, he could see the drivers' faces contorted with yelling and ugly laughter. An object flew through the air and landed just outside the barn, exploding with a flash and boom. Flaco staggered back, ears ringing, and held on to the wall to keep his feet. His head ached and stomach roiled as the trucks spun in ever-widening circles.

A sharp bark punctured the chaos. Cheney was somewhere out in the dark yard and barking with increasing urgency. One truck cornered sharply, and in a flash of the headlights, Flaco saw the big dog bouncing on his front paws at the edge of the torn-up yard.

Was it an accident, or did the driver aim for Cheney? It all happened so fast—the turning tires, the dog's terrible cry, and the truck braking hard. In the headlights, Flaco saw Cheney's muscular form lying still.

The truck reversed and then took off up the steep driveway. The others followed and roared off into the night.

The silence was deafening. Flaco stepped out into the ruin of the yard. The night smelled of wet earth, diesel, and crushed leaves. He couldn't see anything in the darkness. Where was the dog? He listened for any sound.

"Cheney! Good dog. ¿Dónde estás, perro?"

Cheney whimpered softly. Flaco hurried toward the sound and found the big dog lying on his side, tail thumping. Cheney whined and tried to rise, then yelped and fell back.

"Cálmate, cálmate, Cheney. Tranquilo," Flaco murmured.

He placed a hand on the dog's trembling flank and heat rose through the dog's skin into his palm.

What should he do? Where was Jacob? Why wasn't he back yet? Flaco's phone didn't work, and if it did, who would he have called? He didn't know anyone here except Jacob and Señora Evangelina and Señor Sergio, and he didn't know their numbers.

Cheney moaned and Flaco sat in the dirt near the big dog's head, touching his snout gently. Cheney licked his hand and moaned again. Flaco swallowed against the sob rising in his throat. What should he do?

He heard an engine at the top of the road. Were they coming back? He felt sick with fear and rose to his feet. He stood between the oncoming vehicle and the injured dog, feeling skinny and afraid. But he would not let them near Cheney again. He clenched his fists and braced himself.

The truck stopped in front of him and the headlights snapped off. The light of the barn illuminated two people inside. Flaco's breathing accelerated as they stepped out, one tall, the other short. Doors slammed and they came toward him. Cheney's whimpering intensified as they drew closer. Flaco's mind was blank. He stepped forward and screamed at them, as loud as he could. No words, but a warning, a declaration, a battle cry. He would not let them hurt Cheney more.

The people came into the light, their faces open and surprised. It was a man and a woman. The man was tall and skinny, the woman short and dark-haired. Cheney whimpered again, breaking the silence.

The man swore and said a rush of words, but Flaco only understood "Cheney."

At the sound of his name, the big dog whined and tried to stand but collapsed again. Then the two people were on their knees bending over the dog, their voices raised and rushed. Flaco couldn't understand what they were saying.

The man looked up at him.

"Where's Jake?" he asked.

Flaco shook his head. His English had deserted him.

The man said something to the woman and stood. He pulled out his phone, punched the screen, and held it to his ear. Whoever he was calling didn't seem to answer. He called someone else and paced the ground, speaking rapidly and nodding, but Flaco couldn't understand what he said.

The woman was examining Cheney's leg, and the dog cried in pain.

"Okay, okay," she said.

The man sucked in his breath and surveyed the ruin of the yard. He knelt next to the woman and spoke quickly in English. She stood and ran to the truck and opened the door. The man asked something, but Flaco didn't understand. He gathered himself and found the words.

"More slow please," he said.

"Who are you?" the man asked.

Flaco thought of that day in the high meadow when he introduced himself to Jacob. It seemed so long ago now. I am Sebastián Santiago Luna López, he thought to himself. I am from Michoacán,

Mexico. I am the only son of Beatriz López. I am a traveler in need of assistance. I am the best friend of Carlos Cardenas. I am an undocumented minor seeking Special Immigrant Juvenile Status.

Who was he? He didn't really know how to answer the question anymore. But the man was waiting for an answer.

"I am Flaco," he said.

"What happened to Cheney?" the man asked.

Flaco's heart thumped in his throat. He didn't have the words to explain and felt overcome. He thought of the trucks again, feeling sick. The woman came back with a towel. She knelt and slid it under Cheney's head and the big dog moaned.

"What happened?" the tall man asked again and Flaco shook his head.

"No tengo ninguna idea como explicar," he murmured to himself.

The woman looked at him sharply and stood.

"What are you doing here all by yourself, little brother?" she asked in Spanish.

Flaco blinked. His heart flooded with relief at the sound of her voice speaking his mother tongue. His brain shook loose and the words tumbled out.

He was Jacob's guest, he explained. Jacob had gone to town, and three big trucks had come and torn up the yard. One of them hit Cheney and they left. He had no idea who they were or why they would behave that way.

The woman listened, nodding, and translated for the man. Unburdened of his story, Flaco was awash in relief and grief.

"I am so sorry," he said in Spanish. "Jacob loves the dog so much. He will be very angry with me."

He already knew Jacob didn't really want him there. He would make him leave now, and where could he go?

The woman clicked her tongue and shook her head. She stepped forward and put an arm around his shoulders. She was a full head shorter than Flaco, but he felt comforted nonetheless.

"No, no. You didn't do anything, chamaco. It's not your fault." She smiled at him.

"I'm Cece and this is Noah. We're old friends of Jacob's. Don't worry, Flaco. Everything will be okay."

"Cece and Noah," Flaco repeated.

He breathed deeply trying to calm himself. He recalled the photo of the two of them with Jacob in the kitchen. Jacob's old friend, Noah, and his girlfriend, Cece.

"Cece and Noah. Ah, sí. Ruby she say me you make good bread," he said in English.

Noah looked at him blankly.

"Ruby?" he said.

Flaco nodded and tried to think of how to explain.

"When Ruby come for visit."

The man frowned.

"Ruby was here?" Cece asked.

Flaco nodded.

"Yes, yes. Ruby, she come with the baby."

Noah swore and Flaco wondered what he'd said wrong. Cece murmured something to him and then bent over Cheney, who'd begun to whimper again. They all turned at the sound of a vehicle at the top of the drive. With relief, Flaco recognized the sound of Jacob's truck. It sped into the yard and halted abruptly.

Noah ran to the truck and conferred with Jacob, who threw open the passenger door. Noah returned, explaining something to Cece. They crouched on either side of the dog, slid their arms under his body, and stood. Cheney yelped once and then was quiet. Together Noah and Cece got Cheney into the truck on Noah's lap. Jacob called something out the window as he drove away. The silence rang in Flaco's ears as he stood under the star-studded sky. He was exhausted and so lonely.

Cece had remained. She smiled, put an arm around him, and steered him into the house. Flaco sat at the table and watched her dig through the refrigerator. She pulled out tortillas, cheese, onions, and salsa. She heated a can of black beans and made quesadillas. As she stirred, shredded, and chopped, she asked him questions, and Flaco told her everything—how he'd met Jacob on Mount Hood and about his cousin César. He told her about walking the Pacific Crest Trail alone for days. And before that about Bend and Luis's uncle and the illegal marijuana farm. He told her about his journey, and why he'd left Las Lunas. He told her about Alán and Tonio and Carlos. He told it all. It was the first time he'd told the entire story to anyone, and it felt so good to tell it to someone who could understand him. Not just because she understood his language, because the señora and the lawyer did too. But Cece was younger and felt like a big sister, which was a comfort. She listened, nodding, asking questions here and there. Mostly she just let him talk.

She slid the quesadillas onto a plate and set them on the table in front of Flaco. He hadn't eaten since breakfast and was so hungry. He ate in huge bites and she chided him gently, like his mother would have, and smiled.

"Sorry. I have three little brothers who also eat like wolves."

Flaco chewed slowly. He asked how old her brothers were, and she said twelve, fifteen, and nineteen. She leaned her elbows on the table and watched him eat, chin in hands.

"I'm from Michoacán too," she said after a while. "From a tiny town called El Manzanillal. You've probably never heard of it."

Flaco started.

"You're not a norteamericana?"

She smiled, a little sadly he thought, and held her palms up.

"Pues, sí y no. I feel like an American. I don't even remember Mexico. My parents brought me here when I was three. My papá had a green card through work and my mamá was able to apply through him."

"What about your brothers?"

The boys were all born here, she explained, so they were citizens.

"And you?" Flaco asked.

"Technically I'm called a Dreamer. Do you know about that?"

Flaco shook his head, and she explained about a program called DACA, Deferred Action for Childhood Arrivals it was called in English. His heart leapt. Could he apply for DACA? he asked.

Cece shook her head.

"It's for people like me who came when they were little but with their parents. There are about three million of us. About half a million are enrolled in DACA right now."

"So DACA lets you apply for a green card and citizenship?"

She shook her head again.

"No. You can't. If you're enrolled in DACA you can work, and go to college, and you can't be deported. But you can't apply to be a citizen. There is no process for that. It's sort of messed up."

"But you can stay? You have legal status?"

Cece frowned and seesawed her hand.

"Más o menos. But it depends on who is president. Things can change from one election to the next. It's not great. I can't apply for citizenship now. At least not until it changes. If it changes. I'm getting married, so I can apply through Noah, but lots of my friends are just stuck. It's our country, but we don't get that acknowledgment. Some days, I don't know . . ."

She trailed off.

"No tener pies ni cabeza," Flaco said.

"Exactly. Neither feet nor head. It makes no sense."

Flaco felt the weight of that. Cece was already here and had lived in the United States for most of her life. But she wasn't safe either.

Cece brightened and laughed.

"That saying reminds me of 'Diego de Dos Cabezas.' Did you learn that song when you were little?"

Flaco shook his head.

She sang a verse a about a boy named Diego who grew a little head out of his big head. And another about his friend Pedro de Pies who walked on his hands and tied his shoes with his teeth. She smiled as she sang and did a little dance. The silly lyrics made them both laugh. Flaco felt better seeing her sorrow fade.

"So, how do you like it here, staying with Jake?" she asked.

"Jacob, he has been very kind to me."

He told her how he'd helped Jacob with the beehives.

"Ah, sounds so serious. So you've just been here working then? No fun at all?"

She was teasing and he smiled.

"No, Jacob bought me lunch in Odell too. And we went down to the river to the beach. I saw the, what do you call it? The wind things?"

"Ah, kiteboarding," Cece said. "Did it look fun to you?"

Flaco thought of the sand under his feet, the wind against his face, the view of the snow-covered mountain against the blue sky and the steep basalt hills of the north bank of the river. He shook his head.

"No, not the kiteboarding. But the river, the cliffs. It was just . . ."

He didn't have words for it, but there was something about this place that called to him, that made him feel like he wanted to belong there or could want to.

As he searched for the words, the front door banged open, and Jacob and Noah came in. Cece rose to hug Jacob. There was laughter and all three of them talking over each other. Flaco felt the deep ache of being outside of this circle of friends.

Cece turned to him, smiling.

"Cheney is going to be okay. They took him to the vet, and he'll be back soon."

Relief flooded him and he felt a rush of fatigue. Jacob asked her something and she turned to Flaco.

"Can you explain again what happened? I'll translate it for them."

He told the story and Cece translated a few sentences at a time.

He was waiting for Jacob. He didn't say how worried he was or that Jacob had never been gone so long before. He didn't say he was hungry but didn't think he should go in the house uninvited. He explained about hearing the trucks and thinking it was Jacob until they sped into the yard and tore up the ground. He thought it might be la migra, and he didn't know what to do. He described the yelling, the blaring music, and the explosion. He told of the large flag in the back of one truck, twisting and snapping as the truck spun.

Then Cheney appeared at the edge of the yard barking in that silly playful way he had. One of the trucks hit him and he was down and so still. Then the trucks left. Flaco ended the story, swallowing a sob.

When Cece finished translating, Jacob met his eyes, and he smiled.

"Sometimes Cheney is a big dummy," he said.

They all laughed and Flaco hoped no one noticed he might be crying a little bit.

Cece made more quesadillas, and they crowded around the table. Like Jacob, Noah spoke a little Spanish, and when their Spanish failed, Cece translated. Eventually he understood that Cece and Noah had gone to high school with Jacob. They'd been out of town for several weeks visiting Cece's family in Mexico. As Ruby had said, they owned a bakery in town. Nobody mentioned Ruby. Jacob elaborated about Cheney's injury. The beloved mutt had a broken foot and would spend a night or two at the vet.

Even though he laughed with his friends, Flaco sensed Jacob's preoccupation. He could tell that Jacob didn't really want him there. And yet the señora had not suggested anyplace else for him to go. After this bad thing with Cheney, well, it was reason enough for Jacob to ask him to move along, wasn't it?

After they ate, Noah and Cece left and Flaco helped Jacob clear the table. They did the dishes without talking. The quiet was almost unbearable, but Flaco was more afraid of what Jacob would say when he began to speak. When they were done cleaning up, Jacob rolled back to the dining room table and opened a bag Cece had left. Peering in, he smiled.

"Bizcochitos," he said and shook the bag at Flaco. Flaco sat down and took a cookie but didn't eat it. The thought of eating while hearing bad news seemed impossible.

"Thanks for helping with Cheney," Jacob said.

Flaco didn't feel like he'd helped with anything but nodded.

"Those people," Jacob said, spitting the word. "They're . . ."

He seemed to be struggling for the right words.

"They are dangerous. Terrible. I can't even explain."

"With Google?" Flaco asked.

Jacob shook his head.

"Another time. Anyway, we need to talk about the schedule for the week, okay?"

Flaco nodded.

Jacob spoke slowly and paused to use the translation app when Flaco didn't understand a word or a phrase.

"I talked to Señora Evangelina, and you have an appointment with your lawyer next week. Evangelina will take you again because I'm going to be very busy with work. I'll start harvesting honey next week. I'll be gone for most of the day every day and I won't be cooking or anything. Really just coming home to sleep."

Flaco felt cold all over. Now Jacob would tell him he had to leave. He knew he couldn't stay with the señora because of her husband's job. Where then? Homesickness engulfed him. He missed his mother.

Maybe Cece's family would take him. She said she had three little brothers. What was one more?

"I stay with Cece?" he asked.

Jacob shook his head and looked surprised.

"Um, I don't know about that. Why do you want to stay with Cece?"

"I stay somewhere?" he said. "I go somewhere?"

Flaco heard his voice crack.

Jacob ran a hand over his face and smiled, looking tired.

"Oh, no, no. You can stay here. Evangelina and I decided you should stay here while your application is processed. I'm happy to have you."

Flaco stared at him, unsure that he'd understood. Jacob spoke the words into Google Translate.

"Puedes quedarte conmigo. Estoy feliz de hospedarte."

It was fine, he assured Flaco, and Flaco knew he was telling the truth. His heart flooded with relief. He felt something almost like happiness at being allowed to stay. It wasn't home, no. But he was safe here. He was welcome here.

Jacob wrote down his phone number, Señora Evangelina's, and the lawyer's. He explained how to dial from any phone in the United States so Flaco could always reach one of them. Those men probably hadn't even seen him. Nobody even knew he was here at the farm besides the señora's family, the lawyer, and Señor Sergio, Jacob said.

"You're safe here, Flaco," he said.

Flaco went into the guest room, thinking of it as his room, for now, anyway. He took out the pocket atlas of the United States and put it on the bedside table. He pulled the Pacific Crest Trail map out of his other pocket and laid it in top. Lastly, he unfolded a map of the Columbia River Gorge. He looked at the two great volcanoes there—Mount Adams, Pahto, just north, and Mount Hood, Wy'east, to the south. He lay down, head to south, feet to north, feeling himself in the cradle of those two volcanic valleys. He closed his eyes and saw himself in that room, that town, that state, that country, the same continent as home. It helped to place himself there within the physical bounds of this strange and unfamiliar place, made it seem not so strange and unfamiliar.

He said his prayers and lay awake listening. Through the open window, he could hear the frogs singing in the darkness. He thought of the silly songs Cece had sung.

Diego who had two heads and Pedro who walked on his hands. Sometimes the world seemed upside down, but you had to keep moving.

The melody echoed through his mind, and he fell asleep.

21

COLONY DEFENSE

By many estimates, the world's insect population has declined 45 percent in the last four decades.

—LAVIN, *THE WONDROUS WORLD OF BEES*

IN HER RELATIVELY short, six-week life, the average worker bee contributes one to two teaspoons of honey to the hive. This industriousness never seemed more miraculous to Jake than it did during peak honeyflow and harvest. Almost overnight, the humming hives, which had gradually developed deep honey stores, became full to bursting and all from the tiny efforts of these small workers—hour by hour, day by day, week by week.

It began that last week of June. As predicted, the rain let up, the temperatures soared, and the Hood River Valley bloomed extravagantly. Blackberry patches, strawberry fields, and blueberry farms were awash in blossoms. Sunny meadows frothed with Queen Anne's lace and every irrigation ditch was a riot of aster and goldenrod. It was a gorgeous, delirious moment in the season.

The joy Jake would normally have felt was flattened by the fact that harvest was imminent, and he still didn't have a crew in place.

His phone calls to farmers and other beekeepers had yielded nothing. Noah and Cece had promised to spread the word but were desperate for help themselves as they caught up at the bakery after their long absence. And yet, some thought Noah and Cece had come home too soon.

"Mamá would have kept us in Mexico until Christmas," Cece said wryly the night they returned.

The newly engaged couple had dutifully visited the grandmothers and great-grandmothers and the graves of the grandfathers and great-grandfathers. Noah had met the great-aunts and great-uncles and the regular aunts and uncles and the cousins and second cousins and cousins once removed. There were elaborate breakfasts that bled into lunches and dinners that lasted late into the night.

For Noah Katz, who hailed from a small, agnostic Jewish family, the trip had been a crucible.

"Dude, it was . . . just . . . so many people and so much food. So much church. I just, I don't know, I had to stop fighting it. I sort of surrendered. It seemed like I would never get home and I'd spend the rest of my life sleeping on someone's couch or floor while Cece's mom told me where to go next and someone handed me a plate of food and introduced a relative whose name I forgot immediately."

When Mrs. Martinez had suggested a side trip to Lake Pátzcuaro to meet a raft of third cousins and go birdwatching, Cece lost it. Her temper tantrum had been "epic," Noah said, putting his arm around his diminutive fiancée.

"Honestly, I think it made the local news," Noah said. "Certainly, it was the top story for several days on 'Radio Tía,' as we like to call the auntie network."

Cece smiled placidly.

"I was just making my boundaries clear. Sometimes Mamá doesn't listen until I yell."

Though Jake was glad to have his friends home, they couldn't alleviate his problem. Honey harvest, once it began, would be fast and furious, and every minute counted. It was a simple if labor-intensive process. Each honey super had to be opened and the bees carefully brushed off, frame by frame. Those frames were sorted into bins and taken to the shop, where the wax cappings were sliced off with heat knives and transferred into one of three commercial extractors. Spun for several minutes in each direction, the frames would throw off their honey, which would drain into a double strainer. The frames emptied further on large trays before being returned to the hives. And at the end of the process was this golden treasure—a river of raw honey running into five-gallon buckets and then distributed into gallon-, quart-, pint-, and cup-size jars. The wax cappings—secondary bounty—would be processed later into bars of beeswax to sell for soap making and candle making.

Still without staff, Jake did what he could to get things in place in the barn. Flaco helped, and Jake wished he could pay him. He wished he could hire him outright. It seemed silly that he couldn't.

However, when he asked, Evangelina had made it clear that working for Jake could jeopardize Flaco's application for asylum.

"He only gets this one chance, Jacob. We don't want to give the judge a reason to reject it."

There was risk for Jake there too, she said.

"If someone turns you in, you could get fined or face criminal charges."

Ron had agreed with Evangelina, wagging his head ruefully.

"ICE does have a tip line, apparently. People are calling our office too, thinking it's a place to report. It's getting unfriendly, I'm sorry to say."

So Dewitt hadn't fabricated the tip line after all.

Evangelina had reiterated what the lawyer had told her. If ICE came to the farm, Jake had no obligation to let them in the house and they could not force Flaco to speak with them. He should call her or Ms. Vasquez immediately for instructions on what to do next.

But what if Flaco was outside as he had been the other night? Or alone at the farm? Jake thought these things but did not ask. He'd agreed to help and he would do his best.

On July 1, Jake flipped on the radio for the weather forecast and heard Dewitt on a show called *Around the Valley*. The host, Veronica Moncada, was a levelheaded third-generation resident of the Hood River Valley and known for her thorough and balanced interviews.

"... give people a general sense of your intentions," Veronica was saying. "Why should people vote for you? What is it you'll offer the residents of Hood River County?"

Jake turned up the volume.

"It's real simple, Veronica. It's good, God-fearing American values," Dewitt said. "The residents of this county want the same things I do. Freedom from the invasion of illegals and safety in our streets. Look at Texas and Arizona! Those people are just coming over and taking jobs and overrunning the schools and clogging up the ERs. We've all seen it."

"I have to disagree with you, Mr. Dewitt. There's no documentation of an 'invasion' of immigrants, as you put it," Veronica said. "As a matter of fact, the number of immigrants at the U.S. border has dropped in recent months. But let's not forget that their right to apply for asylum is enshrined in our laws. More to the point locally, do you worry that your message might turn off Latino residents and others? I mean, we're at the start of summer harvest. Local orchards have relied on migrant labor for as long as we've been producing fruit. Businesses in a county where more than thirty percent of residents identify as Latino—"

"Businesses?" Dewitt interrupted. "What local businesses need is freedom, Veronica. Freedom to grow and expand to their God-given potential. Take my friends at ZigZag Ridge Hunting Camp. They want to bring joy to people up on that beautiful mountain.

They're already up there, doin' it, and they just want to make things a little better. But no! You've got these hysterical environmentalists standing in the way saying it's a terrible thing. Terrible for who? There's nothing up there but some trees and marmots. If I were sheriff, I'd support such spirit of entrepreneurship."

"With respect, Mr. Dewitt, I have to point out that as sheriff you'd have no authority on that particular issue. The U.S. Forest Service oversees the Mount Hood National Forest and has denied ZigZag Ridge Hunting Camp's permit to construct permanent structures—"

Dewitt talked over her.

"Yes, it was denied, Veronica. You're exactly right. And for no clear reason. A bunch of hysterical liberals. The ZigZag folk are good Christian people, I might add. I told them, I said, look, you boys should stake your claim. It's public land and you're members of the public. You need to stand up for it, stage your own Malheur!"

"Mr. Dewitt, the armed takeover of the Malheur National Wildlife Refuge was a federal crime and left one man dead. Surely you're not lauding the Bundy family's radical approach?"

"But they didn't go to jail, did they?" Dewitt said. "Ammon Bundy is a hero—"

Jake snapped off the radio. He surveyed the earth between the house and barn, which he'd smoothed down with the tractor. If Dewitt himself hadn't torn up the yard that night, his supporters had. Jake thought of the terrible things scrawled on Ron's defaced campaign signs. He felt a creeping worry about Flaco. Had those men seen the young teenager there alone? Was Evangelina worried?

Evangelina seemed sanguine enough when Jake saw her that evening. She'd invited him and Flaco to a birthday party for her mother, Teresa. A small gathering, she'd said. Jake chuckled when he saw more than a dozen vehicles parked outside and thrice as many people spilling out of the house and into the yard. Evangelina greeted

Jake and Flaco with her usual warmth and ushered them to the dining room table, laden with food.

Flaco went outside and hovered near the Ryan boys and their cousins, looking shy. Marco said something to him and the boy's face brightened. Jake turned back to Evangelina.

"I noticed Ron got all his signs replaced along Tucker," he said.

Evangelina nodded, stirring a pot of birria on a hot plate.

"Yes, he and Ronnie and Marco put up new ones. Recycled all the damaged ones."

She sounded so calm, and anger flared in his chest.

"Did you take photos? Ron should talk to the paper or to Veronica Moncada. People should know what his supporters did. Or Dewitt himself!"

Evangelina regarded him calmly.

"There's nothing to be gained from engaging with people on those terms, Jacob. We keep moving forward. We keep working toward the change we want to see and look for the good. We don't give in to fear and ugliness."

Shame and frustration rolled through him.

"It just pisses me off! That disrespect—and especially to your family," he said, fighting to control his voice.

"I know, my darling," Evangelina said, leaning down and wrapping an arm around his shoulders. "That's because your mamá raised you right. Now, no more election talk."

They went outside and joined the wide circle of Ron and Evangelina's family, who were convened around Abuela Teresa. She sat in a seat of honor at the head of the patio, looking imperious—all ninety pounds of her. Her great-granddaughter placed a crown of daises in her hair and everyone sang "Las Mañanitas" when Evangelina brought out the cake. When they reached the last verse, Jake's throat tightened.

"De las estrellas del cielo te tengo que bajar dos. Uno con el que saludarte y el otro para despedirte."

Of the stars in the sky I have to lower two for you. One with which to greet you and the other to say farewell. He thought of Ruby, who hadn't even said goodbye.

On the drive home Flaco seemed happy, searching on Jake's phone for some music Marco had played for him. He sang along, tapping his fingers in time to the music. He'd been so animated at dinner sitting with the Ryan boys and their cousins, smiling and even laughing a little, shy though he was. How lonely he must be at the farm, Jake thought.

He stopped at the mailbox at the top of the driveway. Ron's signs were still in place and the photos of Ron's smiling face were reassuring.

He idled the truck and flipped through the mail—a flyer from Little Bit Grocery about a Fourth of July sale, a postcard from the city reminding people about fire safety, and a letter from an insurance agent soliciting Queen of G's business.

At the bottom of the pile was a postcard for Dewitt's campaign. His stern pink face. His arm around his wife's shoulders and his three mini-me sons around them. Jake remembered seeing Mrs. Dewitt in the store and her haunted look.

"Wishing You a Happy Fourth!" the card read.

Then, handwritten on the back: "Sending you our best, Mr. Stevenson. Here's to keeping Hood River County safe, patriotic, and legal."

His skin crawled and he crumpled the postcard in his fist.

Flaco looked startled, and Jake shook off his anger.

"Junk mail," he said, and put the truck in gear.

He didn't want to frighten the boy, but he couldn't leave Flaco alone at the farm anymore, he realized. Or Cheney either.

At the house Cheney hobbled to the front door to greet them with his front paw still wrapped and splinted. Cheney crawled up into Jake's lap, sighed, and burrowed his snout into Jake's armpit. Jake was so relieved that he was okay. He'd lost Cheney once before, and the dog's recent injury was a reminder of that old heartache.

Jake checked the weather report and knew he couldn't put it off any longer. He had to start harvesting the next day. He sat at the table and sketched the task list for the Mount Hood apiary harvest, which would happen first. It would be labor-intensive, as he had to transport honey frames back to the farm for extraction. That was another reason to charge more for that honey, Jake reasoned. Cheney snored under the table as Jake made lists of equipment and a timetable for the harvest days.

He refreshed his help wanted ad on the Gorge Classifieds and checked his email. Still nothing. He sighed and pulled out his phone to text Cece. Her little brothers were still in Mexico with her parents, but she said she'd work on the Salazar twins if he was desperate.

"Word of the day is: desperación," he wrote.

Instead of texting back, Cece called.

"When do you need people?" she asked.

"Tomorrow morning I'm going to start on the mountain apiary. Tell them they can just come watch," he said.

He thought the twins, who'd refused to get near the hives at the house, might be convinced if they saw how much calmer the bees were in the long hives.

"I'll ask them," Cece said.

"They're in! I'm coming too so they don't flake," she'd texted later.

Manny and Miguel showed up the next morning with Cece in tow. She leaned out the truck window and waved at Jake.

"You're buying me lunch, right?" she called.

"Lunch, dinner. Whatever you want, Cece!" he called back.

He knew how busy she and Noah were at the bakery, and taking time off to help him was no small thing.

"I'm holding you to that, Stevenson!" she yelled, smiling.

Jake led the way up to the field with Flaco in the front seat and Cheney stretched out in the back. The sun burned through the windshield, and the temperature began to climb. It was hotter than it had been the week before the brief rain. The wind was forecast to pick up that afternoon too. Jake could feel the ticking clock of the season. Time was running out and there was nothing he could to do slow it.

They arrived at the meadow at eight, and it was already warm. The rising temperatures showed in the terrain around them. Since Jake had been to the field last, the meadow grass had turned from green to golden brown. The wildflowers were in full bloom still, but the trees ringing the meadow looked dry—pines dropping needles and bigleaf maples looking limp.

He told Manny and Miguel to watch while he and Flaco pulled honey off a hive, hoping they'd be more convinced by what they saw than by his words. Despite his worry, he felt cheerful as soon as he started working. He approached the first hive with that sense of reverence he'd felt the first time, that first day he'd investigated Alice's hives on his own.

"Hello, ladies," he breathed as he opened the top on its hinge, and his heart swelled with gratitude for Naomi Price's hive design. He removed the wool insulation layer and peeled back the canvas cover, marveling at how calm the bees were. He loosened the outside frame of the hive and drew it out into the sunshine. It was heavy with honey, and the sweet smell of it wafted through the morning air. He brushed the bees gently down into the hive and dropped the honey frame into the waiting bin and secured the lid. He moved on through the hive. As he expected, the ten frames on one end of the hive were heavy with capped honey. He found brood on one side of the eleventh and left it, then moved the blocker board up to shrink the space. He replaced the canvas cover and the insulation pad and closed the lid. The process was quick and quiet and easy on the bees.

Jake and Flaco opened another hive and removed the frames with little drama. But the twins remained behind Cece, arms crossed and muttering.

"Oh, for God's sake!" Cece yelled and threw up her hands. She rounded on the boys, hands on hips, and unleashed a scolding in Spanish that Jake couldn't understand most of, though he recognized the word "diapers."

Cece grabbed a hat and gloves out of the equipment pile and strode over to Jake.

"What am I looking for?" she huffed.

Jake gave her a hive tool and explained how to evaluate the outer frames for honey.

"Flaco can show you. Right, Flaco?"

The boy nodded. Cece and Flaco began working the adjacent row. After a few minutes the twins joined them, looking sheepish. Cece explained the process to them, calling to Jake for clarification when needed.

The morning passed and they made some headway, though the twins, Flaco, and Cece were slow. Jake tried to quell his impatience with their pace. Though it wasn't rocket science, as he heard Cece grumbling to the boys, it was all new to them. So it seemed inevitable when Miguel dropped a frame and Manny, who'd refused to put on a canvas jacket over his bare arms, got stung.

He ran across the field yelling and swatting the air, and Jake's heart plummeted as he realized he'd neglected to ask if either of them, or Cece, reacted to stings.

"Cece!" he yelled, and she turned to him, laughing at the fleeing teen.

"Get him back over here, okay? There's an EpiPen in the tool caddy."

She grew somber and retrieved Manny. The boy only had a couple of stingers in him, which Jake removed, and did not appear to be reacting. Still, Jake walked everyone through the safety protocol for bee stings, explaining worrisome signs to look for, showing them the EpiPens and how they worked. Cece translated for Flaco. The boy paled when Jake explained how quickly some people could die from bee venom.

"Flaco had about two dozen stingers in him," he told the others.

"You got lucky, Flaco. It's a pretty powerful toxin in a small creature," Jake said, trying to keep his voice light.

Manny took a swig of water and stood.

"I'm good. Let's get back to it."

Jake checked the time and shook his head. He was so grateful, but he knew it was pointless. Between them, the twins, Cece, and Flaco had managed to pull honey off only ten hives in three hours. Jake had gotten through nearly twice that on his own. But that still left more than 160-odd to go. He just didn't have enough people. Besides, the wind had continued to strengthen. Wind made the bees cranky and harder to remove from the supers. It was obvious; he'd have to surrender here and concentrate on salvaging the harvest down at the farm.

"That's okay, Manny," he said. "I think we should call it a day."

Cece was looking past Jake toward the road.

"There's someone . . . I think . . ." she said.

Jake heard the sound of a diesel engine roaring up the forest service road. Spitting loose gravel, a truck tore past the meadow, music blaring through open windows.

"Proud to be an American! Where at least I know I'm free! And I won't forget the men who died who gave that right to me!"

"Jeez, that's loud!" she said.

"Is there a Fourth of July campout up here?" Miguel asked.

An American flag streamed out the back as the truck roared past followed by three more. Jake recognized the last vehicle—a red Ford F-350 with star-spangled mud flaps. Dewitt.

He thought of what Dewitt had said on *Around the Valley.*

"What local businesses need is freedom, Veronica. Freedom to grow and expand to their God-given potential . . . You've got these hysterical environmentalists standing in the way."

Fear washed over him in a cold wave.

"No, I don't think it's a July fourth thing. There's an OSU research group up there. And those idiots— I better call Ron."

After the incident with the trucks, Ron had said to call immediately if Jake had any concerns. Now he answered on the first ring.

"Hey, Jake. Everything okay with Flaco?"

"Yeah, he's fine, Ron, but there's something else. I'm up at our mountain apiary. I'm pretty sure I just saw E.W. Dewitt and some others heading higher up."

"Well now. What's E.W. doing up there?" Ron asked, sounding wary.

"You know how the forest service denied that hunting camp permit? It's roughly the same area as this OSU research field camp. They're doing a native bee study. Anyway, Dewitt just drove by with several other trucks. I might be paranoid, but I heard him on Radio Tierra talking about staging a local Malheur."

Ron's questions were clipped and concise. Which forest service road? How far was the camp from the turnoff? Could he drop a pin? He said he'd be there as quick as he could.

Jake put his phone away and thought about awkward Abigail Plue and her passion for the bumblebees.

"Everything okay, Jake?" Cece asked.

Jake shook his head.

"No, I think that was E.W. Dewitt driving up. There's a native bee study up near Eliot Glacier and I think he's going up there to harass them to make a statement. Ron is on his way, and he said he'd call the ranger."

He thought of Dewitt and his trolls descending on the field camp. Ron was at least half an hour away. He recalled the protest he and Alice had participated in five years earlier over the county's use of pesticides that decimated local hives. What began as a well-intentioned peaceful demonstration—students, beekeepers, environmentalists, and farmers—had been upended by two dozen thugs. They'd waded into a sit-in and started hitting people. It still made

Jake furious to think about it. He wasn't about to let Dewitt do the same thing without consequence. He felt determined to bear witness to whatever aggression might be happening up on the mountain.

"Look, could you all grab the gear for me? I'm going up to the field camp. One of the researchers is a friend of mine and I've got a bad feeling."

He moved toward his truck and pulled himself up. The passenger door opened and Flaco boosted Cheney in and climbed in after.

"You should wait here," Jake said. "Esperas aquí. With the others."

But the others weren't waiting. Cece and the Salazars had climbed into their truck and had pulled up behind Jake. Flaco shrugged.

"We all go," he said.

Jake sped up the forest service road in the direction the trucks had gone. He covered the first few miles quickly and slowed when the road narrowed into a rough track. He shifted into his lowest gear and punched the accelerator. The truck roared up the incline, clearing the deep ruts and large rocks. Jake dodged the largest boulders and plowed over smaller rocks and logs, grateful for the reliability of his old Dodge. Eventually the track emerged from the tree cover and opened up into a broad field.

Several large trucks were parked between the road and the field camp. He saw the SUV that Abigail had been driving and a large passenger van with the same OSU logo. Jake heard Dewitt's voice, loud and argumentative. In the middle of a group of people, Dewitt was talking to a woman. She was tall and broad shouldered and stood with her arms crossed. He could not see her face, but from her body language, she did not appear cowed. He could hear her voice, lower and calmer, under Dewitt's rising tone.

"Stay in the truck and keep the doors locked," he said to Flaco. "And keep Cheney with you."

He unloaded his chair and considered the uneven ground outside the truck. He slid down into his wheelchair carefully, grateful for his upper-body strength and conditioning. The ground was bumpy, with an angled fall line, and he powered over it. Cece and the Salazar twins soon joined him. As they approached the group, he could see a dozen or more people behind the woman. He heard someone laughing in an unhinged way, which added to the weirdness of the scene.

". . . true spirit of public lands!" Dewitt was saying. "God gave us the Constitution specifically to protect the rights of businessmen like the ZigZag Ridge folks to grow to their potential. Whatever concerns your research might have here, well, they are secondary concerns to those rights."

The woman he was speaking to did not seem persuaded.

"I do believe, Mr. Dewitt, that the Constitution," she said slowly, "was given to us by the framers of the U.S. government, not by God. And the state constitution was given to us by regional lawmakers. And voters."

She sounded like she was trying to explain something to a small child.

"Both state and federal laws protect our presence here, Mr. Dewitt. And while I do admire your creative flights of fancy, they do not change the fact that we are operating on a permit here through tomorrow at noon."

Dewitt flushed red.

"Nothing fancy about it," he growled. "As the presumptive sheriff-elect, I have the responsibility to protect citizens like ZigZag Ridge from nonsense like this, like this little bug you're after. My boy says you've been up here all week and nobody found a thing. Waste of time and tax dollars!"

Abigail Plue stepped out of the crowd with clenched fists.

"That is NOT true," she shouted.

Her gravelly voice carried across the clearing and was even louder than Jake remembered.

"Your BOY, among other things, is a LIAR! And an ASShole!"

Dewitt looked momentarily startled at the force of Abigail's voice.

"Ms. Plue," the woman said.

She murmured something to Abigail, who looked furious but remained silent. The woman turned back to Dewitt.

"I'm going to ask you to leave now, Mr. Dewitt," she said calmly. "And please take your son with you. Dwight, don't worry about your things. I'll have them sent down later. Now, if you'll excuse us, we have work to do."

"Lady, we ain't goin' anywhere," Dewitt said.

He turned to the men standing near him.

"Set up a perimeter, guys, and settle in."

Jacob noticed then that Dewitt and his men were all armed.

Cece swore.

"Okay, Gil," Dewitt said. "Start the live cast."

The man closest to Dewitt held up his phone and panned the crowd and then focused on Dewitt. Dewitt put his shoulders back and rested a hand on his gun. He held up a sheet of paper and began to read, glancing up at the man with the phone from time to time.

"Citizens, join us! We're claiming this public space on behalf of ZigZag Ridge Hunting Camp, a long-established family-owned business that has a God-given right to use these public lands to prosper! We will not be leaving until their permit is approved!"

Behind him, Jake heard the faint sound of sirens. Dewitt seemed to hear them too. He turned and looked toward the road. He met Jake's eye and smiled, his creepy little mustache stretching across his face like a centipede. And Jake realized that by calling Ron, he'd done exactly what this fucker wanted.

22

ROBBING

In the wild, bee colonies may face threats from many quarters—bears, skunks, and racoons, not to mention yellow jackets and wasps. But human-caused dangers are graver and impossible for the bees to combat—things like pesticide use, drought, and habitat loss.

—LAVIN, ***THE WONDROUS WORLD OF BEES***

ABIGAIL FROZE WATCHING Dwight scrabble at the air between them. She felt like she was underwater, her body arrested, her voice silenced, her breath pressed out of her body. The specimen container hit the ground, and he stepped on it, smashing the plastic under his boot. The moment seemed to last forever. She felt she'd spend the rest of her life watching Dwight destroy that gorgeous *Bombus occidentalis*, that one survivor, a rare spark of hope and beauty.

Casey's voice broke the terrible moment apart.

"Dwight! What the hell are you doing?"

She shoved him and he stumbled back.

"What the actual fuck!"

Calm, kind Casey was wild with fury.

"I didn't . . . I just wanted to see it—" Dwight stammered, donning his stupid hangdog look.

"Bullshit, Dwight! You did that on purpose!" Casey said.

He smirked and held up his palms.

"Whoops," he said.

"Why would you do that?"

Casey had tears in her voice.

"It's what we've been looking for, what all of us have been hoping for. The team goal. What were you thinking?"

"All of us, huh? Yeah, all of you, maybe. I'm not on your team, am I?"

His face was mottled and red.

"You know what's bullshit? This whole thing is bullshit. Restricting this piece of real estate for a few insects? Some dumb bug nobody even cares about. Wake up, Casey. That's not how the real world works."

"Real estate? What are you talking about, Dwight?" Casey said. "This is national forest. It's public land! It belongs to—"

"We live in a capitalist system, Casey," he interrupted. "Look, everybody knows the planet is on fire. Our lifetimes are going to be shorter probably, or more miserable anyway. So why fight it? Why not let people have a little fun?"

He gestured around them.

"A hunting camp. Why not?"

"Hunting camp? What hunting camp, Dwight?"

He regarded Casey with contempt.

"You're not from here. You don't get it. Hood River used to be so great. You could speak your mind, do what you wanted. Now you have to be so careful with what you say. Or you upset the Californians who've moved in and bought everything up. They get hysterical if you make a joke about women, or, like, brown people, or gays. Don't get me started about the illegals. It's not fair!"

Casey turned away from him, disgust plain on her face.

"Dwight. I have no idea what you're even talking about."

"What I'm talking about is that none of this matters!"

His voice was a creepy singsong.

"This stupid research project or any of the studies at OSU. It's all just another way for people with power to keep it and not share. To keep white men out. And you all talk about inclusivity."

Abigail listened at a remove. She watched Dwight and Casey as if she were somewhere else. The wind swept across the meadow and the grass undulated. The sunlight fell on a patch of thimbleberry bushes, and her heart shifted. She sighed and Casey turned to look at her.

"You okay, Abigail?" she asked.

Abigail nodded, feeling overcome. She shut the specimen cooler and swept the shattered container into a pile. Casey took the debris from her and tucked it in her pack. Dwight was still droning on, but Abigail didn't listen. She and Casey shouldered their packs and began to walk back to camp.

Dwight fell into step beside them.

"You don't even know that it was a western," he said. "You can tell Dr. Lavin and the others that, but it's really your word against mine."

Casey gave him a murderous look.

"Your word?" she said. "How are you going to spin this exactly, Dwight? That we made it up and smashed the sample?"

He smirked at her.

"Dr. Lavin said she needs proof, and it seems like you have a few photos that might or might not be a western."

Casey rounded on him.

"Dwight Dewitt. You are everything everyone has ever said about you. You are a liar, a creep, and a loser! I don't know why I ever thought otherwise."

Dwight stepped back.

"Oh boo. You hurt my little feelings," he said.

Casey walked on, muttering, and Abigail marveled at the string of profanity coming out of her mouth. She followed Casey and eventually spotted the flags marking camp. As they crested the hill, she saw four pickup trucks parked near the fire circle. Was this a forest service meeting? Or the Mount Hood ranger? As they neared, Abigail could see Dr. Lavin listening to a man with short red hair and a mustache. Several other men stood nearby, none in forest service uniform.

". . . God-given right, protected by the Constitution, ma'am. That's what I believe. That's what these men believe too. My deputies," the man said.

Dwight passed Casey and Abigail and leaned against one of the trucks. Dr. Lavin said something low and terse, and the red-haired man stepped closer. Abigail saw that he and the other men had guns.

The sight of the guns was so alarming it brought her up short. And, as she often did in supremely uncomfortable situations, Abigail started to laugh. Her laughter rang out in short barks across the meadow. Everyone turned to look—the students, Dr. Lavin, and the strangers. Dwight said something to the man with the mustache, and he scowled at her. He scared Abigail, which made it worse, and she laughed even harder.

Casey grabbed her elbow.

"Abigail, stop," she whispered.

She tried. But then Dwight's sweaty face got her going all over again. She couldn't explain the impulse to laugh. There was nothing funny about a group of armed men at the field camp. But she couldn't help it. She pinched herself on the insides of her arms. As Abigail laughed and snorted and hiccupped her way into silence, Casey pulled her toward the other students. The man had resumed talking to Dr. Lavin. She saw Dwight's sneer mirrored in his face.

"My boy says you've been up here all week and nobody found a thing. Waste of time and tax dollars!" the man said.

Abigail felt a shot of white-hot anger. Nothing? They'd cataloged scores of species of bumblebees and native pollinators. They'd identified the plants supporting them—fireweed, bear grass, columbine, and giant rhododendrons. The thimbleberry and huckleberry and salmonberry. How could you call that nothing? And the western bumblebee, the very focus of their search, they'd found one. Dwight was a liar and an asshole.

That's what she was thinking, but she only managed to articulate the last part.

"Your BOY, among other things, is a LIAR! And an ASShole!" she yelled.

It had to be said. It was not A Wrong Thing to say. Still, Dr. Lavin shushed her.

Somewhere in the trees, Abigail heard the sound of approaching sirens. On the far side of the clearing she saw Jake Stevenson with a group of people she didn't recognize. Why was he here? The red-haired man turned away and started talking to the other men. Dr. Lavin beckoned the students.

"We're going to stay calm, people," Dr. Lavin said, looking grim. "I spoke to the ranger, and she's on her way with the deputy sheriff. Stay close and stay quiet."

She looked pointedly at Abigail.

Dwight's dad was making a speech now, and Dwight stepped forward, holding his phone up to film it. His father broke off.

"Dwight, what the hell are you doing? You're blocking Gil. Get out of the fucking way!"

Abigail turned away from Dwight's flushing face. Casey was whispering to Dr. Lavin and weeping quietly.

"We were so close, Dr. Lavin. We had a specimen. A beautiful one. We took photos, but Dwight smashed it."

Dr. Lavin's face didn't change.

"There's no sense in crying about it, Casey. What's done is done. I'll petition for an extension from the forest service, and we might get an extra week."

She did not sound convinced.

"You and Abigail did your best. That's all I could ask for."

"It was such a beautiful bee," Casey whispered.

"Was it?" Dr. Lavin said. And Abigail saw a softness in her face. "I would have liked to see it."

Of course she would. Dr. Lavin, more than anyone, would want to see that particular specimen, to hold it up and view the delicate stergites that wrapped its thorax, to touch the soft, downy pile, to see the healthy young queen that she was. To imagine her helping sustain a hidden hive that would produce a new crop of drones and virgin queens at summer's end. It would have thrilled her to see the small creature, this survivor, that was living proof of hope, or rejuvenation, of some slight victory against the damage being done to the fragile planet.

Abigail thought these things but couldn't speak. It was too much. Instead, she stepped toward Dr. Lavin and opened the specimen cooler and held it up. It was an offering, a sacred gesture—lifting the small plastic cooler so Dr. Lavin could see inside. There lay a single broad thimbleberry leaf, and perched on it was one lovely western bumblebee. The fat, fuzzy specimen that had flown free and landed safely.

"Abigail!" Casey whispered. "You saved her!"

Dr. Lavin leaned in.

"Oh my," she breathed. "Yes, she is a beautiful bee, isn't she?"

Dr. Lavin pulled out a magnifying tool and examined the bee more closely. She held up her phone and asked Abigail to position the thimbleberry leaf. She snapped photos from several angles, made notes, and recorded a short video, holding the bee astride the leaf in her palm.

"On July 2, 2019, in the afternoon, this western bumblebee was located by members of our field team in the northwest quadrant of our study area in the Mount Hood National Forest. She looks to be a healthy young queen, and we can confirm her identity as a *Bombus occidentalis* from the distribution of black and yellow stergites and lack of yellow coloration on the fourth abdominal segment," she said. "This western bumblebee specimen is the first documented since Dr. Hall discovered the presence of the species near this location and it further establishes our sense that this portion of the national forest is key habitat to the western."

Nobody else seemed to notice. The rest of the students were worriedly murmuring to each other or texting. Dwight was filming his father, who was still bloviating, and the men around him were listening attentively.

Dr. Lavin completed her documentation with care. By the time she'd finished, the bee had warmed up and begun moving around on the leaf. Dr. Lavin moved out into the sunlight and handed the leaf to Abigail.

"I think she's about ready to fly," Dr. Lavin said.

The small creature rested on the leaf and cleaned her antennae, pulling them forward with two of her six legs. The small body pulsed slightly. Pollen cached in her corbicula caught the sunlight and glowed like golden treasure. Abigail looked the bee full in the face. The creature gazed directly at her through its large compound eyes. Abigail felt an electric spark in her center.

Wonder, she thought. Delight and Joy.

The creature turned and turned as if finding her bearings. She faced northwest and then rose and droned away across the meadow toward home, a tiny miracle of fuzz and bumble, a survivor.

JAKE LISTENED TO DEWITT WITH rising fury. Did he believe anything he was saying? That the Constitution had been written by God? That public funds were being siphoned for undocumented immigrants, and public lands withheld from entrepreneurs? Or was he just playing to his audience? It was somehow more infuriating that it didn't even matter what Dewitt believed.

The approaching sirens grew louder and then ceased as two sheriff's Jeeps arrived with the ranger's truck close behind. Ron and the other officers got out and moved slowly toward the group. The westerly wind had picked up and Jake saw the tall trees behind them sway in a gust. Dewitt flicked his eyes toward the approaching officers but kept reading his so-called manifesto.

Ceding from the state of Oregon to join Idaho. Requiring each household in the county to own a gun. Fair wages for the faithful members of a deputized posse, like the one assembled here today, paid out of county coffers. He revisited the need to defend local businesses like ZigZag Ridge Hunting Camp from the nefarious abuse of federal laws and from quote unquote scientific claims about threatened species.

"To develop to their God-given potential," he said. "And, if elected to sheriff, you can be sure Ron Ryan would deny them that. And let's not forget his family's deep ties with illegal aliens."

The man recording Dewitt's speech panned to record Ron's reaction, but Ron's face was neutral.

Dewitt stated a list of demands—the immediate disbandment of the research camp, a revocation of their study permit, and the approval of ZigZag Ridge Hunting Camp's request to develop a year-round outfitting operation. Dewitt stepped closer to the guy who was filming and put his hand over his heart.

"As the soon-to-be elected sheriff of Hood River County, this is my way of showing my support for the good Christian people of this community. God bless you all."

He stepped back. There was a long pause and then he scowled at the man with the phone.

"Turn it off, Gil. That was the end, you moron! I told you after the God bless part! Jesus!" he barked.

He turned to Ron, pulled out a can of chew, and tucked a pinch in his lip and spit.

"Afternoon, Sheriff Ryan," he said. "You're a bit far afield today."

Ron scanned the group of students and scientists. His eyes rested briefly on Jake and then he looked away.

"Well. That was . . . something, E.W.," Ron said. "I'm impressed by the magnitude of your vision."

Dewitt scoffed.

"My message has been consistent. It's about commitment to our county."

Ron regarded him calmly.

"I'm not sure I follow. How do federal land-use laws figure in here?"

Dewitt leaned and spit.

"The fact that you even have to ask really says something, Ryan. I'm here to help the citizens of our county thrive. The true locals. County people know I'm on their side. After you supported this sanctuary city crap, they needed someone like me to stand up for them."

Ron took off his hat and ran a hand through his hair.

"Well, Oregon has been a sanctuary state since the eighties, E.W. I'm simply upholding what people voted for. And I don't see what that has to do with—"

"Course you'd say that," Dewitt interrupted. "What with your wife running illegals through that place of hers."

Ron stepped closer, but his voice stayed level.

"My wife is not employing undocumented workers or faking papers for them or anything else you and your friends have attempted to malign her with. She's a stalwart supporter of the migrant workers of this community as well as asylum seekers. She has nothing to hide."

Dewitt chuckled.

"That's not what people are saying, though, Ryan. Folks say she's hiding people at that café. Maybe even at your place too, or with your friends."

He looked at Jake and then back to Ron.

"Illegals are supposed to get reported to ICE immediately, aren't they?"

Behind him, Cece hissed a string of curses in Spanish and English. Jake willed himself not to look toward Flaco in the truck. But Ron didn't blink.

"Actually, no, E.W. Oregon law is very clear that local sheriff and police departments are not meant to enforce federal immigration laws. If ICE has a warrant for someone—"

"Convenient for you to see it like that, Ryan," Dewitt said. "You can just turn a blind eye while our county is overrun with criminals. Is that it?!"

A hard blast of wind carried a wave of heat across the clearing. Jake felt sick and furious. With Dewitt escalating the conversation, Ron couldn't force him to leave the meadow, not with several armed men between the officers and the students. And if Ron left, he'd be abandoning the field camp to a hostage situation. How would it look if the sitting sheriff of Hood River County left a crowd of vulnerable civilians in the hands of E.W. Dewitt and his "deputies"? To Dewitt's people it would be a victory. To the rest of Hood River County, it would look like Ron had lost control of the situation.

He thought of Malheur, three years earlier, which had seemed impossible until it had happened. The armed takeover of a national wildlife refuge had lasted forty-one days and left that small community changed forever.

The wind gusted hugely, knocking over a table and some chairs in the camp. Papers went flying and two students raced to pluck them out of the wind.

Ron was shaking his head and still calm.

"It's true, you are . . . consistent, to use your word. But this scenario, well, it really is a game changer. I mean, to initiate—what did you call it? 'Hood River's Malheur' in a statement of rights for public lands. I mean, I had no idea that you were an emissary for ZigZag Ridge Hunting Camp."

The radio at Ron's hip crackled low.

Dewitt spit in the grass and smiled.

"Yes, I am an ally to their cause. You could call me a Robin Hood of the entrepreneur."

He grinned at his men and chuckled.

"That's really something," Ron said. "I mean, that they asked you to represent their interests and you interceded in this way. To speak for them. I mean, to be willing to take hostages on their behalf."

Dewitt's smile dropped.

"I didn't take any hostages, Ryan," he said.

Ron gestured at the field camp members crowded together on the far side of the clearing.

"Well, it sort of looks that way. I mean, unless you're the guests of the research folks today? Were you invited into the field camp? I can confirm that with Dr. Lavin if you'll let me come through."

"I don't need to be invited! I'm merely exercising my right to carry a firearm on national forest land—"

"As a representative of ZigZag Ridge Hunting Camp?"

"They never *asked* me to represent them," he said. "I just—"

"You just?" Ron repeated, waiting.

Dewitt didn't seem to have an answer.

"You just took it upon yourself to threaten a group of citizens on their behalf?"

Dewitt flushed scarlet.

"Desperate times need boldness. ZigZag Ridge Hunting Camp and the other patriots of Hood River County will understand that extreme measures are sometimes called for!"

Jake's heart dropped. Ron had miscalculated and lost. Dewitt was exactly the kind of person who doubled down when confronted with his own idiocy. His men stepped forward and formed a wall between the field camp members and the officers. Dewitt kept talking, a string of nonsense intended to bait Ron further. Ron turned to confer with the ranger and his radio crackled again.

The wind blew across the meadow, steadily now, and Jake watched a tent roll over and then tumble away. The students raced to secure the other tents and another table fell over.

Jake heard the unmistakable sound of Cheney's warbling bark then. He turned to see his big dog limping toward him, singing a joyful tune of reunion as if they'd been apart for months. Flaco followed, walking slowly and deliberately toward the crowd. He looked so young and so vulnerable. What the hell was he doing? Jake had told him to stay in the truck. Jake wanted to yell at him to stop, or to run for the trees.

"Shit! What is he doing?" Cece whispered.

Cheney yodeled and limped all the way to Jake and then lay his heavy jowls in his lap.

Flaco walked to Ron and stood before him, looking so exposed and so young. He tilted his face up and said something. Jake was too far away to hear what it was, but Ron turned east and looked up, across the meadow, past Dewitt's men and the students, and up into the eastern ridgeline of the foothills. Jake turned, following his gaze, and saw what looked like a rapidly expanding thunderhead high overhead.

IN HIS STUDY OF VOLCANOES, Flaco knew that eruptions could begin in different ways. Magmatic eruptions were the most common—the explosion and outflowing of lava that came from decompression of magma as it rose to the surface. But there were other kinds of eruptions, like phreatic eruptions, during which groundwater, heated by magma, flashed into great columns of steam. Phreatic eruptions could occur with little warning and, because of that, were extremely dangerous.

For a moment, when he saw the plume of white, Flaco imagined it was a phreatic eruption, a spurt of steam into the bright blue sky above the trees on the east ridge. The foothills here were, after all, within the volcanic collar of Mount Hood. It wasn't an impossible idea. But as it grew, it became obvious that it was a thick plume of smoke. As he watched, a bright orange flame spiked up through the center of the plume and ignited a large pine tree. The fire seemed to devour that tree and then spread quickly to the next, and then another, tearing from branch to crown as the flames danced along the ridgeline. The fire moved with grace and speed, a river of flame coursing through the trees, licking and devouring everything in its way.

Flaco was mesmerized by the violent beauty of it, but nobody else seemed to notice. The señora's husband was arguing with the other man, and some were still watching them. Others were running to retrieve chairs and tents blowing around in the wind. The doors on one of the trucks, parked facing him, slammed shut in a big gust. Flaco looked at Jacob and Cece, willing them to glance his way, but they did not. Manny and Miguel were not visible in the crowd either. He looked back to the fire and saw the flames had traveled south to the bottom of a cluster of tall radio towers.

Flaco recognized the towers and remembered what lay below them—that little town where they'd stopped on the way up to the meadow the first time. He thought of Jacob's student working in the food cart and the boys playing fútbol, and that nice coach who'd invited him to practice. He remembered the abuela and the sack of cherries and how grateful she'd been for his help. The street there was lined with tienditas and little houses tucked into the orchards. All that lay on the other side of the hill beyond the rapidly growing fire. As the minutes ticked by, the fire lunged, growing exponentially as it ate its way through the trees.

Jacob had told him to stay in the truck and to keep the doors locked. He had said not to attract attention. He'd told Flaco that the men who'd torn up the yard at the farm and injured Cheney were dangerous. The men in the field had guns and the one talking to the señora's husband looked angry. Flaco knew he should trust Jacob, and that it was safer in the truck, but he couldn't take his eyes off the growing flames. He thought of the abuelita, who'd reminded him of his abuela Patricia.

"*May God bless you, son,*" she'd said.

Flaco opened the door and Cheney jumped down, yelping as he

landed on his injured paw. Flaco hesitated. The angry man was yelling now, and those behind him were holding their guns across their chests. Flaco wanted to run and hide. He wanted to be home with his mother in their little house. He wanted to be anywhere but here. But he was here and he was watching a fire eat up the hillside above the little town of Odell, a fire nobody else seemed to notice.

Flaco got out of the truck and walked toward the sheriff. The wind blew hard against his back and his hat flew off. The dog began to bark and then all eyes were on him. Jacob and Cece waved him back toward the truck. He looked at the armed men and heard the abuelita's voice in his head.

"La migra, they'll snap you up in broad daylight just like that man at the bank!"

But it was too late to retreat. He reached the señora's husband, who turned toward him, his face a question.

"Incendio," Flaco said, and pointed up at the fire racing along the summit.

Everything moved very fast after that. The señora's husband spoke into the radio. He clapped his hands and addressed the crowd. Everyone turned to him, even the angry man. The señora's husband said something Flaco didn't understand. The crowd turned to look at the fire up above them and their voices rose in confusion. The señora's husband shushed them and said something else. He turned back to Flaco.

"Go with Jacob and the others. Go now," he said in Spanish, then he ran to his Jeep. He and the other officers drove away down the mountain, sirens howling in the trees.

People began moving toward the vehicles at the road. Flaco looked for Jacob and could not see him in the rushing crowd. Manny and Miguel ran past.

"Let's go, Flaco!" Manny yelled.

Flaco followed them and jumped into the back seat of their truck. They looked for Cece and saw her running toward them.

"Oh, you've got Flaco!" she said as she climbed in.

Manny reversed and spun the truck around.

"Hang on you guys! Jake is waiting for Flaco," Cece said, twisting in her seat to look back.

"Should I go find Jacob?" Flaco asked Cece.

Miguel was on the phone with someone and turned to his brother.

"They're mustering at the fairgrounds. We need to go there."

Cece leaned forward.

"We need to go where?" she asked.

"I'm training with Hood River Fire," Miguel said. "Everyone has been called to help out. They're staging in Odell."

"What about Jake?" Cece said as Manny accelerated toward the road.

"He's good," Manny said. "He saw us all together."

"You're sure?" Cece asked.

"Yeah, he just waved at us. I'm positive," Manny said.

Flaco looked back and saw Jacob behind the wheel of his truck. He raised a hand, but Jacob was looking away, up at the fire on the hillside. Manny sped up as he followed the other vehicles down the hill. The truck bumped down the rough track and soon they were swallowed up by the trees. They emerged onto the forest service road, which was full of smoke, and Manny accelerated into the gloom. He drove fast, braking hard when taillights flashed in front of them. Flaco held on as the truck jostled and jerked. He looked out the window to find his bearings but could see nothing. Next to him, Cece gripped the door handle and stared ahead, swearing under her breath whenever the truck hit a big bump. She saw him watching and tried to smile.

"Don't worry. He's a good driver," she said.

The smoke lifted and the view cleared as they sped out of the forest and met the road going north, choked with traffic. Cars, trucks, and trailers streamed toward Hood River. A fire engine screamed by heading south, and Manny followed. Soon Flaco recognized the stretch of highway that led to the little town of Odell. They slowed as they passed into the center of town. High above, the hillside was ablaze with running fingers of flame. The fire started about midway up the side of the slope and ran to the summit under the radio towers. The flames were moving fast as the wind blew ferociously over the peak.

Manny pulled into a dirt lot and parked next to an idling fire engine. Then he followed his brother, who had jumped out of the truck and was moving into a throng of people.

"Manny!" Cece called, and he turned. "Where are you going?"

"I'm going to help Miguel. He said they need volunteers," Manny said.

"When will you be back?"

"I don't know! Sorry, Cece!" he yelled. "You should probably get a ride!"

Flaco, unsure what to do, found himself following the twins into the crowd. Fire engines and ambulances were gathered on the fútbol field. Some people had heavy gear while others were in regular work clothes. The man next to him wore a jacket that said, "Bend Fire." A man with a microphone stood at the front of the crowd giving instructions in English. Flaco saw Miguel on the far side of the group and pushed his way over to stand next to him.

"What's he saying?" Flaco asked.

"He said the wind is pushing the fire east and into town. It normally wouldn't burn downhill, but there's so much fuel up there and it's really dry on this side. We need to dig a firebreak to arrest the fire, otherwise Odell can't be salvaged."

The man had finished speaking and people began to move. Flaco was pushed toward a military truck full of tools. A woman in fatigues handed him a shovel and he followed a line of people moving toward the hillside. He ran to keep up with Miguel but lost sight of him in the crowd. Some people climbed up and began raking underbrush and debris downhill. Others started digging a trench in the slope. Flaco struggled to gain his balance on the steep hillside. He found himself in a line of people, and the man ahead of him spoke over his shoulder.

"Dig, chamaco! We want it to be about four feet wide," the man said in Spanish. "Stay right behind me."

Flaco dug. He put his head down and he dug. His shovel bit into the dry earth and he counted as he dug. One, two, three, and up to twenty, then shuffled forward. He dug to keep pace with the man in front of him, trying to find a rhythm in the awkward labor. Above them, the fire gusted toward them in the wind, and he could feel the heat of it through his clothes. The air blew hot and smoky, and the fire popped and crackled as it tore through the underbrush on the hillside.

Flaco kept his eyes on the back of the man in front of him and the sweat stain growing between his shoulder blades. He dug and dug until he felt like he couldn't lift another shovelful of earth. And then he kept going because the man in front and the one behind kept going. The skin on his face and the backs of his hands burned. He choked on the hot, smoky air, and his tongue felt huge in his mouth. Dizzy, he knew he had to stop. He couldn't keep going, but then he did keep going.

He thought of his mother. She would tell him he could do anything if he just put his mind to it. She didn't really believe that, did she? Her sweet insistence on pretending to believe it, like believing in magic or angels, just for his sake, made him want to weep. Maybe he did weep. Maybe it was the smoke burning his eyes or the sweat and snot streaming down his face. It didn't matter. He lost track of time and forgot he was tired. He would have kept going forever. Flaco was just a body in motion among other bodies, digging, shuffling, digging more.

The man in front of him stopped suddenly and pulled on his arm. "Back up, güey!" he yelled.

Flaco joined the others running downhill away from the advancing flames. He stumbled to a stop, panting, and a cheer erupted from the crowd. The man next to him punched him in the arm.

"We did it! We turned it, chamaco! We turned it!"

Flaco looked through the sooty air and saw that the fire had been arrested by the ditch they'd dug in the earth. The wall of flames seemed to stop there and burned back on itself, losing power. Below the firebreak, all was safe—the remaining hillside and the little houses beyond, the playing field, the tienditas, and the fruit stands.

Flaco sat down hard in the dirt and released the shovel. His hands were raw from gripping the handle, and his eyes and nose were streaming. The man sat next to him and handed him a bottle of water. He drank and gazed at the road below, where the big yellow fire engines sat idling.

"Why don't they put it out?" Flaco asked.

"The terrain is too steep," the man said. "They'll stay below in case it comes near structures. They've got birds dropping water now.

"Look," he said, pointing.

Flaco looked up and saw a helicopter buzz low and release a bucket of water. The water splashed down on the inferno. From a distance it looked like nothing.

"But the woods," Flaco asked. "The trees. Won't they burn?"

The man nodded.

"Así es. They can't do much in the thick trees. There's so much fuel up there."

He stood and Flaco returned his water bottle.

"I have to report to my team leader and see where they want us next. You did good, güey."

Flaco followed him down the hill. On the field, people hurried in different directions. The man was there and then gone. Flaco looked around for the Salazar twins. He didn't see the señora's husband either. He felt exhausted and stumbled toward the parking lot in search of the truck and Cece.

Just beyond a line of yellow security tape, a woman grabbed him by the elbow. Older than Flaco, but younger than his mother, she wore her hair in dark shoulder-length curls. She was nicely dressed and seemed out of place in the dirty, smoky parking lot. She asked him in Spanish if he'd been fighting the fire, and he nodded numbly.

"Can you answer a couple of questions?" she asked, and he nodded again.

Only then did he see the camera. Speaking rapidly, the woman introduced herself as a reporter from Univision at the scene of the Middle Mountain Fire south of Hood River, Oregon, and speaking with one of the brave volunteers who'd helped turn the blaze.

"Can you tell us your name, son?" she asked.

Flaco blinked.

"Flaco," he said.

"Do you live here in Odell? Do you work here in the orchard?"

Flaco shook his head.

"No. I was . . . nearby and I wanted to help."

"Can you tell us what it was like up there? Describe the fire line for us?"

Flaco couldn't find the words. Hot and exhausting but also exhilarating. He shook his head.

"It must have been quite an experience for you," she said. "How would you explain it in just a word or two?"

He looked into the camera and felt woozy.

"Smoky?" he said. "And hot?"

He opened and closed his smarting hands.

"So you don't live in Odell or work here, is that right?"

"No, I . . . I want to work here, but I don't have papers yet."

"Are you here with your family?"

He shook his head.

"Only my cousin, but he was . . . they took him to jail and he got deported."

"So you're on your own, then? Where are you living?"

"I'm staying with some people I met in Hood River."

"And how did you end up fighting the fire?"

"I was just helping my friends," he said. "It seemed like the right thing to do. My mother raised me to pitch in."

"And where is your mother?"

"Las Lunas, Michoacán," he said.

And as he said that, Las Lunas felt so far way he might as well have said Mars.

"But you're in Hood River now?"

"Yes, for now. My mother sent me. She thought it would be better here. People have been very good to me. I'm staying on a honeybee farm. But I don't know. I just miss home I guess."

"A honeybee farm?" the woman said, and Flaco nodded.

"What kind of work do you do there?"

Flaco described how Jacob had taught him to add honey supers to the developing hives for the pending harvest.

"They have hives in Hood River and also up on Mount Hood. He's nice, the farmer. But it's not like home."

Flaco was so tired he wasn't even sure what he was saying aloud and what he was just thinking to himself.

The woman continued to ask questions, and he answered them in a daze of fatigue. She turned and faced the camera and kept one hand on Flaco's shoulder as she spoke. She told the camera how this young undocumented minor from Mexico had jumped in to help local firefighters and volunteers save the little town of Odell. Without consideration for his own safety, he'd risked his life for strangers. That wasn't exactly how he would have put it, but she was no longer asking him questions. And then she was done and signing off.

"Thank you, Flaco," she said. "You've been very brave. I appreciate your candor."

She handed him a small card. Flaco gazed down at it and read her name.

"Maria Herrera, KUNP-TV, Univision," it read.

"We should talk again sometime," she said. "Get home safe, little brother."

She hurried off with her crew and then Flaco was alone again. His thoughts cleared and everything he'd said to her came sharply into focus. He was an undocumented Mexican boy alone in the town of Hood River. He was working on a honeybee farm. Had he said Jacob's name? Had he said the name of the farm?

"*You're safe here,*" Jacob had said.

Nobody had known he was at the farm besides the señora's family, the lawyer, and Señor Sergio. Until now. Anyone watching that interview might know where he was, or guess. Panic rose in his throat. They would come for him now, surely. La migra was probably on the way to Jacob's farm this very moment.

He stood in the haze of smoke and watched people moving around the parking lot. He thought of Jacob and the last time he'd seen him in the high mountain field. Jacob had been so kind to him, had given him a place to stay and taught him about the bees. Jacob had worried about his safety and told him to stay in the truck.

He wanted to believe it was good that he'd gotten out of the truck, wanted to believe that it had mattered. But he also wished he'd waited for Jacob in the meadow and ridden back with him. Why had he followed the twins? Jacob would have driven back to the house. If he'd stayed with Jacob, Flaco would not have joined in the fire line. He would not have been able to help, but they didn't really need him, did they? He was just one person. One dumb skinny boy who should have kept his mouth shut. Who should not have said all those things to a television reporter.

Flaco scanned the parking lot, looking for anyone he might recognize—Manny, Miguel, Cece, the señora's husband—but saw no one. He walked across the fútbol field and away from the people and the cars, not sure where he was going. He followed the path of least resistance—downhill and through the opening space, like a river would, or lava from a volcano as it ran out its violence and yearned toward stillness.

"*Get home safe, little brother,*" the reporter had said.

Home? Where was home? Flaco wondered.

When he reached the far side of the field, he glanced over his shoulder one more time looking for a sign of Jacob. Jacob had been so generous and almost felt like a friend now. And Jacob's friends had been nice to him. Even if he could see the silly dog, he'd feel better. But he didn't see anyone he knew.

Flaco wished he'd had a chance to say it had been nice to meet them and thank you. He'd say, Thank you, Jacob, for helping me. Thank you, so much, for everything. Thank you and goodbye.

23

CONFLAGRATION

At peak population, a honeybee hive has up to sixty thousand members. Those thousands of bees work in harmony toward a single goal—the survival of the hive.

—LAVIN, *THE WONDROUS WORLD OF BEES*

WHEN JAKE WAS a senior in high school, his shop teacher took the class to watch the Hood River Volunteer Fire Department burn down an old building near the Pine Grove Grange. It was a training exercise for the volunteer firefighting crew, of which Jake's shop teacher was a member. Jake had expected to be bored. He'd even brought a little weed along with him thinking it might be possible to smoke, what with the burning building to mask the aroma of his Kushmania. Kush was a favorite back when Jake had a deep relationship with weed. He stood with his classmates watching Mr. Sullivan and his fellow volunteers don their gear and scanned the area for a place to light up. But then it started—one of the volunteers approached the old house with a blowtorch and in a moment where there had been a shingled wall there was now a sheet of flame. The fire licked around the other three sides of the old building, cedar shingles popping in the heat, until the whole thing was completely engulfed. In a matter of minutes, it wavered, folded, and toppled with a crash, sending sparks high in the air. The class watched as the firefighters controlled the perimeter to keep the flames from spreading, and before the end of the hour, the building had been reduced to ash.

Jake, mesmerized, hadn't been able to look away. The fire was beautiful and terrible at the same time. He'd never seen anything like it. He was one of the last students to board the bus back to school. He sat near Mr. Sullivan and wanted to ask how old you had to be to volunteer. But he was too embarrassed, not wanting to let on that he actually cared about something. He was like that back then. And Mr. Sullivan didn't talk to him either. At that time, Jake had convinced all his teachers, including Mr. Sullivan, that he was a lazy pot-smoking fuck-up. Because he had been at the time. For long afterward, Jake remembered the speed and power of that fire, the terrible beauty of it.

Now, watching the fire grow on the ridgeline, he did not feel that sense of awe. This was no controlled burn, but a living, wild thing. Tongues of flame raced through the trees and crested the hillside. Within minutes the entire summit above Odell was aflame.

He thought of the mountain apiary, his two hundred hives sitting exposed and vulnerable a few miles north. Beekeepers traditionally used smokers to tend their hives, dousing the top box with smoke to mimic wildfire. The bees would retreat to gorge themselves with honey in case they needed to relocate. He wondered if his bees were doing so now, shoring up their reserves in the event of an emergency flight. Were they sending messages of stress and panic throughout the hive? If so, there was nothing he could do to help them.

Jake heard Ron talking to dispatch, who said Odell was being evacuated and the fire camp was staging in town there. Ron conferred with the professor in charge of the field camp, then directed everyone to evacuate immediately.

"Please be calm and organized, but go now. Help each other out and get into whatever vehicle is available."

Jake saw Flaco standing where Ron had left him, staring up at the fire. As Ron and his men ran to their Jeeps, he stopped to speak to Flaco. The boy turned to watch them go. The field became chaotic then. Dewitt was yelling at his men to stay where they were. Some wanted to leave and they began arguing among themselves. Jake heard the professor calmly directing her students to the university vehicles.

Cece appeared at his side.

"I'll help Cheney get loaded up," she said.

Jake made his way over the rough ground toward the truck. Cece boosted the big dog onto the front seat and slammed the passenger door.

"You good?" she asked.

"I'm good," he said. "I'll just wait for Flaco."

"Okay, I'll see you down in town," she said.

He looked around for Flaco and did not see him. Students ran past, some on their phones chattering excitedly, some crying, some filming themselves. They piled into the university van.

"Leave everything," the professor called over the noise. "Get in the van or the SUV and make room for others."

The SUV struggled forward and emitted a clunking noise before shuddering to a halt. The engine whined with effort, but the vehicle was going nowhere. Abigail Plue slid out and slammed the door.

Jake looked up at the growing fire, momentarily mesmerized by the flames tearing through the trees. Dewitt's men charged by in their trucks, kicking up dust as they passed. Jake pulled his chair into the back seat. The professor appeared at his window.

"Can you take anyone? I'm full up and our second vehicle is out of commission."

Jake scanned the field, which was empty except for Dewitt and three students. Dewitt was yelling at one of them, while Abigail and the other student watched from a remove. Flaco must have gone with Cece and the Salazars.

"Yes, I have room," he said.

The professor ushered Abigail and the other students toward his truck. He looked around for Flaco again, worried about leaving him. But there was no sign of him. He had to have left with the others. He texted Cece just to make sure.

"You have Flaco, right?"

The professor asked him to meet at the Hood River Event Site, then loped off to the university van.

Two students climbed in the back, and Abigail Plue stood outside the truck scowling.

"Abigail, we need to get going," the woman said.

Abigail looked over her shoulder, sighed, and climbed in, slamming the door.

Jake headed down the mountain with the fire in the rearview mirror, glancing back at it until the truck entered the shelter of thick woods and he couldn't see it anymore. Smoke descended like a fog over the road. He checked his phone, but there was no response from Cece about Flaco.

The students in the back seat were silent. Abigail hadn't spoken to him or even acknowledged that she recognized him. Was she scared, perhaps?

"Hey, Abigail. You okay?" he asked.

She twisted around with rage blazing in her eyes.

"Dwight, you are a LIAR and no longer part of our FIELD TEAM!" she yelled. "So why are you riding with US?!"

Jake looked in the mirror at the object of her fury. The guy, who said nothing, looked familiar.

"Abigail, calm down, okay?" the other student said.

But Abigail did not calm down. She twisted farther around, straining in her seat belt.

"Why didn't you go back with your dumb DAD?" she hissed.

The kid mumbled something and stared out the window.

"His dad wouldn't take him," the other student said quietly.

"Too bad, so sad," Abigail said in an angry singsong. "Guess you should have WALKED then."

Abigail huffed and turned around in her seat. There was a strained silence.

"Abigail, we couldn't just leave him. You can't do that. It wasn't right for his dad to do that," the woman said.

Abigail didn't respond. Everyone was quiet as Jake navigated the smoky road. It was a bumpy ride and he was grateful for the old Dodge, which was reliable as always. Eventually the air was clearer, and he could see the road in front of him as the view opened out into the valley. When they passed the turnoff for the meadow apiary, he resisted the urge to go check on his hives and continued down toward town. There was nothing he could do to protect the bees from the fire, and he tried not to think about the hives sitting there, so vulnerable. He reached the turnoff for Highway 35 and found it clogged with northbound traffic from people evacuating from Odell. It took some time to merge, and then they crept along slowly in the stream of trucks, cars, and trailers.

In the mirror, the two students in the back seat were looking away from each other and holding opposite ends of the long body of his dog. Cheney, oblivious to any danger or discord, had lapsed into a snoring slumber.

Abigail sighed loudly. She did not turn around and her voice had resumed a regular tone. Regular for Abigail anyway.

"I know, Casey. It wasn't RIGHT and we could not leave him behind."

They were quiet again. Then Abigail turned to Jake, addressing him for the first time.

"Thank you for driving us, Jake Stevenson. I appreciate the ride."

She sounded like one of his mother's friends thanking him for a lift home from church, not a wildfire evacuation. He suppressed a smile.

"No problem, Abigail," he said.

"Um, you two know each other?" the woman asked.

Abigail shifted in her seat and gestured at Jake.

"Casey, this is Jake Stevenson. He's a beekeeper. Jake, this is Casey Antica, a member of the field team and my office mate. And this—" She pointed at Dwight.

"This is Dwight Dewitt. He is an ASSHOLE."

Jake stifled a laugh and looked at Dwight, recognizing him from his father's campaign billboards.

"Abigail! You shouldn't talk like that!" Casey said.

Abigail turned around and leaned back against the seat, placidly folding her hands in her lap. Now she really did look like one of Jake's mom's church pals.

"Dwight, do you want to tell Casey what you said to me in the equipment room?"

"The equipment room? What is she talking about, Dwight?"

Dwight didn't say anything.

"Asshole," Abigail whispered, her mouth curling into a smile.

It had been such a strange day—Dewitt, the fire, and now Abigail Plue, telling it like it was. Jake swallowed a chuckle.

Abigail flicked her eyes at him and smiled a tiny smile.

He checked his phone again, but there was no answer from Cece.

When they reached Hood River, downtown was backed up from Grace Su's all the way to the event site turnoff. When he finally reached it, the lot was a mass of people and vehicles, horse trailers, trucks towing heavy equipment, and even an open cart full of bleating goats. Hundreds of residents had fled the fire in the valley and the scene was chaotic. Jake looked for the Salazars' truck, feeling increasingly uneasy about Flaco.

As soon as Jake pulled over, Dwight flung open the door and left without a word. Casey leaned forward and pointed.

"I see Dr. Lavin," she said. "I'll go ask her where to meet."

She squeezed past Cheney, who thumped his tail and wouldn't budge.

Jake called her back.

"Can you ask if she's seen my friend? He was with three others, but he's only fourteen. His name is Flaco."

Casey nodded and hurried toward the professor, who was talking to someone in a forest service uniform with a clipboard.

Abigail gazed after her and muttered something.

"Sorry?" Jake said.

She turned to face him.

"Dr. Lavin will try to get an extension for our permit to give us more time," she said.

"More time for what?" he asked.

"To identify the key particulars of the western bumblebee's habitat in the meadow. And confirm the food sources and other elements of the ecosystem that are sustaining it. And hopefully identify a few more specimens."

"A few more. Did you find one, then?"

Abigail's green eyes grew bright with joy. She was quite pretty, he realized, when she wasn't yelling.

"We did," she said.

She pulled out her phone and showed him a series of photos. A bumblebee alighting on a thimbleberry blossom, a close-up shot of the bee's fuzzy, striped torso. A photo of the bee in a plastic container. Abigail was silent, even solemn, as she swiped through the photos. He recognized the reverence there, the same kind he himself felt when he'd first encountered the honeybees at Alice's farm. It was a little like falling in love. He wondered if she'd fallen as unexpectedly for bumblebees as he had for honeybees.

"Congratulations, Abigail," he said.

She put her phone away and leaned back against the seat, sighing.

"Thank you," she said. "Dr. Mora will be happy too and will let me keep working in pollinator research."

"Dr. Mora," Jake said, recognizing the name. "Nicolette Mora, right? I know her. She and her students helped us a few years ago with a pesticide study in the valley."

"I don't know about that," Abigail said.

"Yeah, we had a big die-off. Dr. Mora and her team worked with us to help decrease the impact of pesticides on local honeybees. It was super helpful for beekeepers and orchardists."

Abigail looked thoughtful.

"The Honeybee Lab can be . . . useful," she said begrudgingly.

What was that about? Jake wondered.

"And your mountain apiary?" Abigail asked. "Did your new hives produce as you'd hoped?"

"Yeah, it looks like it."

"Congratulations to you, Jake Stevenson," she said.

He thought about the hives high in the meadow, wondering if the fire had proceeded west. Were his hives alight this very minute? Would he lose everything?

Casey appeared next to Abigail's open window.

"Dr. Lavin says we need to join the group. They have an extra car to take us back to campus," she said.

She looked at Jake.

"I'm sorry, she hasn't seen your friend. I hope he turns up."

Jake's stomach dropped.

"Thanks for checking," he said.

Abigail studied him.

"Your friend," she said. "Was he that boy from the field?"

Jake nodded.

"Yes, that's him. Flaco."

Jake thought of the boy's thin face, his huge eyes as he stood in front of Ron.

"I told him to stay in the truck," he said, more to himself than Abigail.

"Why?" she asked.

How to explain it all—Dewitt, Flaco's immigration status, the election?

"It's complicated," he said. "Anyway, I'm sure he'll turn up."

He said this with false confidence.

"I hope so," Abigail said.

She extended her hand.

"Thank you for your assistance, Jake Stevenson. Good luck with the rest of your harvest."

He shook her hand, stifling a smile. Abigail Plue was odd, and he liked her.

She got out and stood with her friend.

"Thanks for the ride," the woman said.

"No problem. Casey, is it?"

She nodded and then looked south at the plume of smoke that had settled over the shoulder of the mountain. If you didn't know better, you'd think it was a thunderhead.

"Oof. I hope this doesn't get too bad," Casey said.

"Same here," Jake said.

"We have to hope," Abigail said.

They walked away. Abigail did not look back, but Casey turned and waved. She had a nice smile.

His thoughts returned to Flaco. Could he have gone with Ron? No, he had to be with Cece and the twins. For a brief, horrible moment, he wondered if Dewitt had grabbed him. He wouldn't put it past him to take the boy to ICE as a PR stunt.

His phone began to ding and he saw multiple texts from Cece come through.

"Flaco is with us."

"See you downtown!"

"Correction. Manny's driving us to Odell."

"Update: Flaco is with the twins. I'm going home."

"Where is he now?" he texted, but she didn't reply and didn't answer when he called. He called Noah, who was with Cece at her parents' house, but Flaco wasn't with them.

"He rode down with her and the twins," Noah said.

"Yeah, I just got her messages," Jake said.

"They went to Odell to help with the fire. I picked Cece up and brought her back, but Flaco had disappeared with Manny and Miguel."

Cece said something in the background.

"She's texting the twins now," Noah said.

Fuck, he thought. Flaco was in Odell during a Level Three evacuation? He was responsible for the kid. And not just because he'd told Evangelina he'd look out for him. Flaco had become, as he'd told Abigail and Casey, his friend.

"Oh shit . . . bro!" Noah said.

"What? What did they say?"

"No, not the twins. But your boy Flaco is definitely still in Odell. Hold on a second."

Jake could hear Cece's family talking in rapid Spanish over the sound of the television.

"Bro, he's on the news. He was interviewed by Univision. Said he was helping with the fire and . . . that he lives in Hood River and, hang on. Cece's translating."

There was a pause.

"Oh boy. Yeah, he explained that he came from Michoacán to work with his cousin, but his cousin was deported. That he's here alone and undocumented and he's working on a honey farm in Hood River. Yeah, he pretty much just spilled the beans on TV."

Jake felt sick. What was the kid thinking?

"Cece will look up the reporter and try to call her," Noah said. "He's probably with the twins. Or maybe he's back at your place already. Stay in touch."

Jake hung up and called the twins, but neither answered.

"Please call," he texted.

He turned around and drove back toward Odell. The northbound highway remained congested with cars full of families and trucks with orchard workers standing up in the back. The southbound lane was empty and he reached Odell quickly. A roadblock kept him from entering the fire camp, so he cruised outside the parking lot looking for Flaco or the twins. His worry deepened as the minutes ticked by.

He jumped when his phone rang. It was Manny.

"I thought he was with Cece!" Manny said. "I told them to get a ride."

Miguel was still with his volunteer group and Manny was making his way down the hillside to the truck.

"I'll call you if Flaco shows up," Manny promised and hung up.

A guy in fatigues appeared at Jake's window.

"Are you with the fire crew?" he asked.

"No, I'm just looking for someone."

"Sorry, but I need you to turn around. This is an active fire situation, and we need civilians out."

"What's the status?"

"Firebreak turned it back, so Odell is okay. The west side of town is still under evacuation," the man said.

Jake thought about the meadow apiary and Abigail's field camp.

"Will the fire burn back west?"

The man shook his head impatiently.

"Probably not. Should be arresting on the southeast because of the topography and the wind direction. But, sir, I need you to clear out. We need to get fire trucks through here. Please head that way," he said, and pointed Jake to the exit.

Jake cast one last look around the parking lot and headed home. Flaco had his phone number. If he didn't find the twins, he could borrow a phone and call Jake. Maybe Ron had found him and taken him home. Or maybe he'd called Evangelina to come get him. He really wanted to believe that. That someone in the Ryan family had scooped the boy up and he was someplace safe. But why wouldn't they have called Jake to let him know?

At home he descended the driveway and parked in front of the barn. The door was closed, and the shop was dark. Jake felt a deep dread in his gut. What if someone had stopped Flaco from leaving Odell after what he'd said on TV? What if Dewitt had called ICE? He thought of NORCOR and the fact that they housed juveniles there with adults, many of whom were actual criminals and not just detained for violating immigration laws. He felt cold all over. What hazards was the boy facing right now?

His phone rang and it was Evangelina. His heart surged with hope.

"Mijo! I just spoke to Ron and he told me what happened on the mountain," she said. "He's down at the fire now. Are you safe? Are you and Flaco safe? Are you both okay?"

No, they were not okay, Jake realized. They were in the middle of the largest conflagration in the history of the Mount Hood National Forest, and nobody knew the whereabouts of a fourteen-year-old boy named Flaco.

24

FLIGHT PATH

Bumblebees and honeybees share common developmental stages—egg, larva, pupa, and adult. Their development takes weeks, whereas some solitary bee species need months to complete the process.

—LAVIN, ***THE WONDROUS WORLD OF BEES***

FLACO WALKED ACROSS the fútbol field with the town of Odell at his back and the fire burning high above. Mount Hood rose in the south and he could see the top of Mount Adams jutting up over the northern hills. He knew if he kept going east, he'd find the highway. From there he would hitchhike south toward Bend. And then what? Then he'd call Javier, who was in California, who'd given him his number, who'd said to call if he got in a jam. Javier would help him get to the southern border and across. He'd done it many times, he'd said. And Flaco would go home. He would walk. He was young and strong and smart—hadn't his mother been saying so all along? He'd walk back to Las Lunas and back to his old life. What a relief it would be to feel the familiar dust under his feet and hear the town dogs barking at his approach, the tinny voice of the radio outside the tiendita, Frida's little girls playing in the yard, his mother singing as she cooked dinner.

Tired and hungry as he was, Flaco was cheered by the thought of walking into his old house and finding his mother there. She would scold him, but then she would hug him and tell him how glad she was to see him. He'd tell her he'd tried and failed, and she'd forgive him because she loved him.

He heard the clang of chain against metal and saw someone taking the net down on the far side of the field.

"Hey, Oscar! There's no practice today!" the man called in Spanish.

As he neared, Flaco recognized the coach who'd invited him to come practice with the team.

"Oh, sorry. I thought you were one of my boys."

Flaco shrugged and kept walking.

"Hey, can you give me a hand? The net is hung up on that side."

Flaco took hold of the net and lifted it free. He walked toward the coach to fold it in two, then retreated and advanced to fold it again.

"Thank you," the coach said. "Practice was canceled because of the fire. I'm hanging out in case any stragglers show up."

Flaco nodded and the man looked closely at him, and Flaco looked down at his sooty clothes and hands streaked with dirt.

"Whoa, son! Are you okay? Were you in the fire?"

Flaco found his voice with some effort.

"I'm okay. I was helping the firefighters."

"Is your family okay?" the man asked.

"My family is . . . fine," Flaco said, his voice breaking.

In that moment Flaco felt the full weight of his despair, his hunger for home and the people he loved.

The coach asked where he was headed and offered him a lift to the highway. So Flaco walked across the field with him carrying a mesh bag of balls and got in the man's car. They hadn't gone far before the man, who told Flaco to call him Coach Mateo, stopped in front of a neat single-story house. It was one of many similar houses on the street. People were out in their yards, everyone looking up toward the bright flames of the fire on the western hillside.

"This side of town wasn't evacuated," Coach Mateo said. "We're on alert, though."

The door opened and a little girl ran out. She leaned in the window and kissed the man.

"Marta, I brought a friend home. Tell Mamá we have one more for dinner."

The little girl ran back inside.

"Come in for un rato. You should eat something before you go," Coach Mateo said. "It's been a long day, no?"

Flaco did not want to go into the man's house. He wanted to be on his way. But he was aware of his deep exhaustion, his aching body and smarting hands. He nodded and got out of the car. They sat in a pair of plastic chairs in the driveway and looked across the valley toward the fire. Marta brought them water in plastic cups, and Flaco drained his quickly. She refilled it with a pitcher and then ran back inside. Flaco could feel the coach's eyes on him.

"I know you don't live in Odell because I know everyone in this town. Are you here working the fruit season?"

Flaco shook his head and explained he was staying in Hood River.

"How did you end up on the fire line?" the coach asked.

"I was up on the mountain when the fire started and came down to Odell with some people. They asked for volunteers, and I just followed everyone else."

The coach looked toward the mountain, where a huge plume of smoke squatted in the sky.

"That was good of you. Generous," he said. "You're a credit to your parents."

Flaco was silent.

"How are you here by yourself, son?"

Flaco shook his head and explained about César.

The coach clicked his teeth and leaned his elbows on his knees.

"I'm sorry, son. That's bad luck. You were going to work with your cousin, eh? On what orchard?"

"It's called Mount Hood Orchards. He's worked there many seasons."

"What's your cousin's name?"

"César. César Camarillo."

The coach cocked his head.

"César Camarillo. Does he play goal?"

Flaco nodded. César had been a champion portero, his mother always said. The man pulled out his phone.

"César Camarillo? No kidding?" he said, scrolling through his phone. "I know him! We played together in the county league years back. He's a madman in goal, your cousin."

He held up his phone and showed Flaco a WhatsApp contact with César's smiling face on it. It was the same on Mamá's phone.

"Yes, that's my cousin! That's him!" Flaco said.

After so much time trying to reach César, there was pleasure in this—that at least someone else here knew him. The flash of joy fizzled as Flaco thought about how his cousin's trouble had upended everything.

"So what now, mijo? What's your plan?"

Flaco looked toward the mountain.

"I have a friend in California, and I'm headed there. He can help me."

The coach nodded.

"Long way to California," he said.

Flaco shrugged.

"I made it from there before," he said, trying to sound confident, though suddenly the very thought of the journey was exhausting.

"What about your parents? Do you think they'd want to talk this over with you? We could give them a call."

Flaco shook his head.

"I don't want my mamá to worry," he said.

"And your dad?"

"I don't know him," Flaco said. "I haven't seen him since I was little. I don't know anything about him."

Suddenly it made him angry. Why didn't he know more? Why had his father left? Why had his mother never spoken about him?

The coach sighed.

"I'm sorry, son. That is a sad thing in a family," he said.

Flaco kicked the ground with his heels.

"And your mamá, don't you think she'd want to hear from you? Just to know you're safe?" the coach asked.

Flaco didn't say anything. He didn't want to call her. Not yet.

The coach stood and gestured for Flaco to follow.

"Well, let's go see about dinner," he said.

Flaco followed him across the small yard and felt that the temperature had dropped.

"What's your given name, son?" the coach asked.

"Sebastián," he said. "But everyone calls me Flaco."

"Are you named for your father?" the coach asked, opening the door.

"No, for my abuelo. My father's name is David. David Luna. Or was. I don't know . . ." he trailed off.

The coach turned to look at him and held the door open.

"Welcome to our house," he said.

The coach's wife was in the kitchen, and Marta was setting the table. The house smelled of onions and garlic and chili—familiar and comforting aromas. When he called the woman "señora," she laughed and said, "I'm Lupita. And this one is Mateo," she added, pointing at her husband.

During dinner they talked about the status of the fire and which neighbors had been evacuated. Mateo suggested again that Flaco call his mother. He refused politely. She wouldn't know anything about the fire, so why worry her more?

Lupita insisted he stay the night before setting out for California.

"I don't know your mamá, but please let me do this one thing. As a mamá," she said.

Flaco felt it would be rude to say no, and he was so tired. Lupita made him a bed on the couch, and when everyone had gone to their rooms, she came out to turn off the lights. She paused as she passed the couch and whispered good night to him. Her hand grazed his cheek. He missed his mother so much then that he wanted to cry. But he would not. He was grown now. He would have to fend for himself, and men did not cry.

He slept a deep, heavy sleep. When he woke up, the house was quiet and dark. He heard a vehicle outside and Mateo walked through the kitchen and into the yard. Men's voices murmured together in the darkness. Flaco sat up and pulled on his boots, feeling stiff. His hands smarted from yesterday's shoveling. He wondered if someone had come with news about the fire. Mateo had said this part of Odell was still on evacuation alert.

The door opened and Mateo motioned for him to come outside into the yard. Flaco hurried after him.

"Someone wants to speak to you," Mateo said.

He gestured toward the driveway where a man stood next to a blue pickup. He wore a neatly pressed Western shirt tucked into jeans and a white sombrero. He took off his hat, and in the light cast by the streetlamp, Flaco saw he was a little older than the coach. He was clean-shaven and wore his hair combed back. He was nobody Flaco knew, and yet he felt a strange sense of recognition. The man's face crinkled as he smiled and exposed bright white teeth.

"Hello, Sebastián."

Then he said, just as he had all those years ago, "My name is David. I'm your papá."

Flaco felt like he was seven years old again, facing this stranger. He had no idea what to say. He stood in the near dark and listened to

Mateo and David talking about David's drive, and about the latest news of the fire, which flared in the darkness. High on the dark hillside it seemed to hang in the sky. Flaco felt invisible. The sky began to lighten over the east hills and he could hear Lupita moving around in the kitchen.

Inside, they sat at the table while Lupita made them breakfast. Mateo and David chatted about work, fútbol, and politics. Flaco listened numbly, still reeling from the shock of his father's appearance.

Finally, David turned to him, frowning.

"I should explain some things," he said.

Mateo, it seemed, had met David more than a decade ago when they'd first come north. They'd both arrived with a group of young men from Michoacán and had worked the cherry season together their first year. Nights and weekends, they played fútbol.

"There was a crazy pickup game on Sunday afternoons back in the day, no, Mateo?"

He snapped his fingers, remembering.

"¡Chingón!"

About three years after they'd met, César had shown up at the game. He'd come north to work the cherry season, and David had introduced him to Mateo and the other guys as the cousin of his wife.

"I should say, the cousin of my ex-wife," David said.

Flaco blanched and David paused.

"Did she not tell you, mijo? We divorced six years ago."

Flaco looked down at the table.

"Oh, Beatriz," David said, shaking his head. "She should have told you."

Flaco did not speak but felt his gall rising.

"Did she tell you I was here? Your mamá knew I'd been working in Oregon for years."

Flaco shook his head and David sighed, rubbing a hand down his face.

"Well, when you told Mateo about César and then gave him my name, he called, and I drove here fast as I could."

Finally, Flaco managed to speak.

"Drove from where?"

"From eastern Oregon," David said. "I supervise a warehouse at the Port of Morrow in Boardman. It's the second biggest port in the state. We've lived there about three years."

Flaco did not care how big the Port of Morrow was.

"We who?" he asked quietly.

"My family," David said. "Me, and my wife, and our three little ones."

"Your family," Flaco repeated. They felt like the saddest words he'd ever said.

"Of course, you're my family too," David said quickly. "My first-born. That's really special, Sebastián."

Flaco felt a spark of hope.

"Did you come to take me home? To live with you?"

David looked flustered, leaned back, and braced his hands on his knees.

"Ah, Flaco. You know, it's complicated. We have a really small house and none of the kids are in school yet. It's a little crazy right now. I'll need to speak to my wife. She doesn't . . . I haven't told her about you."

That fact hung between them.

"And your . . . wife," Flaco said, hating the word in his mouth. "Is she Mexicana?"

David shook his head.

"She was born here. Her family has been in Oregon for generations."

"So she's a citizen," Flaco said.

David nodded.

"Yes, and I am too. Through her. And the kids were born here so they are too, of course."

"Of course," Flaco echoed flatly.

Lupita appeared holding a plate and asked him if he wanted more. Flaco hadn't touched his food.

He pondered the idea of that. An entire familia Luna with official U.S. papers. And none of them him.

"Flaco, maybe tell your father about your plan to go to California and meet up with your friend?" Mateo said. "David, what do you think of that?"

"Well, he's old enough to make his own choices," David said. "You're nearly eighteen, no?"

Flaco, not yet fifteen, did not correct him.

David leaned forward, pulling out his wallet.

"I'd like to help, mijo. Just to get you on your feet. Support you in your new life, however I can."

Flaco stared at the folded stack of proffered bills in his father's hand. It was a hand he did not recognize, as foreign to him as that of a stranger.

Support him in his new life.

He thought of the lawyer, who would not take his money, and the staff in her office, who were so kind to him. He thought of Señora Evangelina, who'd taken time off work to go to the lawyer's office with him and fed him and lent him her son's clothes. Jacob had given him shelter, and taught him about honeybees, and introduced him to his friends. And Cece had made him dinner and sat with him at the house. All these strangers, reaching out to help him, and yet they felt like intimates compared to this man.

"Yes, there is something you can do, señor," he said. He could never call this man papá.

After breakfast, David dropped him off at the top of the driveway by the mailboxes, as he'd asked. They shook hands as they parted, and Flaco couldn't think of anything to say. This man had driven from the eastern side of the state, propelled by some desire to help, but he couldn't offer the things Flaco most needed. Family, belonging, and home.

Flaco had taken his money and asked for a ride to Jacob's. Before he left for California, he would say a proper goodbye. He knew now one shouldn't simply disappear like his father had. There was risk to showing up at the farm after what he'd said on TV. He'd announced that he had no papers and pretty much told la migra exactly where to find him. But he wanted to be the kind of man who did not leave important things unsaid.

Flaco turned away as David drove off and looked at the campaign sign next to the mailbox. The señora's husband smiled out at him. "Experiencia, Conocimiento, Confiabilidad," it read. If he could vote, he would cast his for Ron Ryan for sheriff. He trusted this man and his wife and their friends. He was so grateful to them. It was a shame he would not get to know them better before he left.

He thought of the dicho his mother so often repeated, her own father's favorite inspirational quote.

"El éxito no es definitivo, el fracaso no es fatal. Es el valor para continuar lo que cuenta."

Success is not final, failure is not fatal. It is the courage to continue that counts.

Flaco walked down the long driveway toward Jacob's house. He didn't know what came next but only hoped he would find the courage to face it.

25

FLORAL FIDELITY

Many bee species engage in floral fidelity,
which is the practice of visiting the same type of
flower species on a single foraging flight.

—LAVIN, *THE WONDROUS WORLD OF BEES*

ABIGAIL PLUE SURPRISED herself. She sat in the conference room of the U.S. Forest Service office in Hood River feeling almost giddy. The windows revealed the Columbia River, its dark green surface roiling with whitecaps under a stormy September sky. She'd spent so much time here over the summer and fall that the view of the water, framed by steep basalt cliffs, was a familiar and welcome sight. She'd become part of something here after the fire. Abigail Plue was a member of a community, it seemed.

People streamed into the room for the meeting, nodding and saying hello to Abigail. They all knew her name now and she knew theirs. They talked to her, listened to what she said, and came to her with pollinator questions. Many even seemed to like her! It amazed her to feel this strange sense of acceptance. For so long she had seemed to disappoint people's expectations—of what she would say or how she might say it. But now she felt welcome just for being herself at this working group following the Mount Hood fire. A team player and collaborator after all.

The working group had first convened under hectic conditions with the wildfire still raging on the mountain. Wild-land crews had contained the eastward growth of the blaze, and the evacuated residents of Odell had been able to return after a couple of days. But the conflagration had continued to rage up in the steep terrain where cliffs and ravines made it impossible for firefighters to approach. They'd done what work they could with water drops over the area. The fire eventually grew to more than fifty thousand acres and had burned for weeks.

Abigail and Dr. Lavin gathered with the other stakeholders to discuss postfire restoration efforts on Mount Hood. Attendees included forest service employees, local Riverkeeper staff, concerned community members, and representatives of recreation organizations—skiing, hiking, mountain biking, and hunting. Abigail had been less than charitable toward the recreation people until Dr. Lavin gently reminded her of the multiuse mission of national forest lands.

"Do not conflate the extreme behavior of Mr. Dewitt and his associates with other recreation groups. It's a shared resource, Abigail," she'd said.

Dr. Lavin was not here today. She'd asked Abigail to present on behalf of the OSU-UW research team.

"You're more well informed than I am about the status of the project. You've earned a leadership role here, Abigail," Dr. Lavin said in their Zoom meeting.

Abigail agreed.

"You are correct. I have worked an average of 30.5 hours per week on the project, which is more than anyone else on the team."

She wondered if that was A Wrong Thing to say, because Casey, sitting next to her, had giggled, but Dr. Lavin only nodded and told her she'd look forward to hearing how the presentation went.

Confident, Abigail thought when she said that. Fulfilled and Empowered.

Abigail liked working with Dr. Lavin, who seemed to understand her thinking patterns in a way that her other supervisors never had. She asked questions that Abigail could answer and always gave clear instructions. Once, Dr. Lavin had told Abigail that she herself was on the autism spectrum and that she felt her autism made her a better scientist because she could focus so intently on her work.

"Some of the best minds in science today are people with autism," Dr. Lavin had said.

Abigail wasn't sure why Dr. Lavin had told her about her autism. She seemed to think Abigail would find that information interesting or useful.

Casey had helped Abigail put together the PowerPoint for the day's presentation, and Abigail would make sure to give her credit for that. She'd also mention Casey's work in the ongoing project she was reporting about—the continued investigation of the status of *Bombus occidentalis* and other pollinators—even though Casey only worked an average of 4.25 hours per week on the project.

Abigail was not being critical of Casey. She was just stating the facts about her best friend's workload, which also included other projects. Abigail loved to think that—that Casey was her best friend. She doubted she was Casey's best friend because Casey had so many friends. But they were office mates and shared an interest in native pollinators. And they also hung out on the weekends sometimes. Hanging out did not come naturally to Abigail, and the first time Casey had asked her if she wanted to hang out, Abigail had asked for clarification.

"What kinds of activities would be involved. And what timeframe?"

Casey laughed, but Abigail didn't feel like Casey was laughing at her.

"I forget about how literal you are! Okay. How about Saturday between ten a.m. and two p.m. and we can do, I don't know, whatever. A movie, a hike, or pickup Frisbee?"

They went for a hike in the OSU experimental forest and out for ramen after. Abigail was home, as planned, by two p.m. She went straight to her calendar and checked off "Hang out with Casey: 10 a.m. to 2 p.m." as completed, feeling Satisfied and Content. She liked hanging out with Casey. For the first time in her life, she knew what it felt like to have a friend she could count on. Miss Ricketts had been right when she'd said Abigail would find her people eventually.

Casey came in now and took a seat next to Abigail. She handed her a coffee and smiled. Abigail had discovered that she did, in fact, like coffee, and Casey was kind enough not to remind her about her earlier, vociferous objection to it. Abigail looked at the agenda for the meeting. She would speak first and then the Riverkeeper people would report on water-quality testing, the hunting group would speak about deer and elk populations, and a wildlife biologist would give data on the well-being of large carnivore populations—bears, mountain lions, bobcats, lynx, and wolverines.

The ranger called the meeting to order.

"Good morning, everyone, and thank you for coming. As you know, I always like to give the fire status report at the start of our meeting. Today I'm so pleased to tell you that the Middle Mountain Fire is one hundred percent contained!"

The room erupted in clapping, whistling, and feet stomping. It was the news they'd all been hoping for, Abigail included, though she thought the stomping and whistling were unnecessary.

"The last visible flames were tamped out yesterday," the ranger continued. "Crews will continue to monitor the area through fall because smoldering root balls can flare up even months later."

Abigail's dad would be pleased to hear this news. He'd taken a keen interest in everything that had happened to Abigail up on Mount Hood. After they'd been evacuated the night of the fire, she called him from campus and asked if she could come over and stay the night. It was unusual for her to make such a request, but she felt shaken after the day's events.

"Of course, sweet pea. I'll come pick you up right now," he'd said.

He'd made her favorite dinner—spaghetti and meatballs from scratch. She watched him cook and tried to figure out how to frame the question she'd felt rising in her heart. The inquiry that had nothing to do with wildfires or bumblebees or selfish, ranting men like Dwight Dewitt and his father.

When they sat down to eat, her dad looked across the table at her and smiled, his eyes crinkling at the corners, so reliable and comforting.

"Dad. Why did she leave?" Abigail asked.

It was a question she'd never known how to ask.

Her father reached across the table and squeezed her hand.

"Abigail, I don't know. I wish I did. She wouldn't tell me at the time, and then she asked me to stop contacting her. She said she'd get in touch with us when she was ready."

Abigail felt the strawberry-size wound just under her heart then and realized it wasn't strawberry-size at all. Sometimes it grew bigger than her whole body. It welled up in her, the sadness of being abandoned at the age of three and never understanding why. Her feelings spilled out of her and took her breath away.

Loss.

Sorrow.

Grief.

She could feel the size and shape of her pain. It swelled until she didn't think she could stand it, but then she did. Her sadness expanded to the far reaches of its borders, and then slowly contracted, absorbed back into her body. Naming her feelings seemed to give her breath back.

"I guess she never was ready," Abigail said.

Her father looked sad.

"Guess not," he said. "But, Abigail, you have to understand—it didn't have anything to do with you. Why your mom left, I mean."

When he said that, Abigail noticed that the pain in her heart diminished—only slightly, but immediately.

"Oh," she said. "I never thought of that."

And she hadn't, but she'd obviously felt somehow responsible for the departure of Elizabeth Plue from their lives. They didn't say anything else about it. For the rest of dinner Abigail told her dad about everything that had transpired on the mountain—the standoff with the armed men, the fire on the ridgeline, but mostly about finding the western bumblebee and how wonderful that had been. That feeling was not lost even amid all the confusion that had followed.

"She was a perfect specimen, Dad," Abigail said.

She'd thought about that western so often over the past weeks. Of the twenty thousand species of bees in the world, this was the one that mattered to her. Yes, the entire species of *Bombus occidentalis*, however small their numbers. But also this one humble bee, the individual that had stood in her hand, its tacky feet prickling her palm as it combed golden pollen down its body. The one bee who had looked her full in the face before turning, rising, and disappearing across the meadow to whatever fate awaited her. Death, certainly, was part of her future. But it didn't seem sad to Abigail, the small creature's short life. Instead, she remained fascinated by the unique particulars of this bee and what she'd accomplished on her own. So solitary for a social bee, this western bumblebee had crawled out of her winter hibernation equipped with everything she needed in life—wax with which to make her honey basket, honey to feed herself until her daughters were old enough to care for her, and the eggs that would become those daughters in her thriving hive. It was all within her, everything just waiting to make life happen.

Now Abigail shifted in her chair and thought about that one lone queen and all the work she must have done for the rest of her short life. Her daughters, surely, were busy locating their individual nests and preparing for winter. Abigail liked to think of them all burrowed down safely in the high alpine meadow, which would soon be buried in snow.

The ranger was wrapping up her introduction and Abigail knew it was almost her turn to speak. Casey whispered something and tittered. She was talking to Jake Stevenson, who had come in late and was sitting on Casey's far side. Though not an official part of the working group, Jake still came to the meetings regularly. He was concerned about the health of the mountain and how the fire would affect all pollinators—honeybees, bumblebees, and other natives.

Like Casey, Jake Stevenson had become a friend. Abigail and Casey had visited his honeybee farm several times that summer and fall. Early on they'd joined a group of undergraduates that Dr. Mora had recruited for his honey harvest. Abigail didn't mind helping with harvest, though she didn't enjoy it as much as everyone else seemed to. It was noisy and crowded working with other people all week. But it had been fun to camp out in the orchard next to Jake's place and listen to Casey point out the constellations overhead each night. And she'd liked helping Jake. This was part of friendship, she understood—helping, even when that helping meant doing something you didn't particularly want to do. At his farm, in the midst of the bustle of the harvest, Jake had seemed excited and happy. Seeing him that way made her feel happy too. Happiness, it seemed, could be shared between friends.

Over time, Jake had explained more about his young friend who'd gone missing the day of the fire. And how the boy, whose name was Flaco and who had been trying to emigrate from Mexico, had put himself in the path of Dwight's father to warn the sheriff about the fire. Jake believed that Flaco's warning had helped save the community of Odell and even his own meadow apiary. Arguably much alpine habitat for native pollinators too. Abigail wished she'd had a chance to thank the boy for what he'd done.

Casey nudged her as the ranger introduced her.

"Break a leg," Jake whispered.

Abigail stood and made her way to the front of the room. She began her report on the progress of OSU and UW's new project—the Pacific Northwest Bumble Bee Atlas. The atlas was a way to mobilize citizen scientists in Oregon, Washington, and Idaho to help researchers develop a clearer sense of the status of native bumblebees across the region. As she advanced the slides, she noticed the lights were bright but wasn't distracted because she'd grown used to them. She saw that people were listening and appeared interested. They sat up, attentive. They did not check their phones or rock in their chairs or sniffle. Or if they did, Abigail didn't notice. She did not find their faces overwhelming either, many though they were. These people had become familiar to her as colleagues and peers. She felt grounded by the sense that she had something to offer.

As she spoke, a warm buzz began in her chest. It grew and rose into her throat and entered her forehead. It was a soundless hum, a warm vibration. She felt, strangely, like she was glowing from within. Was it a feeling or simply a state of being? Whatever the case, she knew what she'd call it if anyone asked her.

Belonging.

26

HONEY RESERVES

Beekeepers must monitor their hives closely to determine when they need to supplement the bees' nutrition and when they are free to take surplus for themselves.

—LAVIN, *THE WONDROUS WORLD OF BEES*

JAKE STEVENSON WAS the first honey producer in the history of the West Coast Food and Wine Classic to decline an invitation to attend. Never mind that 2019 was only the second year that honey producers had been invited to the nationally acclaimed culinary show. It seemed inconceivable to organizers that anyone wouldn't want to come. They'd emailed back and even called just to be sure he understood them. There would be no entry fee for Queen of G Honey, since it had won Best in Show the previous year. And the show would pay airfare and lodging expenses for Jake and Alice. He thanked them and confirmed their regrets. Queen of G had decided to focus on other goals this fall, he said. He didn't feel the need to explain further.

The 2018 Feastie award still hung over the dining room table. Jake had observed it that very morning and with considerable pride.

But with that pride came a pang of understanding that he had other priorities now.

On the drive to Corvallis that September morning, he'd had a chance to consider those other priorities. He drove past the eastern flank of Mount Hood thinking about the little piece of meadow he and Alice had leased. It had been spared by the wildfire, along with Abigail Plue's bumblebee study area. Since the fire, Jake felt more invested in the mountain apiary but also the entire ecosystem of the great glacial peak, the rivers that cascaded down off it, and the trees he was now passing, which were dusted with early snow. His firsthand experience with wildfire had changed how he saw the forest. Though wildfires were increasingly common in the West, it was something else to watch a blaze erupt and threaten a place he loved.

Though the meadow apiary had not burned, Jake hadn't finished the harvest. In the scorched landscape, the bees had fewer resources, so he left the remaining stores of honey in place. Tending to the health of his bees was the most important thing and always had been. After that, the pressure of fulfilling all the orders seemed like a ridiculous thing to have worried about. Queen of G would be profitable that year and satisfy its wholesale accounts and even most of the new restaurant business. So what if they had to disappoint the ecstatic emailers, the honeymooners, and the birthday celebrators? Making the most money possible had never been his goal or Alice's either. They reminded each other of this fact at their first business meeting after she returned from Alaska.

"First of all, congratulations on a whopper harvest, Jake," she'd said as they went over the profit-and-loss report.

"But dammit! Why didn't you call me?"

As much as Jake had tried to downplay his labor shortage, Alice developed a clear picture after talking to Noah, Cece, and Tansy. Especially Tansy.

"I told Jacob he should reach out and let you know that he didn't have a single summer employee by mid-June, but he would not listen to me, Alice," Tansy said.

They both turned to look at him, disappointment in stereo. Sometimes it was like having two moms, though Alice was more like an angry football coach than a concerned parent.

In any case, it was behind them now. The harvest from the home apiary had been a healthy one and went smoothly with help from Dr. Mora and her students. Jake had gotten the idea to reach out to her from his conversation with Abigail. He'd enjoyed working with Dr. Mora five years earlier on a study of pesticide use in the Hood River Valley. To his relief, Dr. Mora was more than happy to recruit students for the harvest.

"It would be a tremendous learning experience for our undergraduates, Jake," she'd said.

With his labor problem solved, his worry had been replaced by the old excitement that harvest always brought. This moment was nothing short of magical. Inside those closed boxes, the bees had assembled their life's work, and by filling out the supers, they showed they had plenty of honey to share. Dr. Mora's students were smart and already well-informed about bee behavior and handled harvest easily. Abigail Plue and her friend Casey Antica had helped too. They and the other OSU students camped in the orchard for harvest week—a glorious, sticky stretch of days. Jake loved the camaraderie of laboring with other bee-minded folk. They worked in teams pulling honey frames, cutting off wax cappings, running the extractor, and managing the bottling process. The days were hot and the sweet scent of honey and wax permeated the air. At the end of each day, they'd eat together outside. In the apiary a cloud of golden bees hovered over the draining frames as they salvaged every last bit of treasure to replenish their stores.

The only disappointment for Jake was that the Langstroth hive design limited his own participation in the harvest. Stacked with double supers, they were too high for him to manage. It irked him to miss this important step, which he felt was an opportunity to offer thanks and gratitude to the bees while carefully removing frames. But he had to be content with what he could do, and overseeing the extraction process kept him more than busy. Next year things would be different, he promised himself.

Nobody had time to cook during harvest week, so Jake ordered lunches from River Daze and dinners from the taquería. The last night of harvest, Evangelina brought the food down herself. She helped Jake put the large trays out on the picnic table as the others finished up the last extractions.

"What's your yield this year?" Evangelina asked, loosening the tinfoil on a tray of enchiladas.

"Back of the napkin, it looks like eighteen hundred gallons."

"Aha! Jacob!" she said, squeezing his shoulder. "That is amazing, mijo! I'm so proud of you."

"Well, the bees did all the hard work," he said.

But he was proud and happy too. Happy for himself and Alice. Happy for the honeybees, which were healthy and thriving. And also happy that this little corner of the world was working, when things felt so dark elsewhere. At dinner, Jake looked around the table. Abigail was talking with Alice about her trip to Alaska, and Cece was telling Casey about the wedding. Noah was offering sourdough tips to a couple of undergraduates. Dr. Mora had surrendered her lap to Cheney's heavy head and was chatting with Tansy. Jake sat quietly, watching them all, and felt more content than he had in years.

After the difficult summer, he was even more grateful for the farm, the bees, and his business. He wanted to focus his energy on those things. To that end, he and Alice sketched out a five-year plan for the company. They laid it all out over dinner at Twin Peaks, their favorite burger joint out by the county airport, starting with their main priorities. Jake took notes while Alice talked.

"Priorities for Queen of G, number one. Health and wellness of owners—i.e., annual vacations, exercise, and relationships," Alice said.

Alice had come back from her trip to Alaska with a new attitude about work. The beauty of the backcountry made her realize how much of her life she'd spent working for the sake of working. She said she wanted to make time to see the world and nurture important relationships.

Jake gaped.

"Um, did you just say 'nurture'?" he asked.

Alice blew her nose and shoved her hanky in the pocket of her overalls.

"Yes, I did. Nurture. So what?" she said, cracking her knuckles. "I'm a nurturing person."

Jake was thinking of the string of profanity that had cascaded from Alice's mouth on the drive up to Twin Peaks when she'd been passed on a double yellow by a motorcyclist. Road rage didn't necessarily rule out being nurturing, he supposed.

Number two on the list was "health and wellness of bees." This one came from Jake and it was a big one. Any beekeeper wanted healthy bees, of course. But for Jake, this priority meant more. He wanted to phase out the Langstroth hive design in favor of Naomi Price's long hive. Jake's records over the season had convinced him that they were better for the bees—survival rates, mite protection, and heat insulation. Their bees would live longer and, hopefully, produce more honey. And this change would allow him to work every single stage of hive tending and harvest.

Number three the two of them had come up with together: "Community." For Alice this meant greater involvement in the Hood River Beekeeping Association, where, as a master beekeeper, she could help train beekeeping apprentices and journeymen, both backyard hobbyists and small farmers.

"That sounds pretty social for you, Alice," Jake remarked.

"Prepare to be amazed," Alice said.

True to her word, she'd signed up to be a mentor to a new class of backyard beekeepers. At the first meeting, Jake was a little awed at how good she was at conveying the basics of beekeeping, once she got into the swing of it and stopped scolding people for talking while she was talking.

For Jake, part of community involvement was driving to Corvallis on this Wednesday morning. That afternoon he'd be touring an experimental pollinator garden on the OSU campus, a project headed up by Casey, whom he'd met through Abigail. Casey was researching native plant species that could best support native pollinators, and especially hardy perennials that were drought resistant and resilient to wildfire. She said the Middle Mountain Fire had sparked her interest.

"No pun intended," she said, smiling to reveal a dimple on her right cheek.

Casey smiled often, he'd noticed in the short time he'd known her. He also knew she liked jazz, but the old stuff, not modern like Jake played on his trumpet. Also, she was a passionate fan of the national curling scene, which Jake thought was hysterical. The only time he'd seen Casey get the slightest bit defensive about anything was when he laughed about curling.

"But seriously—the urgent ice sweeping and all the yelling!"

"You have to be from Minnesota to understand," Casey said, sounding miffed, but she got over it.

Jake liked Abigail and Casey—fellow pollinator people but also bonded to him, it must be admitted, by their unpleasant experience with E.W. Dewitt.

Jake wondered what would have happened if the wildfire hadn't broken Dewitt's standoff with Ron. In the end, Dewitt had done himself in. His manifesto video had gone viral mostly because of his proximity to the fire above Odell while he was giving it. And in the fickle machinery of social media, some accused Dewitt and his posse of delaying the response to the fire by distracting Deputy Sheriff Ryan. Someone suggested Dewitt and his cronies had actually set the fire. Jake knew this wasn't true. The Mount Hood ranger had confirmed that the fire was ignited by fireworks. Some teenagers at a dispersed campsite near Odell had been setting off bottle rockets over the river—despite the fireworks ban and the clearly posted fire danger signs.

But Dewitt's real downfall occurred after it came to light that he'd misused campaign funds. A story in the *Hood River News* detailed how his new Ford F-350 had been paid for by his unwitting supporters alongside personal trips that he'd claimed were for business, like going to see Toby Keith perform in Las Vegas. He'd stayed in the penthouse of the Red Rock Resort and not in the company of his wife. Some thought it was Cindy Dewitt herself who sent this information to the newspaper right after she left town with the two youngest boys. Others thought his oldest son had leaked it. Jake had asked Abigail if she thought that was true and she shrugged.

"I do not care what Dwight Dewitt does or doesn't do," she said evenly. But he heard her whisper, "Asshole," under her breath.

Whatever the case, watching Dewitt defend himself had been truly satisfying. In the online comments, people turned on him. Eventually he shut down his Facebook page. He moved away, though nobody seemed to know where. Dewitt's name remained on the November ballot, which had already been printed, but Ron was expected to win by a healthy majority.

A couple of weeks earlier the Ryan family had their traditional Labor Day party at the taquería. All of Evangelina and Ron's family were there—Ronnie and Marco, as well as Evangelina's mother, and so many cousins and second cousins on both sides that Jake could never keep them straight. Even Victor was there—home from Seattle and beefy as ever. Seeing him made Jake think of Flaco because Vic had been skinny like that boy when he was the same age. He wished Flaco were at the party to meet Vic and to see the family all gathered like that. Flaco would have loved it, Jake knew.

He missed the boy. The house seemed so quiet without him, even though Harry was back from Texas and living in the bunkhouse. They hung out often and gamed sometimes in the evenings. But even now, he caught himself thinking about what he and Flaco could eat for dinner, before remembering the kid wouldn't be there when he got home. He'd come to feel responsible for Flaco, and he'd liked it. He'd liked taking care of the kid—feeding him, teaching him about the bees, talking with him in Spanish and English. Though he was only nine years older, Jake understood how his age, his advantages, and his life experience obliged him to help him. Their brief time together had changed Jake. It made his throat feel tight, thinking that.

At least he was seeing more of Noah these days since Noah had asked him to be his best man. Their planning sessions mostly entailed hanging out when Mrs. Martinez was coming over to talk to Cece about the wedding. Cece didn't mind and understood it was Noah's way to escape her mother's granular attention to detail. She did ask Noah and Jake to put together a playlist for the rehearsal dinner, though.

One night as they scrolled through potential songs, Jake asked him what it felt like—being engaged. Was it different?

"No, I mean, we've been together so long I already feel married," Noah said. "I love Cece, but I don't really care about the wedding part. It's important to her, so I'm down."

Noah paused on a song and flicked a sideways glance at Jake.

"I never asked about that night Cheney got hurt. How was it seeing Ruby?"

Jake exhaled.

"Jesus. Yeah. That, well."

Noah had been there through it all—the first time Ruby had left and the aftermath of last year's visit. Jake blew air through his lips.

"She needed somewhere to crash for the night. Didn't want to wake up her grandmother. Her and the baby," he said.

"Baby must have been a surprise," Noah said.

Jake laughed, feeling a sob rising beneath it.

"Yes, it was. For a hot minute I thought maybe he was mine."

Noah whistled.

"Yeah. But no. Not Neals's either. Just some casual thing, she said."

"Ouch," Noah said.

"I even thought—" he started and then stopped.

"Thought what?" Noah asked, starting a new song.

"It was so stupid. I thought she might stay, and I could help raise the baby, you know? I don't know what the hell . . ."

He trailed off.

"But she took off without even saying goodbye."

"Bro?" Noah said.

Jake laughed again and ran his hands over his face.

"You'd think I'd have seen that coming, right? I spiraled for a few hours, but then I came out of it. Faster than I expected."

"Well, that's not bad, is it? Why do you think?" Noah asked.

Jake held up his palms. The gesture encompassed so much—the two hundred healthy bee hives, the high mountain meadow spared by the fire, his friends.

"I decided not to let Ruby rob me of everything good in my life. Not again, not after how hard I worked to come out of it last time. Anyway, I have to take care of myself. There's so much I want to do."

"I get you," Noah said.

Now Jake took the exit for Highway 26 and glanced up at the south face of Mount Hood. Early snow covered the crooked peak of the mountain completely. Under the gray skies the glacier glinted blue. The massive volcano was comforting—a signal of stability amid so much change and uncertainty. And yet he knew even that was an illusion. Flaco had told him that geologists monitored the seismic activity deep in the core of the mountain and that the landmass was continuing to move, imperceptibly and irrevocably north.

Change was the only constant. Jake knew that, had witnessed it in his own life, in the annual cycle of his bee colonies, in his family, and in his relationships. Change would come. And loss, and surprising moments of joy. Always. We never really know what will happen next. For some reason, at that moment, this unpredictability gave life, his life and all lives, a kind of wild beauty. He drove west, toward the ocean, toward the future, wondering what might come next. Knowing he couldn't know. And finding peace in that.

27

HOMING INSTINCTS

The queen, colony unifier, is the mother to all.
While she is in good health, her pheromone links
all hive inhabitants in connection and belonging.

—LAVIN, *THE WONDROUS WORLD OF BEES*

FLACO KNEW HE should have been hungry. After the physical challenges of the past two days, not to mention the heat, he should have been ravenous, should have been fantasizing about the most delicious dishes he could think of. Or at least taking what he could get of the meager offerings now at his disposal—crackers, lukewarm water, an apple. But he couldn't eat, not a bite. He felt nauseated and woozy, like he hadn't since that time after he'd eaten those hongos up on Mount Hood. It was just nerves, though, and he knew it would pass.

He stood up from the bench he'd been occupying for the past hour and stretched. His calves threatened to cramp, and he jumped about in place to loosen them. He looked around, hoping he hadn't attracted attention, but nobody was even looking at him. Everyone around him was absorbed in their phones. Even the people who were obviously there together were seemingly in separate worlds, staring down into their little glass screens.

An announcement blared overhead in English, and he didn't catch it, and then it repeated in Spanish. "Damas y caballeros," it said. "Ladies and gentlemen. For your safety and security, please report any suspicious activity to airport security."

He glanced around. How would you even know what suspicious activity was? Did he seem suspicious? He stopped jumping and sat back down and flexed his feet.

Coach Mateo had told him he didn't need to be here so early—two hours before the flight. Coach said he could drop him off later, and that Flaco should come out and eat with all the other guys before the team headed back to Hood River. But Flaco said no, thank you. He wanted to be there early.

He liked Coach Mateo and he liked his teammates. That Labor Day weekend in southern Oregon, they'd dominated a preseason tournament of Class 5A teams. Flaco loved playing fútbol again and like this—on a proper team. They had jerseys and warm-ups with their school name on them, and water bottles even. Flaco, though the youngest member of the Hood River Valley High School varsity team, was starting striker. It felt so natural—like being back home playing with his friends. Only now there was strategy and practice and drills. There were adults like Coach Mateo helping them get better. Flaco could never have dreamed it, this team, his place on it, and some start of a new life here in Oregon.

That day, months ago, when his father had left him at the top of Jacob's driveway, Flaco had no plan beyond returning to say thank you to those who'd helped him before he left. It was a risk, he knew. His television interview could have sealed his fate and la migra might have been waiting for him at the farm. But that's not what happened.

Instead, he'd found Jacob's house crowded with people. Everyone was talking over one another, and nobody saw him come in the door. Noah and Cece were sitting at the kitchen table with the twins. The señora was there too and some other people he didn't know. He could hear Jacob but couldn't see him amid the throng. And then Cece's shriek pierced the room.

"Holy shit! He's here! He came back!"

Then she was hugging him and crying, and everyone was yelling and trying to high-five him, which he never got right. The señora grabbed him tight and Jacob came out of the kitchen behind her whooping. Everyone looked so happy. It took a while, but Flaco soon understood that they'd been looking for him. After seeing his TV interview and not knowing where he was, they'd all convened at Jake's to search. Some of them had been up all night looking for him on foot and in cars, others making phone calls to family and friends to see if anyone had spotted him—a fourteen-year-old boy alone leaving Odell.

Flaco felt terrible then that he hadn't asked the coach to call Jacob. He hadn't even thought of it, but nobody seemed mad at him. On the contrary, they seemed happy to see him. Their happiness made him feel even worse about leaving. While la migra had not come knocking yet, Flaco was convinced it was just a matter of time. That night he lay in bed in Jake's guest room and had the strangest sensation, a kind of homesickness at the idea of leaving Hood River, Oregon.

He watched Jacob make breakfast the next day and wished he'd had a chance to learn how to make pancakes for his host. But there hadn't been enough time. They had the radio on to listen to news of the fire. Jacob told him the señora was coming by. He was happy and sad at the same time. At least he would be able to say goodbye to her and thank her before he left. He tried to eat, knowing it might be a while before he had such good food again, but he felt sick and only picked at his food.

The señora arrived and the lawyer was with her. They were smiling at him and seemed weirdly happy.

"Flaco, Señora Evangelina told me you saw your father at Coach Mateo's place and that he's living in eastern Oregon," the lawyer said.

Did they think he'd lied to them about not knowing his father?

"I'm sorry," he said. "I didn't know. I hadn't seen him since I was little."

The señora squeezed his shoulder.

"Oh, it's okay, Flaco. We know. Your father explained."

"You talked to my father?" Flaco said.

The lawyer was positively beaming now.

"We did," the lawyer. "We had a conference call with him and an immigration judge. Flaco, I have really good news for you."

She explained that Flaco's father had agreed to sponsor him in becoming a U.S. citizen. Because his father was already a citizen, he could do this. It was much easier than Special Immigrant Juvenile Status, and the papers had already been filed.

"It's a clear path forward for you, Flaco. I'm really hopeful for you," the lawyer said.

Flaco thought about the application for Special Immigrant Juvenile Status, the section accusing his mother of neglect and abandonment.

"What about the other forms?" he asked.

"We don't need them. This is a better way, through your dad."

Flaco pondered the idea of his father's involvement.

"So will I go live with him now?"

The señora and the lawyer glanced at each other.

"No, he says that is not possible, Flaco," the señora said slowly. "Not just now."

He nodded, silent. It hurt less to hear this a second time.

"So what happens next, then?" he asked. "What do I do?"

The next step was to wait, the lawyer said. She hoped things would move quickly, but she couldn't make any promises.

For the time being, he needed a local sponsor and Coach Mateo had offered to be that person. He said Flaco could come live with him and his family in Odell. And since he was the coach at the high school, he would help get Flaco to school once the academic year started. So he should be thinking about classes and maybe even playing on the soccer team.

"Coach Mateo and Lupita want to help," the señora said. "Mateo came here as a young man and he knows how hard it can be to get through the immigration process. He's a good person. And a great coach! Our high school team is excellent!"

Flaco listened silently. He thought about Coach Mateo and his nice wife, Lupita. Their daughter, Marta. They had been kind to him. The idea of staying with them was tempting. More certain than simply heading south on his own, especially since he'd been unable to reach Javier in California. When he called the phone number, the person who answered said he didn't know who Javier was but wished people would stop calling.

"So, I would stay with Coach Mateo," Flaco said.

Jacob spoke then.

"You can stay here, too," he said. "Estoy feliz de hospedarte, Flaco."

Jacob smiled and Flaco felt so happy. Despite their language barrier, there was a bond between them. Jacob felt like a big brother or an uncle now. He was someone Flaco could rely on. Unlike his father, and unlike Tonio, who had once occupied that space in his life. It felt good to have a friend like Jacob.

Flaco spent the summer living at the farm. He did chores around the place and made friends with Cece's brothers and their neighbors, Manny and Miguel. They invited him to play pickup fútbol and cruise around town some evenings. And when school started, he went to live with the coach and his family and he joined the team. With each passing day he felt more at ease in Hood River, though it wasn't perfect. Many people at school spoke Spanish and most of the white kids were okay. Occasionally someone said something rude about Mexico or called him an "illegal alien." But for the most part it was fine. Around town there were lots of Mexican people and familiar food and music. On weekends, he hung out with his new friends. Some of the places they went it seemed everyone was white except for him and Cece and her brothers and the Salazars. He lived in a strange in-between land and wondered if he'd ever get used to it.

He felt ambivalent, too, about his father, David Luna. In one way, his father had given him the biggest gift, helping sponsor his application for citizenship. And yet he'd let him down in so many other ways—leaving when Flaco was little, for one thing. And now he was just a few hours away but had not invited Flaco to visit or meet his wife and other children.

"Soon, mijo," he'd said the last time they'd spoken on the phone. But Flaco didn't really believe him.

He told Jacob about the conversation afterward as they sat outside near the apiary on a beautiful if slightly chilly day. He reported what his father had said—that he was keeping in touch with the lawyer and that things looked good regarding his application. As for a visit to Boardman, maybe Christmas, he'd said.

Flaco thought he was recounting the conversation straightforwardly, and only when he finished did he notice the tears sliding down his face.

"I'm sorry, dude," Jacob had said then. "My dad," he started and then stopped. He looked out over the beehives in the field and then back to Flaco.

"My dad wasn't great either. Dads can let you down, you know," he said.

Flaco felt slightly better when Jacob said that. He'd met Jacob's nice mother, who was divorced, he knew. They never spoke of Jacob's father.

Then Abigail had said something in her loud, strange voice. Abigail, Jacob's friend, was visiting that day. She was the one who'd driven the SUV into the field long ago, angry for reasons Flaco still didn't understand. Abigail was a bit odd, Flaco thought, though not unfriendly.

She looked at Flaco and repeated whatever she'd said. He asked Jacob to translate.

"She said not all fathers are bad and that hers is a very good father," Jacob said.

She told them her father was kind and caring and always helpful. Flaco began to feel terrible all over again about his own father.

"My mother—" Abigail said, and stopped abruptly, looking down at the table. And then she said something else. She looked at Flaco and her wide eyes looked so sad.

"She said her mother left when she was three and she doesn't know why," Jake said. "She said you should understand it wasn't you. You shouldn't think your father left because of you."

Hearing that, Flaco felt released from a weight he hadn't known he'd carried. Of course he hadn't caused his father to leave. He was just a little kid then.

His mother had agreed when they'd talked about it on the phone.

"Of course not, mijo. Your papá and I were just so young. I'll explain more when you're older."

He knew she would too. She always told him the truth. As she did when he asked if she'd known his father was in Oregon when she sent him north. She'd sighed and said yes, she did.

"Pues, sí. I didn't know where, but I hoped César might," she'd said.

She apologized for not telling him and promised not to hide such things anymore. He believed her. She always did what she said she would do, his mamá. Like she was today, this day he'd dreamed about for months. During this long, strange journey to this place where he'd known nobody and through all that had transpired, he'd thought of her. When he felt so terribly lonely and out of place, he'd held on to this hope. Today it was happening. His mother was coming.

The lawyer had helped with her tourist visa, which Flaco didn't really understand. All he knew was that his mother, Beatriz López, was landing any minute at Portland International Airport.

Coach Mateo had told him where to wait and where to meet the car he'd reserved to drive them to Hood River.

"I look forward to meeting your mother," the coach had said, and left to take the team to lunch before heading back to Hood River.

The minutes crawled by and somehow turned to hours. Flaco passed the time by imagining his mother's plane flying north from Mujica International Airport toward the United States. He imagined the volcanic peaks she'd see from the plane: Volcán de Colima, Volcán Parícutin, and Volcán Ceboruco. Then Mount Shasta, Mount Bachelor, Mount Jefferson, Mount Hood, and Mount Adams. He would tell her the Indigenous peoples called Mount Hood Wy'east and Mount Adams Pahto. He had so much to tell her.

He must have dozed off because he had to open his eyes when he heard her voice. He looked up to see her hurrying toward him. There she was—Beatriz López, his mother—looking even more herself for being in a crowd of strangers. She ran to him and dropped her bags. Flaco had to stoop to hug her because he'd grown so much. And she was laughing and crying and so was he. He buried his face in his mother's neck and smelled the familiar and precious scent of her—cinnamon and vanilla and soap. He felt her strong, slender arms around him, and he felt something he hadn't felt in so long. Forever, it seemed.

He felt like he was home.

ACKNOWLEDGMENTS

THIS BOOK WOULD not have been written without the help of many people.

Heather Carr, thank you for offering early encouragement and for always being available to answer questions and chase away worries. I appreciate your thoughtful edits, which brought forth the story I'd hoped for. Molly Friedrich, thank you forever for your straight talk, sense of humor, and inspiration. I believe I can do anything with you in my corner. Marin Takikawa and Lucy Carson, thank you for all you do to support me and my books.

Lindsey Rose, deepest gratitude for welcoming this return to Hood River and honeybees. Thank you for your thoughtful suggestions and changes, which elevated the story. It's a joy to work with you. Charlotte Peters, I appreciate all your wrangling of permissions, author questionnaires, copyedits, and the many other details that bring a book together.

Emily Canders, huge thanks for your incredible support through media outreach, events, and publicity. I'm grateful for all you do to garner attention for my novels in a busy book landscape. Nicole Jarvis, thank you for all your work in marketing, advertising, and promotions to aid my books.

In my research to create the character of Sebastián Santiago Luna López, aka Flaco, I'm deeply indebted to many people. MariRuth Petzing and Garrett Sharp, thank you for fielding my questions about U.S. immigration law and immigrants in Hood River County. For insight into the experience of Hood River County's Latinx immigrant residents, I'm so grateful to Carlos Alvarez, Tina Castañares, Alfredo Magaña, Juan Reyes, Gladys Rivera, Amber Rose, and Martha Verduzco. My dear Barbara Moran, thank you for answering my many questions about Spanish language and Mexican colloquialisms and for connecting me with Isabel Perez Vieyra, who offered helpful details particular to Michoacán. Thank you, Isabel! To Noemi Martinez and Juan Reyes, many thanks to each of you for your thoughtful reads of the manuscript. For other concerns, thank you Michael Condino and Sarah Kellems.

To Jennifer Larson, thank you for inviting me to the Oregon State Beekeepers Association Conference, where this novel began. Your own work with honeybees and native pollinators planted the seed for a story about the shared world of these distinct groups.

I'm so grateful to Naomi Price, whom I met only briefly and whose beautiful hive design is featured in this story. To Vivien Hight, thank you for your mentorship with the Valkyrie hive.

A big thanks to all the book clubs who've hosted me over the years and wanted to know what happened next with Jake. Your questions helped me find my way into this story. And to anyone taking the time to read this book—thank you so much. In the words of Rebecca Solnit, "Books are solitudes in which we meet." Reading is an act of community in a fragmented world.

Thank you to my dear friends and family for your love and support.

Matthew Lore, from the beginning and always, I thank you.

Special thanks to Nancy Foley—you are simply indispensable.

And wonderful Brendan Ramey, early reader, cheerleader, and the best person I know, thank you for everything, every day. I'm so lucky to have you.

ABOUT THE AUTHOR

EILEEN GARVIN is the author of the national bestselling novels *Crow Talk* and *The Music of Bees*, as well as the acclaimed memoir *How to Be a Sister*. Born and raised in Washington State, she lives in Oregon.